MW00769461

A WEREWOLF ANTHOLOGY

Published by Horrific Tales Publishing 2020

http://www.horrifictales.com

A CIP catalogue record for this book is available from the British Library

ISBN: 978-1-910283-23-3

This book is a work of fiction. Names, characters, businesses, organisations, places and events are either the product of the author's imagination or are used fictitiously. Any resemblance to actual persons, living or dead, events or locales is entirely coincidental.

Cover Artwork by Patrick Cornett

Illustrations by Michelle Merlini

Edited by Lisa Lane and Graeme Reynolds

CONTENTS

For Charlotte, my amazing wife.

The only person who can calm my inner monster and makes
my life worthwhile.

Love you always.

The Dead Brother Situation

A Gilson Creek Story

Glenn Rolfe

Brenda chased him as far as the front door, but the howling blizzard outside prevented her from venturing further. He needed her to back the hell off. She didn't understand he was doing this to keep them safe.

"Alan!" she shouted, though her cries were quickly muffled and snuffed to a whisper beneath the wind.

Ignoring her, he climbed behind the Suburban's wheel, put the truck into gear and headed out of the driveway. He glimpsed her dropping to her knees in her housecoat.

She'd never understand.

She could never find out. It would ruin everything.

There was no Rick, no Carson, no Bryan. All his "friends" were bullshit. This was no weekend hunting trip, at least not the way she thought.

There would be plenty of tracking, plenty of blood, and if all went well, enough meat left over to feed them for the next couple months. He'd been getting overzealous the last two outings and bringing home nothing but scraps. He told himself he was still in control. He was the beast and the beast was him.

Alan. Shit, she didn't even know his real name. And the boy, well, the baby had something in his blood, something in his DNA that she'd figure out sooner or later. The truth always rears its ugly head whether we want it to or not.

He was very interested to see how that would all play out. Would the kid wolf out as a child? He sensed puberty would trigger it, but who the hell knew? Maybe it was like other traits, and the damn mongrel in the boy would lie dormant until he had kids of his own.

Did he love them? It was a fair question. One he wasn't completely sure he could answer. He cared about them, but not above his own... issues. He'd always believed to love you must put those you care about above all else. So, in that scenario, no, he did not love them.

The Suburban plowed through the heavy snow pounding the little backwoods town roads. He never traveled in this kind of weather without his chains on. Brenda didn't realize that he couldn't stay home, not without putting her or Nicholas's lives in danger.

He headed west. These old roads were a disaster, and plows wouldn't make it out this way until morning at best. Still, he had no choice but to push on through. Two hours into the drive, he found Canyonville Road and turned right. The cabin of one of his earliest victims was about a mile down the road, just off the lake. When he'd mutilated that man, Matthew Lacey, he'd worried someone would come looking. But he'd returned to the cabin numerous times over the past two years and no one had ever shown. The place remained untouched as far as he could tell. Lacey's stuff still filled the corners, but no one had come to claim it. He'd at least expected to find a bank notice about foreclosure, but it looked like Lacey must have owned the place outright.

When his headlights found the mailbox, he glanced up the drive to see if he could spot any lights through the trees. He always did a drive-by, just in case. The snow looked to be about a foot high, but he was confident the truck would make it through, and per usual, the old home sat in perfect darkness.

He slowed the truck before pulling a U-turn and heading up the driveway. He feared the vehicle wouldn't make it for a split second, but the chains caught and clawed their way to the foot of the stairs.

He'd left a good stack of wood inside last month and found it nice and dry against the far wall as he pushed through the door. He loaded the wood stove and got a good fire going. It was freezing, and he wouldn't be changing until sometime tomorrow. If he didn't heat this place up like Hades, he'd be dead by dawn.

Once the fire was stoked, he fetched his bags from the truck. He'd have to shovel the driveway, at least around his truck so he could swing it around get back down to the road. But there was no sense taking on the arduous task now; the snow was supposed to fall until somewhere around four in the morning.

The hunger was with him. He'd packed four good-sized steaks and a pork loin that he'd found stuffed in the depths of their freezer.

He dug out the cooler of meat and retrieved two of the steaks. The scent of blood traveled up his nostrils and tickled something deep inside. He was salivating as he peeled back the cellophane, picked up the dripping hunk of meat and bit into it.

He enjoyed every succulent piece, making a damn mess of his beard and his sweatshirt as he devoured the meal. He swallowed it down with four Budweisers. Filled and feeling the slightest touch of a buzz from the beers, he made sure to lock the door, tossed a few more logs in the fire and lay down atop the sleeping bag he'd brought.

His dreams were filled with all the things he'd grown accustomed to on the nights before the change. Old haunts, old foes, old kills, but also the more jarring images of Brenda and Nicholas. He stirred in his sleep as the visions of their deaths at his hands served as reminders of why he left them every month.

When he awoke to the voice asking, "Who the hell are you?" and having the business end of a rifle in his face, he tried his best to keep the smirk from his lips.

"I asked you something, you son of a bitch," the man holding the gun said. "Who the hell are you and what the fuck are you doing in my brother's cabin?"

Another man, about half a foot taller with a dirty looking peach-fuzz mustache, chimed in, "The hell you smilin' about? Huh?"

"Shut up, Shea," the brother Lacey said. "I'll handle this."

Shea backed away with his hands up and mumbled, "Sure, man, okay. Whatever."

Brother Lacey put a boot into Nick's ribs.

"Get up," he ordered.

"Okay, fella, I'm getting up," Nick said.

"You know my brother?"

"And you are?" Nick asked, rising.

"Paul Lacey, but that don't fucking matter to your ass. Do you know my brother? Answer the damn question."

"You mind not aiming that thing at my face?" Nick said.

"You answer me, and I'll consider it."

"Fine, no. I don't know your brother."

"Then what the fuck are you doing in his house?"

"There hasn't been anyone here in months. I figured it would be cool if I just sort of camped out here while I was hunting."

"My brother's been missing going on two years. And by the looks of you, you've been here more than just last night. You know where my brother is?"

"I told you—"

"He heard what you fuckin' said, trespasser," Shea said.

Nick clenched his jaw and bit his tongue. This was all too good. He'd been wanting to unleash on some fucking assholes. Chasing down bear and moose and deer had its uses, but putting motherfuckers like this in their place, well, that fed a whole other beastly hunger.

"Matthew Lacey," Paul said, still aiming the rifle at his face. "This is his cabin. He came up here two winters back to do some huntin'. Ain't been seen since. You know something, you better fucking spill it now or me and Shea here are gonna have to exercise some good ol' goddamn street justice."

"And why you got blood on your shirt?" Shea added.

Nick looked down at the stains on his grey sweatshirt. "Told you I was hunting. Had a little dinner last night. That okay with you?"

Shea stepped up to him and kneed him in the balls. Nick dropped to a knee and clenched his fists.

"Ah, ah," Paul said. "Don't even think about it."

Nick thought about it. He thought about hulking out and burying his teeth into these fuckers. But the butt of the rifle smashed into his forehead and dropped him to his back. Before he could react, the butt came down hard again and caused the world to go black.

***

He awoke tied to the chair in the corner, stripped to his underwear. His head ached, but he knew it wouldn't be too long before these sons of bitches got what they had coming.

What did surprise him was that both Paul Lacey and his "more than just friends" buddy, Shea, were also stripping down.

"Hey, Paul," Shea said, "Looks like ol' Bright Eyes is coming to."

Glenn Rolfe

"Well, well, well," Paul said. "We were gonna wake you with a helluva surprise, but guess you get to see it coming."

The snickering both men let out sent a tendril of nausea into Nick's guts. No way. No fucking way was he winding up the fly in these Pulp Fiction wannabe motherfuckers' web. He knew he'd turn today—sooner than later, he fucking hoped—but that slim chance of these assholes trying to fuck him before he could unleash upon them with great fury, well, it was slightly terrifying.

"You want a sneak peek?" Shea asked.

Nick tried to free his hands, but the ropes were too damn tight. He gritted his teeth and dropped his gaze to the floor as Shea pulled out his stiff cock and waved it back and forth.

"What's a matter, tough guy?" Paul asked. "You ain't afraid of a little dick, are ya?"

"He looks hungry to me, Paul. What do you think, huh?" Shea said. "You want a last meal, trespasser?"

Paul charged across the room in his tightie whities and slapped Nick.

Nick tasted the blood from inside his cheek as Paul sank his nails into his jawline and raised his chin.

"You got one last chance to tell me what happened to my brother," Paul said. "One. And if you keep this act up of 'I just found this cabin,' I'm gonna fuck the hell out of your ass until you're cryin' like a baby here on the floor. And then, after Shea has his way with you, and only then, will I put you out of your fucking misery and kill you dead."

"Where have you been?" Nick mumbled.

"What's that?" Paul said.

"Your brother's been dead almost two years. How come you and your boyfriend are just showing up here now?"

"Motherfucker," Shea said, stepping past Paul and hammering a right hook into Nick's face.

"Wait, wait!" Paul ordered. "Goddammit, Shea, fucking hold on."

Nick spat blood on the floor.

"You do know, don't you?" Paul said, his eyes wide, a flurry of rage flickering through them like a wildfire coming to full blaze.

Nick nodded and smirked. "Yeah, I know just what happened to him. I was there all right."

"Say it. Say it, you bastard," Paul said. His eyes were glistening.

Another shot from Shea mashed Nick's nose.

"Goddamn it, Shea," Paul said shoving the asshole with his dick still hanging out.

"What?" Shea said. "This asshole here just admitted to killing Matthew."

"I heard him, dickhead. Put your cock away."

Shea did as he was told. Nick thanked the Gods for small blessings. He was sick of looking at the loser's pecker.

"He said he was there," Paul said. "Ain't that right, Bright Eyes?"

"Shit," Shea gasped. "He does have fucked up eyes. What's up with that? They didn't look like that a minute ago."

Nick knew what Shea was talking about. He could feel the first hints of his other side. The way his blood surged to his muscles, he smelled intimate things he didn't care to smell coming off these two hillbilly perverts, he heard their quickened heartbeats, sensed leeriness. They noticed the changing tides.

"Fuck," Paul said, "who gives a shit about his eyes?" He stepped to Nick, pulled his head back with a handful of his hair and said, "Now, I wanna hear it outta your grinning mouth. Say it."

Nick nodded again. "Yeah, I was there."

"And?" Paul asked.

Nick stared Paul in the eyes. "And I ripped his fucking throat out and ate what was left."

The rage faltered in Paul's gaze. His eyes widened; awareness on some deeper level clicked into place.

Shea looked from Paul to Nick and back to Paul again, like a child not sure how to react or what to do in a suddenly dangerous situation.

And this was certainly a dangerous situation.

"Shea," Paul said, letting go of Nick's head, and beginning to ease away. "Get my rifle."

Nick inhaled deeply through his nose, and as he did his muscles rippled beneath the flesh. His shoulders gave an audible crack, like a fresh branch being stepped on, followed by something that sounded like grinding teeth.

"Hey, shit," Shea muttered.

His breathing became heavy, grunts accompanied his hollow laughter.

"G-g-get my g-gun," Paul's voice, barely above a whisper, but Nick heard it loud and clear. Fear. These pussies were about sixty seconds from pissing their stained undies.

Nick's jaw snapped as he began jerking his head from side to side. His gums ached as the teeth dropped to the hardwood floor in a rain of enamel and blood.

"Jesus fuck!" Shea said. He'd yet to make a move for Paul's weapon.

Nick's body tensed and grew, popping, snapping, grinding into his werewolf form. His face went tight. His snout pushed forth from his nasal cavity. Black hairs slid from their dormant home below his skin, his clawed hands snapped free of their bindings.

The two men trembled before him. Shea yellowed his undies, his piss flowing to the floor. Paul cried out a high whine before turning for his gun.

Fully transformed, Nick Bruce kicked the chair free from his feet and launched at Shea, swiping upward and eviscerating the weasel from navel to chin. His body flew across the room, slamming against the wall, where he collapsed dead to the floor, his innards spilling out in a pool of crimson. His hands twitched as his pathetic mind was cast into the great beyond.

"You're a-ah-ah-you-you're a wer...." Paul sputtered, the gun forgotten in his arms. He dropped it to the floor with a thud that was swallowed by the guttural sound emanating from the creature standing before him.

"Puh, puh, please... I don't want to d-d-die," he whined.

Nick reveled in the beast's power. Felt it vibrating through his body, his muscles, his veins. He'd never driven a classic sports car, but he imagined the thrill coursing beneath the black fur was something akin to sitting behind the wheel of a souped-up Charger or Mustang. It was intoxicating. He revved his engines, his growl growing in volume, his hulking body flexing before the coward piece of shit before him.

Paul's wide eyes slimmed. The fool suddenly remembered he had a pair between his shaky legs.

Nick welcomed the asshole's momentary bravery with a garish smirk, being sure to show the man his set of flesh-rending teeth.

Paul dropped to his knees and snatched up the rifle. He had it up and aimed directly at Nick's chest as the beast side-stepped the well-placed trajectory and, with one swing of his claws, severed the arm holding the weapon and sent it across the floor, the weapon discharging as it sailed to the ground. Nick grabbed Paul by the throat and lifted him so that they were eye to eye. He could see the beast's yellow orbs reflecting in this poor fuck's watery eyes.

Nick sank his claws into the man's flesh until the blood overflowed from the wound and dripped from his fur to the hardwood floor in a crimson dribble.

Paul's eyes gave in to the inevitable. His feet twitched then stopped. Satisfied, Nick slammed the dead man down and sank his mouth into his chest.

He'd devoured much of the two weaselly men before bursting out into the dying light of the day and chasing down any other unfortunate creatures in the vicinity.

The two men were enough, but when you only got out once a month, gorging yourself on so much fresh meat was essential.

**

The next morning, Nick Bruce woke inside the cabin. Naked and freezing, covered in the crimson delights of his latest hunt. He climbed to his feet and shivered. Gazing around the weekend home that had served him well, sheltering him and giving him a camp for his beastly adventures, he knew it was time to turn the page. The remains around him were more work than he felt like dealing with this morning. He would burn the place to the ground.

Forty minutes later, dressed and standing at the tail of his Suburban, he smiled as he warmed himself before the conflagration rising high in the sky, dancing with the black smoke. It had been more than a year since he'd killed a man. The ecstasy it produced was incomparable. And if he

16

was going to be returning his sights to the most dangerous game, there was one place he had to go, one man he had to pay a visit to, for old time's sake

He walked around the truck and climbed in behind the wheel.

Driving away, the raging fire in his rearview mirror, Nick knew where he was going on his next hunt.

There was unfinished business in a little town called, Gilson Creek.

He'd figure out what to tell Brenda, if he told her anything at all. There was such a thing as fate. Nick believed in it full heartedly. And his fate was waiting for him farther south in a place that he'd last seen slicked in blood and rain.

Glenn Rolfe

ABOUT THE AUTHOR

Glenn Rolfe is an author from the haunted woods of New England. He has studied Creative Writing at Southern New Hampshire University and continues his education in the world of horror by devouring the novels of Stephen King, Richard Laymon, Brian Keene, Jack Ketchum, and many others. He and his wife, Meghan, have three children, Ruby, Ramona, and Axl. He is grateful to be loved despite his weirdness.

He is a Splatterpunk Award nominee and the author of The Window, Becoming, Blood and Rain, The Haunted Halls, Chasing Ghosts, Abram's Bridge, Things We Fear, Boom Town, and the collections, Slush and Land of Bones.

Look for his new novel, Until Summer Comes Around, coming from Flame Tree Press in May of 2020.

Twitter: @grolfehorror

Amazon:http://author.to/Getrolfed

Patreon: www.patreon.com/getrolfed

HUNTER'S MOON

David Wellington

Orange light glimmered on the snow that lay heaped under the windows of the Yellowknife diner. A thick smear of condensation obscured the glass, preventing anyone outside from seeing what was happening within, but the black smoke roiling out of the front door might give them an idea. Men and women still trying to pull their coats on spilled out into the street.

Inside, Laura Caxton ducked as a cast iron skillet flew over her head. She straightened up again and snapped off a single shot from her Beretta, knowing it would go wide. She just wanted to keep the vampire in the kitchen, if she could.

The kitchen was on fire. Fire might not kill Bava, not if he'd drunk blood recently. It could hurt him, though. Slow him down. If he slowed enough, she might get a chance to shoot him through the heart and end this.

The fire had been his idea. She'd tracked him here, walked in and caught him just as he was about to slaughter every living person in the place. One look at her and he'd dived over the counter, even as she drew her weapon. He'd tossed some old towels and bar rags onto the range, maybe thinking she would be more afraid of burning than he was.

He still didn't know her very well.

Caxton was pushing forty. She'd definitely slowed down since her heyday as a vampire hunter. She hadn't forgotten much, though. She knew how hard it was to kill a vampire. She knew if you wasted your chance on being afraid, you might not get another one.

A glass jar full of pickles arched over the counter to smash near where she crouched. Some of the brine splashed on her leg, but she couldn't smell anything but smoke. The kitchen was a raging inferno and the air inside the diner was getting thick.

Caxton evaluated her chances. If she could get a clear shot—

Then Bava screamed and jumped over the counter. For a second he looked like a comet rocketing through space. His arms and back were on fire, the flames spreading across his dry flesh. He made a run for the door and he was outside, running barefoot through the snow. He tore at his lightweight jacket and his shirt, throwing them behind him. They fluttered like fiery birds as they fell to the street.

Caxton dropped to one knee and fired three times into his back, pausing between each shot to recover her aim. If she could pierce his heart with one of those shots—

He skidded on some ice and ran down a side street, out of view.

She climbed back up onto her feet, her knee protesting vigorously, and ran after him.

That was when she heard the scream.

She came around the corner with her arms out for balance and saw a woman lying in the street, the snow around her dotted with blood in a hundred places. The woman had stopped screaming by the time Caxton arrived, but she was still conscious. She was staring at the stump where her right hand used to be. Blood flowed in a thick stream from the ragged wound.

Caxton looked up and saw Bava, already a block away. He was still on fire, still burning brighter than the half-full moon. She couldn't catch him on foot, but she might get close enough to get another shot at him.

"Pl-please," the injured woman said from behind her.

Caxton grimaced.

Ten years ago, she wouldn't have stopped. Ten years ago, nothing would have mattered except Bava.

Ten years ago... for ten years now, she'd thought she could live a different kind of life. That her work was over.

Ten years is a long time.

"You're going to be all right," Caxton said, dropping to kneel next to the hurt woman. She yanked off her own belt to use as a tourniquet. "You're going to live."

Down the street Bava disappeared into the night.

***

They didn't cuff her. Caxton figured that was something, anyway.

A very polite local cop named Gord had led her to an interrogation room. He'd offered her coffee and then apologized about the wait. Then he left her there to stew. Caxton had been stuck in enough cop shops in her time to know what that meant. Gord had to wake somebody up and drag him in to talk to her.

That somebody turned out to be a Corporal of the Mounties. Apparently, he was the ranking guy in town. He was a big guy who looked like he might have had real muscles once, but now he was running to fat. He wore a navy-blue uniform and a baseball cap, and he didn't even have a holster on his belt, much less a weapon. He sighed and toyed with a pen before he even sat down. Before he even looked at her.

"This kind of thing doesn't happen in the Northwest Territories," he said, and let out a short, surprised laugh. "The town of Yellowknife wasn't prepared for you, Ms. Caxton."

Caxton had been law enforcement, once. She knew how this was all supposed to play out. She didn't have time for that.

"Listen. I know your instinct—your cop reflex—is to charge me with something. Maybe a firearms violation. We both know that's just about stalling. Don't do that. You need to cut me loose and let me chase this bastard down. What happened at the diner—that was just the start. Bava will kill again. I was called in by the Edmonton cops to find him and put him down. I followed him all the way here, and if I don't catch him soon, he'll kill again. He isn't going to lay low. He's not going to stop until—"

The Corporal had his hands up in front of him. Telling her to stop.

"Ma'am," he said, "if it wasn't for you, Peg Caulson's kids would have had to come to the morgue tonight instead of the hospital. You saved her life."

Caxton was already regretting it.

Except—

"Whatever you need," the Corporal said. "Whatever you think is best. The Yellowknife Municipal Enforcement Division is here to help."

***

Too bad not everyone in town felt the same way.

Yellowknife was the capital and the biggest town in the Northwest Territories. It was a transportation hub for the entire Canadian Shield, a big stretch of mostly nothing between Alberta and Nunavut. There weren't many roads out there, so that meant small planes were the only way to get around—and the only chance she had to find Bava. Bush pilots congregated down on the river, leaning on the floats of their seaplanes. They hauled cargo or tourists all over the wilderness, whatever came along. When they saw Caxton coming, a lot of them decided to walk away for a smoke break.

Some of them stuck around to laugh at her. "You want to go where?" a pilot named McMurphy asked. A big tough guy in a sleeveless padded coat.

"What the heck would he go there for?" a pilot named Jackson asked. Jackson was young and had spiked hair he scratched at as he spoke. "There ain't much out there but trees and little lakes too small to land on."

"Permafrost and muskeg that'll suck the boots right off your feet." Harris, an ex-marine from Alaska, spat into the water at the very idea.

"No people up there," Tyrone told her. Tyrone was Dene First Nations and, according to local legend, the best pilot in the Territories. Caxton had thought maybe he would be her man. She was wrong. "No *people* go there, if they're smart."

She didn't understand. She asked the Corporal what that meant—no *people*.

"It's dangerous," he said. "Dangerous terrain and... and there's legends, you know. Old stories. That maybe might actually be true."

"Stories?"

"A couple hunters went out that way a bit ago. They didn't come back. Not just your weekend duck killers, mind; these were big-city guys, professionals who specialized in hunting big vermin."

"What, like rats?"

"Bears and coyotes," the Corporal said. She could tell he was circling around something. Something that had rattled him. What the hell was she missing?

"Wolves," one of the pilots said. One she hadn't noticed there before. "He's worried you'll laugh at him if he says what those hunters were really after. They came hunting werewolf. Didn't bag any."

He was a big guy, but very skinny, with a glorious head of pure white hair he pulled back into a tight ponytail. He wore sunglasses with carved wooden frames.

"Werewolves," Caxton said. "There's never been a werewolf attack in North America."

The skinny pilot turned his head to the side, as if he wanted to look at her in his peripheral vision. She felt she was being judged. Evaluated.

"So they say," he told her. "Said vampires were extinct, too."

"I take it you know who I am," she said.

"Might be." He stuck out a hand. His nails were surprisingly long and carefully manicured. "Jesse Det'anichok," he told her. "I'll take you up there. But you follow my rules, okay?" He turned to give the Corporal that same side-eyed look. "Wallace," he nodded. "You're good to cover my expenses? Fuel and incidentals, that's all I ask."

The Corporal nodded eagerly.

The pilot looked at Caxton straight on and took off his sunglasses. His eyes were colorless, and she couldn't help but flinch when they looked straight into her. "Peg Caulson's a good woman. Damned shame what happened to her hand. You follow my rules to the letter, I'll make sure you find this vampire of yours. Do we have a deal?"

Caxton looked down the bank of the river, at the pilots and their little planes. None of the other pilots looked back.

"Deal," she said.

***

Werewolves or no werewolves, she could see why it took a certain kind of pilot to chase down the vampire. There was no point flying during the day—Bava would be inactive then, hiding in a tree stump or an old bear's den, and there would be no chance of spotting him. Instead they had to search at night, and from a low altitude. Jesse seemed to have no problem skimming the treetops, but for Caxton it was an exhilarating—not to say gut-clenchingly terrifying— experience.

They quartered the region northeast of town, making long, sweeping passes over a moonlit realm unlike anything she'd ever seen. A primal place, untouched by roads or towns or any sign a human being had ever been up this way. A terrain dotted with a million lakes and tiny ponds that caught the moon and then winked out into darkness, so that the land seemed to sparkle.

The trees—mostly conifers, black spruce, jack pine, tamarack—grew tall up here, fifty feet and more. They stuck up at seemingly random directions, like fingers pointing at random stars. "Permafrost," Jesse told her, when she asked why. "Except it ain't, anymore."

"What?"

"The ground here used to be frozen all year round. Permafrost. Now every summer it melts a little. The ground slides around, soil gets loose and the trees, they lean and stretch. Pretty crazy, huh?"

"Sure," Caxton said, and went back to staring out her window. Looking for any sign of Bava. White skin, she thought, pale as the belly of a fish. It ought to stand out against the dark background of trees and cold water.

After the first hour, the first pass, took them fifty miles from town and she'd seen nothing, she fought not to let herself get discouraged. They were searching a huge region for something very small. Jesse banked them around to head for another pass, and she tapped on the glass window with her index finger, impatient.

How far could a vampire run, how fast? Faster than a human, but still... he could only run in the dark, and even he would have to keep an eye out for low-hanging branches and watch his footing. There was no reason to think he knew this country, either.

So why had he come here? Before he died, before he

became a vampire, Jerry Bava, Jr. had worked as a truck driver down in Alberta. He'd had no living family, and few friends. Once she caught his trail, he'd headed steadily north, always north.

When she'd caught up with him in Yellowknife, she'd assumed he was just running to get away from her. When she imagined a map, though, and plotted his trail, it was clear he had been coming here, to this desolate place. A region where there were no people to prey on, no blood to be spilled.

Why? Did it have something to do with werewolves? Had he heard a rumor about lycanthropes at large in the north country? Caxton knew very little about any kind of monster except vampires. What did a vampire want with werewolves?

Jesse stirred in his seat and grabbed something from behind him, which turned out to be a thermos. Coffee, straight-up black, still pretty hot.

"It might be a long night," he said, his voice distorted by the roar of the engine. "Just don't drink so much you need to pee."

***

She was fast asleep when Jesse nudged her. She jerked awake and looked around the tiny cabin of the plane. Asleep? On a manhunt? That was... that had never happened before.

She tried to rub sleep out of her eyes and face, but Jesse was pointing through the windscreen, saying something over and over. "There, look!" he said, starting to sound exasperated. Caxton sat up and stared out into the moonlit forest. And saw nothing.

"Where?" she asked.

But then she saw it. A patch of white, fluttering between the trees. Jesse eased them in closer, shedding altitude until Caxton imagined she could hear the tops of the trees brushing against the plane's undercarriage.

And there he was. Bava. Running fast. He glanced back over his shoulder, his eyes burning red with hatred.

In a second they shot past over the vampire's head. Jesse turned them around for another pass. She reached behind her and grabbed one of the rifles. "Keep it as slow as you can, and as low," she said. "I probably won't drop him with the first shot."

"Try," Jesse told her.

She rolled down the window next to her, and freezing air burst into the cabin, waking her up, finally. She leaned out through the window, both arms cradling the rifle. The air whipped into her eyes and she had to blink away tears. She closed one eye tight and pressed the other to the rifle's scope.

There. She held her breath. Gently squeezed the trigger. She saw him in the crosshairs, saw white flesh part as her bullet went right through his shoulder. Closer than she'd expected to hit, closer to his heart. Not close enough. The wound closed over and healed without so much as a scar. Goddamned vampires.

In a moment she'd lost him in the trees.

"Where'd he go? Do you see anything?"

"Hold on," Jesse said. He banked so hard Caxton felt like she was going to fall out the window. "Do you see him?"

"No," Caxton said. "No—he's gone, he's—"

Then Bava emerged on a long slope of naked rock, dashing right out into the open. She ejected her brass and loaded another round in the rifle, but before she could aim again, he did the one thing she hadn't expected.

The stretch of rock was perched above a tiny lake, a wide patch of utter blackness undisturbed even by moonlight. Bava didn't even slow down, he just ran up to the edge and off into space, arms pinwheeling, knees tucking up under him. He hit the lake and its surface was shattered like a broken mirror, the water catching a million tiny images of the moon before it settled again.

"Can you put us down on that water?" she asked.

"It'll be tight," Jesse told her. "And this is a bad time for it—"

"What are you talking about? He's down there right now. This might be our only chance!"

Jesse swore, but he banked around. Cut the throttle and put up all his flaps. The engine wound down, and suddenly she could hear everything—she could hear the silence of the Arctic night. The plane's floats hit the water hard. Caxton was thrown forward against her seat belt, and the rifle flew from her hands, clattering against the plane's dashboard.

Jesse twisted the yoke back and forth, cutting s-turns through the dark water. The far side of the lake suddenly looked way too close, a solid wall of tree trunks. Caxton threw an arm up across her face. It wasn't a voluntary motion.

But then—with a sudden, rocking silence, the plane came to a stop.

Caxton threw her door open and jumped down onto the plane's broad float.

She took a moment to look around. To see where she was. If she'd thought it was silent before, when the engine stopped—the lake seemed to eat all sound, now. As she moved around the float, it was like her boots were striking a drum. She tried to be still. To focus. She lifted the rifle to her eye and scanned the dark, surging water. She couldn't see anything below the surface.

Ice had formed along the margins of the lake. The water

had to be near freezing. The smell of the trees was heady, almost intoxicating. The stink of the sap and the fallen, moldering needles hitting her like a strong cup of tea. She could feel the skin of her face starting to freeze as she stood there. Waiting.

Then—she heard something.

She heard something breathing in the woods, at the edge of the lake. No, not breathing.

Panting. Like a dog.

She glanced upward and saw the moon rising over the treetops, half full, its dark edge blurred by shadow. Werewolves were only supposed to come out during a full moon, right? They were human at all other times. That was what she'd seen in a dozen movies.

Then a pair of eyes blinked into existence, just beyond the treeline. Cold green eyes that did not move.

"Caxton," Jesse said, from inside the plane. "You'd better—"

A howl filled the air, so sudden and so close it nearly knocked her off the float, into the water. It didn't sound exactly like a wolf's howl. It was long and throaty and very, very angry sounding. Like a prolonged snarl more than anything.

Caxton's blood froze inside her veins.

"Caxton!" Jesse switched on the plane's engine, and it came to life with a belching roar that couldn't compete with that howl.

"We won't get a better chance," she said. She looked down at the black water.

And saw the reflection of a wolf, standing right behind her.

She whirled around and saw it wasn't nearly as close as

31

she'd thought. It was at the edge of the water, two long legs spread out in front of it, as if it was bowing. Its coat was a mottled brown and black. Its paws were enormous where they kneaded the muddy shore. Its teeth—

Jesus, Caxton thought. No wolf on Earth had teeth that big, that sharp.

"Caxton!" Jesse shouted. "They can swim!"

A second wolf launched itself out into the water. The one with the green eyes. Its coat was mostly black, with patches of silver. The water splashed high around its muzzle as it rushed towards her.

A hand grabbed the strap of Caxton's rifle. Jesse yanked her backward, inside the plane, her legs still dangling across the float. He didn't wait a second longer but opened the throttle and taxied at full speed down the length of the lake. In a moment they were up in the air.

Behind them the wolves raced along the ground, effortlessly matching their pace, jumping up to snatch at the air with those teeth, those giant teeth.

***

"Whenever the moon's up," Jesse told her over a stack of pancakes. He cut a huge bite and stuffed it in his mouth. "Don't matter what phase, if the moon's in the sky, they change."

Caxton's cup of coffee had gone cold. She wasn't hungry.

"Not just when the moon is full," she said. Needlessly. Jesse nodded in agreement.

She leaned forward across the table. Around her people were talking, pointing at her. Their table was next to a window, and there were more people outside, people in parkas, just watching her not eat. She was a celebrity in Yellowknife now.

She ignored them all.

"You know more about werewolves than I do," she said.

He nodded happily.

"You know more than you're telling me."

He reached for the syrup.

"You want to go back, and we can do that," he said. "But remember: I set the ground rules, right? Which means we wait for the moon to go down. That means going in the daytime. How's that suit you?"

Caxton shrugged and looked away from him. Outside a little girl in a big fur ushanka waved at her. Caxton took a deep breath, then waved back.

They liked her here. They thought she was going to save them from the big, bad vampire. She would see how long that would last if she didn't catch Bava soon. If he killed somebody first.

"Fine," she said. "He'll be vulnerable when the sun's up. Harder to find, maybe. He'll have to go to ground somewhere, find a hiding place, but if I catch him during the day, it'll be a lot easier to kill him."

Jesse nodded and lifted his coffee cup. "Hey, miss?" he called. "How about a refill for the fearless monster hunters?"

***

The trees and the water were the same, but as Caxton stepped out onto the float again, she barely recognized the little pond. No vampire, no giant wolves stalking through the underbrush. She heard a bird off in the distance, and its song was like a signal blasting the all clear.

She took a second and just stood there, breathing in the smell of the pines.

She reached back into the plane and took out the hunting rifle and slipped its strap over her head.

"Six hours," Jesse told her. "You have a watch?"

Caxton frowned. "Six hours until what?"

"Until the moon comes up again. You be back here by then, now."

Caxton checked the Beretta in its holster at her belt. Then she jumped down from the float, into the shallow water between her and the shore. She'd picked up some waterproof boots, but still the cold seeped through them, startling her a little. Summer was over, and she had a feeling it wasn't going to get any warmer as the day went on. She hurried up onto a mossy bank and headed between the trees, ducking as a leaning birch brushed her hat and her shoulders.

Ten steps into the forest, and she couldn't see the lake or the plane behind her. Ten more long strides, and she might have traveled back in time a million years. The ground was soft under her feet, the trees always moving. There was no trash on the ground, no old, dirty plastic bags, no tin cans. As she walked along under the trees, she felt almost like she was violating sacred ground. Had a human being ever walked this way? Ever?

Vampires didn't belong in a place like this. Vampires needed human blood, and that meant they tended to stick close to towns and cities. She didn't understand Bava. Always before she'd stalked vampires by learning their stories, by knowing who they'd been as humans. Unless she literally tripped over his hiding place, she had no idea how she was supposed to find this one.

She headed down a gradual slope, a place where the soil had given way. A big tree had fallen, and its roots stuck up in the air like hair matted with clods of old dirt. The smell of sap and raw earth was overpowering. The roots wove together like an arch over her and she looked deep into the hollow they made. Something small and mammalian stirred in there, some little furry thing. She resisted her city girl urge to jump back, to be scared of a mouse or a shrew, maybe.

She continued down the slope until she reached the edge of another pond, this one no more than twenty yards across. The trees swayed over it, watching themselves in its dark mirrored surface, shedding needles that floated on top of the perfectly still water. She took a step down towards the edge of the pond and peered in, thinking maybe Bava was sleeping down there, at the bottom. Instead she saw her own face staring back at her. She'd reached a point in her life where, when she saw her reflection, she was always surprised by what time had done. She saw the deep wrinkles forming under her eyes, the permanent crease in her forehead that made her look worried all the time.

She sighed and sank down on her haunches, thinking of the old times. The times when she'd thought nothing of running through a dark forest all night, pistol clutched in one hand, a flashlight in the other. She thought of Clara, at home in Pennsylvania, waiting for her to come back. When the call had come in, when the Canadian government had asked her to come look into a vampire sighting, it had been late at night and Clara had turned over in the bed, pulling her knees up to her chest, pretending, pointlessly, she was still asleep.

They'd both felt the tension, the old, way-too-familiar change in the air.

I have to go, Caxton had said, rubbing Clara's arm.

You really don't, Clara had told her. Then she'd gotten up and gone to kitchen and made some coffee, because that was all the discussion there was going to be. Clara understood. She knew who Caxton was.

Now her reflection in the dark pond frowned, because—

There was another face floating in the water. A woman's

face, and for a moment Caxton thought she was looking at her younger self over there, on the far side of the pond. But the hair was wrong, brown and shoulder-length and soft-looking, as opposed to Caxton's random mess of black spikes.

She looked up and saw a naked girl lying on the moss by the water, one arm curled under her head like a pillow.

Naked—because an hour ago, when the moon was up, this girl had been a wolf. She must have been sleeping there when the moon went down, and of course the wolf didn't have any clothes.

"Shit," Caxton said, out loud. She licked her lips, unsure of what to do.

The temperature out here couldn't be more than forty-five—seven Celsius, as the Canadians would say. Close enough to freezing and yet this other woman wasn't wearing a stitch.

The girl opened her eyes. Saw Caxton. She didn't move, but there was a tension in her, a readiness, as if she might spring up at any second, leap across the pond, snarling and ready to kill.

Then something changed. The eyes softened. The girl pushed herself unsteadily up onto one arm. She folded the other across her breasts, and Caxton realized that she was staring at a naked woman, and as dumb as she knew she was being, she couldn't help but look away. To try to give the girl some illusion of privacy.

"You need to leave," the girl said. "You aren't welcome here."

Caxton still couldn't look at her. "What's your name?" she called out.

"Chey." The girl cleared her throat. "Cheyenne. You're in serious danger here, and you need to leave. I don't know why you came, but you must have heard the stories."

"I know you're a werewolf," Caxton said. "Believe me, I don't want to intrude on your... your hunting ground?"

She could tell she'd picked the wrong words, because the girl stiffened. Caxton could see it in her peripheral vision.

"This is where we live. Our wolves hunt, we just..."

The girl's voice trailed off. Caxton's stomach flipped over and she twisted around to look, but of course—of course—the girl was gone. The lowest branches of a fir tree swung back and forth, disturbed as the girl brushed past them.

"God damn it," Caxton said.

She raced around the pond, hot on the girl's trail.

If she was going to find the vampire, she needed to talk to the werewolf. She needed to ask the right questions.

Because suddenly she was pretty sure she knew why Bava had come here.

She tried to keep her eyes on her feet. She stumbled once, but managed to hop onto her other foot and keep her balance. There—just ahead—she saw a flash of brown hair between the grey trunks of the trees.

It seemed impossible that she could have caught up to the werewolf so quickly. Her instincts kicked in and she could feel something was wrong. But she had no plan other than to keep running.

Caxton jumped over a thick tangle of tree roots and hurried down a slope littered with pine needles that slipped away under her feet, then grabbed at the branches of a fallen trunk, pulling herself up, clambering over to—

A hand like a steel vise grabbed her ankle and pulled her down. She landed hard on her back, breath exploding out of her mouth.

"Wolves hunt in packs," someone said. She saw a flash of a face in silhouette, a man's face with icy green eyes. "They're very good at setting up ambushes." Then big, strong hands grabbed her by the front of her parka and hauled her into the air.

He was a man, just a human being with neatly trimmed hair and no beard. Not what she'd expected. A rough wool blanket hung from his shoulders, his only clothing.

She tried to struggle, to get away, but he pushed her back with one hand, and she might as well have been tied to the tree. She wasn't getting away, not until he let her go.

"I'm Montgomery Powell. Does that name mean anything to you?" he asked.

She shook her head.

"Damnation. What did they tell you in town? What did they tell you about us? You came here with—let's see." He grabbed the rifle off her shoulder. He easily held her in place with one hand while he worked the action and ejected the long bullet.

"This isn't even silver."

Caxton had slowly regained her breath as he spoke. "I not here for you. I came for the vampire."

Powell's eyes narrowed, and a low growl started up in the back of his throat.

He tossed the rifle far away into the trees. The bullet dropped between them, useless. "I could scratch your skin. That's all it would take, and then you'd be like us. Cursed forever. You'd have to live up here the rest of your days, far away from civilization. Is that what you want?"

Then he stepped back, releasing her. Maybe daring her to come at him, to fight. She kept her hands well clear of the holster at her belt.

His eyes never left hers. He didn't even blink.

He took another step back. Behind him the girl—Chey—stepped into view. Caxton stayed exactly where Powell had left her. She knew better than to make any sudden moves.

"Bava's a killer," she said. "I don't know what he told you. He came here last night." She decided to put her cards on the table. "He must have come here asking for sanctuary. Right? He wanted your protection? You shouldn't believe anything he says. Vampires lie all the time to get what they want. They lie—and they murder people."

Powell's mouth had been a hard line before. Now it curled up at one corner. "You think any of us up here have clean hands?"

Then the two of them, the werewolves, turned and dashed off into the woods. So fast they were gone from sight before Caxton could even take a step forward. She stood there for a long time, breathing heavily.

Eventually she headed back to the pond, to Jesse and the plane. It was the only thing she could think to do, even though she had no intention of leaving.

***

It turned out Jesse had an idea.

"There's a house about two miles up that way," he said, pointing northeast with his knife. He had been whittling a fish spear out of an old, dead tree branch. He made one last, long cut, tested the point of the spear against his thumb, and nodded. "You really want to commit suicide, that's where you should go."

Caxton squinted at him. Then she looked up at the sky. The sun was setting fast. It would be night soon, and an hour after that the moon would rise. The timing was bad. Maybe she should just wait until tomorrow, when she'd have more sun—but she'd been chasing vampires long enough to know that if you gave them a chance to get away, they would take it. They were survivors, beyond anything else.

39

"This house. You spotted it when we were flying around?" Caxton asked. "It's where the werewolves live when they're, you know, human?"

"Mmm," Jesse said. He stood up on the plane's float and looked down into the water. He wasn't wearing his sunglasses, but all the same, Caxton didn't see how he could spot anything in the murk down there.

"You think Bava's at this house," Caxton said.

"Mmm." He didn't look at her.

She considered the pilot for a long time. There were things about him she'd decided not to question so far. Maybe that had been the wrong move.

"You know more than you're telling me. You see things other people miss."

He smiled, but he didn't lift his eyes from the water.

"What are you?" she asked.

His whole body tensed, every muscle locked in place. Then he moved with explosive force, jabbing his spear straight down into the water so cleanly it didn't even make a splash. When he pulled it back, there was a big, silver fish writhing in panic, stuck on its barbs. Jesse smacked the fish's head against one of the plane's struts and it stopped moving.

"I'm hungry," he said, hoisting his catch in the air. "And this, right here? This is dinner."

***

The two of them crept through the forest, moving into the wind. "They can smell you nearby, sure," Jesse whispered. "They'll know you're close. They won't be able to pinpoint you, though."

Caxton kept her head down and her rifle in her hands.

The house didn't look like much except old. Its eaves sagged, and piles of pine needles and leaves had collected on its roof. There was a big stack of firewood against one wall, and a couple of windows showed darkness inside.

There was also somebody she didn't recognize sitting in a rocking chair on the porch. He was a big guy dressed in a massive fur coat. He had a wooden mask over his face. He just sat there, rocking back and forth. He wasn't armed.

She turned and glanced at Jesse. "Who?" she asked, her voice so low she wasn't sure if he could hear her.

The pilot gave her a big, chilly smile. Then he stood up to his full height and walked forward in plain view of the house.

"Musquash, old buddy!" he called out, his arms spread wide.

The man on the porch stopped rocking. He pulled his mask up, revealing a wide, friendly-looking face. At least, Caxton assumed it would look friendly if it wasn't wracked by terror.

"Eagle," the masked man said. "You're... you're here."

"Took me a while to find you. But I'm patient. Where are your pet werewolves? They going to make trouble for us?"

The man on the porch rose slowly to his feet. "They're... around here somewhere. In the woods. Listen, um."

"Oh, I'm listening."

Musquash smiled. It wasn't a very convincing smile. He opened his mouth as if he were going to speak.

Then Caxton's eyes went wide. She'd seen plenty of strange things in her career as a vampire hunter. Nothing like this. Musquash shrank down into his furs. His mask slipped down over his face, and then it *was* his face, except it didn't look like a mask anymore—

41

Meanwhile Jesse lifted both arms in the air and shook them until they became broad, strong wings. With a piercing cry, he shot through the air straight at Musquash, who was already running for the trees as fast as his legs could carry him. His four legs.

"Oh, come on," Caxton said as Jesse—Eagle—disappeared between the tree trunks, both flying and running at the same time. "Vampires and werewolves weren't bad enough?"

But she didn't have time to puzzle out what she'd seen. It sounded like the house was deserted—unless Bava was inside. Sleeping. This might be the best chance she'd ever get.

She rushed across the needle-strewn clearing and threw open the house's front door. It wasn't locked.

She still had about ten minutes before sundown.

***

A wood stove was burning in the kitchen, warming a pot of what smelled like stew. Caxton hadn't eaten in a while, but she was too tight with nerves to even think about food. She moved through a rustic living room, the furniture all made of wooden logs with the bark still on.

She drew her pistol and kept it low, by her hip. Hopefully she wasn't going to need it, but she liked to be prepared.

There was an inclined ladder in one corner, which headed up to a bedroom on the second floor. A king-sized mattress lay on the floorboards, strewn with sheets, blankets and old dog-eared paperbacks. Apparently werewolves liked to read.

There was a door on the far side of the bedroom, presumably leading to a bathroom. The door was closed but not locked. Caxton turned the knob slowly, knowing what she was about to see.

In the old stories, vampires slept in their coffins like good little corpses. In the movies they always looked so clean.

Caxton pushed the door open. There wasn't a lot of light in the bathroom. She could see a claw-footed club, its white enamel slightly luminous in the shadows, and a big washbasin on a stand. No running water, of course. If you wanted to take a bath in here, you needed to fill the tub by hand.

There was no water in the tub now, even though it was full. The smell of what was in there was like a punch to the throat. She forced herself to take a step closer.

There he was. Bava. In his truest form.

The tub was half full of a pale, viscous liquid, stained here and there with tiny clots of blood. Pure, liquefied protoplasm. Maggots twirled and swam through the putrescence. Floating in the grotesque stew were human bones. A skull crested one end of the tub. Femurs stuck up near the bottom. Ribs were like shadowy fingers reaching up from the bottom of the tub.

And there in the middle of it all was Bava's heart. His one vulnerable part. It floated in the exact center of the tub, black and flaky with ash. Connected to nothing.

But beating. Slowly, inexorably beating. As it might forever if she didn't end this, right now.

While the sun was still up, she could tear the heart to shreds with her bare hands. It would be enough. It would kill Bava. Put an end to his murder spree.

She reached for it, at which point, Chey grabbed her forearm and slammed it down against the side of the tub. Hard enough that Caxton cried out in sudden pain, thinking her arm must be broken, snapped in half.

Then Chey grabbed her by the hair and dragged her out of the bathroom. Tossed her down on the mattress. Caxton struggled to get back up. Through the bathroom door she could see movement—a human skull slowly rising over the lip of the tub.

"No!" she screamed. "No!" It was too late. The sun was down, and night had begun.

Chey kicked the door shut, cutting off Caxton's view.

***

The darkness outside was the darkness of a wild place. Profound. The only illumination came from a single kerosene lantern burning inside the house.

She could see Bava, the vampire, just fine. He nearly glowed in the dark. He crouched on the porch of the little house, not moving. He was whiter than the snow, except for his blood-red eyes. His ears came to sharp points. There was no hair anywhere on his body.

He watched Caxton. Studied her, as if trying to figure out why she had been so persistent in chasing him down. Or maybe he was just wondering how good her blood would taste.

Given her experience with vampires, it was probably the latter.

The werewolves hadn't really hurt her. Her arm wasn't broken, it just hurt like hell. They'd knocked her around a little in the process of dragging her out of the house, but then they'd just thrown her up against a tree and left her there, under the vampire's watchful eye. They'd made no attempt to restrain her. Why bother? They could chase her down if she tried to run. They'd taken her weapons, and she could hardly win a fistfight against one monster, much less three.

"Have you seen Dzo? I thought he was going to meet us here," Powell said, coming around the side of the house. He was dressed now, in a flannel shirt and dungarees. "I can't find him anywhere."

"You never know with our pal, the musquash," Chey said, coming up from behind Caxton's tree. Maybe she'd been back there setting up an ambush, in case Caxton did try to run. She'd dressed, too.

"My pilot chased him off," Caxton told them. Her continued existence pretty much depended on the werewolves, so she figured she would be helpful if she could.

"Your pilot?" Powell asked, stalking toward her, his face pinched with anger. Maybe she should have kept her mouth shut after all.

"Jesse Det'anichok," Caxton said.

Chey looked confused, but Powell just nodded, as if Caxton had explained everything.

"What are they?" Caxton asked.

"Animal spirits," Powell said offhandedly. "Creatures from the old stories of this part of the world. Your pilot is the personification of the eagle. Dzo—he's the musquash, the muskrat. An animal eagles prey on. If you wanted to get on my good side, you really failed, bringing eagle here. Dzo's our friend. He helps us out. The only thing up here we can talk to because our wolves have no interest in killing him."

"Your wolves?"

Chey sighed. "That's how Powell talks about them. It makes him feel like he's got some ownership over his curse. Instead of the other way around. By making them separate from us—"

"I am not that *thing*," Powell insisted. "Enough." He came over and squatted down next to Caxton. "We warned you. We told you to leave."

"You're harboring a vampire," Caxton told him. "I'm a vampire hunter. That's what I came here for."

Powell shook his head and stalked away. He couldn't seem to stand still. Instead he paced back and forth, nearly panting.

Chey, on the other hand, looked tired out. Ready to end things. She leaned against the side of the house, her face pressed against the rough wood. "I was a hunter, originally. I came up here hunting a werewolf. Look how that turned out."

Bava spoke, and everyone turned to look. A vampire's voice was one of his most deadly weapons. They could hypnotize with their words. Enthrall.

"She's not a hunter. She's a murderer. She's killed so many of us... I might be the last of my kind."

"Good," Caxton said.

"Do you see?" Bava demanded. He jumped off the porch and threw his arms up in the air. "She only wants to destroy. You should kill her."

The werewolves wouldn't meet his gaze.

Interesting, Caxton thought.

Bava hadn't said, "Let me kill her." He hadn't suggested they let him drink her blood.

"What did he tell you?" she said, trying to catch Powell's eye. "What did he promise?"

"Nothing. He asked for our help."

"Uh-huh," Caxton said. "Did he say he was one of the good vampires? That he didn't want to hurt anyone, that he just wanted to be left in peace? It doesn't work that way. He needs blood. He *has* to have it. Eventually he's going to kill somebody to get it."

"He hasn't tried to hurt us at all," Chey pointed out.

"Sure," Caxton told her. "Because you're not human. He

needs human blood."

"In a minute there's going to be plenty of that around here," Powell pointed out. "The moon's coming up. Our wolves will tear you to pieces. You can't talk to them. You can't make *them* any promises. They hate anything like you. Anything human."

"Then we need to finish this now," Caxton said.

Powell turned his gaze on her, and it was almost worse than looking straight into the eyes of a vampire. There was no magic in those cold, green eyes, but there didn't need to be. There was, in them, the look of a predator. The look of humanity's oldest enemy, the wild animal, and it fixed her to the spot.

"There are times," he said, very slowly, very deliberately, "when I think my wolf has a point. I've been living up here most of a century. There's never been a time when humans weren't coming up here to kill me."

He walked over and put his arms around the vampire's shoulders. "When Bava came and spoke with me, he bowed his head. He begged for my help as a fellow outcast. You—I don't know you. You came here with guns. You came to kill. I have one thing in common with my wolf, definitely. I'm just trying to protect my pack. And right now, he's part of my pack."

Caxton understood. She knew she was never going to convince the werewolves to give her Bava. Because she had her own pack—in this case, the people of Yellowknife. She thought of the little girl in the big fur hat, waving through the window of the diner. She thought of Corporal Wallace, who believed in her when she needed it the most.

She would do anything to protect those people.

Even the stupidest, riskiest thing she could think of. She had no weapons, no way to kill Bava like this, but she did have one thing that might change the balance of power.

She had five liters of blood in her veins.

"He's not your friend. He's nobody's friend," Caxton said. Before Powell could respond to that, she lifted one hand to ask him for a moment's patience.

Then she brought the hand down hard against the tree's trunk, dragging her skin across the rough bark. Then she brought her hand up to where she could see it in the near dark. She flexed her fingers, willing her desperate ploy to work.

"I'm not interested in games," Powell told her. He moved toward her and grabbed her arm, pulling her to her feet. "We need to make a decision, now."

"Kill her," Bava said.

The werewolves both froze in place. Listening to that voice.

"She'll never stop, not until I'm dead," the vampire insisted. "We have no choice."

"You'd know about not having any choices," Caxton told him. She flexed her hand again, squeezing the abraded skin on the ball of her thumb. She felt a faint wetness there, just a few drops where she'd broken the skin against the tree bark.

It would have to be enough.

She flicked her hand out, toward Bava. Her blood flicked through the air.

And then it happened. The change. She'd seen it before. Had been counting on it.

Vampires looked almost human. They sounded reasonable when you talked to them, like rational human beings. But they weren't. They were hollow inside, their personalities scraped out by the need. The desperate, undeniable craving.

Bava's nostrils flared and his eyes went wide.

"What is it?" Chey asked. "What did you do to him?"
"Oh, look," Caxton said, holding up her hand. "I've cut myself."

Bava's lower jaw distended like that of a snake trying to swallow an egg. His lips drew back, revealing row after row of sharp, glassy teeth. Like the teeth of a shark, not a human. Every muscle in his body tensed, and she thought of Jesse standing on the plane's float, waiting to spear a fish.

Except Bava had no intention of waiting. He launched himself through the air, so fast it looked like his feet were barely touching the soil. Then he was right on top of Caxton, his hands reaching to grab her, to pull her apart. She'd known he wouldn't be able to resist the smell of blood, and she'd known it probably meant her death.

For the little girl in the fur hat, she was willing to make that sacrifice. If it showed Powell and Chey what Bava really was—

Just before those claws dug into her, before the teeth could rip her throat out, Caxton saw a blur of motion and then heard a sound like two sides of beef smashing together. Bava went rolling across the clearing, with Chey on top of him. She had grabbed both his hands and was trying to pin him down.

Maybe she wasn't human. Maybe Bava had no desire to drink *her* blood. His head lunged forward and he tore at her body with his fangs anyway. She howled, an animal sound, and rolled away as he tore a huge chunk of meat from her shoulder and arm. She crashed to the snowy ground, cradling her mutilated flesh.

Bava started to get to his feet, his eyes locked on Caxton's bleeding hand. He took a step forward—and that was as far as he got. When Powell hit him, it didn't sound like meat on meat. It sounded like a hammer hitting an anvil.

Bava's left leg shattered under the force of the blow, the bones snapping audibly and ripping out through his papery skin. No blood flowed from the wound, but Caxton could see his translucent muscle fibers tearing.

The vampire didn't care, though. He staggered up onto his feet, the compound fracture healing almost instantly. As Powell came for him again, he was ready. Powell charged in with his head down, clearly intending to pick Bava up and then body slam him into the ground. Instead Bava jumped out of the way at the last minute, the claws of one hand extended.

The claws tore Powell's stomach open, side to side, spilling Powell's guts into a steaming mass at his feet. The werewolf tried to scream, but then he choked on his own blood.

Caxton could only stare in horror. She couldn't move.

Not until Chey crawled up toward her, her damaged arm dragging in the dirt.

"You... need to..." Chey closed her eyes as her face rippled with a wave of pain.

"You're hurt." It sounded stupid even as she said it.

"The moon'll... it'll fix us. But you need to run!"

Chey looked up, at the top of the trees. Caxton saw a smudge of silver light there, the first beams of a rising moon.

Powell had fallen to his knees. Bava had one hand on either side of the werewolf's head and was squeezing—crushing Powell's skull. It would be enough to kill any human. But the change had already begun.

Powell's flesh grew transparent. Illusory. Caxton expected the transformation from man to wolf to involve a lot of tearing skin and howling rage, but Powell looked peaceful, almost happy as he seemed to transform into a smoky, silver-lit version of himself. Bava's hands passed right through him as if he were a ghost, and the vampire staggered back in surprise.

Then Powell's clothes fell to the ground, right through him.

Caxton looked down and saw that Chey had gone through an identical transformation. Her eyes were closed and her lips parted, just a little, as she let out an almost orgasmic sigh.

Caxton was already running through the trees when behind her there came a flash of silver light, and then she heard the howl of a dire wolf. That unmistakable predatory screech she'd heard the night before, when the wolves came through the trees and tried to attack the plane.

She glanced back only once. In that moment, under the rising moon, she saw Powell's wolf, with its green, green eyes. It lunged forward and tore Bava open from shoulder to groin with one savage snap of its jaws. The vampire started to fall—but even as he did, his skin began to knit back together, closing the wound.

Powell's wolf didn't give him a chance to heal. It dug its massive snout deep inside Bava's chest and then pulled his heart right out, the aorta snagging on the wolf's massive, grinding teeth.

Bava was dead.

But Caxton would be too—if she didn't move.

In the dark she could barely see the branches of the trees whipping at her face. She kept her hands up as she ran, even though every time a branch caught her across her hurt arm she wanted to cry out in agony. She stumbled on a tree root, but she was so full of adrenaline she just jumped into the air, vaulting forward to land, still running.

Behind her the wolves howled and cried. She could hear

their bloodlust, hear their jaws snapping at the air.

It wasn't far to the pond where Jesse theoretically waited with the plane, but it felt like it could have been on the far side of the world. She tried to control her breathing, tried to fight through the fear.

Then she saw a pair of green eyes racing parallel to her, through the forest. Powell's wolf, so close she could almost have reached out to stroke its fur.

Caxton tried to veer off, to run away from the wolf, even if that meant she would miss the pond, maybe lose it in the dark. She had no choice. She stared forward through the darkness and saw a tree trunk rushing towards her face and just managed to dodge sideways. The wolf leaped over a dead, fallen tree and it was right on her heels. She changed her course again, but she could have sworn she felt its hot breath on her back.

The female wolf—Chey's wolf—howled in the night somewhere off to her left. Were they playing with her? Setting up an ambush?

She should have expected as much. All the same, when it came, she was surprised. She half-ran, half-jumped between two trees, and there was the pond, a clearing of pure black ahead of her. The moon's reflection shivered on the icy water, and she heard the roar of an engine. Jesse was already taxiing across the water, getting ready to take off—without her. She waved her arms and shouted for him.

And then Chey's wolf ran right across her path, knocking her off her feet into a pile of fallen needles.

Caxton jumped up, but the wolf was right there, its mottled coat gleaming in the pale light. Its teeth—its teeth —so huge, so sharp—

The wolf lunged forward, right at her throat. There was no way she could have escaped that attack. She closed her eyes and waited to die.

So she heard, rather than saw Dzo, the muskrat spirit, erupt up out of the water in a great splashing crescendo. When she opened her eyes, she saw the fur-clad spirit grab the wolf by her hind legs and drag the animal back into the water. Chey's wolf let out a startled yelp, her jaws snapping shut.

Caxton didn't bother wondering what had just happened. She jumped over the two of them where they wrestled on the pond's bank, jumped into the water. The plane was only a few yards away, moving fast, now. The water surged around her and she felt it sucking her down, but then the plane's float was right in front of her. She ducked her head to avoid its propeller and grabbed onto the float, grabbed on for all she was worth, her arm shrieking in agony as she hauled herself up to a place where she could clutch the strut that connected the float to the plane's fuselage.

Powell's wolf came out of the trees and threw up both paws to try to catch the plane, but it was already in the air, climbing almost vertically.

As the plane carried her up into the air, Caxton looked down at the trees below her, the drunken forest leaning in every direction, the countless little patches of water, every one of them glowing with a tiny reflection of the moon.

***

Jesse set down in another lake, just long enough for Caxton to climb up off the float and drag herself inside the tiny cabin. The pilot—the eagle in human form—didn't even look at her. He was too busy getting them airborne again.

Once she sat down and strapped herself in, Caxton closed her eyes and just tried to breathe for a while. She hurt in a dozen places and she was freezing, her parka soaked through, her body wracked with chills. But she was alive.

"He saved me," she said. "Musquash. He—he saved me.

I thought... I thought you came here to kill him. Maybe eat him."

Jesse frowned. "Eat him? Nah. Hell, no." He seemed almost offended by the idea.

"But—the way he ran when he saw you—"

"He owed me three hundred dollars," Jesse explained.

Caxton couldn't believe it. "You came all this way, helped me kill a vampire, just to collect on a debt?"

"Three hundred dollars is a lot of money." Jesse shrugged. "And I didn't even get it in the end. He didn't have so much as pocket change. So instead I told him we'd call it even if he agreed to help you out."

Caxton's chest heaved. She thought it was just another chill at first, but then a laugh exploded out of her mouth.

"When we get back to Yellowknife, you're buying the beer," Jesse said.

Yellowknife. Caxton kept laughing, but she peered out her window, looking for the lights of the town. The town full of people—her pack.

Always before, throughout her career as a vampire hunter, she'd fought alone. She'd considered people to almost be expendable. She'd used them as bait if it meant her getting closer to her quarry.

Maybe it was time to start rethinking that strategy.

Because she knew that while she was aging, slowing down, there would always be more vampires. More for her to do. But from now on—maybe she didn't have to go it alone.

ABOUT THE AUTHOR

David Wellington is the author of over twenty novels, which have appeared around the world in eight languages. His horror series include *Monster Island*, *13 Bullets*, *Frostbite,* and *Positive*. He has written fantasy and thrillers, and has also worked in video games and comic books. His most recent novel is *The Last Astronaut*, a work of science fiction and horror. He lives and works in New York City.

http://www.davidwellington.net

@lasttrilobite

The Original

David Watkins

"You're a long way from home, Roman."

Marcus stopped walking and gazed into the trees. He was on a well-worn path, wide enough for three men to walk abreast, which meant the Celts would consider it a road. Dense trees lined the way, with branches joining overhead. They provided some cover from the persistent rain, but not enough.

His thick cloak covered his battered armor and weapons. All markings showing his unit were long gone, though if they were erased by time or battle was unclear. He drew back his cowl, revealing dark, long unkempt hair and a weather-beaten face. His beard had seen better days — ones before he'd got on the road.

"And you are not hiding as well as you should," he said. His baritone voice befitted his hulking frame.

"Is that a threat?"

Marcus shrugged. "Make of it what you will. It is late; I am tired. If you wish to rob me, I hope you have brought more men."

The man hidden by the trees laughed — a false and empty noise. It sounded more like someone clearing their throat of phlegm than genuine mirth. "I'm 'ere to give a friendly warning. You've 'eard of the Beast, down in Isca?"

The Beast. Marcus studied the tree line, waiting for the man to show himself. He knew that at least two more men stood hidden in the forest behind. Marcus pulled his cloak back, revealing his gladius and rested his hand casually on the hilt.

"Ho, no need for that, Roman."

"My name is Marcus Remus Pelasgus," he said. "You should know who you are dealing with."

"That name means nowt to me. So, Marcus, why're you 'ere? Is it the Beast?"

Marcus shook his head. No sense in telling them the truth. "My countrymen are coming this way in large numbers. I wanted to see this" —he gestured around him— "before it's gone."

At his words, rain thudded harder on the leaves.

"Very noble. You're obviously alone. Not much of a scout, are you?"

"I am not a scout. Show yourself."

A branch moved, and the man stepped into view. He was dressed in various animal pelts, with a necklace of teeth dangling halfway down his muscly chest. In his right hand, he held a vicious-looking spear, and he was grinning.

"So, Marcus the Roman. Should've I 'eard of you?"

Marcus shrugged again. "Whether you have or have not is of no consequence. Tell your men to come out."

"Very good, Roman," he nodded in appreciation. Glancing over his shoulder, Marcus saw two large men carrying spears emerge from the undergrowth. They looked well fed, their arms strong. Maybe this wasn't going to be as easy as he'd assumed.

"I have told you my name," Marcus said. "Can you grant me safe passage?" He smiled. "Protection from your Beast?"

"Now that depends on what you're offering us in return," the man said.

"Your lives."

All three men started laughing, and this time it was

genuine.

"Just one of you, my friend. You're outnumbered."

"Not for the first time." Marcus' hand shifted, so he held the gladius tightly. "Nor the last."

***

Marcus saw the smoke from the huts long before they came into view. Thick black smoke rose to the sky, its tendrils reaching out to ensnare the clouds. It had finally stopped raining, and he would have been glad were it not for the need to wash blood out of his cloak. When the road had turned into a path, then a trail, he had used his new spear to turn branches out of his way. The weapon was well balanced — almost as good as his javelin. Given that he hadn't seen his javelin since Germania, this one would serve as an adequate replacement.

The trail started to rise, gently at first but then increasing in gradient. Marcus climbed out of the undergrowth and stopped at the top of the hill. He longed for the warmth and security of Rome. It had been many years now since he had last seen it, with the Legion taking him far from his home. Originally, it had been a choice — a chance to see the world and escape the suspicion at home. Now, something else drove him forward.

The Beast, always the Beast.

A ring of huts sat in the hollow in front of him. All were round and seemed to be made of mud with occasional lumps of stone protruding from the walls. Thick straw made up the roofs. They were little more than hovels, especially when compared to the houses in Rome. They looked dirty and unkempt. Who would choose to live like this? The source of the smoke lay in the center of the huts: a large fire with a deer strung on a crude spit over it.

He could see some people moving around the huts, two women and a child playing some sort of game. Mud was not just used to build here: Celts were covered in it. Did they bathe in mud or only cover themselves in it for fun? Men sat near the fire, probably congratulating themselves on such an excellent kill. The smell of the venison cooking made Marcus' stomach grumble. He stood on the rise, waiting for them to see him.

A shout went up, and three men stood, approaching him quickly. All three carried iron-tipped spears, and the third also had a small knife. Marcus held his hands out at his sides, not moving and waiting until they were close enough to hear him.

"I did not come to fight," he bellowed.

"Romans are not welcome here," the man with the dagger said.

"I have not come for Rome," Marcus said. He took a step forward and was met with the point of a spear touching his chest.

"Where d'ya get that spear?"

"Some men tried to rob me. I took it from them."

The men exchanged an uneasy look. "What happened to them?"

Marcus shrugged. "I am trained, they were not."

Pressure from the spear tip eased as the man lowered it.

"You killed them?" Dagger said.

"It was not difficult."

The expressions on the men's faces said that they disagreed. Shock turned to awe as they realized Marcus was serious.

"Then we're in your debt. Come and join us."

***

Marcus sat on a log, pulling strips of venison off the

bone with his teeth. Juices ran down his chin and hand, coating his arm. He didn't care. It was delicious - the meat smoked from the flames and full of flavor. He thought, perhaps, he could eat the whole deer by himself, but the Celts might then not be quite so welcoming. After a long time on the road, it was good to eat something other than berries and stale bread.

A fire crackled in a pit in front of him, its warmth welcome after the rain of the day. The sun hung low in the sky: It would soon be dark. The clouds had finally cleared, leaving a cold night ahead. Another reason to be grateful for the fire.

"So, Marcus," Caratacos, the man with the dagger, said. "This ain't your 'ome."

"No," Marcus shook his head. He watched the group for a moment. Two women, four men and at least three different children. Who the parents were was anybody's guess. Everyone stank of manure, dirt and filth. Caratacos, in particular, reeked with an ammonia stench that burnt Marcus' nostrils. "I have not seen Rome for over twenty years."

"Why?"

"The Legion keeps marching. Caesar wants more lands."

"He'll never take this one," one of the women spat.

"Hush, Alane. He's helped us. We'll not be rude."

The woman gave a look that could have curdled milk, but she did not speak again.

"You're alone," Caratacos said. "Why?"

"My men are gone. In Germania." Marcus grimaced at the memory. The endless forest, then Germanic Celts moving out of the trees, throwing spear after spear. Everywhere his unit had tried to retreat to, there were more Celts. It had been a massacre. He'd barely survived and had been forced to salvage equipment.

"The might of Rome beaten by our cousins?" Caratacos smirked.

"They had help," Marcus grunted. "A man called Arminius showed them what to do to defeat us. We had educated him. A traitor to Rome."

"And yet you survived."

Marcus nodded.

"How?"

Marcus shrugged. "I got lucky." He fell silent, and it was clear that he was going to say nothing more on the subject.

"They'll kill you for desertion," Caratacos said.

"I did not desert," Marcus said softly.

Caratacos snorted. "If you ran, then you deserted. How can you go back?"

"I have heard tales of your Beast." Marcus glared at the Celt, hiding the abrupt change of topic with his stare.

Alane took a sharp intake of breath and made a strange gesture with her hand. The other woman stood and disappeared into the hut. She was followed by the two men, and Marcus could hear them telling the children to be quiet.

"What've you 'eard?"

"The usual tales from men deep in their cups. A Beast, 'the like of which you have never seen before, ferocious and deadly.' They say those who cross its path are never heard from again. They say its howls at night are the only evidence it exists." Marcus took another chunk of venison and looked Caratacos in the eye. "They say it can change shape. Sometimes a wolf, sometimes a man."

Alane made the symbol with her hand again and spat on

the floor.

"These woods are full of stories," Caratacos said. "You shouldn't believe 'em all."

"Your woman would seem to disagree."

"She's no-one's *woman,* Roman. You'd do well to remember that."

Marcus' lips were a thin line, but he kept quiet.

"Tell me of the Beast," he said, voice insistent. He let his hand drift to the hilt of his gladius.

Caratacos shook his head, then glanced at one of the huts.

Marcus shifted his gaze, but the dark was absolute. A change in the evening breeze brought a fresh assault on Marcus' nose, and he gagged. He took shallow breaths and tried to control his anger. He drew the gladius, although he did not need it, and snarled, "Tell me."

"Sit down, Roman," Caratacos said. "We're not your enemy."

"Then who is back there?" Marcus pointed to the hut with his sword. "Show yourself."

"We're farmers," Caratacos said, "not warriors."

"Then why hide?"

Caratacos shrugged. "We stick together. Our families need to be kept safe."

"Why do you keep looking at the huts? What is back there?"

"I sent someone to check your story. He's returned."

Marcus grunted. "You do not believe me?"

A howl shattered the coming night. The Celt turned to

the sound, face suddenly pale beneath the grime. Marcus followed his gaze. The small rise he'd come over earlier was now shrouded in dim light, with the first strands of mist rising from the ground. Something moved on the brow of the hill — or was it a trick of the light?

"Inside," Caratacos said softly. His hand was trembling as he reached the spear closest to him. Animal teeth were wrapped around the shaft, and they clinked together softly as he lifted it. Alane moved quickly, glaring at Marcus.

Another howl echoed through the night. A different noise, lower in pitch. There were at least two creatures out there. Now, movement on the rise — and this was definitely no trick of the light. Something was moving, slinking through the shadows. Marcus frowned, squinting as if to help his eyes focus on what he was seeing.

Moving slowly and deliberately, the shape emerged from the shadows. It was huge: easily the biggest wolf Marcus had seen in a long time. With a snarl, it revealed two rows of razor-sharp teeth.

"Don't let it bite you," Caratacos said. He was holding his spear tightly, fear a mask on his face.

With a roar of his own, Marcus charged, gladius outstretched before him. The wolf snarled again, muscles tensing, ready to jump. Marcus thrust the sword, and it bit deep into the wolf's side as it leaped at him. The wolf's momentum carried it through its jump, and it landed on Marcus, sending them both crashing to the ground. Teeth smashed together in front of Marcus' face, narrowly missing his nose and cheek as he turned his face away. Wolf spittle dribbled onto his face.

Marcus pulled at the sword, but it was stuck in the wolf's side. It bit down again, and Marcus jammed his free arm between the teeth. The wolf shook its head, trying to rip Marcus' flesh, and Marcus shouted at it. He released the sword, leaving it buried in the wolf's side, and punched it in the head. It didn't release its grip, so he hit again and again. Finally, he rolled, heaving with all his strength, pushing against the wolf. The creature twisted, and Marcus was suddenly on top of it. He reached down for his sword and yanked it free with a sickening squelch. Blood poured from the wound, and the animal whimpered as it released his arm.

"Your arm!" Caratacos cried.

Marcus held up his left arm, revealing the armor plating covering his forearm. Dented in a multitude of places where the wolf had tried to gain purchase on flesh, the armor was still intact. Marcus grinned at the Celt, but then he saw something move between the huts behind him.

"Behind you!" he roared.

Caratacos started to turn, swinging his spear, but the gap between the huts was too narrow for such a long weapon. Hidden in the shadows until now, another wolf charged, growling and baring its teeth. It would be on Caratacos before he could bring the javelin to bear. Marcus shouted again and threw his gladius. The sword sang through the air, hitting the wolf in the head and sinking deep into its skull. It fell to the ground, whining as it hit the earth. Marcus closed the distance between them in a few long strides. He pulled the gladius free and then swung it in an arc over his head. The blow separated head and body, blood pouring from the stump. The wolf's eyes gazed at him venomously, despite their lack of life.

"You saved my life," Caratacos said, breathing hard.

"I killed a creature," Marcus said as if it were nothing. He kicked the severed head away from the corpse then turned to the other wolf. "Are these the Beast?"

The wolf's breathing was ragged and shallow. With every breath, more blood pulsed out of the wound. It whimpered, watching Marcus with a baleful eye. Drool slipped out of side of its mouth, and it blinked twice. Its eye seemed to focus more clearly on Marcus now, and the horrible rattle of its breath was slowing, with each inhalation weaker than the last.

"That one is," Caratacos said, pointing. "They heal. The other thing doesn't."

As Marcus watched, the blood squirting out of the beast's side slowed then stopped. The fur was knitting back together, but almost immediately it started receding, flowing back into the wolf's body. Its snout shortened and forelegs shrank. The hind legs elongated, but there was no sound: no crunching bone or cracking skin. In seconds, a naked man lay in the mud, a long scar adorning his side. He stood slowly, bones popping as he did so. Stretching his muscles out, he grinned at Marcus.

"Hello again, Roman," he said, getting to his feet. "Did you really think I'd be that easy to kill?"

The would-be thief. He was naked but made no effort to cover himself. A sly smirk sat on his face as if he wanted Marcus to see his body. Marcus grunted and closed the distance between them in a few quick steps, shaking as anger surged through him, mixing with adrenaline to banish weariness from his limbs. He swung his sword in a wide-sweeping arc, moving so quickly the Celt had no time to react. The gladius sliced deeply into his exposed neck, severing muscle and bone as it went. His head flew clear off the body, blood erupting from the stump of his neck and spattering to the ground with a noise not dissimilar to the earlier rain.

Marcus kept the gladius sharp and well-oiled for a reason.

"You killed him," Caratacos said, his voice full of awe.

"Twice," Marcus grunted. He kicked the corpse, which was still oozing blood. Kneeling in the mud, Marcus picked up the severed head and examined it. "He is human," he said.

"Sort of." Caratacos joined him. The Celt was still

looking at Marcus with wide eyes. "He's the Beast you've 'eard of, but you killed him."

"I am a little disappointed."

"You've saved my life, and 'ave killed the Beast," Caratacos said. "These things are not disappointing to me, my friend."

"I was going to take it to Rome," Marcus said.

Caratacos laughed. "To Rome? For your emperor? It would've killed you long before you even got to Isca."

"Not for Caesar," Marcus muttered. "For me."

"You?"

"Never mind." Marcus was weary now as the adrenaline started to fade. "I should take my leave. It is a long journey back to Isca."

"There are more of these things in the woods. If you leave now, you'll not see the dawn." Caratacos took the head from Marcus and tossed it onto the fire. Flames danced over the skin and hair. Soon, the skin was blistering then black. Fat sizzled and spat in the fire. The smell of roasting flesh almost overwhelmed Caratacos' odor.

Almost.

Marcus grinned. "More?"

"They live in the depths of the woods, away from the main paths. We leave them alone, and they usually leave us in peace. Sometimes they eat our sheep, sometimes something more precious."

Marcus watched the man as he stumbled over the word "precious." So few children here. Even with winter approaching, there should have been more.

"I want one alive," Marcus said.

"They're dangerous."

"So am I," Marcus said with a snarl. Caratacos looked away and then held up his hands to try and calm the Roman.

"Why must it be alive?" His eyes were wide, pleading. "They'll kill you."

"I want to take it back to Rome. It will fight for me in the Colosseum." Marcus pointed at the scar on the dead man's body. "He healed so quickly, he will be more than a match for any of our gladiators."

"This is about money?" Caratacos was aghast. "That's impossible! You ain't got no men."

"I have no need for them."

Caratacos scoffed. "How'd you get it to Rome?"

"It will come with me." Marcus smiled. "I can be very persuasive."

"They don't listen," Caratacos said.

"Money changes many people's minds." Marcus' grin widened. "We will make a fortune."

"This is madness, my friend."

Marcus gestured at the huts. "Are you saying you do not need the money?"

"You've got money?" Caratacos laughed and pointed at Marcus' battered clothing.

"Enough," Marcus said.

"And you'll bring the money back 'ere to us?" He laughed again.

Marcus reached into his tunic and pulled out a small bag of coins. Despite its size, it was heavy and the coins within clinked together. It was more wealth than the Celt had ever seen.

The Original

"I can show you to their lair at first light."

***

First light was actually the vaguest glimmer of sunrise. The land was still dark under a heavy grey sky, but the golden hue on the horizon signaled the coming day. Marcus stretched as they walked, feeling the weariness of months on the road deep in his bones. Caratacos stayed close to Marcus — too close. The man's stench had not improved with sleep. He was quiet as they walked, a shadow of the talkative man from the night before. That suited Marcus just fine, as he was sore from the excitement of last night. Not much of him *didn't* ache: His arms and legs felt especially heavy today. Sleep had not come easily to him, not now his quarry was so close.

The Beasts.

Plural. For so long, Marcus had tracked all mention of them, and now they were close. An entire family of them. Marcus had not thought it possible; in his experience, the Beasts lived in small groups. One Beast and its pack — it had seemed to be a rule. Never had he heard of more Beasts together. Until now.

The thought excited him. As they trudged through the forest, the ground still damp with morning dew, he mulled over what he knew about the creatures. The Beasts were powerful: Healing was only part of it. They could also create lesser beings — what Caratacos and the others had fought before. Wolves in human form, created when the Beasts did not kill their prey. A single bite would do it. If the human survived, they became wolf-men. It was how the Beasts grew their packs. In Rome, they had been called Originals — apparently descended from Lycaon himself. Even there, very few people had heard of them.

"It's not much farther," Caratacos said, breaking the silence. "Deeper into these woods, there's a cave. You'll find them there."

"You are not coming?"

"No," Caratacos said. "I'm no fighter. You took the leader; the others will fall easily to your mighty blade."

Marcus grunted. The Celt's disgusting smell hid his fear, but Marcus was too old to be fooled by someone complimenting him so blatantly.

"Follow the path," Caratacos said, pointing. "It's wide enough for the Beast, it'll be wide enough for you."

Marcus followed the point with his eyes. Lush, green trees grew thick and wild, branches and leaves intertwining to cover the way ahead. He frowned and looked closer. Slowly but surely, a path revealed itself. Bare grass here, a broken branch there. Now he knew what he was looking for, the route was clear.

He took a breath and started to walk along the path. His heart was beating with a ferocity that surprised him. He forced himself to calm down, breathing deeply and trying to keep his muscles relaxed even as he walked. By Marcus' reckoning, he'd walked for a couple of hours, and so the sun should be up. Its rays were not penetrating the covering of the foliage: Neither light nor warmth reached Marcus in this gods-forsaken place. He used his sword to push back low branches and tried to avoid stepping on any twigs or sticks on the ground.

Marcus moved quickly for a big man and made good progress through the forest. Mist hung around the undergrowth, increasing the feeling of gloom that pervaded from the trees. This was not a happy place. He found the skeleton of a sheep, picked completely clean of all flesh, its white bones looking silver in the mist.

Nothing moved in the forest except Marcus. He heard no birds singing, nor did he hear any evidence of other creatures large or small. Usually, he would hear a big animal crashing away from him or birds taking flight in a flurry of squawks and feathers.

Here, all was silent.

The air cooled further as he walked, and he knew he was near. Now, the stench of rotting flesh overpowered the freshness of the forest air. He pushed a thick branch out of the way and saw a large cave. Trees had hidden the rise in the land and rocks hugged the opening, looking like ill-formed teeth.

As the hill ascended above him, the entrance beckoned, leading into the cave. It was dark, but Marcus wasn't afraid of that.

"Come out!" he bellowed. "Come and face me!"

His voice echoed around the cave, and he took another step toward the darkness. Almost immediately, the ground fell away before him, a steep, rock-filled path leading treacherously downward. A rustle in the trees behind him and an assault on his nose made him turn.

"I thought you'd need this," Caratacos said. His smile revealed his teeth — many were missing, and those that remained were black. He held a thick branch toward Marcus, and the top was covered with moss and straw. A torch. It smoldered now, faint twists of black smoke coiling their way into the air. Caratacos blew onto the branch, and the embers glowed fiercely then burst into flame.

Marcus grunted his thanks. He'd been waiting for his vision to adjust to the gloom, but there was no way for the Celt to know that.

"You coming?" Marcus asked.

"With you at my side, Roman, I've nothing to fear," Caratacos said with a grin.

Marcus squinted at him. Caratacos' newfound bravery disappointed him. You knew where you were with a coward. Marcus drew the gladius and stepped into the cave, Caratacos close behind. Loose stones gave way under his feet, and he slipped, skidding a few feet into the mouth of the tunnel. To his credit, Caratacos did not make a sound, although the flames showed the concern etched on his face. Marcus found firmer footing and nodded at the Celt. His meaning was clear: *Watch your step.*

Farther down the slope, the path started to level out and open up. Marcus found himself in a large circular cavern. He frowned — the cave showed nothing, no bones or any signs of animal life at all. Where were the creatures? In the center of the cave sat a large slab of stone covered in ornate carvings. The biggest showed a horned man holding a torc in one hand and a snake in the other. Marcus moved toward it and then stopped.

Something was wrong.

The cave was brightening. Marcus turned to see Caratacos lighting more torches. He moved with the certainty of someone who knew what they were doing. These were set into the walls of the cave on crude metal brackets. They gleamed in the light. Bronze, he realized. Why were there torches down here?

Caratacos beamed at him, and then Marcus detected something else, hidden by the Celt's horrific stench. There were more people here.

Lots more.

Something whistled through the air, and Marcus moved to his left. A spear flew past his head, narrowly missing him. More spears flew out of the darkness where Caratacos had not yet reached with his torch. Marcus tried to dodge again, but there were too many. One took Marcus square in the chest, thudding through his armor. A second landed in his stomach, doubling him over as a third struck him in the side. More spears whizzed through the air.

Marcus staggered, holding the first spear, trying to remove it from his chest. If he could, then he had a chance. Falling to his knees, Marcus struggled to gain purchase on the spear with hands now slick with blood. His own blood, something he had not seen in such a long time it fascinated him. Something tugged around his neck, and he fell to the floor, hands slipping from the spear.

One of the Celts threw a rope, and it landed over Marcus' head, tightening around his neck. The Celt kept his distance, though, which meant he wasn't stupid. Torn between removing the spears and rope, Marcus turned his head and caught Caratacos' eye. The Celt shrugged and grinned his disgusting grin.

"You know we can't let you live," he said. "We know what you are."

Marcus laughed. How could he have been so stupid? His excitement and greed had clouded his judgment. There were no more Beasts. They lived alone — perhaps surrounded by underlings, but never another one of them. Marcus knew this.

Marcus knew everything about the Beasts.

Another rope whistled through the air and landed around his arm. He tried to move away, but it slipped tight around his wrist and held fast. Marcus felt weak now and knew he had to prioritize the spears. Get the spear out and let the healing happen. If it hadn't hit his heart, it was close. He was losing too much blood. He rolled, breaking the shaft of the spear in his side. Marcus didn't care — that wasn't the one doing the damage. He felt the rope around his wrist tighten as the Celt tried to pull on it. His bindings gave slightly, and Marcus pulled his arm again, putting as much of his draining strength in as he could. A Celt stumbled toward him, letting go of the rope.

Marcus gave in to his frustration and rage and made his face *change*. His jaw extended, stretching the skin until it split and fur burst through the wounds. His nose and cheeks elongated until he had the face of a wolf. The stumbling Celt had no chance. Marcus bit his face off with one snap of his powerful jaws. Blood and chunks of flesh filled his mouth, its effect immediate. Energy coursed through him. The spear in his side clattered to the ground, while the other two started to slide from his body, where his flesh was already knitting together. His body would heal eventually all by itself, but another piece of juicy Celt would accelerate that process.

Screams of the remaining Celts filled the air, terror clear in their cries. The German Celts had screamed like that, as he'd made his escape. Two of them dragged the corpse just out of his reach.

More Celts surged forward and grabbed the end of the rope around Marcus' wrist. They pulled on the line, turning him toward them. A boy darted toward him, slipping the end of another rope onto his other arm and then retreating. Marcus' jaws snapped closed but snagged only air and no flesh.

Marcus forced himself to change. He felt the Beast within straining for release, and he gave into it. His equipment and armor fell to the ground as the wolf burst out of him. Only then did he realize that the Celts had a tight grip of his forelegs and he stumbled. The Celts' intricate knots slipped tighter around his forelimbs, digging into flesh hidden by thick fur. He shook his head violently, feeling the rope slacken. His current neck was much thicker than his previous one. He snarled. The groups holding his arms pulled backward, muscles straining as Marcus tried to resist. They had strength in numbers: He was strong, but not strong enough.

His hind legs scrabbled uselessly on the floor, claws clicking on stone. Marcus howled in frustration. His legs and back hit the rock, and he slipped, his legs giving way. He landed heavily, feeling the hardness of the cold stone shock through his body. A huge Celt ran forward, clutching a large rock and screaming. He threw it onto Marcus' back, and something cracked. His legs went cold, and then he could not feel them anymore. Back broken, legs refusing to obey, and now he was moving again, sliding inexorably forward and up.

They had pulled him onto the slab of stone.

A new feeling rose in him, one he was unaccustomed to.

Fear.

The Celts pulled again, heaving on the ropes, wrenching his forelegs outward, away from his body in a movement they were not meant to make. Marcus howled as he felt muscles tear. Now the healing would take longer. Too long. Caratacos stepped forward, watching him thrash with as much interest as he would show watching an upturned beetle trying to right itself. Marcus changed back to a man and screamed at Caratacos. The change brought a momentary respite from the pain and prevented his ribcage from splitting open, but he could still feel the damage across his chest. His body was trying to repair the damage from the spears, but he knew he was in trouble.

"Let me go, and you live," he snarled.

"No. Your kind's time's done."

He stood aside, and a woman came into the light. Alane. She had a single blue line painted down the middle of her face, but a cloak covered her hair and body. Her hands came out of the fabric now, pressed together as if she were praying. She whispered something in a language Marcus did not understand or recognize. Something ancient. There was a power hidden in her words.

"There're no more like you on these lands," Caratacos said. "Go back to Lycaon and tell him these lands aren't for your kind."

Marcus grunted. "Lycaon is a myth. It is just a story." He turned back, the Beast emerging once more. Marcus snapped at the ropes, but the Celts tightened their grip. The ropes were thick and well made. His teeth sank deeply into them, but the lines, while weakened, did not break. Now he could discern their scents from beneath Caratacos' stench, he knew how afraid they were.

"Pull!" Caratacos shouted, his voice echoing around the chamber.

Marcus realized too late that he had played into their hands. In this form, he was stronger, but his forelegs could not be moved sideways. He felt the muscles tear further and white-hot pain coursed through his torso. Caratacos darted forward and stabbed him in the middle of the chest, just to the left of where the remains of the spear jutted out. His gladius.

Caratacos had stabbed him with his own sword.

Alane opened her hands and raised her arms to the ceiling. Her voice rose as she did so, still speaking the ancient tongue. The shadows rippled like they were moving and then he saw why: spiders. Huge, black spiders with thick legs and bulbous carapaces scuttled across the ground toward him. They surged past the Celts like an eight-legged ocean and started to climb onto the altar. Marcus tried to pull away, but his body refused to move with his back and legs ignoring all instructions. The spiders crawled over him, and he felt sharp pain where they moved.

They were biting him.

Caratacos pulled the gladius free as Marcus lost the last of his strength. Blood spurted out his mouth, splashing onto Caratacos. The Celt grimaced but swung the sword again, and the blade bit deep into Marcus' neck. More of his body went cold as he lost feeling, and this was not due to his broken back. Caratacos heaved, and the sword came free, spilling Marcus' blood over the stone floor.

A noise like the wind sighing signaled the sword's final descent.

***

Caratacos bowed to Alane. "'Tis done," he said. Two of the stronger Celts lifted the severed head and carried it to the back of the cave. A narrow tunnel led further into the dark there. Caratacos knew it led to a much smaller part of the cave but hoped the distance would be enough to stop the Beast from healing itself.

Alane scowled at him. "It's never done with these Beasts. The Guardians'll watch over the bones." She pointed at the spiders, who were scattering away from the corpse, skittering into the shadows between the torches. "Seal the cave." Alane headed for the entrance, moving with a grace she usually hid from view.

Caratacos took a last look around the cave. The torches were spluttering out now, their light growing dimmer by the second. He could see no sign of the spiders. The two big Celts ran back into the main cave, brushing their bodies and faces full of revulsion. Caratacos shared the disgust: The spiders were horrible creatures, but they would not hurt anyone unless they tried to take the bones. In the dying light, he could see the white of the skeleton that had been the Roman. The spiders had eaten every bit of flesh, picking the bones completely clean.

Not a Roman, he reminded himself. One of *them*, disguised as a soldier. Hiding in plain sight. The Beasts were getting more devious as their numbers dwindled.

He bowed to the altar, nodding at the face of Cernunnos carved into it. "Protect us from this evil," he whispered. Caratacos left the cave and heard the strain of the others as they moved the rocks, sealing the cave off. He grinned as he walked away, heading toward the river to get clean.

ABOUT THE AUTHOR

David Watkins lives in Devon in the UK with his wife, two sons, dog, cat and two turtles. He is unsure of his place in the pecking order: probably somewhere between the cat and the turtles.

There are two novels in The Originals' series: *The Original's Return* concerns an ordinary family man becoming the God of Werewolves and the follow up, *The Original's Retribution*, covers the immediate aftermath and consequences of Jack's actions in the first book. Both novels are highly rated on Amazon.

David's latest novel is The Devil's Inn: a chilling tale set on Dartmoor during a fierce snowstorm. Has the Devil really come to Devon?

He is now working on a new stand-alone novel, set in Exeter. He hates referring to himself in the third person, but no-one else is going to write this for him.

David can be found on Twitter so please drop by and say hello @joshfishkins, where you'll find him ranting about horror, the British education system and Welsh rugby, but not usually at the same time.

Social Media links

Twitter: @joshfishkins

Facebook: https://www.facebook.com/originalsreturn/

The Kiss of Divna Antonov

Jonathan Janz

Clark paced the living room, the latest humiliation from the university curled in his right hand. With his left, he dragged trembling fingers through his oily, overlong hair. He'd thought the cut would make him look like Cary Grant, but instead, he only looked like a desperate version of himself, Clark Lombardo Coulter, Ph.D.

You're not a Ph.D. any longer, a voice whispered.

"No," he said aloud and peered through the window, where snowflakes swirled in the dying dusk. "They can't take that away. Not that."

You're not a professor anymore, the voice insisted. *No self-respecting institution in America will hire you. Not after the book.*

"Dammit!" he cried. He cast a feverish look about the room, but there was no help there. Just his grandfather's settee. A fire in the hearth. His books. And a comfortable chair in which to read them.

They don't matter, the voice declared, louder now. *No wife, no kids. And now no job or reputation.*

He seized the hair at his temples, knocked his spectacles askew, but the rolled sheet of paper in his hand scraped against his skin. He jerked it away and glowered at it. He didn't need to read it to remember the wording:

If your office is not cleared by the last of the month (January 31st, 1940), the custodial staff will donate or dispose of any possessions left inside, excepting any university property they discover.

Bastards, Clark thought. *Soulless, plotting bastards.*

The letter was signed Columbia University Anthropology Department, but Clark knew who was behind the unnecessary belittling.

Dr. Robert Spates.

Otherwise known as Blustering Bob. At least to those who saw through his blowhard demeanor.

His face twisting, Clark strode to the fireplace and cast the letter into the flames. As if to taunt him, the curled sheet of paper caromed off the dog grate and landed half out of the hearth. He stared at the paper, sure it would catch fire and go up in a brilliant flash, but it didn't, the message having landed text up and facing him as if Bob Spates had somehow bewitched it.

Teeth bared, Clark extended a foot and attempted to toe the letter toward the fire. He could feel the heat seething through his sock and knew he should use the iron stoker, but he'd left that in his bedroom.

A fresh wave of disgust shivered through him. A few nights ago, he'd carried the stoker to bed with him for protection—protection from what, he dared not consider—and then, not knowing where to store the iron rod, he'd laid it in bed beside him, where a wife should have been. For whatever reason, he'd never interested a woman enough to get married. And here he was, fifty-seven and alone, his only companions his ridiculous hairstyle and an iron stoker. If ever a man needed to end things, it was Clark. He'd made his preparations. It was a simple matter of heading upstairs to his study, of mounting the chair and fitting the noose under his chin...

Pain in his big toe shocked him back to the moment. He glanced stupidly at the smoke rising from his sock. Sucking in a breath, Clark danced away from the hearth, flailing his foot and cursing his negligence. He slumped in the leather chair and tore off the sock. The toes beneath were bright red, no blisters yet, but obviously burned.

Idiot! He thought. Clark massaged his toes and shook his head at the absurdity of it.

Burning his foot in the hearth, he realized, was an apt metaphor for how he'd sabotaged his career. He'd discovered a fascinating subject, one so original no other scholar had written of it. He'd thrown himself into the fire, so spellbound by the possibilities that he hadn't considered how unbending, how close-minded the academic community was at its core. Yet he'd ventured into the flames with the starry-eyed naivety of a child.

And been incinerated.

Clark sighed and let go of his aching toes. It was the book. That damned, execrable book.

He swiveled his head and glanced at it, still proudly displayed on his shelf.

Lycanthropology.

The book on which he'd wasted the past six years of his life. His passion. His obsession.

His downfall.

Clark's throat tightened at the sight of it. No scholar had worked as hard on a project as he had on this one. No one had gone to such extreme lengths to verify his findings.

Remembering those years of research, Clark's temples started to throb.

The subject matter had rendered the pursuit well-nigh impossible, but he'd known this at the outset. Nevertheless, steadfast in his beliefs and exhilarated by the prospect of illuminating truths no one had ever discovered, Clark had staked his reputation and his career on the project. He'd traveled to France, England, into Hitler's fanatical Germany; he'd ventured farther, to Slovakia, Hungary, Romania.

Eventually, he'd arrived in Belarus.

It was there he'd discovered the glittering black heart of his book.

The tale of Twelfth-Century Berstuk. The story of the Antonov sisters.

His whole body cold despite his heat-raw toes, Clark thought of Divna, the eldest Antonov sister. The young woman who'd been sexually abused. The one who'd suffered at the hands of a brutal patriarchy, the village of Berstuk, a mirror of the rest of the world: dominated by power-mad men, the women subjugated and silenced.

Clark shifted in his chair and scraped a hand over his stubbly jaw. In retrospect, that's what had doomed him. Oh, the subject alone—for what self-respecting anthropology professor believed in werewolves?—was enough to place his career in jeopardy. But Clark was sure it was his denouncement of the patriarchal social construct that had doomed him. Critics like Bob Spates and Dominic Headley only mentioned Clark's views on female empowerment in passing, but Clark knew that was what had truly ended his tenure at Columbia.

The wind gusted outside, a willow branch whipping and scratching at the window. Clark sat up straighter, not because of the wind but because he could have sworn he'd heard footsteps on the cobblestones outside...

A staccato knocking—*tap tap tap tap*—sounded on his front door.

Why get it? The mocking voice demanded. *You're ending things tonight anyway. Why delay the inevitable?*

Clark stared at the door, his fingers gripping the leather armrests tighter.

Tap tap, the knock sounded. A pause of perhaps fifteen seconds. Then, *Tap tap tap.*

Clark pushed to his feet and was about to answer it when he caught sight of himself in the gold-flecked mirror above the mantle. His glasses sat crookedly on his nose. His dress shirt was unbuttoned to the navel, his t-shirt beneath rumpled. A five o'clock shadow dusted his face, the lank, greasy hair a series of inky commas on his forehead. True, his hair was still black. In that respect, at least, he looked like something other than what he was.

A broken-down laughingstock.

The rapping came again, this time so loud and rapid he found himself hurrying to answer it. As he made his way there, he straightened his spectacles, buttoned his shirt, and dragged a hand through his messy hair. He knew it wouldn't do a damned bit of good, but why not make this last encounter with his fellow man as dignified as possible? He didn't want his visitor to tell tales at the inquest: *Oh yes, he looked just awful! Clothes disheveled, hair unkempt. I knew then he wasn't long for this earth. But then everyone knew he was losing his mind. Why else would he write such a frightful book?*

Clark opened the door and felt his jaw drop open.

The woman staring back at him was the most stunning he'd ever seen.

It wasn't her clothing. In fact, her simple wool overcoat and her snow-spattered pumps might best be labeled as "sensible." Yet despite the plainness of her attire, the woman's sculpted features, her shapely figure, most of all her impressive height—she was at least six feet tall, the gray woolen hat adding another several inches—conspired to conjure a striking sight. She wore little makeup, and he suspected the cherry-red lips were natural. He could make out only a hint of blond hair above her ears; she'd pinned the rest of it under her hat.

Her neutral expression betrayed nothing, nor did her posture. Her black-gloved hands dangled at her side, her feet planted shoulder-width apart on the snow-dusted stoop.

The woman stared at him.

Clark attempted a smile. "Good evening. Are you lost?"

Suave, he thought. *Even in your final moments, you still exhibit that same unflappable charm.*

"Am I disturbing you?" the woman asked.

Clark hesitated. That accent... he couldn't place it. There were traces of German and Eastern European in it. But one thing was certain—this woman wasn't from Manhattan.

"You aren't disturbing me," he managed. "Would you..." He stepped aside, nodded over his shoulder. "I have a fire going. I can fix you a drink if you like."

She surveyed him with good humor. "You make a habit of inviting strangers in for drinks?"

Snowflakes wafted down around her, but they seemed to avoid her wool coat. Clark suspected they'd melt the moment they landed on her.

He opened his mouth to say something winning, but finding nothing, he said, "I'm afraid I don't entertain very often."

Her eyes lowered, flicked up again. "Where's your other sock?"

Clark goggled at her. "I was scooting a paper toward the fire and..." He swallowed and shrugged.

She appraised him for a long moment. One corner of her mouth twitched. "I don't drink alcohol."

"Oh. I..."

"But if you have water, I'd like a glass. I've traveled a goodly distance."

Not trusting himself to answer coherently, he stepped aside and motioned her into the house. She passed him, her chin raised regally, her limbs moving with a graceful fluidity that reminded him of an accomplished professional athlete. He'd once seen Lou Gehrig play at Yankee Stadium, and though no one would accuse this ethereal creature of resembling the Iron Horse, the manner in which she entered the house, the unconscious ease with which she pivoted and perused his living room reminded him very much of the Yankees slugger.

"Can I take your coat for you?" he asked.

She unbuttoned her coat and peeled it off her shoulders, revealing a bloodred blouse. Beneath that, a black skirt clung to her hips. She was curvy, what Clark's male colleagues would have called voluptuous, at least when there no women around. In the presence of women, men like Bob Spates and Dominic Headley folded their hands and nodded respectfully. But the moment a lady was out of earshot...

"I'm a fan of your work," the woman said.

Clark glanced at her. She clearly hadn't read his book, wasn't familiar with the public shaming he'd endured. If she were familiar with it, she certainly wouldn't be here tonight.

He adjusted his glasses. "May I take that for you?"

She relinquished her coat, which was more substantial than he'd anticipated. He started away but stopped. "Would you like me to—"

"I'll keep the hat," she said without looking at him.

Clark bustled away and draped the coat on a closet foyer hanger. When he returned, she was sitting in the wine-colored brocade chair near his own. Seeing her there, he paused, aware of how often he'd daydreamed of someone occupying the chair, someone who enjoyed his company, a woman who not only valued his conversation but also had no interest in university politics. My God, to talk like regular people rather than verbal sparrers, constantly maneuvering for greater prestige.

He stepped over to his chair and eased into it. "You said you're a fan of my work?"

"I value boldness," she said, her eyes inspecting the bookshelves on either side of the eastern window.

He waited for an amplification. When none came, he asked, "Is there an article in particular you found?"

"*Lycanthropology,*" she said.

Clark tightened. So it was a setup. He should have known it was too good to be true. Spates and Headley had put the blonde up to this. A final indignity to heap upon the mountain of insults.

He pushed up his glasses, leaned forward, and braced his forearms on his knees. "When they threatened to take my possessions to the dump, I figured they'd degraded me to their satisfaction."

The blonde looked at him. "Professors Headley and Spates."

In the back of his throat, the sour taste of bile began to boil. "You're not even going to deny it."

She continued to watch him, her expression inscrutable.

He leveled a forefinger at her. "You're no better than they are, taking money to play these games."

"What do you believe I came here to do?"

Her fingers lay on the armrests, the cardinal-hued fingernail polish a striking contrast to the burgundy chair fabric. They looked powerful, those fingers, capable of ripping a novel in half.

In fact, he couldn't shake the feeling he was now living in a novel, one of those lurid potboilers with an alcoholic P.I. and an enigmatic femme fatale. His visitor certainly looked the part. He imagined her spinning a yarn about an abusive husband and a murder plot aimed at seizing her inheritance. In the novel, she'd throw herself at Clark's mercy, and he'd oblige her, both sleeping with her and investigating her case only to find himself the patsy, the blonde duping Clark and her husband and winning in the end.

But that was absurd.

Clark cleared his throat. "Miss..." He raised his eyebrows, but she didn't supply her name. "Miss Whatever-Your-Name-Is, I appreciate you have a job to do, but I really do have important matters to attend to, and you're keeping me from them."

"Like taking your own life?"

His body went numb, the chair beneath him disintegrating. For a long moment, he experienced a sensation of weightlessness, of having transformed into some sort of ghost or vapor, one that merely hung in the air, as insubstantial as a puff of smoke.

The woman folded her legs. "I've been patient with you. You've endured much, and your thoughts have turned bitter."

Even had Clark known what to say, he didn't have the power to articulate a response.

"I've seen it more times than I've cared to." A new light seemed to shine on her face, her gaze razor keen. "The moment someone threatens established ideas—particularly wrongheaded ones—the uproar swallows him up, devouring the revolutionary notion."

Clark tried to breathe but couldn't. It was as though she were staring into the dark purple scar of his suffering.

"Ordinarily, I make a practice of remaining apart from human matters." A rueful shake of the head. "Ephemeral lives leaving neither a glow nor a stain on history."

The weightlessness grew more severe. Had he the strength to glance down and take stock of his body, Clark would not have been surprised to find himself floating a foot off his chair.

"But this," the woman said, "is different."

"Different," Clark repeated.

A nod. "Our species rarely intersect non-violently. Your kind is too narrowminded to confront the eternal without fearmongering."

Unbidden, an idea flitted through his mind, and at the thought, Clark grunted breathless laughter. "I'm sorry. You did say my 'kind'?"

The woman merely watched him.

He ventured a smile. "Your wording... you believe we're two different species?"

There was no perceptible change in her expression, but when she spoke, her accent was more pronounced. "You would be wise to alter your attitude."

At her tone, Clark drew back and sat up straighter. "You're telling me those wiseasses from the university didn't put you up to this?"

"I never do anything unless I desire to."

Clark opened his mouth to ask a question, but the woman beat him to it.

"My name," she said, "is Divna Antonov."

***

Clark knew he should wait for her to utter the punchline, but he couldn't avoid repeating the name. "Divna Antonov."

The woman stared back at him.

He smiled, riffled through several scathing responses, but the seriousness of her gaze somehow forbade them all. He ran his tongue around his mouth and said, "You're the alpha wolf, the first of your kind."

When she didn't answer, he continued. "Born in the tiny village of Berstuk during the time of Eleanor of Aquitane and Richard the Lionheart. That would make you"—he narrowed his eyes—"nearly eight hundred years old. Am I correct?"

The woman did not smile, nor did she exhibit signs of outrage. Still, he couldn't help but notice how—he could not escape the word—*queenly* she seemed. The idea she'd been sent here by Bob Spates and Dom Headley recurred, and though hiring an actress to play the part of *Lycanthropology*'s central and most fascinating figure would have been a stroke of genius, he couldn't shake the feeling that such a plot was beyond the imaginative powers of his former colleagues.

Yet if it hadn't been Spates and Headley who'd put her up to this...

But that was madness!

Clark scratched the back of his neck. "Look, Miss... I won't deny you're a terrific actress, but surely you don't think I'll—"

"You don't stand by your work?"

He felt his scalp tighten. "Of course, I do. If I hadn't, do you think I'd be unemployed?"

"They asked you to disavow it."

He twitched a hand at her. "Sure, they did. 'Just admit it's a work of fiction, Clark, and we'll let you off with a six-month suspension.'"

"You refused."

Clark pushed to his feet, began to pace. "You're

goddamned right, I refused. I spent years on that project."
He crammed his hands in his pockets and shook his head.
"Funded most of it myself. I spent every vacation day for
half a decade traveling Europe... staying in bug-infested
inns and choking down some of the most wretched food you
can imagine."

From the corner of his eye, he saw her grin. "I
understand hunger."

"You do, do you?" He rounded on her. "Do you
understand willful ignorance? Base jealousy disguised as
intellectual integrity?"

"I'm looking at it right now."

"Looking at what?"

"Willful ignorance."

"You know what, Divna? I don't need this. I don't need
your derision."

"I thought you'd be different."

He spread his arms. "Well, I'm not, okay? I'm just as
awful as the rest of us humans. Now, why don't you go tell
Bob and Dominic that their stunt was successful."

She rose, crossed slowly to the foyer.

He spoke to her back, his voice rising. "Tell them
anything you want. That I believed you, that you pretended
to transform, and I fell to my knees and begged for mercy."

She opened the closet door, reached inside.

"Vicious bastards," he muttered to himself. "Never
enough. They took my job, my reputation. Made sure the
critics piled on..."

The woman began sliding on her coat. Though still tall,
she didn't appear as strong as he'd at first assumed. His
inferiority complex, he suspected, had led him to magnify

her stature. She was just a woman. An actress hired by cruel men to play a prank on him.

The woman buttoned her coat.

Clark exhaled. It wasn't her fault. Not really. Many people struggled to make ends meet. If Spates and Headley had paid her handsomely, he couldn't begrudge her that.

So say something!

"Hey, Miss?"

Her elbows, which had been stirring as she buttoned the coat, grew still.

He took a step toward her. "I'm sorry. I've had a rough time of it."

She didn't move.

"That's no excuse, though," he said. "Can we still... would you mind having a drink with me?"

"I told you I don't partake of that poison."

Unaccountably, he felt a wry smile forming. "Then will you partake of water? I'd like some company tonight."

Slowly, she pivoted around to face him. "Will you accord me the respect I deserve?"

"Yes. I was wrong not to."

"Will you attempt to disabuse yourself of the lies perpetuated by your meager species?"

"Absolutely."

"You still don't take me seriously," she said, "but in time, you will."

He nodded. "Fair enough."

She didn't seem appeased, but she did begin unbuttoning her coat again.

He started forward. "Should I—"

"I'll do it."

He stopped, nodded. "I'll get the water?"

The woman slid the coat off her shoulders. "Yes, Clark. You get the water."

When he returned from the kitchen, glass in hand, she was standing before the hearth, a book spread before her on the mantle. *Lycanthropology*, he saw as he drew up beside her. Why this should surprise him, he didn't know. Still, he paused a moment before offering the glass.

She accepted it but scarcely looked up from her reading. "You got much correct, Dr. Coulter. How were you able to trace us back to Berstuk?"

Still on that, are we? He thought. *Fine then. Let's prolong the charade.*

"I did what a good detective always does," he answered. "I worked backward."

"From *The Prosperity*?"

Despite the ludicrousness of the notion—a werewolf standing beside him reading his book about werewolves—Clark experienced a chill at the name of the ill-fated trans-Atlantic steamer. Ninety-two passengers and crew members murdered during the voyage, nary a soul left alive to tell the tale.

He coughed into his fist. "That's right."

She glanced sidelong at him. "What linked the *Prosperity* to werewolves?"

He chewed his bottom lip. "It's not a pleasant story, I'm afraid..."

She lowered her chin, her frank stare unwavering.

"For one thing," he said, "the carnage was too

spectacular to have been perpetrated by mere man."

"Perhaps a group of them?" she asked.

"Too vicious. Too widespread. Even a coordinated effort by twenty stout men couldn't have achieved the bloodshed discovered in Boston Harbor that night. Only the werewolf is capable of such evisceration, such wanton violence."

Her gaze returned to the book. "Wanton," she said softly.

"Why yes," Clark said, moving nearer. "When in thrall to the change, the werewolf succumbs to its maniacal bloodlust. It kills in a frenzy, leaving no living creature in its wake."

"Is that so?" She flipped the page.

"Yes," he answered. "Do you disagree?"

Instead of answering, she flipped the page again.

He read the title of Chapter Six—"The Sensuality of the Lycanthrope"—and felt his cheeks burn. "We need not linger on that section. It's more speculative than—"

"Why should you be uncomfortable with sensuality?" she asked, her fingertips caressing the page. "You wrote this."

"I don't have much proof that it's true."

"You believe werewolves are libidinous creatures."

His eyes wandered to her blouse, which was open at the chest. He caught a glimpse of a black brassiere before averting his gaze. "I think lycanthropes are like any other animal, and most animals are driven by the need to reproduce."

"That's not what you say in here."

"Well…"

"It says *here*"—the tip of her forefinger came to rest at

the bottom of the page—"that lycanthropes engage in 'amorous activities' not for reproduction, but for pleasure."

The skin at his collar burned. "Lycanthropes must keep their numbers down, mustn't they? Too many of them running around, they'd risk detection."

"They kill their sexual partners?"

He knew the blush in his cheeks was deepening, but he managed to say, "Out of necessity. Once a human learned a lycanthrope's true nature, extermination would become the only logical course of action."

"How do you think that feels?"

He drew back slightly. "What, death?"

"To destroy one's partner after making love." Something permeated her voice, darkening it. "To share the glorious bonds of flesh and spirit, only to snuff out that warming glow moments later."

Clark swayed on his feet and found that only by gripping the edge of the mantle could he keep himself from falling. The woman had barely moved, yet now he felt as though her warmth, her vitality, had enveloped him, had kindled within him a reciprocal heat. Her eyes—were there flecks of gold banked down within the irises?—cocooned him, swaddled him with their lethal grace. He wanted nothing more than to remain inside them, the gilded flecks igniting a new blaze inside of him. Coaxing him back to life. Animating what was long dormant.

She was still staring at him when a rapping sounded from the entryway.

He jerked from his trance, passed a hand over his mouth, and murmured, "Better see who it is."

He moved to the foyer, opened the door, and felt his good spirits curdle.

Bob Spates and Dominic Headley stood on the porch,

each with his arm around a woman, one of them a redhead, the other one's hair a lustrous black.

Bob grinned at him. "Met a couple new acquaintances at the club, Clarky. Thought we'd bring the party to you."

Without waiting for an invitation, Bob barged past him, his gorgeous new acquaintance in tow. With a muttered, "Hey, Clark," Dominic Headley led his companion through the door too. When Clark caught up with the new arrivals, they were shaking the snow off their coats and looking around the foyer.

"Not exactly the Biltmore Mansion, is it, Clarky?" Bob remarked.

Clark ignored it, Bob Spates' other methods of belittling him long ago outfacing the irritating nickname.

"I dunno," Dominic said, eyes scanning the coffered ceiling. "The place has got potential. It just needs a little love. Right, gorgeous?" Dominic took his date's hand and pecked it with a kiss.

The woman smiled and said, "Give me an hour, and I'd have it scintillatin'."

Dominic and Bob exchanged a surprised look. Dominic said, "You hear that, Bob? *Scintillating.* Our Stella's got a brain, hasn't she?"

Clark glanced at Stella to see if she was annoyed with the condescension, but if she was, she gave no sign.

"Here, darling," Bob said to the other woman. "Let me help you with that."

"You're such a sweetie," the woman answered.

"So Maxine," Bob said, taking both his date's coat and Stella's and toting them over to where Clark stood by the foyer closet, "this is the guy we were telling you about. Dr. Clark Lombardo Coulter." Bob pushed the women's coats into Clark's arms, the melting snowflakes wetting Clark's shirt.

"He still a doctor?" Maxine asked, tossing her red hair over her shoulder. "I thought you said he was disbarred."

Dominic stifled an embarrassed smile, but Bob grinned and set about unbuttoning his own beige coat. Cashmere, Clark noted without surprise.

Eyes never leaving Clark's, Bob said, "Professors don't get disbarred, dear. You're thinking of lawyers." Bob peeled his expensive coat off his broad shoulders and added it to the heap in Clark's arms. "Professors just get let go, like any other job. Isn't that right, Clarky?" He gave Clark a chummy pat on the shoulder.

Clark had begun the job of hanging the coats when he heard Dominic utter a surprised gasp and say, "My goodness—I didn't see you there." Turning, Clark saw Dominic had discovered the blonde, whom Clark assumed was still positioned beside the hearth. Dominic, Clark noted without surprise, had donned his oily smile, the one reserved for undergrads he intended to deflower. Dominic Headley was, in the words of his best friend Bob Spates, an "inveterate skirt chaser."

To Clark, he'd always just seemed morally bankrupt.

Clark finished hanging the coats and shut the closet door in time to hear Bob say, "Hello there, miss! Wherever are Clarky's manners?"

Clark emerged from the foyer in time to see Bob Spates reach the blond woman and extend a hand. Rather than taking it, the blonde merely fixed Bob with an impassive gaze.

Bob grinned. "I won't bite, darlin'."

The blonde did not shake hands.

Bob turned to frown at Clark. "Now see what you've done, Clarky? You've prejudiced your guest against me." A tutting sound. "That's not very Christian of you." Bob glanced at Maxine and gestured toward Clark. "See, honey? I told you he'd hold a grudge. Some people can't let things go."

Clark mastered an urge to retrieve a heavy bookend from the shelf and brain Bob with it.

"So what's your story?" the one named Stella asked the blonde.

Stella, Clark noted, was quite attractive herself. Prominent cheekbones, sensual mouth. Nearly as tall as the mysterious blonde. Raven-colored hair that was very long and very straight. Too bad Stella also spoke with an exaggerated Bronx accent and worked her bubble gum like a farm animal chewing its cud.

The blonde didn't even glance at Stella; instead, she kept her pale blue eyes fixed on Bob Spates. Was the blonde attracted to Bob? Clark wouldn't be surprised. The man was a boorish caveman—more than once, it was rumored that when a woman wasn't willing, Bob forced her into compliance—but he was confident, and in Clark's experience, women tended to respond to confidence.

"Why ain't ya talking?" Maxine demanded. Like Stella, Maxine boasted an attractive face and an athletic figure—a figure accentuated by her clingy green dress—but her voice, Clark decided, sounded more like Maine than New York.

Clark wished they'd all go home.

Dominic stepped up next to Bob and introduced himself. "And these," he told the blonde, flourishing a hand at Stella and Maxine, "are our dates."

"We met at the club," Stella said around her wad of gum.

"Picked us up is what they did," Maxine said and snorted laughter.

Dominic lowered his face and exhibited an embarrassment that was, Clark suspected, wholly feigned. "At any rate, it's nice to meet you, Miss..."

"Antonov," the blonde answered. "Divna Antonov."

Dominic blinked at her. "Say... that sounds familiar. Does it sound familiar to you, Bob?"

Bob grunted in the negative. He was eyeing the blonde like a mountain climber appraising a particularly challenging cliff face. "Is that vodka in your glass, Miss Antonov, or are you too prim and proper for that?"

Divna—was Clark to think of her as Divna?—didn't answer him.

"Well, *I* ain't too proper for a drink," Maxine announced. "What do you got, Clarky? Whiskey? Scotch?"

She was, Clark realized, slurring her words. Stella had also, judging from the way she swayed as she sauntered over to his bookcases, already imbibed her share of alcohol.

A thrill of misgiving whispered through him.

Relax, Clark told himself. *It doesn't matter. None of it matters.*

That was true, he realized. Besides, he would be beyond the jibes and machinations of Bob Spates and Dominic Headley soon enough. Just let them all have a drink, and he could get on with what he had to do.

Fingering the spines of his rarest books, Stella said, "You must like old stuff, huh, Clarky?"

"That's right," he said. "I like old stuff."

"But you're not *that* old, are you?" Bob said over his shoulder. "Sixty isn't over the hill."

"He's fifty-seven," Divna said.

Bob turned to her, and in the mirror above the mantle,

Clark could see the surprise in Bob's face. "You must know each other better than I thought."

"I know him better than you."

Bob grinned. "Is that right? You two go way back, do you?"

"The bond we share transcends time," Divna answered.

At her words, the saliva in Clark's mouth dried up.

"Well, listen to you," Bob said. His smile reminded Clark of an abusive father removing his belt for a good hiding. "You've got spirit, haven't you?"

"You could never fathom what I have," Divna answered.

Bob stared at her, his brow creased. Even Stella and Maxine seemed at a loss.

Then Dominic clapped his hands lightly and said, "How about those drinks, Clarky? They in the kitchen?"

"Uh-huh," Clark said softly. He moved away from the group, and the last thing he saw before the hallway darkness swallowed him up was the blonde who claimed to be Divna Antonov staring at Bob Spates.

**

When he reentered the living room, the tray of glasses held before him and Dominic trailing just behind, he was relieved to find Bob Spates in conversation with Stella and Maxine. Divna stood alone between the bookcases, her back to the group, her gaze riveted on the snowswept window. It wasn't yet a blizzard, but it might soon be. Clark resolved to get this over with so his unwanted visitors wouldn't be forced to spend the night.

"I hope brandy is acceptable," Clark said, placing the tray of snifters on an end table.

"No bourbon, Clarky?" Bob asked.

"Now Bob," Dominic said as he plucked a snifter from the tray and began to pour, "let's not be too hard on our former colleague. After all, he didn't expect us tonight."

"Brandy's swell," Stella said. She accepted the snifter from Dominic, leaned down, and plopped the chewing gum into her palm. She glanced about, a frown darkening her pretty features.

"Here," Clark said, fetching a napkin from the tray and holding it out for her.

She deposited the pink wad of gum in the napkin and winked at him. "You're a sweetie."

He mustered a smile and handed Dominic another snifter to fill. It occurred to him, not for the first time, that Dominic Headley was rarely as unpleasant as Bob Spates. If you didn't mind his loose moral compass and his snakelike habit of speaking ill of you when you weren't around, you could almost believe Dominic was a decent guy.

Almost.

Dominic proffered the next snifter to Maxine, then Bob. After filling one for Clark, Dominic prepared a snifter for himself and raised it to the group. "To friendship."

"To friendship," Stella and Maxine repeated, but Bob shook his head and waved everybody off.

"No, no, no," he said, moving toward Clark. "To hell with friendship. Let's drink to second chances. Shall we, Clarky?"

With a supreme effort, Clark kept his agitation from showing.

Bob tossed back his drink, most of it gone in a swig. Dominic imbibed a much more urbane amount, and their two dates merely swished the brandy around their snifters to warm it.

Wiping his lips with the side of his hand, Bob stalked

over to stand beside Divna. "Since you and Clarky are old acquaintances, you no doubt know about his shame?" Clark noted that Bob had loosed his necktie at some point and unfastened the top two buttons so that a tuft of black hair peeked out from atop his barrel chest. "Yeah, Divna, Clark always was a bit of a rabble-rouser, but we had no idea just how radical he was until that book of his."

"Are you familiar with it, Miss Antonov?" Dominic asked over his snifter.

"What kind of book is it, Clarky?" Stella asked.

"That's the best part!" Bob said. "Girls, you're not gonna believe this."

"It's about werewolves," Divna said without turning.

Bob scowled at her back. "Thanks for stealing my thunder, sweet cheeks."

"Her name is Divna," Clark heard himself saying.

Bob glanced at him with mild surprise. "Is that right, Clarky?" Bob began to stroll toward him. "And is Divna familiar with your views on the subject?"

"What's a werewolf?" Maxine asked.

Bob whirled on her. "What's a *werewolf*? Honey, don't you go to the movies?" He shot a look at Dominic. "What was the one we saw a few years ago? It starred that guy... Henry Hill."

"Hull," Dominic corrected. "Henry Hull." An indulgent smile. "It was titled *Werewolf of London*." A wink at Stella. "Very macabre."

"Ma-what?" Stella asked.

Bob chuckled. "A werewolf, Maxine dear, is a man who turns into a wolf every full moon."

"Unless he imbibes the juice of a rare flower before he

changes," Dominic put in.

Stella frowned. "Turns into a wolf?"

"Like, he walks on all fours?" Maxine asked. "He howls at the moon?"

"Yes," Bob said magnanimously, "the whole thing. He goes prowling naked through the countryside and hunting for fresh victims."

"You mean *people*?" Stella asked.

"Why, of course, darling. The more people, the better."

Dominic gulped his drink. "But you better hope it kills you."

Stella made a face. "Why?"

"Because if you're bitten, you become one," Bob answered.

Maxine asked, "Isn't that better than getting eaten?"

"Not really," Dominic answered. "The werewolf's life is a curse." He began to pace as he spoke, much the way, Clark assumed, he did when lecturing about the indigenous peoples of the Amazon Rain Forest. "Made an outsider to society. Relentlessly persecuted, constantly on the run. What man would ask for that sort of existence?" He glanced at Divna and laughed. "Or woman, for that matter?"

Bob slipped an arm around Maxine. "And Clarky here believes in all of it. He wrote a book on the subject." He gave Maxine's waist a squeeze. "It's called *Lycanthropology*."

Clark sighed and stared into his snifter.

Bob tossed back the rest of his drink, released Maxine, and returned to the tray, where he poured himself another brandy. As if Clark weren't standing three feet away from him, Bob said, "The book caused quite a stir, too. We knew

Clarky'd been working on something for ages, but we had no idea what it was. When the university got an advance copy,"—he took a sizeable swig from his snifter, bared his teeth—"when me and Dominic took a gander at what Clarky had been up to... all those trips to parts unknown..."

"I dare say we were kinder than the rest of the academic community," Dominic said.

Clark noticed the brandy-fueled flush on Dominic's cheeks, the relaxed way he'd draped an arm over Stella's shoulders. For her part, Stella was neither smiling nor encouraging Dominic's advances. She appeared stiff, perhaps disapproving of the current run of conversation.

And as Clark watched her, he noticed something else. She wasn't drinking. She had brought the snifter to her gaudy red lips, but she wouldn't drink, wouldn't even sip.

He glanced at Maxine and saw that although she still clutched the brandy snifter and was swirling the alcohol around, she wasn't drinking either.

Bob finally seemed to notice the women's discomfiture. "Drink up, darling," he told Maxine. "The night is young."

Dominic approached the tray. "Stella and Maxine are right," he said, refilling his glass. "This is no topic for polite company."

"Who's polite?" Bob asked. And before she could react, he planted a wet kiss right on Maxine's mouth.

Maxine neither reciprocated nor pulled away, but when it was done, Bob turned to the group and said, "How about some music, Clarky? Please tell me you've got a Victrola hidden around here somewhere."

Though Divna had her back to him, Clark could see her reflection in the window she faced. And despite the frost reefing the edges of the panes and the ghostly flakes swirling outside, he had the distinct impression she was watching him.

Jonathan Janz

Watching him and awaiting his reaction.

"On the north wall," Clark said. "Under the built-in."

"Hot damn," Bob said and crossed the room at a jog. He yanked open the cabinet door and found the Victrola. Coming out with it, he said, "Why Clarky, you've got a hell of a collection! I never suspected you for a music lover."

Dominic and their dates joined him beside the cabinet.

As Dominic set up the Victrola, Bob stooped and came out with an armful of albums. "Lookee here, girls. Benny Goodman, Al Jolsen..."

"The Andrew Sisters!" Stella called.

"Bing Crosby," Bob went on. "Tommy Dorsey."

"Ooo," Maxine said, plucking an album from the pile. "I love Duke Ellington."

Dominic accepted the album from her and favored her with a gallant smile. "Then Duke Ellington it shall be."

Moments later, Dominic and Stella were dancing to "It Don't Mean a Thing (If It Ain't Got That Swing)." When he'd purchased the album several years ago, Clark had enjoyed the song's upbeat tone, but tonight the tune bored into his skull with the persistence of a power drill. While Dominic and Stella moved nimbly about the small space, Bob and Maxine were dancing more intimately, their midsections pressed together, his big hands roving freely over the small of her back and her shapely rear end. If she minded, she wasn't letting on.

Halfway through the song, Bob teetered over to the tray, swatted Clark on the chest, and muttered, "You sure know how to show a lady a good time."

Clark's throat contracted. He had been toying vaguely with the notion of asking Divna to dance, but something in her posture seemed to forbid it.

Clark passed a hand through his hair. He glanced at his fingers, noticed they were slick with sweat, and when he looked up, he realized that Stella was watching him. Dancing with Dominic, but watching *him*. Dominic swayed with her and let his hands rove over her back, but Stella merely gazed at Clark, her eyes imploring.

It got him moving.

When he reached Divna, he saw her reflection in the window more clearly, and yes, she was watching him too.

He cleared his throat and said, "Would you mind dancing with me?"

Behind him, he heard Bob mutter something that sounded like "Clark finally grew a pair," but Clark scarcely heard it. Divna was turning and fixing him with that profound gaze.

She said, "May I choose the song?"

"Of course," he said. The Ellington record was barreling to a close.

Divna stepped over to the stack of albums and had only glanced at three titles before making her selection. With a deftness he admired, she unsheathed the vinyl disk, placed it on the turntable, and nested the Victrola's needle.

The song was one of his favorites: "They Can't Take That Away from Me," by Fred Astaire.

Mesmerized by the song's opening notes, he went to her. There was only Divna and the music and the sultry atmosphere of the living room. Clark's fingers threaded with Divna's, his other hand on the curve of her lower back. The fire was blazing, and as Clark and Divna began to revolve, he sensed the others watching them, the women with silent approval, the men with barely suppressed disdain. She moved closer and said at his ear, "Is this the last night?"

He started to pull away, but she clutched his body to her. The question hung in the air between them, and Fred Astaire sang about how you wear your hat and how you sip your tea, and Clark uttered the first words that came to his head: "Who are you?"

Divna let go of his hand and laced her fingers around the back of his neck. Her lips an inch from his ear, she said, "My tormentor was Radomir. He was the most respected man in our village."

Berstuk, he thought. *Jesus Christ. She really does believe she's Divna Antonov.*

"You were right about the abuse," she said. "Only it was worse than you could imagine."

Clark's muscles hardened. There was no way this woman was centuries old, but the notion of her being sexually assaulted... that he could believe.

"He fixated on me," she said, "but I knew he would soon prey on Militsa and Stanislava. They weren't yet of age. Of course, I was just twelve."

Fred Astaire sang of beaming smiles and singing off-key. Dominic muttered something about another drink.

"Divna," Clark said. "I appreciate your reading my book —"

"You will make a decision," she said. "By the end of the song. Just as I had to make a decision. Would I allow the foul order to continue as it had for ages? Would I allow my sisters to be treated as I was being treated?"

"Plant one on her, Clark!" Bob shouted, his voice thick with drink. "Unless you're a sissy," he added in a very audible undertone.

Divna's body was glued to his, and though there was sexual desire there, far stronger than that was the idea that this was right, this was natural. Holding Divna was like holding the sun and the trees and the water. Holding Divna was embracing everything good, clean, and true. "I want to believe you," he said, "but I need proof."

"No proof," she said, her tone sharper. "No proof. By the end of the song, you must decide."

Clark's head swam. The intoxicating scent of Divna's hair, her skin, her breath conspired to dilute gravity, to send him floating into the air, her body affixed to his, to rise above the house and dwell in the sky.

"I had always communed with the wolves," Divna said, her lips ever closer to his ear. His skin there tingled. "They understood me in a way the villagers did not. My sisters sometimes joined me, but mostly I went alone. I felt…" She paused, and Clark knew he held his breath. "I felt that here was truth. Here was understanding. Have you ever felt that way, Clark?"

Right now, he thought.

"Come on now, Maxine," Bob said from behind them. "Don't be that way."

Divna's body stiffened infinitesimally, but she continued. "I performed a ceremony. Alone in the dark with the wolves, I undertook the rites. I didn't know what I would do until I did it, but when I was finished, I knew I had changed. Have you ever been governed by instinct, Clark? An impulse deeper than thought?"

He swallowed. There was a brief commotion from the direction of the others, but all his attention was on Divna. Fred Astaire crooned about how you hold your knife.

"The song is ending," Divna said.

And it was. Divna's lips brushed his ear, his cheek, and for an endless beat, they stood there, the song's last notes dying away, new, feral energy surcharging the room.

Clark turned and stared at the others.

It was Bob—of course, it was Bob. He had a forearm braced behind Maxine's back, his other hand wrestling with hers. A sick parody of a slow dance. Maxine's lips were twisted in pain. Her body was trembling violently.

"Let go of her," Clark said.

Bob paid no mind. Stella, he noted, stood a few feet off from Dominic, who swilled his drink appreciatively and watched Bob manhandle Maxine the way a ranch hand would admire an expert wrangler subduing a recalcitrant colt.

Clark started forward. Behind him, the Victrola needle bumped, bumped as the finished album continued to spin.

"Please stop," Maxine said.

But rather than stopping, Bob let out a hungry growl of laughter. The arm around her waist began to rub, his hand pawing roughly at her buttocks.

"Goddammit," Clark said, seizing Bob by the collar, "I said back *off*."

Bob spun too quickly for Clark to react. Before he knew he'd been struck—a vicious right hook—Clark was lying on the floor staring up at Bob. Maxine stumbled away, but Bob seemed not to notice. He was grinning savagely down at Clark, his shirt unbuttoned to the belly, his pomaded hair jutting up at wild angles.

"Look at the disgraced crackpot," Bob said, looming over him. "Wants to impress some call girl." His glittery eyes flicked to Divna. "How much is he paying you? A dame with your looks, you can't be cheap."

Clark pushed to his feet. "Don't talk to her that way."

Bob aimed a gleeful grin at Dominic. "You hearing this, Dom? Pitiful little Clarky trying to prove his mettle."

"It doesn't suit him," Dominic said.

Bob stepped closer, his nose three inches higher than Clark's. "Well, let's go then. Show the ladies what you can do."

"He already has," Divna said.

And so forceful was her tone that Clark turned and looked at her. Divna had never looked more regal than she did at that moment. Taller than all of them, limbs lithe and girded with a vitality he sensed rather than saw, she smiled and said, "Go ahead, Militsa."

"Who the fuck's Militsa?" Bob said.

But Clark realized Divna was addressing Maxine, who was shuddering more violently than ever. Moments earlier, while Bob was assaulting her, Clark had assumed her quaking was born of fear or revulsion.

Now he understood there was something deeper at work.

Maxine—

(*Militsa, Divna called her Militsa*)

—was shaking like a storm-plagued jib, her body bent double, her hands scratching the air as though entombed by some invisible coffin.

"Allergic reaction?" Dominic asked.

In answer, Maxine's body gave a great heave, and her green dress split at the shoulders.

"What the hell?" Bob asked.

Maxine uttered a weird moan and sank to all fours, where the paroxysm grew more severe. Her hands whirred so rapidly Clark could hardly trace them; her hair... her scarlet hair seemed to be growing. And not only from her head, he saw with a leap of dread, but from her hands and wrists and back.

Militsa, he thought. *Oh my God*.

Dominic was watching in awe, but Bob had darted for the foyer.

"Stanislava?" Divna said.

Stella reached the foyer in five loping strides. Clark was shielded from the front door, but he heard Bob fumbling with the lock and the door *whishing* open. Then there came a strangled cry, a grunt, and the door thumped shut.

Stella—Stanislava?—reappeared from the entryway. She was towing Bob forward by the wrist, despite the way he slapped at her hand, despite his attempts to dig his shoes into the hardwood floor.

When Clark's gaze returned to Militsa, he felt his legs melt to jelly. She was rocked back on her knees, her face upturned, her now-hairy fingers ripping at her dress.

"*Let...go of me*," Bob demanded. But his efforts were in vain. Stanislava held him in place as though he were a leashed terrier.

Her cheekbones expanding and pulsing, Militsa turned her face heavenward and bellowed. Dominic dropped his snifter.

No one paid attention to the shattered glass. All eyes remained on Militsa, whose torn dress now revealed a torso furred in brilliant red strands. The sight would have been magnificent if it hadn't been so terrifying. From Clark's vantage point, he could just make out one heel, broken free of its pump, the Achilles tendon stretching, the foot itself stretching, elongating.

You were right, a voice declared itself in Clark's head. *Incredibly, impossibly, you were right*.

I was, he thought. *But I wish to hell I hadn't been*.

Because what was taking place ten feet away was an abomination. Now at least a foot taller than she'd been,

Militsa's body was a riot of sinew and scarlet fur. Her eyes, when her chin tilted down, now glinted gold. Her overlarge teeth were pallid scythes. Yet worst of all was the hunger in that amber gaze. The desire to rend and feed.

Dominic's trance broke. He started for the kitchen, but his foot slipped on the shattered glass and alcohol, and with a bound, Militsa was on him. Clark was positive she would tear him apart on the instant, but instead, she grabbed him, rolled him over, pinned his arms above his head, and roared into his face. Dominic let loose with a yodeling shriek as the werewolf's slaver pooled over his face.

"Please let us go," Bob was moaning. "Please don't hurt us."

"Hurt you?" Divna asked.

With Stanislava still clutching his wrist, Bob faced Divna on his knees. He reached toward her with his free hand. "Please, miss." He winced as Stanislava gave his wrist a squeeze. "*Please*. I beg you."

"I like that," Stanislava said.

Bob looked up at her, wide-eyed.

"I like it when you beg," she explained.

Bob's face crumpled. "Please," he sobbed. "Don't hurt me. I'll do anything."

Divna lowered to a crouch and studied Bob's mucus-slicked features. Clark expected her to take Bob's head off with a swipe, but instead, she brought her face right up to his.

"Radomir," she breathed.

Bob's eyes widened. "Huh?"

Divna rose to her full height and began to unbutton her cuffs.

Bob looked around the room, perhaps searching for a sane ally. "Who the hell is Radomir?"

"You are," Clark said. He turned to Dominic. "So are you."

Pinned under Militsa, Dominic could only wail.

"Help me with my zipper?" Divna asked. Clark noted before he stepped behind Divna that her irises had taken on a golden hue.

"Are you surprised?" Divna asked.

Clark drew down her zipper and noted how the knobs of her vertebrae pulsed and undulated. "Yes," he answered.

"Your work is validated," she said.

He completed the zipper's downward path.

Across the room, Dominic howled in terror. Divna shouted, "Wait!"

Clark saw how close Militsa, her lycanthropic transformation now completed, had come to biting Dominic's face. Her teeth, which had actually closed on Dominic's chin and nose, withdrew just enough to allow him to thrash his head from side to side and wail for mercy.

When Clark's eyes returned to Divna, she was nude from the waist up. Tossing aside her black brassiere, she said to him, "Whatever happens, you must not interfere." She pushed her dress the rest of the way down her legs, then removed her black underwear.

Confronted with her glorious body, Clark found it difficult to formulate an answer.

Blond hair had begun to slither out of Divna's bare flesh. When she spoke, the hint of a growl tinged her words. "We watched you for a month."

He frowned. "How..."

"We can be furtive when we wish to be." The ghost of a smile appeared but was gone just as swiftly. "We witnessed your downfall. Your last days at the university. The shameful treatment from these two cowards." A contemptuous nod toward Bob and Dominic. Bob, Clark noticed, was wrestling with Stanislava, grappling with her to release her grip. But Stanislava merely applied more pressure, and beneath Dominic's cries for mercy, Clark heard the dull snap of Bob's wrist. Bob screamed and sank down onto his side.

"We will take our time," Divna said, her voice now gravelly, her incisors and canines too long for her mouth. "You may watch or wait for us upstairs, according to your preference."

Bob must have caught this last because he looked up at Divna, who now stood six inches taller than before, and said, "Watch *what*?" His pain-glazed eyes darted from Divna to Clark. "What's he supposed to watch?" Bob glanced at his captor, and he sucked in a breath. "Please stop. Whatever you're doing... please stop!"

Clark saw without surprise that Stanislava had begun to alter as well.

Divna stalked toward Bob. Even in her half-werewolf form, her beauty was stunning. "We learned about you," she said to Bob. A glance at where Dominic lay pinioned under Militsa. "We learned about Mr. Headley."

Bob brought up an imploring hand. "I don't know what you think you know about me, but it's not true."

"It *is* true," Divna said, her voice deepening. Her sculpted buttocks were barely discernible beneath the glorious blond fur. "You're a rapist. And a monster."

Bob gaped at her. "Who's calling who a monster?"

Divna pitched forward and landed on all fours. She snarled, and her knees gave way, twin gouts of blood splattering the hardwood as her legs hyperextended.

Jonathan Janz

"Call her off!" Bob shouted at Clark. "Call them all off!"

The words were barely out of his mouth when Stanislava, in the throes of the change, jerked on Bob's arm. Clark heard a meaty pop and knew from Bob's scream and the unnatural way his body twisted that his arm had been pulled loose from the socket.

"Come, Radomir," Divna growled, crawling toward Bob. "Offer me your succulent meat."

"Who the fuck is Radomir?" Bob screamed.

Stanislava had sunk down beside Bob, and though she didn't relinquish her hold on his broken wrist, she had entered the terminal stages of the change. Her pink dress had ripped open in a dozen spots, where black fur poked through in lustrous tufts.

Bob thrashed to escape from Stanislava, but the vise grip on his wrist kept him tethered to the transforming werewolf. Her jaw elongated, her eyes a luminous gold. Bob's eyes were gaping orbs. "Oh...my...GOD!"

The change completed, Stansislava turned and snarled at him.

A crunching sound and a shrill scream tore Clark's gaze from the grisly tableau. He saw that Dominic had gotten an arm between his face and Militsa's rapier-like teeth, and in response, Militsa had bitten down on his forearm. Dominic was shrieking, shrieking, and Militsa's jaws were working, grinding, splintering Dominic's radius and ulna as though they were soup bones. The blood coated Militsa's radiant red fur in a cherry-colored spray. Dominic's eyes were riveted on his mangled forearm, his screams devolving into a phlegmy wail. Militsa's head jerked, and most of Dominic's forearm separated near the elbow. An upsurge of brandy and gastric juices spilled from the corners of Dominic's open mouth, the auburn-hued liquid only a shade darker than Militsa's fur. Militsa jerked her head again, and the forearm came off in her jaws. Dominic began to choke on his own vomit, but his staring eyes never left his severed arm. The fingers of his lost hand twitched as though playing an unseen piano.

"Do something, goddamn you!"

Clark swung his head around and realized Bob was shouting at him, Bob, who was swatting feebly at Stanislava, the raven werewolf, while she dragged him under her. Clark marveled a moment at how gigantic Stanislava had become, how long and broad she and Militsa had grown. Deep down, in the region of his brain where reason still resided, a mystery that had long plagued him found a resolution. Despite the frenetic vigor of the lycanthrope, despite its supernatural power and unbridled bloodlust, Clark had still not been able to reason out the scope of some of the werewolves' more extreme attacks. An entire village destroyed in Berstuk. A small town ravaged in Hungary. A transatlantic steamer reduced to a floating abattoir.

Now he understood.

Somehow, someway, the werewolves grew to obscene dimensions when in thrall to the change. That's how they killed so prolifically.

"Let me go!" Bob shouted, and as Clark's eyes refocused, he witnessed a horrifying sight: Stanislava, now a gigantic black werewolf, pairing Bob's wrists with one of her taloned hands, while with the other, she reached down and grasped the front of Bob's trousers. With a yank, she tore Bob's pants off, and with another quick swipe, she shredded the crotch of his boxer shorts.

Bob gaped down at his exposed genitalia.

Just in time to see Stanislava grab hold of them.

Bob screamed, "OHMYGODPLEASEDON'T—"

But it was too late. The raven werewolf merely tugged on Bob's genitals, and the skin around them gave with a wet snap. Blood fountained up from the ragged hole, and Stanislava, her golden eyes gleaming, popped the glistening member and testicles into her maw.

Bob threw his head back and wailed.

Standing beside Clark, Divna roared in triumph.

And as Clark peered up at the alpha werewolf, a passage from *Lycanthropology* recurred: *When in thrall to the change, the lycanthrope succumbs to its maniacal bloodlust. It kills in a frenzy, leaving no living creature in its wake.*

Holy God, he thought. *I'm going to die.*

His legs numb, he started for the kitchen. To his left, he saw Bob jittering, Stanislava's head now buried in his crotch and burrowing deeper. Bob's fingers still grasped clutches of the werewolf's shoulder fur, but Bob's grasp was weakening now. Tears of agony streamed from his eyes.

Staggering, Clark made it past Bob and Stanislava, but now he beheld Dominic Headley, his throat a mangled goulash of flesh and tissue. Militsa lapped greedily at the blood spray, her auburn hair matted from chin to chest.

Moaning, Clark weaved around the pair and headed for the kitchen. He knew he should escape through the back door, but an image of Divna tackling him from behind and devouring him in the snowy backyard forbade this route. And anyway, the back door boasted three different locks, and he could hear the heavy clatter of Divna's footsteps behind him. Closing in. At any moment, she'd reach out and
—

With a cry, he veered left, away from the back door and onto the staircase. He took the stairs three at a time, and as he reached the second story, he heard the alpha werewolf panting at his heels. There was no escaping, no resisting the beast's onslaught.

Still, he made it to his bedroom, spun, and slammed the door. With shaking fingers, he managed to slide the chain lock into place, but as he backed away from the door, he marveled at the futility of the gesture.

Without thinking, he reached out, pulled the lamp chain. The room brightened, but not by much. Clark stared at the door, a childish hope arising in him that the werewolf would leave off the hunt. Something to his right drew his vision, and when he beheld the noose dangling from the ceiling, he clenched his teeth at his stupidity. My God, he'd almost killed himself over a job. Over a pair of idiots like Bob Spates and Dominic Headley, *dead* idiots who never should have—

The door exploded inward.

Shards of wood spiraled through the bedroom. Instinctively, Clark covered his face with a forearm and stumbled toward the bed. Snarling, the alpha werewolf launched itself at him. Clark lunged toward the window and only avoided the beast's talons by inches. Nauseated by fear, he shambled toward the ruined doorway, but he knew it was pointless. The creature would destroy him within moments. His shoeless feet slipped on fragments of the shattered door, and behind him, he heard the werewolf scramble to its feet.

Clark was almost to the doorway when he heard the werewolf speak, its voice something from the darkest depths of hell: "*I will run you down.*"

He froze, one foot in the hallway, the other balanced unsteadily on a shard of door the size of a baseball bat. His mind raced, and the urge to flee was nearly overmastering, but beneath that, in a psychological realm long dormant, he felt a stirring. Though he couldn't see the blond werewolf, he sensed her watching him from across the room.

Waiting for his next move.

Clark closed his eyes, drew in a deep suck of air, and

turned to face Divna Antonov.

In the honeyed lamplight, her blond fur shone a rich gold, her glorious body towering more than seven feet. The lambent irises glowed like gilded embers, the fangs mere alabaster glints within the pink-black gums.

Clark's breathing steadied, an unaccountable calm settling in his limbs. He bent down and grasped the long shard of jagged wood.

The shard clutched in his right hand, he took a step toward Divna.

The werewolf's mouth formed itself into a ghastly leer.

"Finally," Divna growled, *"you fight."*

Clark launched himself at her and plunged the shard at her chest. Divna swatted his hand aside, the shard skittering across the floor. Clark's momentum carried him straight into Divna's chest, and before he could recover, she thrust him away and sent him skidding on his back toward the doorway. She strode toward him, but he scrambled to his feet and lurched toward the far side of the bed.

The side on which lay the iron fireplace stoker.

She swiped at him, and a bright fire bloomed in his shoulder. He staggered forward, dove toward the nightstand, and right behind him, in the space he'd just vacated, he felt the whoosh of air from the werewolf's swooping talons.

Clark reached out for the stoker, and though his fingers closed on it, the chuff of the werewolf and the click of its toenails on the floor told him he'd never be able to spin around and swing the iron implement before she fell on him.

He scuttled sideways under the bed, pushing the stoker before him, and a split second later, the werewolf slammed onto the floor. Grimacing, Clark wriggled toward the far side of the bed. To his left, the beast groped for him, the wicked talons snagging his shirt. Clark jerked away. In answer, the monster uttered a bellicose growl. Clark continued to drag himself sideways, the space beneath the bed oppressive, but his stark terror lending speed to his movements.

He felt the bed over him shift, and he threw a glance at the werewolf. With numb shock, he realized the monster was forcing its way under the heavy bed. Desperately, he glanced to his right and saw how the gap beneath the bed's edge and the floor was narrowing. The werewolf was tilting the whole bed as it shoved itself after Clark.

Clark scrambled toward the gap but realized it was too late, the whole bed tilting upward now, the werewolf pushing to its feet and overturning it, and then the beast was glowering down at him, the bed crashing over and taking the lamp with it. There came an ear-splitting clatter as the antique nightstand was crushed beneath the bed, and beneath that, a sizzling *pop* as the lamp's bulb shattered.

The bedroom steeped in near-darkness, Clark rolled over and gazed up at the werewolf.

Its eyes glowing a brilliant amber, it fell on him.

Clark thrust the stoker at its chest, and though its weight drove the iron rod through his grip, its handle braced on the floor, and the iron tip plunged deep into the werewolf's chest.

The werewolf crashed down onto him, and its mouth opened in a deep, bone-rattling howl. Clark shoved with all his strength to escape, but the werewolf's bulk kept him trapped and deprived of air. The monster howled again, and Clark felt its arms bruising over his pinned body. He was sure the beast would open his ribcage, but then the werewolf's fingers closed over the stoker handle, and it rolled off of him.

Clark gasped, the ability to breathe again unutterably wonderful. He pushed to all fours, his chest heaving, and peripherally he saw the werewolf staggering to its feet. There was brackish blood coating Clark's hands and wrists, even more of the stuff pooled on the floor where he and the werewolf had lain. The creature had its back to him, and from the way its elbows moved, he could see it was trying to extricate the lodged stoker. Clark swayed to his feet and made for the door, but there he paused, his breath coagulating in his throat.

The other two creatures were waiting for him just outside the doorway. Their massive forms were tensed. Their lowered snouts and their slitted eyes advertised their desire to rend him to pieces.

Yes, he realized, backpedaling. Divna was their sister, their leader, and Clark had grievously wounded her. Their lips curled in twin snarls, the scarlet and raven-haired werewolves were milliseconds from destroying him.

Clark jumped as a bruising *thunk* sounded behind him. He spun, hand on heart, and saw the iron stoker glistening with blood but no longer lodged in the blond werewolf's chest. The blond werewolf—

(*Divna, her name is Divna*)

—staggered toward the window and slumped against the casement ledge, its huge chest heaving and its shoulders shivering.

A floorboard creaked, and Clark glanced behind him to find the scarlet and raven werewolves—

(*Militsa and Stanislava*)

—stalking through the doorway, the scarlet in the lead, but the raven soon joining its side, the pair of them forming an impenetrable rampart of fur and muscle through which Clark had no hope of passing.

It's the end, he thought. But though he'd planned on this

eventuality, now that it was here...

The scarlet and raven werewolves closed in. The blond beast was slumped over the windowsill, and as Clark watched, one great, muscled arm rose, and the long, knobby fingers grasped the casement crank. The blond werewolf worked the crank until the frost-kissed air ghosted over her. Through the rectangular opening, Clark discerned wind-blown flakes swirling, swirling, and he thought, *Not ready. I'm not ready to die.*

The hackles at the base of his neck rose, the scalding, copper-tinged breath of the werewolves swarming over him. He sensed their closeness, not only from the phlegmy rattle of their growls but from the atavistic reaction of his skin, his flesh drawing taut in nubby goosebumps.

Clark jolted when a hand grasped his shoulder. He began to twist, but another hand seized his upper biceps and drew him into the waiting fur. Carrion breath clouded over him. His eyes watered, and his gorge rose at the smell, but struggle though he might, he could not break the werewolf's hold. Whether it was Militsa or Stanislava that gripped him did not matter. All that mattered was their wrath. He'd injured Divna, and they would repay him with a gruesome, protracted death.

Clark steeled himself and closed his eyes, waiting for the merciless puncture of fangs on his neck.

"*Cease*," a voice rumbled.

Clark opened his eyes, and though he found Divna still before the open window, her posture had altered. Rather than hunched over and wracked with pain, she appeared enervated but calm, resting rather than suffering.

An answering snarl at his ear told him that at least one of Divna's sisters was opposed to sparing Clark, but Divna turned now and spoke again, her voice less bestial: "Release him."

His captor hesitated a long moment, and then, blessedly,

the talons fell away, and unsupported, Clark sank to his knees.

Divna, her face nearly returned to its divine-human beauty, scowled. "Will you kneel?"

The words dug at him, and before he knew it, he was standing again. "Hell, no," he answered.

Divna nodded, turned away, and shivered in the frigid January breeze. Clark watched her shoulder blades dwindle, the blond mane that had furred her skin receding like golden thread drawn through the eye of a needle.

Soon the blond fur was gone, and the gory wound in the middle of Divna's back was visible again. Yet even as he watched, the injury seemed to knit, the flesh tendrils swimming over the ragged hole, joining, and soon all that was left was a shiny patch of fresh skin.

Nude, her body unblemished, Divna stood erect and faced him. In the ghostly luminescence pouring through the casement window, Divna was somehow more imposing than she'd been in her werewolf form.

"If I grant you life, will you promise to keep our secrets?"

"*Divna*," a half-bestial voice behind him snarled, "*we cannot—*"

"Enough," Divna said, her voice calm.

Clark glanced uneasily over his shoulder and saw the speaker had been Stanislava. Like Divna, she was returning to her human form. Militsa, too, he saw with a quick look.

Neither sister looked happy with Divna's decision.

"You must write a letter," Divna said to him. "The authorities will find it and pronounce you dead. You must never reveal your identity, nor may you return to New York."

"Okay," he managed.

Divna stepped closer, her body ethereal in the moonglow. She stopped before him, her eyes on a level slightly higher than his, her breath now fragrant and somehow reminiscent of wild coniferous forests, of pink April flowers and clear, clean water.

Her mouth close to his, she said, "You are the first human to respect our glorious species. For this, I offer you life. But it must be a secret life."

Clark hadn't the foggiest notion of what this meant, and anyway, the sight of Divna's supernal beauty had robbed him of speech.

"Life," Divna whispered and put her lips on his. The kiss was long and deep, and at one moment, exhilarating, and in the next, there was a pang in his bottom lip. But he was intoxicated, and when Divna released him, it was as though a curtain had fallen on a sylvan wonderland, one he'd only dreamed possible in fairytales and myths.

"Go now," Divna said. "We must prepare your house. And you must begin your new life."

He hesitated, the ghost of Divna's kiss still entrancing him.

"*Go,*" she said, her voice firmer this time.

It was the look in her eyes that did it, the subtlest hint of gold.

Clark fled the bedroom, and within a minute, he departed his home for the last time.

As he raced down the snow-tufted street, he was tempted to glance over his shoulder, to search the upper windows of his home for a glimpse of Divna.

But his promise—and his fear of what would happen if he broke his promise—kept his eyes on the street ahead and his feet trudging through the bitter night.

Jonathan Janz

***

Clark was seated in the kitchen, nursing a mug of steaming black coffee, when movement from the lane drew his gaze. The boy he paid to bring the newspaper was scurrying up the cobbled walk, the boy's legs tremoring the geraniums and butterfly weeds that had just begun to bloom. The promise of a lovely April was what had drawn him to Michigan, the childhood memories of flowers and fresh air and mornings exploring the forest near his Ann Arbor home.

Of course, he couldn't risk returning to Ann Arbor—he was supposed to be dead, after all—so Clark had settled for Newberry, a quaint upper-peninsula town he'd once visited with his grandparents during the summer of his sixth year.

And Newberry had proved to be ideal. Civilized enough to support a library and a few restaurants, yet isolated enough to allow him to remain anonymous. Just a retired academic returning to his home state to live out his remaining years in comfort and peace. Thus far, no one had inquired about his teaching career, and when the time came, he figured he could keep the details vague enough to avoid arousing suspicion.

Of course, if the head of the Newberry Public Library kept showing interest in him, it might be challenging to keep his past a secret...

Clark frowned.

He brought his fingertips to his bottom lip, the movement unconscious, but once there, he allowed the pads of his fingers to play over the thin scar, the centimeter of raised pink tissue, the place where Divna's canine tooth had pierced his flesh.

Clark let his fingers fall and thought back to the night before, how on a whim he'd driven the old Roadster into town. After a bite to eat, he'd found himself at the library, where Madeline Stone—*Please, she'd reminded him, call*

128

me Maddie—greeted him with her overbright smile and her unsubtle probings about his past. No, she wasn't rude or offensive. And under other circumstances, her attention would have been flattering.

But when you were supposed to be dead... when multiple newspapers had printed your obituary, and the world believed you'd ended your life with a leap off the Brooklyn Bridge... when you'd even left a suicide note bequeathing the contents of your home to the owner of a local animal shelter...

He'd cleared his bank account the morning after his encounter with the Antonov Sisters, had liquidated his investments, and disappeared into anonymity. The circumstances were bound to provoke suspicion. He mustn't do anything to compromise his new existence.

After exchanging niceties with Maddie Stone, he'd wandered to the periodicals, to the collection of gloriously illustrated pulp magazines Maddie ordered. There, Clark had discovered a new issue of *Unknown*, where he'd found the tale that had almost ruined everything: a novelette by Jack Williamson called *Darker Than You Think*.

The problem wasn't the writing. Williamson was damned good, and the tale was exceedingly well told. Yet, like all lycanthropic literature, the story was crammed with prejudice against werewolves and commonly propagated misconceptions about their habits. Clark had been reading in the back corner of the basement—alone, thank God— when he'd become aware of a low growl emanating from very close by. Jerking to his senses, he'd cast wild glances around him, certain Divna had returned to revoke the mercy she'd granted him. When he'd found the aisle empty, he'd frozen, a sense of cosmic horror enveloping him.

The growling was coming from *him*. A glance at his knuckles revealed wiry black hairs that hadn't been present before reading Williamson's story.

The truth had come crashing down on him in a flood:

He'd been correct about the catalyst of the lycanthropic change. Werewolves didn't transform because of the moon or the scent of blood, or any other foolishness popular fiction would have the world believe. Lycanthropes transformed due to a powerful negative emotion. Lust, guilt, greed, sorrow.

Or in Clark's case, rage.

He'd flung the magazine away and stumbled into the claustrophobic washroom, and only with a titanic effort had he calmed himself sufficiently to reverse the transformation. Before he had, however, he'd caught a glimpse of himself in the cracked and filmy mirror over the sink.

What he'd seen was a creature of nightmare. Crazed. Satanic.

Now in his kitchen, Clark shook his head to clear it of the image, and for something to do, he crossed the room to refill his coffee.

It did not escape his notice that his knees no longer ached, and his back was no longer stiff. Many nights he'd been gripped by an overwhelming urge to shed his clothing and scamper into the nearby forest. To run and leap through the crisp spring night. He imagined Divna joining him, the two of them bereft of clothing, a pair of feral lovers lapping from the creek, and making love in the caressing bluegrass.

Returning to his chair, Clark sipped his coffee and opened the newspaper to the second page, and there he saw it, the account of the moonshiners outside Sudbury, a Southern Canadian town.

As with the other stories, the details were strikingly similar:

The men who ran the still were individuals of ill-repute, most of them with violent criminal records. Something— either a Grizzly bear or a pack of starving wolves—had attacked the men in the dead of night and left behind a scene of unimaginable gore.

Just like Albany. Just like Syracuse. Like Kingston and Peterborough. Over the past few months, the atrocities were moving gradually west.

Toward Michigan's Upper Peninsula.

Clark gripped the newspaper tighter. There could be no doubt that Divna and her sisters were coming for him.

The question was, for what purpose?

Clark remembered the feel of Divna's lips on his. Remembered the depths of her blue eyes, the eyes that glowed gold when she turned bestial.

Clark stood and strode toward the back door, through which he passed and moved to the rear of his property. The cottage sat on twelve acres, but beyond that was wildland, lush forests unspoiled by man and his corruption.

Yes, he thought, gazing into the woods. He would run tonight. He would remember Bob Spates and Dominic Headley and the injustice that had occurred at Columbia.

Clark would revel in his rage, and he would allow the change to come.

And he would master it. If Divna and her sisters were not seeking him, he would begin a new life with Maddie Stone, with her books and her wry sense of humor.

But if Divna did come, he would be ready. If she wanted to mate, he would mate. If she wanted to fight, he would fight.

What he wouldn't do—what he'd never do again—was live in fear.

Clark balled his fists and felt his arm muscles twitch.

He smiled and willed the night to come.

ABOUT THE AUTHOR

Jonathan Janz is the author of more than a dozen novels and numerous short stories. His work has been championed by authors like Joe R. Lansdale, Brian Keene, and Jack Ketchum; he has also been lauded by Publishers Weekly, Library Journal, and School Library Journal. His ghost story The Siren and the Specter was selected as a Goodreads Choice Awards nominee for Best Horror.

Additionally, his novel Children of the Dark was chosen by Booklist as a Top Ten Horror Book of the Year.

Jonathan's main interests are his wonderful wife and his three amazing children. You can sign up for his newsletter, and you can follow him on Twitter, Instagram, Facebook, Amazon, and Goodreads.

@JonathanJanz

https://www.facebook.com/jonathan.janz.3

https://jonathanjanz.com/

The Great Storm

T W Piperbrook

"Are they gone?" Silas peered over the snowy incline, past a cluster of trees.

Katherine pressed her flashlight against the snow, disguising the thin beam. Her body shook from fear and cold. Her winter jacket was snug against her. If it was later in the season, she and Silas might've received the new coats Mom had promised. But no one had expected the early October snowstorm, just as no one had predicted the terrifying creatures that came with it.

None of it could be real. Could it?

Katherine shuddered, closing her eyes and reopening them as falling wet snow stuck to her eyelashes.

"I'm scared, Katherine," Silas whispered, his breath misting the air between them.

Katherine couldn't muster the words to tell him that she was scared too.

Pressing her light further into the snow, she reached over and pulled her six-year-old brother tight. It was all she could manage to do. Peering over the top of the incline, they stared through the trees at the house they'd left behind. The moonlight illuminated the large, rectangular colonial. Only a few wisps of smoke graced the sky from the chimney. Shortly after they'd awoken to the cold and the storm—after the heat and the lights went out—Dad had started a fire. Those moments spent in front of the hearth with her parents seemed comforting compared to what came after.

That was before the monsters arrived.

Before her mother and father had pushed her and Silas

out of the back door and told them to run.

Her Dad had shot one of the creatures, but it hadn't died. Instead, it had come toward him as if he were a meal, its red eyes blazing in the beam of his flashlight, its face and body covered in a dark, coarse fur. More creatures had battered the front door and windows, breaking inside.

They must be monsters.

What else could they be?

Katherine scanned the dark windows and the open back door from which they'd come, but the house was silent.

Were Mom and Dad dead?

Something inside the house crashed.

Katherine let go of Silas and put two hands on the flashlight, flicking it off. She scanned the distant house, holding her breath.

Movement.

For a brief, hopeful moment, she wondered if it was Dad coming to tell them everything was okay.

An enormous figure emerged from inside the house, silhouetted by the moonlight. Thick, black hair covered its body. Large ears poked from the top of its head. Hot breath plumed from its long snout. At first, it stood upright, walking a few steps before lowering its front paws to the snow and moving on all fours. The thing loped across the yard and toward the woods where they hid. Katherine reached up, wiping away more of the pelting white flakes that stuck to her eyes. Could it see them?

The creature kept coming, narrowing the two-hundred-foot gap to the tree line. Katherine held her breath, reaching out for Silas, squeezing him close. She didn't need to warn him.

Stay quiet! Stay quiet!

The creature stopped.

Frightened tears ran down Katherine's cheeks.

The creature arched its back and raised its elongated snout, turning in their direction.

It didn't need to see them. It could *smell* them.

"Run!" she cried to Silas.

Katherine forced herself out of the deep snow, pulling her brother upright. Together, they flew down the small slope and into a thicker patch of woods, faintly illuminated by the moon, until darkness forced her to turn on the flashlight again. Thick, multi-branched trees surrounded them. A few hundred feet of forest separated their house from the next neighborhood, which ended in a cul-de-sac. Maybe they could reach her friend Maddie's house, and then her parents could help them. It was a desperate hope that she had to believe.

A crack rang out from above. Katherine swayed the light to see an arm-sized limb crash to the ground nearby. The weight of the leaves and snow was wreaking havoc on the pines and oaks.

Nothing was safe from the storm's wrath.

"Come on, Silas!" she whispered, clutching his skinny wrist.

They tore through the deep snow, plunging their slippers in and out of the thick, white landscape. If Mom hadn't insisted they wore coats in front of the fireplace, they would've only been in pajamas. They were lucky to have slippers.

Hidden branches threatened to trip them up, but they avoided falling, finding new places to step. Katherine didn't dare glance over her shoulder. Growls echoed behind them. At any moment, the creature would pounce and tear them apart.

Please let us escape...

They passed several clusters of trees that she and Silas had climbed when the weather was warm, where they played tag.

The trees thinned.

An open expanse of white appeared in the distance.

They'd crested the top of the hill, reaching a spot a hundred feet from the edge of a cul-de-sac. New noises reached Katherine's ears.

Car tires whirred. People screamed.

The creatures were on Stillwell Drive, too.

Men, women, and children spilled out of the lightless homes, screaming. Dark, furred monsters loped from the doorways after them, visible in the moonlight and the glow of some people's flashlights, as well as the headlights of some cars stuck sideways in the snow. In horror, Katherine watched two of the fur-covered beasts smash a car's front windshield, drag a man from inside, and gut him on the hood. Another woman's long shriek filled the night air as a beast tackled her to the ground and buried its face in her belly, pulling pieces of her stomach out and holding them to the sky. A pajama-clad man ran across his yard before a pursuing beast tackled him and cut his cries short.

Katherine searched the line of dark, silhouetted homes for a place to run. Nowhere was safe.

The snorts and growls of the creature behind them grew louder.

"Come on, Silas!"

She veered to the right of the cul-de-sac, heading for the backyard of the first lot, where there was less commotion. A car alarm went off, blaring above the screams.

Somewhere in the din, gunfire split the air.

Whatever these creatures were, guns didn't seem to stop them.

Their only hope was to lose the creature behind them and avoid any others.

Katherine pulled Silas along as fast as she was able. They'd gone thirty more feet when a man she recognized intersected with them on the front corner of the first house's lot, aiming his flashlight.

Mr. Cancelmo's gray hair stuck up wildly. His sweatpants stuck to his legs. "They're everywhere!" He looked past them, preparing to run for the woods.

"It's not safe back there!" Katherine warned.

Her words died in the frigid air. Mr. Cancelmo darted past them without listening.

The creature pursuing them loped across the snow from the tree line.

The beast crashed into him.

Mr. Cancelmo's flashlight fell.

Beast and man landed in a tangled heap, writhing. Mr. Cancelmo's agonizing cries were lost in the frenzy of his evisceration. The fallen flashlight revealed the man's severed stomach and his insides, which the beast tore out and threw on the snow. Tears Katherine had no time to process slid down her cheeks.

Move, or die.

"Keep going, Silas!"

She pulled her brother on the path they'd started, looking over her shoulder, keeping half a terrified eye on the feasting creature.

Reaching the shadowed backyard of the first house,

Katherine pulled Silas after her, leading with her flashlight. A deck protruded from the house's back. Katherine's beam illuminated a covered grill and a pair of sliding glass doors. She looked over her shoulder. The shadowed creature hovering over Mr. Cancelmo had finished its meal. Or maybe it was looking for something else to hunt. Its red eyes glowed as it looked after them.

"Shut off the light!" Silas hissed.

Katherine flicked it off.

For a moment, they stood in silence, watching the creature.

Don't see us. Don't see us.

Slowly, the creature stood.

It bounded in their direction.

Katherine frantically scanned ahead. In the next yard, she saw a small, fenced-off garden and a shed on the right-hand side of the property.

A memory came back to her of playing hide and seek with one of her friends in the neighborhood and running past Mr. Grant's shed. Mr. Grant sometimes watched Maddie and her brother when her parents were out. A few times, he'd even let Katherine take vegetables home from his garden. Maybe they could hide in his small shed.

Silas stumbled next to her, taking shorter steps. She pulled him along faster, certain that the beast would leap through the air, land on their backs, and fillet them.

They closed within thirty feet of the shed.

Twenty.

A panicked thought struck Katherine. What if the door was locked? Heading for the entrance, Katherine got her answer. The double doors hung open. A figure lay diagonally up the snow-covered ramp, blocking the threshold. A quick beam from her flashlight revealed the details.

A man she didn't recognize lay on his back, his eyes wide and unmoving.

It wasn't Mr. Grant.

The man's face was frozen in an expression of death. Blood covered his shredded stomach and the perimeter of his body, staining the snow red. Whoever the man was, the shed hadn't saved him, and would probably be just as useless for them. With another cry, Katherine pulled Silas away from the dead man and down the row of houses.

She looked over her shoulder.

The creature entered the edge of the first yard.

They continued away from the bloodied body and across the snow, running over other people's tracks. Silas's arm shook under her grip. If not for the adrenaline caused by the creature behind them, Katherine might've felt the cold, or the snow creeping around the top of her slippers.

Right now, she felt only panic.

She glanced sideways at the dark house to their left. A set of snow-covered steps led up to the back door. Veering toward them, she pulled Silas up onto the porch and tried the door handle.

"Locked!" she cried to Silas.

"Up there!" Silas called. "Someone's in the window!"

Katherine looked up the side of the house, her heart pounding. A light shone from upstairs. A woman looked down at them from one of the windows, her mouth agape, her flashlight pressed against the pane.

Katherine waved her arms. "Down here! We need help!"

The woman was in a panic of her own.

141

A shadow appeared behind her.

The woman screamed.

Her body crashed through the window in a rain of glass, falling two stories and landing near Katherine and Silas. Her limbs twisted at an ugly angle. She didn't move. A snarl echoed from the open window. Growls rang out from behind.

"Run, Silas!"

Katherine and Silas tore away, skirting around the fallen, lifeless woman and toward the next yard. Looking over her shoulder, Katherine saw the beast passing Mr. Grant's shed. It loped steadily, but it didn't overtake them.

Not yet.

Katherine recalled the dog her parents had for several years when she and Silas were younger. Mister Bones had been a great pet to them indoors, but he'd almost been a different animal when they walked him. She remembered how he'd stalked some squirrels in the neighborhood, tracking them and waiting to pounce, just like the creature was doing now.

Perhaps it enjoyed the hunt.

"Hurry, Silas!"

A row of arborvitaes separated them from the next property. Reaching the row of hedges, Katherine listened for screams or snarls. She heard nothing on the other side other than faraway panic. She and Silas picked a spot between two bushes and squeezed between. Their scraping branches felt like claws, tearing at Katherine's coat.

And then they were in an empty yard.

A metal playscape sat in the center of the property. The swings and slide sat empty. Were the children already dead?

She suppressed an ugly thought she didn't have time for. Silas shook underneath her grasp. She wanted to stop and hold Silas's arms as she looked in his face, telling him to be brave the way Mom did when he needed a shot, or when he scraped his knee, but a lost moment would mean the creature catching up.

A crash ripped their attention left. Past the fifteen-foot gap between two houses, in a front yard, a man and a creature circled around each other in the moonlight. The man hefted a shovel, swinging it at the beast. He grunted and struck air.

"Stay back!" he yelled, rearing back his makeshift weapon.

He might as well be screaming into the wind.

The creature lunged for the man's midsection, taking him to the ground, knocking the shovel astray. The man's painful screams were lost in the beast's snarls.

Katherine looked over her shoulder.

The creature behind them was out of view.

They were only a few houses away from Maddie's. If they could get to her friend's house, maybe they could find help. It was a frantic hope that she had to believe.

They passed two more sheds, skirting around an aboveground pool. Crashes and snarls came from several of the houses, but the backyards were quiet, especially the next one they approached.

All around them, dark shadows lay in the snow. A smell Katherine recognized hit her nose: a coppery, metallic odor she knew from scraping her elbows and knees.

Blood.

"Are those...?" Silas whispered, unable to say the word.

Katherine didn't need him to say the word, "bodies."

143

Steam rose from the gutted figures' insides, mingling with the white snow around them. Her slippers pressed on something squishy.

An awful realization struck Katherine as she glanced over her shoulder at the above-ground pool.

Her body clenched.

She looked from the bodies in the yard back to the pool.

If the pool was two houses down, that meant that Maddie's house was...

"No..."

Katherine's legs buckled.

All at once, she was leaning down, fighting nausea in her throat. Silas bent down next to her, frantically looking around at the dead people—two larger bodies and two smaller ones.

"What is it, Katherine?"

Katherine couldn't speak, nor could she turn on the flashlight to verify what she knew was true. Her body was numb. She felt as if she might close her eyes and never wake up from fear. She looked over at the house as if she might be mistaken, but she recognized the back porch and the windows leading to the mudroom, where she and Maddie spent time playing Connect Four or Candyland. Even the house hadn't saved Maddie, her parents, and her brother.

Tears flowed down Katherine's face as she realized the end result of their night. They'd never escape the beasts because Maddie and her family hadn't.

She and Silas were on their own.

"Katherine!" Silas whispered, leaning down next to her. "Katherine!"

Katherine smeared away her tears, looking up at her brother in the moonlight. He fidgeted and wrung his hands. He consoled her to no avail.

And then he grabbed her arm.

Katherine's attention riveted back to the pool. A creature snuck around the perimeter, close enough that she could make out its massive, lumbering form and its protruding snout. She stood upright, taking a retreating step.

"Katherine, I don't want to die," Silas whispered.

His words were like a shot in the arm.

Katherine couldn't let the thing get them.

They couldn't end up like Maddie and her family.

Glancing over at the house, she saw only a place of death, where too many in the neighborhood had been trapped. An idea struck her, so hard and fast that she couldn't deny it.

The woods...

***

Operating on muscle memory, Katherine led Silas between the trees behind Maddie's house. The long, protruding oak branches looked slightly different in the moonlight, but she was able to navigate through them. Memories flashed through her head of her and Maddie pretending the wild was their home.

The last time she'd been over, she and Maddie had hiked deep into the woods, passing Maddie's treehouse and reaching the main road beyond. Katherine knew those woods as well as the ones in her own neighborhood.

"This way!" Katherine told Silas.

"Where are we going?" Silas asked.

"To get help!" she said.

Once or twice, Katherine flicked her flashlight on, but mostly, they kept it off. A crash echoed behind them. The skulking beast's shadow crept through the trees, coming in and out of view.

She'd seen how fast it took down Mr. Cancelmo.

Why hadn't it tackled them yet?

It must be toying with them, biding its time.

The main road was a ten-minute hike away. Maybe they'd get lucky and find a policeman, a large group of people, or someone else—anyone—that might give them a chance.

Animal feet crunched over the snow.

Snarls filled the air behind them.

Maybe she was wrong, and the creature was done with its predatory game, after all.

Katherine searched through the dark tree trunks ahead. The road felt like a faraway place that they'd never reach. The creature would eat their bones as well as their flesh, and no one would ever find their bodies.

Katherine was so caught up in her thoughts that she almost didn't recognize the enormous, moonlit oak in front of them. When she did, another idea struck her.

Maddie's treehouse.

"This way!" she told Silas, tugging him toward it.

They passed several more trees until she reached the tall oak where she thought the treehouse was located. Looking up into the dark foliage, Katherine couldn't see the outline of the small structure.

Katherine felt around the enormous trunk with her cold fingers, searching for the rectangular boards that gave them access to the house. Nothing. Maybe she had the wrong tree. Frantic, she snapped on the flashlight. Relief flooded her as she saw the wooden planks, nailed to the bark.

"Climb, Silas!" she hissed, her heart pounding and out of breath.

Silas hesitated. "I-I can't!"

"If we don't go up, we'll die!" she whispered. Holding Silas tightly, looking into his eyes, she said, "I'll be right behind you."

Silas hesitated again, wiping his eyes.

"Silas! You have to go up!" Katherine bent, putting on the tone her mother used when persuading them to be brave. "I know you can do it. Start climbing, and I'll make sure you reach the top."

Silas looked at her a moment, shaking.

And then he complied.

Letting go of her, Silas found the first step, reaching with his hands for the next one. Katherine guided his way with the light. Lifting the beam upward, she expected to find the treehouse blown away by the storm, or damaged. But it was there, nestled in the crook of several larger branches. The four pieces of plywood that made its sides wouldn't keep the monster out, but it was better protection than staying on the ground. Or at least it seemed that way, at the moment.

Silas took another step, balancing on the slippery snow that covered the top of the planks. His boot slipped. He cried out, kicking the air. Frantic, Katherine prepared to catch him if he fell, but he found purchase and kept climbing.

It was Katherine's turn.

She lifted a boot and found the first step.

Snow crunched behind her.

Katherine spun as a dark, snarling shadow bounded toward her.

Crying out, she fell from the first plank to the forest floor. Just in time, she skirted around the base of the tree, avoiding its raking claws.

"Katherine!" Silas screamed from somewhere above.

On the opposite side of the treehouse, Katherine backed away from the tree. The beast's glowing eyes penetrated the moonlit forest as it circled the old oak. Silas's urgent screams blended with the creature's hungry snarls. Katherine looked from the beast to the tree. In an instant, she realized she'd never make it up the tree after her brother.

A thought more frightening than her own death caught hold of her.

The creature would gut both her *and* Silas if she didn't do something.

She couldn't let the creature get to him.

Mustering a shout through her fear, Katherine said, "Over here!"

She waved her arms and her flashlight, drawing the beast's full attention. Her heart beat a frantic rhythm as she took a step backward in the deep snow and the creature followed. The beast raised its claws, advancing another step.

She turned and ran.

And then Katherine was on another terrifying chase. With a flood of new panic, she predicted how this one would end.

***

Katherine ran away from the oak tree and into the woods.

She was no longer on a path. She was just running, scanning the dim forest for anything that might help her. Her heart hammered so hard she thought it might explode. Beyond the area with the treehouse, the woods took a downward slope. She recalled Maddie's father's warnings. He'd always told them to go no farther than the treehouse.

Of course, she and Maddie hadn't listened, and they'd explored.

The area was dangerous, full of fallen trees and sharp sticks that might injure them. Katherine skidded on the snow as the forest took a steep decline, shining her light. Fallen trees lay everywhere on the ground, like kindling sticks for some enormous fire. Broken branches stuck up from all angles. She veered around several of them, losing speed, clinging desperately to her flashlight, afraid to lose it, lest she plow into some obstacle.

Her fears came true.

Katherine fell.

One minute, she was running; the next, she was on the ground and rolling.

Bursts of pain shot through her body as she turned over and over, hitting rocks and sticks under the snow. She thudded against a fallen tree, coming to a stop. The light jolted around in her hands. Looking behind her, she recognized a hollow, fallen oak in which she and Maddie had discovered a few stuffed beer cans.

The stump was even more rotted than when she last remembered. Sharp, half-broken branches stuck up from its sides. A gap underneath led to the other side.

She turned, managing to get up on her feet.

The creature stopped about ten feet away.

This time it had no other focus.

Its red eyes burned through the semi-darkness.

It raised its claws.

The chase was over, and they both knew it.

Katherine aimed her flashlight at its face, hoping to ward off a monster worse than any nightmare. For the first time all night, she got a good look at the creatures stalking them. The beast's face was covered in black fur, its eyes red and rabid. Long, sharp teeth stuck out from its open jaw, stained with the blood of its kills. Slowly, the beast rose to its hind legs, raising its long claws.

It hesitated.

It wasn't attacking; it was blocking the light.

Katherine sucked in a breath and glanced over her shoulder.

The spark of an idea became a hope. Jabbing the flashlight forward, she shined it brightly on the beast's face for a lingering second, thinking of Maddie's dead family, and of Silas hiding in the tree. She thought of Mr. Cancelmo's dying screams. Even if Katherine failed and died, maybe she'd distract the beast long enough that it forgot about Silas in the treehouse.

Yelling as loudly as she could, she said, "Over here! Come get me!"

The beast took a plodding step through its blindness.

She spun and dove.

Katherine slid underneath the gap between the ground and fallen trunk and to the other side. She kept her head down as the beast crashed on the tree above her.

A deafening screech pierced the air.

The tree shook as if it might collapse on top of her.

And then the beast's yowl ceased, and the forest grew still.

Katherine hunkered beneath the tree, afraid to move, afraid to breathe. She waited until her legs were stiff and sore before she scooted backward and stood, shining the flashlight on the tree, fearing that she'd find the beast waiting for her, its red eyes scanning her face, its claws raised. The creature was gone.

Where the beast had been, a naked man lay facedown on the tree, a jagged, broken limb protruding from the center of his chest. Blood poured from the open wound, dripping from the tree onto the snow. With a shudder, she recognized the naked, seemingly dead figure.

Mr. Grant?

Shock coursed through her. Katherine spun and looked around, expecting to find another vicious creature—some explanation for what she couldn't believe.

Somehow, the beast and Mr. Grant were the same.

Maybe that had explained the slow manner in which he stalked them. Perhaps he had recognized them through his hunger. Katherine couldn't reconcile the friendly neighbor she'd known with the beast chasing her.

She didn't have time to contemplate it. She needed to get back to Silas.

Katherine rushed through the forest, still making sense of what she'd seen and the man she thought she'd killed. Several times, she turned, expecting to find something behind her, but she saw nothing. She traced her path up the incline, clutching the flashlight, her only possession— the one that had saved her.

Reaching the tree where she'd left Silas, she shone her light up the wooden planks. Her eyes roamed to the top of the ladder, which disappeared to the fort's underside.

"Silas?" she called.

No answer.

Her hands shook on the flashlight as she climbed up the slippery steps, scanning the tops of the boards for signs of blood, signs that she was too late. She whispered her brother's name again as she climbed plank to plank. She looked upward.

Still no answer.

She was starting to think she'd lost Silas forever when her brother's familiar face peered down from the hole in the fort's bottom.

"Katherine?"

Relief flooded her.

"Silas!" she cried.

Katherine climbed up the rest of the fort as fast as she was able, scrambled onto the familiar floor, and hugged him tightly.

***

They waited in the tree fort for what felt like an eternity. It felt like a protective fortress from the distant snarls and screams.

In reality, it was a small comfort, and one that wouldn't stop a beast if another one found them.

Katherine knew that, and yet she needed something to believe.

Huddled inside the treehouse with Silas, Katherine's breath plumed the air. Several times, she considered heading down the ladder and searching for help, but she thought better of it. The inside of the fort smelled of the plywood Maddie's father had used to build it, along with the faint scent of a perfume she and Maddie had spilled. An old memory returned of her playing with some of Maddie's dolls up here when they were younger.

Maddie.

Katherine wiped her face as she considered her dead friend and her parents lying in that yard. She'd never forget that sight, just as she'd never forget the sight of Mr. Grant, who had tried to kill them.

Eventually, the pale wintry sky brightened.

The sun rose behind the clouds.

The screams and snarls stopped.

The snow petered to a light flurry.

Katherine and Silas peeked out from the windows of the tree fort, scanning the leaf and snow-covered trees as some of the night's chill receded. They examined the ground. They saw nothing other than an errant slipper track by the base of the tree that the snow hadn't covered and one of the prints of the animal that had chased them.

The beast seemed gone, and so were the others, by the sound of it.

A new noise hit Katherine's ears.

For a moment, she thought she was mistaken, but Silas heard it, too. Shaking, he raised a finger and pointed.

"Are those sirens?" he whispered, looking in the direction of the faint noise.

"I think they are," Katherine said, unable to believe it.

They climbed down from the fort.

***

Katherine and Silas ran through the remainder of the forest, intent on reaching the source of the noise. Katherine kept a wary eye on the trees, still not sure a snarling creature wouldn't run out at them and raise its claws. Maybe Mr. Grant wasn't dead, after all, and he'd return to kill them.

They saw nothing.

Soon, they reached a patch of land preceding a two-lane road leading to Savarese Street, which led into town.

An enormous red fire truck sat in the center of the road. Outside, a large man helped two people into the vehicle's cab. Finding her breath in the cold, Katherine shouted, "Help!"

She waved her hands and her flashlight.

She and Silas shouted several more times before the fireman heard them, turned, and hurried in their direction. They didn't wait for him to get to them. They plunged their slippers in and out of the snow.

They didn't stop running until they reached the truck.

"My name's Al," the fireman said with a grim smile, as he helped them into the vehicle.

Al's voice was the most comforting thing Katherine could ask for after a night filled with panic.

Katherine and Silas huddled beneath the blanket he gave them. Beside them in the backseat, an elderly couple held each other tightly, wearing the same haunted expression as the burly fireman. Katherine looked outside. Several other cars were stopped in the road. Their doors hung open, but Katherine saw no occupants. It felt like they were the only survivors of a shared nightmare.

Checking on them as they warmed up, Al asked, "Are you okay?"

Despite his words, she saw him shaking, too.

"I think," Katherine said, rubbing his oversized gloves together.

"I have another stop to make, and then I'll take you to the hospital," Al said, in a reassuring tone.

The truck started with a growl that reminded her too much of the beasts that had stalked them, since those fateful moments after they'd awoken.

"Where are we going?" Katherine asked.

"To the Knights of Columbus," Al answered.

The elderly man spoke up to explain further. "We heard some people were using it as a shelter right after the power went out. We're going to help them." He beckoned to himself and then the woman next to him. "I'm Abraham, and this is my wife, Sally."

"It's going to be all right," Sally told them. "You're safe now."

"Our parents are still out there," Silas whispered, looking over at them with wide eyes.

"Where are they?" Sally asked.

"At home," Katherine said. "On Lindsay Street."

"I'm sure they're fine. We'll help them. Al will help them." Abraham nodded.

Despite his words, Katherine heard a shimmer of doubt in his tone. She hugged Silas tight. From somewhere in the distance, a long howl echoed through the trees.

**The characters in this prequel story appear in the OUTAGE series, Books 3-5.

ABOUT THE AUTHOR

T.W. Piperbrook lives in Connecticut with his wife, his son, and a Shih Tzu named Remy, who is decidedly not a werewolf. He is the author of the OUTAGE werewolf series, the CONTAMINATION series, and co-author of THE LAST SURVIVORS, as well as the author of THE RUINS. In his former lives, he has worked as a claims adjuster, a touring musician, and a business systems analyst for a Fortune 500 company.

Now he spends his days fighting zombies, battling werewolves, and roaming post-apocalyptic cities. You can connect with him on Facebook at :

http://www.facebook.com/twpiperbrook

or find him at www.twpiperbrook.com.bart

The Hunt

Thomas Emson

1995

Leon Maguire skulked into the Esso service station at 10.15 p.m. on April 23.

As he shook off the rain, he eyed the girl behind the counter. She kept her gaze down. Didn't move.

Reading some stupid magazine, Leon thought. *Head in the clouds like all these dumb birds.*

Leon's gaze flitted around the interior. He clocked the security camera in the far corner. A red light blinked above the lens. Leon swallowed, his mouth dry.

"Can I help?"

He flinched, darted a look toward the counter.

The girl was staring at him. Her eyes were dark and piercing. They drilled into Leon.

Without any reason, he shivered, and the cold feeling went right down into his balls.

He said, "You what?"

"I said, can I help?"

"Just lookin'."

She shrugged and went back to her magazine or whatever it was she was reading.

Leon didn't budge. He kept looking at her. She was pretty, with her black hair pulled back into a ponytail, an oval-shaped face — and those eyes. He was in a trance.

Slowly, she lifted her head, fixing on Leon again.

"You still looking?" she asked.

He got all flustered and ducked behind some shelves. There was something unsettling about the girl.

Hunkering down, he fidgeted with the biscuit selection, not really focusing on them but thinking about the girl.

She was about eighteen or nineteen. His age. Maybe he could ask her out. His legs shook. Things fluttered about in his belly. He always felt like this when he liked a girl, so he must like this one.

He shook himself down, trying to get a grip. Barry would batter him if he could see Leon right now. His cousin had sent him here to do a job. To check the place out. See who was on the ten-'till-four shift.

"That's when we'll do it," Barry had said. "It's quiet, dead of night. And it'll probably be some student, someone who really doesn't want to be there, so they ain't going to put up a fight. We walk in, like nightmares, be really aggressive, wave the fucking piece around. Easy. They'll just be fucking throwing the cash at us, boy."

Barry always said it would be easy. He called what they did "hunts" because "we're hunters and they are the prey," he'd say.

But it never was easy. It never felt like a hunt, either. They were usually the ones being hunted — by the cops.

They got caught the last time. And the time before that. Ended up in a young offenders institute a couple of times.

"Next time, it will be prison," the judge had warned the lads after they'd broken into a village post office.

Scared the shit out of the old bird running the show. She'd howled and whined while Barry rifled through the till, and Leon threatened to batter her with a baseball bat.

He didn't plan to hit her, but the way she was shrieking

and waving her arms about, he seriously thought about it — anything to shut the old cow up.

Barry had said, "See? She was just prey, and we were the hunters," and he laughed.

But they were holed up in the YOI by then, so Barry's boast didn't sound like much.

Maybe this time we'll get it right, Leon thought as he shuffled around the service station, checking out the few pies and sandwiches they had left in the fridge.

Maybe this time, they could be hunters. No shrieking grannies. No cops on their tail.

Just this girl.

As he approached the counter, he got more of a swagger on. His heart raced, though. Sweat ran down his back. Those things, whatever they were, still swirled around out in his belly.

He came round the corner of a shelving unit. As he did so, the girl looked up. Lifting her head so slowly again. Locking eyes with him. The way she did it made icicles run down his spine.

"All right?" she said, looking him up and down.

"Yeah." He shuffled from foot to foot, gnawed the inside of his cheek, scratched his chest, scanned the cigarettes and the booze. "You all right?"

The girl said nothing.

"Just asking," Leon said.

She tilted her head to the side. Like dogs do when they're trying to work something out.

"Twenty Bensons, babe."

"What?"

161

Leon flinched. Took a sharp breath. He thought he saw something in her eyes. Something he couldn't describe because he'd never seen it before. He shook it off. It was only there a second. He was probably a bit shaky. He blew air of out his cheeks, pulled himself together.

He said, "What?"

"What did you say?"

"I said twenty Bensons."

"Please, yeah?"

"What?"

"Twenty Bensons, please, yeah?"

"What d'you mean?"

She tutted, turned around. And with keys she unlatched from her belt, she unlocked the cabinet where the tobacco and the booze were kept.

Leon watched carefully. He watched the key slide into the lock, watched it turn, watched the concertina grill slide away. Watched the girl's delicate hand with black-painted fingernails reach out, clutch a pack of the cigarettes; watched her spin round, wisps of hair fluttering, vein at her temple pulsing; watched her slam the cigarettes down on the counter.

"Two-seventy," she said.

Leon grabbed the packet and raced toward the door. It thumped as he got to it, the double lock ramming into place. Leon tried the handle anyway, yanking at it. Yeah, it was locked.

He turned to look at the girl. She stood, arms folded, behind the counter. He smiled and shrugged at her.

"Worth a go, yeah?" he said.

"Two-seventy, mate."

162

He sauntered back to the counter.

"Just testing."

He slapped three pounds on the counter.

"Testing what?" the girl asked

"Keep the change, babe."

He swaggered toward the door.

"Call me babe again," she said.

Leon stopped and looked at her. "What?"

"Call me babe again."

He looked into her eyes again, and he saw things in there he couldn't understand. His throat became suddenly parched, and his balls felt as if they were shriveling, actually fucking shriveling.

"Call me babe again," she said for the third time.

He didn't.

***

Laura Greenacre smelled him right away. His sweat, his hair gel, his tobacco-stained fingers - his fear.

His scent made her eyes water.

It leached out of his pores.

He was a long piece of string who had to duck his head slightly when he entered the shop.

But she didn't flinch when he came in. The odor coming off him alerted her to the fact he was up to no good. So she kept her cool. Let him do his thing. It was nothing to her. She had been in this kind of situation before. If he thought he could strut in and intimidate her, he had made a grave error.

She had teeth, and she wasn't afraid to bite.

Laura eyed him as he skittered around the aisles like a hamster in a cage.

But the youth didn't do anything, only try to nick some smokes.

As he made a run, Laura pressed the big red button under the counter to automatically lock the door.

He couldn't get out. Prey caught in a trap. He strutted back to the counter and paid for his cigarettes.

She got it, though. Got the gist of his little performance. He was testing her, checking out the security.

After he left, she returned to her reading material.

The book was called *A History Of Lycanthropy: Werewolves In Our Midst*.

***

They murdered her entire family when she was four years old. Wiped them out in a single night. Armed killers raiding homes throughout Britain. Slaughtering without mercy. Men, women and —

Laura didn't know how she got away. But she remembered leaping on the back of the man who had knocked on her door. She was a tiny thing but filled with rage and fury, her teeth sharp in the man's nape, her little claws raking his cheeks.

His blood in her throat.

Instinct drove her to attack. She had no idea where the power came from — the fangs, the claws. They were just there, sheathed weapons.

She didn't remember much about growing up. She moved from one foster home to the next. Never settled. Everything was a blur.

The Hunt

But when she was eleven, something happened.

She started to change.

Other girls at school had whispered things about "change," about growing up, about becoming women.

But Laura didn't really expect it to involve bones twisting, nerves stretching, muscles bulging.

She never thought sharp canine teeth would pierce her gums and that her hands would twist into claws.

And the fur bursting through her skin absolutely terrified her. Not just hair, but fur. Coarse, black fur.

This started to happen every month. But after being scared at first, Laura learned to control the changes. She could actually make them happen whenever she wanted. And by the age of fourteen, she could shapeshift at will.

And what a shape it was.

A huge wolf-like creature. A werewolf, maybe. That's what they called it in the movies, in comic books.

But could such beasts be real?

Laura was real.

The stuff happening to her was real.

The man she had torn apart at a care home three years previously had been real.

The staff finding her distraught among his remains had been real.

The looks on their faces — horror, confusion — had also been real.

The running away was real. The sleeping rough was real. The crying herself to sleep was real.

Her life was real.

But there was nothing, nowhere, that would actually explain to her *why* it was real. How it could possibly *be* real.

Not even in this book.

She made a bored as fuck noise while reading about the Etruscans. It was heavy going, but at least the book contained clues to what she was. It told her about werewolves.

She shook her head.

Is that what I am? A werewolf?

60AD

"Those animals on that island, Quintus, are not Britons," said Marius Victor. "They are the descendants of the Etruscans, a tribe whose roots are older than Rome by thousands of years."

Quintus, fourteen and *Cacula*, or servant, to the Tribune, Marius Victor, listened intently to his master.

The twenty-four-year-old aristocrat was a *tribuni angusticlavii*, a lower-ranking tribune from the equestrian class, just one class below the senators who ruled back home.

He was one of five of his rank in the legion. They were young, ambitious men with military nous who were climbing the political ladder.

Quintus watched as the tribune dipped bread into a bowl of wine and chewed it nonchalantly.

They were camped a mile from the shoreline on the mainland. It was the twelfth hour of darkness. Hardly anyone slept. Tension sparked in the air. Another hour, and it would be sunrise. The attack would begin.

The Hunt

The 5,000-strong *Legio quarta decima Gemina,* led by the general, and governor of Britannia, Gaius Suetonius Paulinus, would cross the straits that separated the island from the mainland.

The infantry would traverse the waters on flat-bottomed vessels constructed of wood from nearby forests.

The cavalry would wade across on horseback, or swim next to their steeds.

Waiting for them on the island, which the Romans called Mona, were armed warriors and their leaders, religious fanatics called the Druids.

The Druids wielded too much power, according to the authorities, and attempts to temper them had failed.

Rome was perfectly amenable to local religions - as long as they weren't fanatical and a threat to order.

The Druids were.

They had to be destroyed.

Or at least that was the official version.

Marius Victor was now telling his young servant the truth about this campaign - or this "hunt," as the tribune called it.

"The Etruscans' lineage goes back to dark times, when the gods had not yet forged man properly," he said. "They were still perfecting us. And in doing so, they created terrible things that were somewhere between man and beast."

Marius Victor gazed across to the island in the distance. The moon cast a silver shaft along the surface of the water. Fires blazed on the island, and if you listened carefully, you could hear noises. Terrible noises. Screams, howls, sounds made by humans in pain, sounds not made by humans at all.

He said, "There were two brothers. Etruscan princes. In-between creatures, part men, part wolves. The brothers were proud of their Etruscan heritage, their wild streak, the animal in them. But soon after the founding of Rome, one of them wanted more power. He wanted to be part of the establishment. The Etruscans were slowly assimilated into the Roman way of life. So this brother, like many Etruscans, became Roman. His descendants became Roman."

Marius Victor looked Quintus in the eye, and the boy felt a chill.

"*We* became Roman, Quintus."

He looked toward the island again and went on.

"The other brother and his descendants were furious. It was a betrayal of their heritage, they said. And the family inevitably went to war. One branch stood up for civilization, for order, for Rome. The other represented chaos. Civilization won that first battle. The wolf-men had to flee. Their culture was suppressed. Their history stamped out. But they're still out there, Quintus. They are still spreading their plague, their depravities."

"But you hunt them," Quintus said.

Marius Victor looked at him. "*We* hunt them. It's my family's responsibility. It's our calling since the first brothers declared war on each other. We are hunters, they are prey. The hunt is my life, my duty."

"Master?"

"Yes, boy?"

"Can you still change?"

Marius Victor gawped at his servant. The boy flinched. He was sure that for a split second, the tribune's eyes had turned yellow, the iris a black slit. But it was only for a split second. They were green again now. Green and full of passion, full of fire.

"No," said Marius Victor. "Why would I want to?"

***

"But," the writer said, "these are quite clearly folk memories and tribal traditions, much like the tribal traditions we find throughout the world."

Laura blew air out of her cheeks and slammed the book shut. She checked her watch. Ten to one in the morning.

Outside, it was dead. A lost world. The pumps, ancient pillars. The streets, a land forgotten.

She felt alone all of a sudden, and the impact of her isolation struck her in the chest like a hammer.

She gasped, and tears welled.

As she was about to grab her rucksack and go AWOL again, the car, its headlights turned off, glided into the garage.

Laura watched the Golf do a circuit of the forecourt, slowly crawling around as if the driver were taking his or her time to select a pump.

Round it went again before it drove to within a foot of the front door and stopped.

Name stickers on the windscreen declared the driver to be BARRY and his passenger CLARE, though the vehicle could have been stolen.

Two figures clad in dark clothing lurked in the vehicle's front seats. The passenger didn't look like a Clare. It was a male. They were both males.

Laura knew what was coming. Her hackles rose. The adrenaline coursing through her body made her shake.

The driver and passenger, both wearing hoodies and scarves wrapped around the lower part of their faces, leaped out of the Golf.

Laura recognized the passenger immediately. He was lanky, clad in the same hoodie and trackie bottoms he had worn a few hours earlier during his recce.

His companion, the driver, was a snippy little wasp - all sharp edges and jerky movements.

He was also carrying a sawn-off shotgun.

They barged in, the driver first.

"Put your fucking hands up, cow," he shrieked as he stormed toward the counter, pointing the gun straight at Laura's face.

The passenger smashed the security camera at the far corner of the store with his baseball bat.

The driver shouted, "I don't want to see you fucking move unless it's to empty the cash into my mate's bag."

The passenger barreled toward the counter, wielding the bat and a duffel bag.

Laura's nostrils flared. She picked up their scents. The tall one smelled like he had earlier; scared and unwashed.

The driver - maybe he was Barry after all - reeked of fear too. His blood buzzed through his veins. Sweat glands worked overtime.

The passenger tossed the duffel bag on the counter.

"Fill it with your cash, bitch," the driver said.

Laura glanced at the bag before lifting her head to look the driver right in the eye.

Something he saw in her gaze made him flinch. His pupils flared. His eyes widened.

She said, "You know that you're both going to regret this."

The driver said, "Don't talk to me, bitch. Fill the fucking bag up."

"I need you to be aware," she said calmly, "that I am going to eat you alive, the both of you."

The driver thrust his sawn-off shotgun in her face.

"Put the fucking cash in the fucking bag."

His friend shoved the baseball bat in her face too.

He said, "Do as he says."

"I recognize your voice," she told him.

"Dumb cunt, Leon," said the driver.

Laura laughed. "And are you Barry?" she said to the driver.

The crooks jerked. Men hated women laughing at them, Laura knew that. It was the worst thing you could do to a man, laugh at him. Not that these two were truly men. A pair of deadbeats who had walked in on their worst nightmare, more like.

The thugs seethed. Barry especially. He was shuffling from foot to foot, lifting the shotgun to his shoulder, lowering it, lifting it to his shoulder, lowering it. His breath came hissing out of his mouth. His chest heaved.

Leon wielded the baseball bat as if he were ready to hit a home run using Laura's head as the ball.

"Fill the bloody bag," he screamed at her.

"You got families?" Laura asked.

"You what?" said Barry.

"We all do, don't we, somewhere. I'm trying to trace mine. Trying to find my roots, you know. I know a little bit about what I might be, but I'm trying to work out where I came from."

"What the fuck are you on about?" Barry said.

The one called Leon said, "We gotta get goin', man."

Laura picked up the book, *A History Of Lycanthropy: Werewolves In Our Midst*, and said, "It's all in here."

The would-be robbers' eyes widened with confusion, with fear.

Laura hurled the book directly at the shotgun. It knocked the barrel away from her face.

Barry reeled. Leon stumbled. Laura sprang.

By the time she was leaping over the counter, her canines had already sheared through her gums, and her hands were curling into claws.

***

You could hear them from the mainland. They were massed on the beach, a devilish horde, screaming, raging.

It was dawn, and the island lay little more than a quarter of a mile away.

It was densely covered in forest, and now, this early in the morning, low clouds draped above it.

Led by Suetonius Paulinus, the legion gathered on the shoreline.

They were silent and still while the enemy across the water howled like beasts.

Marius Victor, astride his white stallion, asked, "Are you prepared, Quintus?"

"Yes, master," the youth said, never having been less prepared for anything in his life.

"See them, among the throng?"

Quintus scanned the thousands of painted and partly

naked warriors, men, and women.

Weaving through the mob, Quintus saw tall, black-cowled figures. They were like ghosts, almost floating among the crazed warriors.

"Yes, I see," Quintus said, his throat dry with dread.

"This is what happens when we let the wolf lead us," Marius Victor said. "Look at those savages. They have taken on the nature of beasts."

"Master, are those hooded things beasts?"

"I am ashamed to say that they are my very distant cousins, Quintus. Those who chose depravity a long, long time ago."

Quintus looked along the line, left and right. Hardened troops who had seen action throughout the empire gasped at the sight.

A voice rang out: "Men of Rome, do not quail."

Quintus searched it out. It was the general himself.

Gaius Suetonius Paulinus, governor of Britannia, the first Roman commander to have led troops through the Atlas Mountains in Northern Africa.

The general went on. "They are frenzied women, that is all. Screaming furies, painted fools. You are Rome. We cross these waters, and we crush them, we burn them, we destroy their groves that are devoted to inhuman superstition, to the sacrifice of children. Who are we?"

"Rome," cried the men, 5,000 voices.

"Again."

"Rome."

"Who?"

"Rome."

Thomas Emson

"Meus caparum Romanus — Ad Victoria!" yelled the general, sword held high.

His words echoed in Quintus' head: *My Roman troops - to Victory!*

But what hope did they have against those monsters across the water?

While Quintus worried about it, the legion moved forward.

Horses neighed nervously as they approached the water. But the cavalrymen drove their steeds into the straits.

Infantry, supported by auxiliaries, launched the flat-bottomed vessels they had been constructing over the past few days. They were flat-bottomed because the straits were thought to be relatively shallow.

They will soon find out, Quintus thought as he cantered his mare into the waters.

Across on the other side, the savages shrieked and waved their weapons around. Ferocious-looking women were now racing back and forth brandishing flaming torches, pointing at the troops, then at the flames, suggesting they would burn their enemies.

And the hooded things continued to prowl among the frenzied mass.

Quintus wondered if they were Druids, as all the troops and their generals claimed, or if they were the monsters Marius Victor described.

His horse jerked and brayed as it was forced into the water, now up to its flanks.

Quintus gritted his teeth against the temperature; it was bitingly cold. He looked at his master. Marius Victor was pushing ahead. Only his stallion's head and neck were above water by now. The tribune was up to his chest in the waves. He held his sword above his head. He looked to

174

Quintus like a sea god rising out of the ocean.

In a line stretching half a mile, the legion forded the inlet on horseback and on the rafts.

Quintus' heart was in his throat. His horse paddled across. The water was up to the servant boy's waist now. It went right to his bones; his teeth chattered.

To desperately create some warmth, he thought of his home in Pisaurum on the Adriatic coast, where the sun always shone.

He wished he could be there now, running around with his brothers. But his father chose this life for him. And here he was in cold, grey Britannia, wading across cold, grey water, headed for a terror that made his bowels fall out.

The horde on the other side of the sound shrieked and railed, and the closer the legion got, the more terrifying their enemy appeared.

Quintus could see the whites of their eyes. Mud and paint plastered their flesh. Most wore nothing, even the women. They had rotten teeth and matted hair.

And they made such a dreadful noise.

"Stay close to me, Quintus," yelled Marius Victor, his tunic and armor soaked as he and his horse reached the shallows.

Some of the savages were crashing into the water, charging at the boats and horses.

Hostiles clambered aboard one raft, hacking at the infantrymen on board with swords, screaming as they stabbed and sliced.

The troops fought back. A pitched battle erupted on the raft, which buckled and see-sawed on the water.

Blood spouted from terrible wounds. Limbs floated like driftwood. Screams filled the air.

Marius Victor galloped toward the raft. Quintus held his breath, realizing he would have to follow his master.

The tribune, with one swing of his sword, sliced the head off a savage.

Blood sprayed from the stump. The head splashed into the waves, bobbed along.

"Wake up, Quintus," came the cry.

His master rallying him. Quintus came round in time to see a furie charging through the water toward him, brandishing a blazing torch.

She snarled, showing a mouth full of rotten teeth. Her eyes were ablaze, her face painted blue.

She screeched as she splashed toward him, breasts bouncing, hair fanning out.

Quintus' horse reared in terror. It shrieked. Quintus fell. The tide swallowed him. The cold hit him like a bolt. He sucked in water. He panicked, yelled underwater. A hand grabbed the collar of his tunic. It was going to force him under, drown him. But instead, it yanked him to the surface. He panted, looked into the eyes of his master.

"Get a grip of yourself, Quintus. You need your wits about you, boy."

Quintus nodded. Floating past him, the body of the furie who had attacked him was face down in a patch of red water. Blood drained from a deep wound across her back that exposed bone and entrails.

"Now get back on your horse," Marius Victor ordered.

Quintus grabbed his mare's reins, and as he mounted, the battle around him intensified.

Initially, the savages had the upper hand. The chaos helped them. Their unruly tactics - primarily just charging at the enemy - had worked. But once the legion had hacked its way onto the shore, once the *Aquilifer*, bearer of the legionary eagle, was on dry land, it began to apply the formations and strategies that had made the Roman army the most formidable in the world.

The *Aquilifer* waved the eagle and cried out, *"Ave Caesar*!"

Cries of *"Ad aciem - Pugna - Celeriter"* filled the air as officers — tribunes and centurions — ordered battle lines formed: "Battle! Quickly!"

Once formed, those battle lines were sent into action.

"Parati — Oppugnare!"

And they *were* ready, and they *did* charge.

Orders flew around the killing ground.

Rome took control of the battle from the savages, who vastly outnumbered them.

By now, the legion had butchered its way to the tree line, leaving behind piles of mutilated corpses.

The savages were being forced back by Rome's discipline, its deadly tactics, its ruthless strategies.

Quintus, protected by a couple of *Triarii*, spearmen who would jab and pierce any savage coming too close, sought out the hooded figures he had seen from the mainland.

He could see none, neither among the piles of the dead nor among the living, some of whom were starting to flee into the woods.

But then a terrifying howl pierced the air and made many of the fighting men cower.

Screams came from the trees. They chilled Quintus' blood. He looked for his master.

A thick, dark cloud must have swept across the early morning sky. Everything darkened.

Quintus looked up. His throat clogged with horror.

It wasn't a cloud.

It was five huge, black beasts, all slashing claws and snarling fangs, sailing through the air to pounce on the troops.

***

Leon hurtled toward the door, his legs wet with piss.

Barry shrieked like a baby behind him, and his cries were mixed in with tearing sounds and snarling.

Leon moaned with horror. He tried to forget what he had seen leap over the counter, to pretend it was a horrible nightmare. But he still had to escape it, and he hurled himself at the door.

It wouldn't open.

He yanked and yanked, not daring to look to where the appalling noises were coming from.

Panic squeezed his heart. He could smell his own urine that had gushed out of his bladder when the girl, leaping over the counter, appeared to change in mid-air into a thing that looked like a wolf.

Not really a wolf, though. Snout like a wolf. Teeth like a wolf. Teeth to eat you. Claws to tear you. Black fur. Hindquarters like a wolf, those that went back at the knee like dogs had. But this thing walked on two legs. And it was way bigger than a wolf.

It had pounced on Barry, who'd fired the shotgun but missed his target.

Leon had initially stood frozen to the spot while the black mass enveloped Barry, who had yowled and shrieked.

The monster seemed to be fucking Barry at first, grinding, pounding. It was almost funny. In that way that mad people find things funny and just howl with laughter all the time.

But actually, Leon quickly realized that Barry was being eaten alive.

That's when he ran for the door.

Now, as he tugged at the handle, he wanted to yell at Barry to stop screeching.

To stop screaming, "Kill the bitch, kill the fucking bitch, help me, Jesus, help me."

It was doing Leon's head in.

Stop fucking screaming, he thought.

And who would have believed it? Barry did just that. He stopped squealing.

It was suddenly lovely and quiet.

Leon stopped pulling at the handle.

He slowly turned to look to where the beast had been eating Barry.

He had kind of hoped to see the girl there, just normal and cute and scared shitless, and Barry with the duffel bag full of cash, proving this whole fucking wolf stuff had been a bad trip brought on by the dope he'd smoked earlier.

No such luck.

Leon's knees buckled. His bowels gave way, and he shat his pants.

The black-furred monster — *Werewolf? Is that what a werewolf looks like?* — was standing up, staring at Leon, teeth bared. It was six and a half feet tall, at least.

Blood and gore spilled from its mouth. Flesh and clothes hung on its claws.

What was left of Barry lay at its feet. He looked as if he'd been pulled inside out. All his guts were on display. Even his ribcage, though most of the bones were shattered. His head was craned back and his eyes were open, staring at Leon.

One of Barry's arms must have been torn off because it was on top of the bread on a shelf, the shotgun still in the bloody hand.

Leon felt he had studied this display of atrocity for long enough.

He started to scream for help and pulled at the door again.

The beast sprang. It hurtled toward him, looming large, becoming the only thing in Leon's eye line. Nothing else. Not Barry's remains. Not the Esso service station they had planned to rob. Not the outside world where he lived with his mum and sister. Not the young offenders' institutes he'd called home. None of these things existed now. They had been wiped out completely by the monstrosity that was coming at him at breakneck speed.

He froze, facing the creature. He shrieked — short, sharp sounds that ruptured his vocal cords.

The creature sank its teeth into Leon's shoulder, picked him up, and shook him like a cleaner shaking out a blanket.

It hurled him across the store, and Leon crashed into the biscuit display, and his brain, in some weird way, took him back to his recce a few hours back when he fidgeted with these cookies while the dark-haired girl watched him from behind the counter.

Blood poured from his shoulder. His collarbone had been snapped in the beast's jaws. Pain sawed through Leon's arm and chest. Tears poured down his cheeks.

The monster fell on him again, and Leon silently screeched while its claws plowed deep furrows in his chest, excavating down through ribs to lungs and heart.

And the last clear thought he had through the blazing pain tearing through his body was, *You fucked up on the hunt stuff again, Barry.*

***

The *Sagittarii* let fly with their arrows. The unit, hired from the African empire, brought down the wolf-beasts. When the creatures hit the ground, dead or dying, infantry fell on them with swords and spears to make sure.

And then startled troops reeled as the beasts, mutilated, became human again.

Quintus gawped. He locked eyes with his master. Marius Victor's look said, *Now do you believe me?*

He followed his master deep into the woods while the Legion spread out across the island to destroy the Druids' sacred groves and kill any savage they came across.

"Where are we going, master?" Quintus asked as they galloped through the forest. "Aren't they all dead, the monsters?"

"They were males," Marius Victor said. "There's always a she-wolf at the head of the pack. The she-wolves are dangerous ones. She can't hide. This is an island, we'll find her."

"Is she the last one?"

Marius Quintus gazed into the dense forest ahead, where darkness was deep and death lurked.

"Perhaps," he said.

***

One Twenty-Three a.m., April 24, 1995.

The emergency call operator, looking forward to the end of her fourth twelve-hour shift in a row so she could chill out for three days, answered the call.

Cries and gasps came down the line. Not unusual.

"Hello, darlin', can you tell me your name? Are you all right? Are you able to speak to me?"

A girl whimpered, calming down, identifying herself as Laura and "something terrible has happened here, Esso service station, Wakefield Road, Chester, blood everywhere — "

"Blood, Laura? Your blood?" said the operator, dispatching police, and paramedics immediately to the address while she was talking to the girl.

"Blood everywhere. Like an animal. A monster. Torn them apart. Oh, God, please help. They've been, like, eaten alive."

***

They gave Laura the same looks she had seen at that care home three years ago - horror, confusion.

They gave the victims - or what was left of them - the same looks too.

They tried to put two and two together, but it just didn't make four for them. It just couldn't.

A girl like her could not have caused carnage like this. No girl could do this; no human.

A paramedic checked her out. No injuries.

The paramedic cleaned her up, gave her a set of overalls because her clothes were shredded.

Forensic officers took what remained of the garments away in bags. They took what remained of the armed robbers away in bags too.

The paramedic wiped her face and smiled.

"You look okay, no wounds. You see what came in here? Did this?"

The paramedic knew she shouldn't be asking these questions. It was the police's job.

And although there were no outward signs of injuries, the victim, this girl, might be traumatized. Asking her to recall the events could re-traumatize her.

But the paramedic had never seen anything like this and would be talking about it with friends and colleagues for years.

Laura said, "I don't remember."

"No, okay, I'm sorry, I'm very rude for asking," the paramedic said, smiling.

Laura smiled too.

The paramedic furrowed her brow. "You've got something in your teeth. Let me just get it for you?"

With tweezers, the paramedic plucked whatever it was out from between Laura's teeth.

"Bit of meat," the paramedic said.

Laura tutted. "Didn't chew my supper properly."

ABOUT THE AUTHOR

Thomas Emson has published eight horror thrillers, including Maneater, Prey, the Vampire Trilogy (Skarlet, Krimson, and Kardinal) and Zombie Britannica. He's also self-published The Trees And Other Stories on Amazon, as well as How To Write A Novel In 6 Months, a guide to helps aspiring authors achieve their writing goals.

You can contact Thomas on Twitter @thomasemson. He'd be more than happy to come and talk to your writing group about his books, and can teach you the ins and outs of his writing method in a couple of hours.

Website:

thomasemson.com

Twitter:

@thomasemson

Outside of Nowhere

Ray Garton

This story is for my friend

Randy Eberle.

They sat in a walnut orchard about forty miles north of Bakersfield, under a silver half-moon, two strangers passing a joint back and forth and talking quietly in the dark.

"What brings you here?" she said.

"I'm camping with a group on the other side. How about you?"

She shrugged as she held the smoke in for a long moment, then let it out. "I like walking alone at night. Not always the safest idea in the world depending on where you are, I know, but I figured this was safe enough. Safer than walking the streets at home." She passed it back to him.

"City-dweller?"

"Yeah, if I can help it. These places in the middle of nowhere—they give me the creeps. I mean, we're in the middle of fuckin' *nowhere*, but people still live out here."

"I know what you mean. People who live in places like this—" He stopped to take another hit and shook his head dubiously.

She nodded enthusiastically, saying, "Yeah, you gotta wonder about 'em. What kind of people are they? There's nothing here, not even a small town, but you drive along, and you see a house over here, another one way over there, all separated by miles of nothing. What the fuck do they do with their lives?" She took the blunt from him when he offered, took another hit.

He said, "Reminds me of that episode of *The X-Files* with the inbred family that lived out in the middle of nowhere and kept their mom under the bed."

Smoke exploded from her as she began to cough, nodding rapidly and pointing at him in agreement. "Yeah, yeah, yeah, that episode was *so* fucked up," she said when she stopped coughing. "That's what I mean, that's exactly the kinda thing I think about when I'm in a place like this. Because people like that—that's not just TV, people like that exist, and they don't live in cities, they live in places like *this*." She handed it back to him. "There's plenty of crazy, sick people in the cities, sure, but most of 'em aren't that hard to spot. You know what you're dealing with and who to avoid because people in the city, y'know, they just let their freak flag fly. Nobody gives a fuck, which is why I like living there. Out here... I don't know, it's just too fuckin' creepy."

Another hit, a pause, then a long exhalation of smoke followed by a few light coughs. "I'm Leo, by the way. What's your name?"

"Emily. Nice to meet you, Leo. You scared the shit outta me earlier, but it's nice to meet you. I was just going for a walk. I didn't expect to find anybody here."

"I didn't mean to creep up and scare you like that. I'm sorry. I should've spoken up sooner. What do you do in the city, Emily? And what are you doing here tonight?"

She accepted the joint again and took her time with it as she decided on how to answer those questions. Tilting her head back, she exhaled the smoke toward the silvery moon gleaming through the skeletal branches.

Emily liked him, and they probably would never see each other again. He was obviously a cool guy, walking around in an old walnut orchard in the middle of the night with a joint—how cool was that? And the one thing Emily wanted, no, *needed*—not just that night but in her life in general—was someone to talk to, someone to tell everything to without worry that it would be repeated or she would be criticized for it, someone she trusted. A friend, she needed a real friend. She had not had one of those since she was a kid, since before she was kidnapped. She knew nothing about Leo except that it was unlikely they would meet again, which was a kind of false substitute for trust.

"I'm a criminal," she said in a dramatic whisper.

He smiled. "Am I in danger?"

"No, you're not in danger. But if I tell you the truth about myself... well, you might not want to be around me then."

"We'll see. What led you into a life of crime?"

"Didn't have much of a choice. I was kidnapped when I was twelve." Leo's smile fell away and his eyes widened, and before he could ask, she said, "No, I'm not shitting you." A thought struck her with such force that she actually flinched. "Y'know you're the first person I've ever told that to? In eight years, the first person. Hell of a thing to keep to yourself, huh?"

"Look, Emily, I've got a phone. I can call the police right now if you want and you can—"

"Oh, no, I can't do that."

"I'm sure you're afraid of them, both the people you're with and the police, but we can get you some protection and—"

"No, it's not that. I have a phone of my own anytime I want to make a call like that. It's the kids. I've got kids to take care of."

He frowned now and began to look at her as if he might be wondering if she were crazy. "Kids?"

"That's what we do." She lowered her head.

"Trafficking. Human trafficking, I mean. Mostly kids." Lifting her head slightly, she peered up at him. "See what I mean? It's awful, and you probably think I'm awful, but that's why I can't leave, see. We've got a moving van full of kids, and they're my responsibility."

Emily took a long hit on the joint, handed it back, and held the smoke in a bit longer than usual. After blowing it out, she said, "When they took me, we were at the lake one day that summer, my family and me, and then for the next... I don't know, it seemed like weeks even though it probably wasn't that long, but for a while after I was taken, I was just raped. That's all, nothing else. It was just raping and beating for days. I was sure I was gonna die. I wanted to. I think... I think part of me has been disappointed ever since that I didn't."

"They broke you," Leo said before finishing off the joint.

"Yeah. They gotta get everything good out of you, including your soul if possible. Once you're empty, they start to use you. They put me to work right away. Prostitution first, then they had me running drugs back and forth to Mexico for a while, then finding kids for them to take and doing what I could to groom them. Then they put me to work taking care of the kids they were trafficking. It's the only work I've ever enjoyed, managing the kids. That's what I've been doing ever since and all I want to do from now on. I like kids. They're always honest. I love that. Until they grow up, of course. Then they learn to be ashamed of the truth. I've thought about getting the fuck out first chance I get, y'know, running like hell. But I... I can't. I just can't do that knowing I'd be leaving all those kids behind with nobody decent to take care of 'em. 'Cause if I don't, somebody else will, and you gotta believe me, Leo, they're awful, all the other people who would do that, they're fucking monsters who shouldn't be anywhere near kids. I know what would happen to those kids, some of them, anyway, if other people in our group were in charge of them. It makes me sick to my stomach. So I protect them as much as I can. I make sure they're not being... y'know, abused. Not while I'm taking care of them, anyway."

Staring at her, eyes wide with astonishment at her story, Leo slowly tipped backward until he was leaning against the trunk of the tree. "I'm not saying I doubt you, but... but it's all so hard to believe. What you've been through, it's awful; no one should have to experience any of that, *especially* at such a young age, and I... I don't know what to say."

"You don't have to say anything. I can tell you're a compassionate human being."

He smirked, chuckled, shook his head. "Don't be so sure. You don't know anything about me."

"That's true, I don't. So tell me about yourself."

"I'm not done with you yet." He produced another joint, rolled as tightly and neatly as a cigarette. He lit it, took a hit, and they began to pass it back and forth as they talked. "What about your parents? Have you been in touch?"

She shook her head.

"Why not? You could call them, or write. Something. Just to let them know you're alive."

"Mickey always said they sold me. Mickey's one of the guys who kidnapped me, runs the operation we've got now. I never believed him, of course, because, well, y'know, that just couldn't be true, my parents *selling* me to someone. Then, about a month after I was taken, the story of my disappearance fell out of the news and Mom and Dad, they didn't, y'know, make any efforts after that to find me. It's like the whole thing just... went away. And lately, I've been thinking about my life before I was taken, what was going on in our house. There was a lot of fighting. Dad lost his job and had trouble finding another one, and Mom went to work, which pissed Dad off, and he started drinking a lot more, and that just made everything worse. And then Dad said we were gonna lose the house, and there was a lot more fighting after that, because we'd have to move into some low-income apartment if we were lucky, a motel if we weren't, and that would only be for as long as we could *afford* a motel, and I remember around that time I was thinking a lot about what it would be like to be homeless. And then we went to the lake one day, and I was taken."

"Was a trip to the lake unusual?"

"For my family? Yeah, I guess it was. By then, anyway. When I was little, before my sister was born, we used to do it pretty regularly during the summer. Once I started school, though, not so much. It was pretty rare by the time I was taken."

"And you just up and went to the lake one day?"

"Yeah. Dad's idea. He'd go through these periods where he tried to pretend everything was fine and we were still a happy, functioning family, and he'd do something like scrape together enough money to take us to the movies, or like that day, we'd go to the lake. I thought that was it; I thought he was going through one of those periods. But now... I'm not so sure. It was even more sudden than one of those days when he wanted us to be a happy family. Usually, you could see that coming, y'know? He'd get all bouncy and smiley first thing in the morning and you'd know, oh, it's gonna be one of *those* days. But it wasn't like that. One minute, he's on the phone talking to somebody, the next he says, 'Okay, let's pack up for the lake, we're going to the lake.' And we went to the lake."

"You believe Mickey?"

"Yeah. He's probably telling the truth."

"You... you really think your parents would do that to you?"

She shrugged. "Who knows what anybody would do? We can never know people, not really. Right? And parents are just people; having kids doesn't make them special. And people... they're fucked up as hell. You never know what they'll do, period."

"That... well, I imagine that must hurt?"

She smiled. "Doesn't everything?"

"Tell me something. If it was just you and the kids, and you could do anything you wanted, what would you do? Where would you go?"

"Well, I couldn't take care of them myself—that would be unrealistic. I'd have to take them somewhere... y'know, somewhere institutional, I guess. But first, I'd like to take them to Disneyland, or a Six Flags, some big amusement park where they could have a day to forget everything and just have fun. Most of these kids are from Mexico, really poor kids. Most of them don't even speak English. Some of them are sick and need care. Some were sold by their parents. It's not that uncommon. Happens all the time. It just doesn't get talked about because it's not something a Kardashian would do, it's not very entertaining, and we all want to be entertained, right? These kids wouldn't know what to do with themselves at an amusement park. That would be something to see."

"These people you're with," Leo said, "are any of them friends? People you care about?"

"A couple I just tolerate. The rest make me want to puke. They're all trash."

"And the children you have with you—you say they're in a moving van?"

"Yeah. A big U-Haul, except it's not a U-Haul anymore, it's been repainted green. Why?"

"Just curious."

They passed the joint back and forth in silence a few more times until it was finished. Then Leo got to his feet saying, "Well, I should get back to camp. The others are going to be wondering where I am."

Emily stood, too, brushed herself off, picked up her

flashlight. "I managed to hog the whole fuckin' conversation. You're taking off before I've had a chance to learn anything about you."

"That's no great loss. I'm not that interesting."

"Where are you and your friends headed?"

"South. Los Angeles."

"That's where we'll be going, too. When we're done here, I mean. That's where we're from."

"Who knows, maybe we'll run into each other again. It's been my pleasure, Emily."

When they parted, they went in opposite directions.

***

When he left the orchard, Leo climbed a slight ridge and, from the top of it, saw his camp. He loped down the other side, entered the camp, and headed straight for Lupa's tent. It was the largest in the group because of her high status in the pack. It was the color of charcoal, with the entrance flanked by two bright lights and two security guards. One of the guards waved him in.

Lounging on a couch reading, Lupa looked up when he entered.

Smiling, he said, "Lupa, I've found something you're going to like."

***

Mickey Schenk, Glock in a shoulder holster, sat gazing pensively into the fire, which was where Emily had left him when she had gone for her walk. He fidgeted in the folding lawn chair, smoked too many cigarettes, and felt his nerves become more and more frayed. Every now and then, he sat up straight and gazed into the darkness around him, looking for signs of ambush or random intruders. Then he would slowly wilt back into his hunched posture, frowning into the fire.

Mickey's father had him cooking and selling meth by the time he was ten years old. By fifteen, about the time his family, involved mostly in drugs and prostitution up to that point, branched out to human trafficking, Mickey was helping his dad manage the entire operation. He had never known anything else and had never strove for anything else because it had never occurred to him that anything else might be possible. He was given a task early in life, and he was still carrying it out with single-minded fervor, still living by his father's advice.

"Just get as much money as you possibly can in this life, no matter what," Dad had told him. "Fuck everything else. Fuck friendship, loyalty, love, morals, all that horseshit. They never got nobody nowhere. People will always let you down—never forget that, Mickey, *always*, no matter who they are. All you have to do is give 'em enough time. Money is the only thing you can count on. And even that's iffy these days, so get as much as you can."

They had sounded like wise words to Mickey when he was eleven, so he took them in, absorbed them, made them a part of himself. He had been striving to live up to them ever since.

He had never known his mother, although he was curious about her. He had asked his dad about her the first time during that same conversation: "Who's my mom?"

Dad, with a poker face, had said, "Well, I'm sorry to bring shame on you, boy, but truth is, I'm your father, but... we don't know who your mother is." Dad waited a moment, watching him with an expressionless face, then laughter exploded from him and he slapped his thigh a few times. Mickey understood the joke now, but it had escaped him back then. He had just wanted to know who his mother was. Dad had told that same joke every time Mickey asked about her. He never did learn anything, and even now at age thirty-three, his mother was a mystery to him. It was one of those things, like Dad's death, that only ate at him when he thought about it, so he didn't think about it.

He always had enough to do to keep his mind off troubling thoughts, and that night was no exception. He was nervous as hell about having to sit there and wait for their pick-up to come. He felt too vulnerable. Mickey was never completely comfortable unless he was in his heavily secure compound in the desert just outside Los Angeles, the one his father had built and left to him when he was shot dead by a cop on his birthday four years ago. But tonight, he seemed to have too many distractions, the worst of which was being parked there in the middle of nowhere, with a load of children on their hands, no less, waiting for a goddamned pick-up.

He stood up from his seat beside the fire and looked around for Emily, then remembered that she was off taking her walk. He needed a stronger distraction than his worries, something like sex, at least some head, anything that involved some wet skin-to-skin friction. With Emily gone, he would have to settle for one of the newer girls. They might be hotter, but nobody gave better head than Emily.

"Hey, Bunny," he called, peering through the dark to look for her. After turning away from the fire and into the dark night, he was temporarily blinded and waited for his eyes to adjust.

Chuck and Angie canoodled under some blankets near the pickup truck, and Roger was tinkering under the hood of the motorhome in the glow of a work light. That last sight reminded Mickey that buying a new motorhome needed to be next on the agenda, something a lot better and roomier than the old Winnebago they had been using. It would be a good investment in the business.

Where was Bunny? Usually, her platinum blond hair showed up even in the dark as a pale, floating blob, but he couldn't find it.

At the other end of the motorhome from Roger and his

work light, Mickey saw what appeared to be a figure hunkering down by the left headlight. "Bunny?" he shouted. "Get the fuck over here."

From inside the motorhome, she shouted, "I'm on the fucking toilet—do you mind?"

Mickey turned toward the sound of her voice. Then, frowning, he turned back to that hunkering figure, but it was gone.

It was never there, idiot, he thought. *Too much weed tonight.*

He took his smartphone from his pocket to check the time. When had Emily left? How long had she been gone? It was after eleven, getting late. Usually, she was gone an hour, hour and a half at most.

With a sigh so heavy it was almost a groan, Mickey sat down by the fire again to wait just as Emily emerged from the surrounding darkness.

"Get over here," he said, unzipping his fly. When she didn't quicken her pace, he growled, "I said get the fuck over here."

She hurried to close the distance between them and dropped to her knees beside the fire without having to be told.

***

When Emily was a little girl, the house next door had burned to the ground one summer, and the plot stayed like that for years, with the blackened skeleton of a house jutting up from it for a while, then with an empty spot where the skeleton had been. But there was a treehouse in the backyard that remained untouched, and whenever she felt down or upset for any reason, Emily had taken her one-eyed Manx cat, Max, and some books to the treehouse to read and enjoy the peaceful isolation. It was her happy place.

Emily returned to that treehouse in her mind whenever she needed to, like right now as she knelt before Mickey and gave him head. She glanced up to see if he was happy. The orange light of the fire shimmered over his face, and she could tell by his expression that she was doing her job well.

She was suddenly jarred from that reverie as Mickey bolted to his feet with a ragged gasp, knocking her over. As she clumsily stood, Emily said, "What's wrong?"

Mickey stood beside his chair staring intently into the darkness beyond the fire. "Somebody was standin' there watchin' us. Just *standin'* there. In the dark. I saw 'em."

Footsteps crunched over the ground, and Emily spun around with a jolt to see Chuck and Angie hurrying toward them.

"We just heard something on the other side of the truck while we were sitting there," Chuck whispered. "Didn't sound like an animal. Sounded like somebody walking around."

"Okay," Mickey said, drawing his gun, "let's take a look."

Emily stayed put while Mickey and Chuck looked around with flashlights on and guns in hand. Emily knew Angie felt as vulnerable and scared as she did while they waited silently.

The guys returned before long.

"Nothin'," Mickey said, returning to his chair. He pointed silently to the ground before him and Emily returned to her spot between his knees.

Chuck and Angie wandered off.

Shoulders hunched, Emily's head moved up and down. She looked up again to see how things were going. Mickey looked the same as he had before the commotion, as if she had never stopped. Before she could close her eyes again, movement caught her attention as something rose up out of the darkness behind him.

Emily was uncertain, at first, what she was seeing, but it stood behind Mickey and towered over him, a dark shape in which the shifting fire revealed glimpses of dark, fierce eyes and a hairy, twitchy face. Then, with a rush of movement, more fangs than she had ever seen in her life plunged downward out of the darkness and sank into the right side of Mickey's neck.

A scream rose from another part of their camp. She recognized it as Angie's.

Emily threw herself backward, away from Mickey and the creature attacking him. She crawled clumsily sideways over the ground, face-up, away from Mickey in front of her and the fire behind her. A pale, tattooed arm tumbled through the air—Angie's left arm, to be precise; Emily recognized the Grateful Dead skull with a crown of crimson roses tattooed on the back of the hand—leaving pinwheels of bloody spatter in its wake before bouncing and rolling to a rest on the ground.

Angie began screaming for her mommy somewhere in the night.

The fangs sank deeper into Mickey's neck and shoulder as the head that held them jerked viciously from side to side, growling wetly and tearing at Mickey's flesh and bone. Parts of Mickey crunched between the jaws.

Emily had never heard or seen Mickey scream before. Yell and rage, yes, but never scream. Now, his mouth yawned open and his eyes bulged as his long, wailing shriek tore through the night.

But her eyes were drawn to the creature biting him. Its black nose glistened at the end of its snout and firelight sparkled in its moist, dark eyes, which had too much white showing as blood bubbled up around its buried fangs and thin, black lips.

Mickey's scream went on and on, until it broke and collapsed in gurgling agony. A large, hairy hand with long fingers that ended in curved, black claws, slapped onto his head and pulled as its muzzle noisily chewed into his neck.

When Emily realized the creature was trying to pull Mickey's head off, she was unable to hold in her scream. But it was cut off when two arms wrapped around her from behind, lifted her off the ground, and pulled her rapidly away from Mickey and the other screams that were breaking out in the camp.

Only a few seconds had passed from the moment that Mickey had shot to his feet after seeing someone watching them in the dark, seconds that had stretched on and on but were now shattering as someone dragged Emily away from it all, as Chuck's agonizing wail joined the screams coming from Mickey and Angie.

"You're all right, don't worry, you're all right," Leo quickly assured her as he swept her away, arms wrapped around her from behind.

Her feeling of panic subsided when she recognized Leo's voice. He continued to carry her away from the camp and further into the dark night, and with surprising speed. When he finally stopped and placed her feet on the ground, she turned to him.

He said, "I wanted to make sure you were clear of the scene because... well, to be honest, we sometimes get carried away while feeding and aren't too concerned with what we're eating. Or who."

Crashing sounds erupted from the camp, a distance away now, followed by more screaming.

Emily began to tremble, and she was surprised when her knees suddenly gave way beneath her. Leo caught her as she began to collapse.

"You okay?" he said.

"No! What the fuck is happening? Who *are* you? What's going on?"

"We're trying to help you."

Then she thought of the children. "Oh, God, the kids, the kids—"

"Don't worry, I've got someone watching them. Like I said, we sometimes get carried away when we're feeding, so I wanted them to be—"

"Feeding? Who are—*what* are you?"

They stood only inches apart in the deep darkness, just close enough for her to vaguely make out the features of his face and see him smile.

"Lycanthropes," he said.

"Lycan—look, I didn't get much education, so—"

"Werewolves. We're werewolves."

Her lips silently formed the word as she stared at him. It was a word from fairy tales and old movies, and she stood momentarily paralyzed by the sincerity with which he had spoken it.

A burst of rapid-fire screams from Chuck punched through the night repeatedly, then suddenly fell silent.

"We've been traveling and haven't found a lot of food in this area," Leo continued. "It's been hard to find enough without risking exposure, which we want very much to do. So... well, your friends will be, um... shared. By the pack. With gratitude, by the way."

The screams had stopped.

"What about me and the kids?" Emily asked, her voice raspy because her throat was suddenly dry as sandpaper. "What... what'm I gonna do?"

"Well, once I'm given the all-clear, we'll see to it that you can take the children out of here in that motorhome. You can take them to—"

He stopped speaking when a strange sound pierced the night's newly minted silence. It was a high whistling sound, like a tea kettle going off on a stove. Other whistles immediately joined in until they rose in a chorus.

Emily winced at the shrill sound, her head turning toward it as it went on and on, rising and falling and rising again.

"Oh, shit," Leo whispered at about the time that Emily identified the sound.

"No!" she cried as she spun around and threw herself forward, trying to run back to camp, to the moving van. To the children. But Leo grabbed her, held her back, wrapped his arms around her, pinning her arms at her sides and holding her forcefully in strong arms. "No. I'm sorry. It's too late now. There's nothing you can do." She continued to struggle as if she had not heard him. But she had, and she did not doubt him.

The screams of the thirty children (minus one little girl who had not survived crossing the border) packed into the moving van back at camp began to die out. The sound diminished rapidly, one voice at a time, until only one remained, a single, high-pitched voice that continued to scream pleadingly. And then it stopped.

Emily went limp in his arms as another sound cut through the night: the long, plaintive howl of a wolf. It was joined by another, and another. Then, from a greater distance in the opposite direction, more howls rose in response.

"Oh, God," Leo whispered. His arms fell away from her, and she slipped to the ground in a weak heap. He began muttering to himself. "They told me they'd protect the children, but... but now..." He began to pace in the dark.

The howling stopped, and a dense silence rushed in to fill Emily's ears. The children were gone, or they would still be screaming. Mickey was gone. So were the others. And now Leo was pacing frantically in the dark, muttering to himself.

"They promised, but it was a lie, because I'm just not important enough to them, they were just stringing me along and, and, and—"

Emily struggled to her feet feeling as if she had been beaten up and then kicked while down. Turning to him, she said, "What's wrong with you?"

He kept pacing a few feet this way, a few feet that way.

"I-I was trying to make myself... valuable to them. I asked them to save the kids for you, and they said they would as long as they got the others. But I-I don't thuh-think they ever intended to do that. Which means they were just using me be-because I'm not... important enough."

"Important enough?"

"They don't... respect me. I... I'm afraid."

"Of what?"

"Of how they'll treat me when I go back. I'm afraid... to go back."

Emily stepped in front of him and forced him to stop pacing.

"You know what?" she said. "I hope they tear you to pieces."

She brought her right foot up in a swift kick that connected hard with Leo's groin. He doubled over with a grunt and a rushing exhalation of air, then fell sideways to the ground.

Clutching his groin, Leo rolled back and forth on the ground making an angry growling sound. Emily could tell, even in the dark, that something was happening to him. She took a step closer, looking down to see his face had distorted and grown hairy. A muzzle grew from it and a pointed ear stood on each side of his head. He spat and frothed as he growled, rolling in pain on the ground.

Werewolves. We're werewolves.

Emily turned and started walking in a hurry through the dark in what she believed to be the direction of the road. Everything she'd had, as dubious as it may have been, was gone. She headed now for whatever was next.

ABOUT THE AUTHOR

Ray Garton is the author of the classic vampire bestseller *Live Girls,* as well as *Scissors, Sex and Violence in Hollywood, Ravenous,* and dozens of other novels, novellas, tie-ins, and story collections.

He has been writing in the horror and suspense genres for more than 30 years and was the recipient of the Grand Master of Horror Award in 2006.

He lives in northern California with his wife Dawn where he is at work on a new novel.

http://www.raygartononline.com.

@RayGarton

Blood Relations

A High Moor Story

Graeme Reynolds

24th November 1991. High Moor, England. 22.35

Marie's eyes snapped open at the ominous creak of the staircase leading to her attic room. She glanced across at the glowing green numbers of her alarm clock then stretched out with her senses to ascertain whether the threat she anticipated was real or imagined. A lingering fragment of a nightmare perhaps?

No. Not imagined. Very real, indeed.

Her father, Norman, stood on the landing with one foot on the staircase, almost frozen in place as if he were playing a game of musical statues. Even without enhanced senses, she fancied that she'd be able to tell he was there. Whiskey fumes billowed from him, mingling with the stink of his body odor to create a unique and unpleasant smell. His heart raced in his chest, and his breathing was deep and rapid as if the mere act of ascending to the first floor had exhausted him.

Norman Williams was not a small man nor a particularly healthy one, and the years of alcohol abuse had taken their toll on him, especially in the years since Marie's brothers had died. The beatings had, if not stopped, at least lessened in frequency and severity, certainly compared to the violence she could remember him inflicting on Michael and David. In their place, however, something else had formed. A seed of temptation had taken root within her father. There had been glances that had made her feel uncomfortable. Hugs that had perhaps gone on too long. And now, beneath the stink of her father's unwashed body and the miasma of whiskey fumes, she smelled something else. The unmistakable, musty stench of arousal. Then the staircase creaked again.

Oh God!

Marie's head span. She must be imagining things, she reasoned. He might be a disgusting, violent drunk, but he was her *father*. There could be any number of reasons why he might be climbing the staircase to her room in the middle of the night. It didn't mean that he intended to... *oh god!* Her mother had just turned the volume up on the fucking television downstairs. Turned it up *loud*. She knew what the bastard was going to do to her. Her own daughter. Her last surviving child, and she was going to let her fat, sweaty husband come up to her room and rape her. Push her down into the old mattress while he climbed on top of her and...

No. No fucking way was she going to allow that to happen. She'd die first. Or kill. Deep inside the darkness of her subconscious, she felt something stir. A presence that she'd lived with for almost five years. The other part of her, a gift that her brother, Michael, had passed to her on the night that he died. She glanced down to the four thin, silver scars that circled her forearm and let out a small snarl. Let him come. She still held on to the hope that she was wrong — that Norman Williams was simply coming upstairs to check on her (as if!) or yell at her over some transgression (more likely), but if there was anything more to it than that, then he would find that he had more to contend with than a scared thirteen-year-old girl.

The creaking of the stairs increased in frequency. Whereas to begin with, there seemed to have been an ocean of time between each step, he was now ascending at a normal, if slightly stumbling pace. She could hear his heart thumping in his chest. Smell the adrenaline mingling with the other scents emanating from him. Then he reached the top of the stairs and paused for what seemed like minutes but, in reality, was probably no more than a couple of seconds, before he reached out and turned the door handle.

Marie wanted to throw up. There was no doubt in her mind as to her father's intentions now. As he'd lost more and more of himself to the booze, the barriers between right and wrong had eroded under the liquid onslaught. And being honest, those barriers had only been paper-thin at the best of times. She remembered the beatings that he'd dished out to her brothers. Especially once, when he'd hurt David so severely that by rights, the boy should have been hospitalized. He probably would have required medical attention if he'd ever made it home. Norman Williams had left her beloved older brother bloodied and broken before throwing him out of the house to retrieve a bag of tools that David and Michael had left in the treehouse they'd been building. David had stumbled from the house, clutching his ribs with tears streaming down his face, and that was the last time that anyone had seen him alive. That was the start of the nightmare that cost her not only her two brothers but John, her best friend (and secret crush). It all stemmed from the routine, casual violence dished out by this brutal thug who was supposed to protect them. The same fucking animal that even now was standing in her doorway, his grotesque shaped silhouetted against the light from the hallway.

Marie had thought about pretending to be asleep, but instead simply said, "What do you want?"

The directness of her tone seemed to knock Norman off guard. "No, need to be like that, Pet. I just wanted to look in on ye. I thought you'd be asleep."

"I was. You woke me up. Can you go now? I've got school in the morning."

Norman seemed to be taken aback by Marie's response. He was, after all, used to having his commands obeyed and was treated, if not with respect, then certainly with caution. He stood motionless in the doorway, seemingly uncertain as to how he should proceed. Marie felt a small twinge of satisfaction as she perceived an increase in his heart rate, and just for a moment, a tiny stab of fear permeated his scent. Unfortunately, it was a short respite. Norman seemed to be fighting against himself, but the fear and guilt he felt quickly transformed into a small flame of anger that began to burn away the conflicting emotions.

He stepped into the room. "Don't you tell me what to do in my own house, girl. If I want to come up here, then that's exactly what I'll fucking do. Am I making myself clear?" With the question left hanging in the air, Norman closed the door behind him then turned back to Marie.

The terror she felt at that moment threatened to paralyze her. With the door closed, her father had, to all intents and purposes, shut out the rest of the world. All that existed to them both at this exact moment in time was contained within the four walls of Marie's bedroom. What had always been a refuge for her now seemed unbearably small. The air was thick and stifling, and the distance between the thing that had masqueraded as a parent and herself was nowhere near enough. Then Norman took another step forward.

"I said, 'Am I making myself clear?'"

The presence in the back of her mind roared to the surface, and it took every scrap of willpower she had to stop herself from tearing the bastard's throat out where he stood. Instead, she pushed back her duvet and got to her feet until she was standing before her father, meeting his lascivious gaze with defiance. "Perfectly clear. Now, was there something you wanted... Dad?"

"I think," he snarled at her, breathing a nauseating mix of alcohol fumes and halitosis into her face, "that you need to learn some respect, girl." He reached down and began to undo the belt to his trousers. Marie couldn't help but notice his erection. "Now, turn around, bend over and take your medicine."

Marie moved so fast that, even if he had been sober, there would have been no way Norman would have been able to react in time. She stepped forward and shot both her hands out, palms open, into her father's chest, shoving him as hard as she could. The effect was dramatic. Norman Williams flew through the air as if he had been attached to a bungee cord that had reached the limits of its elasticity, and crashed into the door to Marie's bedroom, splintering the frame.

"Don't you fucking touch me," she growled at him. "Don't you come near me again. What the hell is wrong with you? *I'm your daughter!*"

Norman picked himself up from the floor, his face flushed red with embarrassment and barely contained rage. "Who the *fuck* do you think you are? You think you can take a couple of karate classes down the rec and tell me what to do? *In my own fucking house*! Girl, I'm going to teach you a lesson you'll never forget. You mark my words. This will stay with you till your dying day!"

Marie could see now that she really didn't have a choice. Whatever had remained of her father, as flawed as he had been, was gone. All that stood before her now was the physical embodiment of rage, desire, and a lifetime of humiliation, fueled by half a bottle of cheap blended whiskey. Before she'd fought back, she was sure part of him was convinced that what he was going to do to his daughter was going to be an act of love. Now he was going to make sure that he hurt her. The pretense of caring had evaporated with his rage, leaving only the desire for violence and control.

So be it.

Marie relaxed control of her wolf and let it come surging to the surface. They existed in symbiosis, the wolf entity and her. In ways she couldn't quite understand, they were a single consciousness. She often brought the other part of her to the surface so that she could use its strength, speed, and senses without fully committing to the transformation, but at least once a month, she would go into the woods and allow things to run their course. Let the wolf out of its cage to run and hunt. The bones in her hands snapped and

213

reformed in an instant. Vicious claws burst from beneath her fingernails while coarse golden hair flowed from her pores. Her jaw dislocated and extended to make room for the array of gleaming fangs that split her gums in a spray of foam and blood.

"No, Dad," she managed to growl through her mangled jaws, "I'm the one that's going to teach you."

She took an unsteady step forward as the bones in her legs elongated. She'd always been stationary when she'd turned before, but fury impelled her forward toward this man who, at that moment, seemed to be the cause of everything that had ever gone wrong with her life. Norman pushed himself backward, against the broken door frame, his eyes bulging from their sockets. And then, before Marie could complete her change and destroy the evil bastard that had dominated her entire life, he clutched his chest and slid to the floor.

Marie stopped, caught in an intermediate state between human and wolf. Her father lay face down on the floor of her bedroom and was not moving. She couldn't hear a heartbeat and could already sense the drop in the temperature of his body. The bastard was dead. She'd killed him, and she hadn't had to lay a finger on him. She wasn't sure how she felt about that. The part of her that was wolf wanted to tear at the body, dig through the layers of rancid fat to find the juicy muscle tissue beneath, but the human part of her felt nothing but revulsion at the thought. No, she was never going to have any part of that bastard inside her. She would satisfy neither his urges nor the wolf's. She was the one in charge. Despite her distorted facial structure, she somehow managed to smile.

Then the door to her bedroom swung open, and her mother saw the body of her husband and the monster that her daughter had become.

Marie took a step forward and reached out to her mother, desperate to calm and comfort her (despite the fact that she had turned up the volume on the television to mask what her husband was going to do to her daughter), but the woman recoiled in horror and let out a long, terrified shriek that only stopped long enough for her to suck more air into her lungs. Marie realized then what had happened and pushed her wolf back down into the depths of her subconscious, quickly turning back into a thirteen-year-old girl. However, the damage was done. When she tried to approach her mother again, the woman crawled into a corner and the shrieking, if anything, got louder.

The realization of what had just happened hit Marie like a hammer blow. Her father lay dead on the floor, and her mother, having witnessed the truth of what her baby girl was, had quite literally lost her mind. Soon a neighbor would come to investigate the noise and find her father's corpse and her mother screaming about monsters. Given the history of High Moor, that would not be a good thing for her. She only had one choice left to her.

She quickly emptied out her school rucksack and stuffed as many clothes as she could get her hands on into it, then stepped past her mother onto the staircase. She looked back at the screaming woman and said, "I'm sorry, Mum. I'm so, so sorry." Then she ran down the staircase, out of the back door, and disappeared into the night.

Two Years Later...

26th October 1993. Prague, Czech Republic. 13.47

Marie shoved her way through the crowd, sending a heavy-set man in a thick wool hat crashing into the street food vendor's cart behind him. She muttered an apology in broken Czech and shook her head in anger at herself. It had been stupid to try this in the middle of the day, in one of the cities' most crowded areas. It was stupidity, however, born of hunger and desperation. She hadn't eaten more than scraps for three days now, and with the cold evenings drawing in, she was going to need to buy some warmer clothing and blankets if she was to stand a chance of surviving the winter. Still, she should have realized that tourists would be on their guard in a busy place like the

Tyn Church. Marie was a reasonable pickpocket, but she was under no illusions that she was great at it. She'd almost been expecting it when the American grabbed her wrist as she fished for his wallet.

She risked a glance over her shoulder and made eye contact with the two police officers that were pursuing her. *Shit!* The cries of the police and the shrill tone of their whistles rang in her ears as they increased their efforts to apprehend the young pickpocket. The crowd behind her began to part, and she felt her heart thud in her chest. The police officers may be wearing the nice new, dark blue uniform of the *Policie České Republiky,* but she was only too aware of the fact that the men wearing them were the same thugs that had served in the communist NSB a few short years ago. To the waves of tourists that had flocked to the Czech Republic since the Velvet Revolution, Prague was just another fascinating European capital to visit. However, beneath the shiny new veneer, many of the old attitudes persisted. You could not change the way a country thought in just a few short years, and Marie knew that if the police managed to catch her, then the very least she could expect was a few nights in the Old Town police station and a severe beating. There may also be questions raised about what a fifteen-year-old English girl was doing stealing wallets from American tourists in their city, and that was something she really couldn't afford to have happen.

The police officers were gaining on her, but Marie had not spent the last two years living on the streets without learning a few tricks. Instead of trying to force her way through the crowd, she dropped onto all fours and began to weave through the forest of legs, using her hands to steer herself in much the same way that she did when in her wolf form. While the cries of surprise and alarm from the crowd increased, the sounds of pursuit soon faded away. Once she was satisfied that she'd evaded the police, Marie ducked down a side alley, straightened her clothes, and checked the American tourist's wallet. She could not believe her luck. The expensive leather wallet contained almost three thousand Czech koruna and a hundred-dollar bill. Enough money to keep her fed for weeks, if not months. She pocketed the money, threw the wallet into a nearby trash can, and then headed southeast, away from the cities bustling Old Town, toward the vast *sídliště* concrete estates of the suburbs.

***

Marie leaned back on the café's metal chair in a vain attempt to alleviate the discomfort of her swollen belly. She had been starving when she made it back to the Jižní Město housing estate and had decided to treat herself to a steaming bowl of *halušky*. Unfortunately, as her mum would have said, her eyes had been bigger than her belly, and almost half of the thick stew remained in her bowl uneaten. She half-heartedly dabbed a chunk of bread into the steaming liquid and let herself relax for the first time that day.

She liked Prague. When she'd first fled home, she'd gone south and tried to blend in with the other homeless people in London. However, it felt as if her life was simply on hold. She was too young to even contemplate looking for work, and the thought of turning herself over to the authorities terrified her even more than the lecherous advances of the pimps and drug addicts she'd had to deal with since arriving in the capital. She also realized that eventually, people would begin to ask questions about why the mutilated corpses of drug addicts and pimps began showing up in the River Thames. After a few months, she had come to a decision. She needed to belong somewhere, and it made sense to her that she couldn't be the only one of her kind, so she stowed away on a cross-channel ferry and began to make her way east. If there were going to be other werewolves anywhere, she had reasoned, then they would be in the countries where the legends had originated. However, she had been in the Czech Republic for almost eighteen months now and had not heard a single report of anything that sounded even vaguely like another lycanthrope beyond some vague stories from the early nineteen eighties.

I'll leave in the spring, she decided. The collapse of communism and the burgeoning property market in Prague had meant that a lot of the prefabricated *panelák* flats in the city had been bought up by foreign investors, however the renovation infrastructure was not quite in place yet, so thousands of them remained empty (their previous occupants kicked out to fend for themselves). It meant, at the very least, that she was never short of a roof over her head, even if it did mean moving from squat to squat when she was discovered. Once the biting cold of the winter had subsided, she would leave Prague behind and head southeast, through Slovakia and Hungary to Romania, and resume her search.

She nibbled at the broth-soaked bread and let her senses expand. It was a habit she'd picked up in London and now practiced almost subconsciously. Better to know who was in your immediate vicinity and their likely intentions than be taken unawares. The number of unexplained bodies in the British capital had reduced dramatically after she had come to that realization. In her mind, she stitched together a picture of the world around her. The scent of oil, metal and fresh sweat from the factory workers outside. The sharper, acrid stink of old dirt from the street children huddled together beneath a tarpaulin in a nearby park. Snatches of conversations from the people in the café. Workers grumbling about the spiraling prices of food or their bosses. Young couples whispering secrets to one another. And then the word that she'd been listening out for ever since she arrived in the Czech capital. *Vlkodlak*. Werewolf.

She tilted her head and focused on the speaker, blocking out every other voice than the one she sought. The word had been faint, barely audible above the whistling wind outside, the dull rumble of the old soviet era vehicles on the road outside and the murmur of conversation in the café, but she reached out with her wolf senses until she heard it again. A child's voice. No, several children. The street kids sheltering in the park were speaking to each other in hushed, fearful tones in much the same way that children

218

would share scary stories around a campfire in the UK. But rather than these stories being told for fun, she could sense a genuine undertone of fear in their voices. She got to her feet, paid for her meal at the counter, and purchased the café's entire supply of stale, cinnamon sugared pastries before she left. Then she stepped out into the cold autumn air and hurried across the street toward the park.

The children had constructed a makeshift shelter beneath an old horse chestnut tree. A large canvas tarpaulin had been draped over a rough frame of wooden fruit boxes then secured with whatever had been to hand. Rocks, concrete breeze blocks, and twisted steel bars all contributed to help the shelter resist the gusting wind. Either one of the children had attempted to camouflage the improvised tent with fallen orange and brown leaves, or the children had been camping there for several weeks, and the leaves had formed the cover on their own. Regardless of intent, Marie reasoned that they would make a generous extra layer of insulation for the occupants of the shelter when the winter arrived. She could see drag marks in the earth around one corner that indicated the entrance, so she lifted the flap and quickly ducked inside.

There was a cry of alarm from a young girl, no more than seven or eight years old, and she scurried toward the back of the makeshift shelter, while an older boy, possibly thirteen or fourteen years old, positioned himself between the other children and the intruder.

He glared at Marie, although some of the tension left his posture once he realized that the newcomer was simply another street kid rather than a police officer (or worse). "There's no more space in here," he spat, "Go find your own shelter."

"Relax, I've got my own place," she said, casting her eyes over the other occupants of the makeshift tent. There were six children in total. The belligerent teenager boy, with another boy just behind him and four younger children aged between eight and ten years old who regarded Marie with curiosity. The two older boys and one of the younger girls were clearly related.

The older boy snarled at her, "Then what do you want, English?"

"I heard you talking about a *vlkodlak* just now, and I wanted to hear the full story. That's all."

The younger children huddled together once more, and even the brash teenager's face paled. "Why should we tell you anything?"

Marie summoned her sweetest smile and produced the bag of cinnamon pastries from behind her back. "Because if you tell me what you know, I'll make it worth your while..."

30th October 1993. Divoká Šárka Nature Reserve. 20.52

Marie shivered as she peeled off her layers of clothing and stuffed them into a pair of plastic carrier bags. This, she decided, was the worst part of being a werewolf. Stripping off in the middle of bloody nowhere before the change and quite literally freezing your fucking tits off until you grew your own fur coat. She stepped back and tied the bags closed to protect her clothes, then felt a thorn pierce the soft flesh of her foot. She cursed, plucking the sharp piece of wood out before the skin healed over it, and thought about what the street kids had told her.

Two orphans had been begging a few weeks earlier at the Dívčí Skok Pub, which was a local tourist attraction. The pub was at the bottom of a sheer cliff where, according to local legend, a female warrior called Šárka had thrown herself to her death after losing what was known as the Maiden's War, and in fact, the name of the entire nature reserve translated as "wild Šárka" after she had famously slaughtered the opposing male army by drugging their mead. As a result, the pub got a lot of trade both from locals and tourists keen to sample Czech culture, and two girls — Magda and Helena, had decided to try their luck assuming that there would be less competition for spare coins (and fewer hostile police officers) than some of the more central tourist attractions. Neither girl had arrived back to the city, and what remained of their corpses had been found a few days later. The police were calling it a bear attack, but even Marie knew that any large predators in the Czech Republic had been hunted to extinction centuries before.

The street kids assumed that the culprit was a werewolf after a spate of similar deaths eleven years earlier, and Marie had decided that it was as good a lead as she'd had in almost two years. However, she had spent the last three nights scouring the reserve in her wolf form and had discovered precisely nothing. It was possible that even if a werewolf had been responsible, they had left the area when the bodies had been found. Tonight, however, was a full moon, and Marie knew that if the other werewolf were still in the area and had been lying low, then tonight they would have no choice but to transform if they had not done so in the preceding month. That the girls had been killed on the night of the last full moon seemed to support this theory. If she found nothing tonight, then she would abandon the search, spend her energy getting ready for the winter, and head east again in the spring.

Once she was sure her bags were sealed, she reached up and placed them securely in the lower branches of a beech tree, crouched down on the cold, wet ground, and allowed the transformation to begin.

Despite the moon not yet having risen, she could feel its influence on her wolven self, feel its almost irresistible pull. She had turned many times already this month and so could have resisted the urge to transform if she wanted to, but the call of the full moon was like a song in her blood, and she gave in to it freely, almost joyously. The pain of turning from human to wolf was immense, but over time, Marie had gotten used to it — in fact, in some strange ways, she almost enjoyed it, if not for the experience itself, then for the end result. She almost grinned as she felt the bones in her fingers and toes shatter and then reform into taloned paws rather than human hands. Her spine cracked and warped to something more suited to four legs than two, while coarse, golden fur began to snake from the pores of her skin and the color drained from her vision to show the forest in stark monochrome. In total, the change took less than two minutes to complete, and another thirty seconds for her to adjust to the flood of information her new canine senses flooded her brain with. She could hear the racing heartbeats of the rabbits and deer that sensed the predator in their midst. Smell the delicious acrid tang of their fear on the breeze. The forest around her came to life in a way she could never experience as a human — even when she used the wolf to enhance her senses, as if her humanity somehow filtered out the majority of the sensations. She let out a long, joyous howl then bounded off into the forest in search of her prey.

One of the biggest problems she faced after she turned was the hunger. Over the years, she'd learned that it was a constant, no matter how much food she'd consumed in her human form before the change. Once she became a werewolf, the hunger was there at the forefront of her mind, and it was almost impossible to ignore. She had no idea if the effort of transmutation burned up anything she already had in her stomach, or whether her wolf form had a completely different digestive system, but the second her change completed, she was ravenous and had an almost overwhelming compulsion to hunt, kill, and feed. This, in part, was why she had decided to come to the nature reserve two hours before the full moon crested the horizon. It would give her time to stalk and kill her own prey, and with any luck, the scent of fresh blood in the air would act as a lure to any other werewolves in the area.

Marie picked up the scent of a small family of deer further into the reserve. Four scents, bunched together for warmth and protection against the cold autumn night and the predator lurking in its shadows. She darted through the undergrowth until she was within a few hundred yards of the animals then began to advance more cautiously, her belly low to the ground as she silently moved in for the kill. She was within a few feet of the deer when a change in the wind brought her scent to them, and they exploded from their hiding place, fleeing into the forest. Marie launched herself at the adult doe but missed her target as the animal rapidly changed direction. Instead, she lashed out at one of the fawns that had strayed too close to her in its panic to escape. Her talons opened a gash on its hindquarters, and the force of the blow knocked the fawn off balance. As the animal struggled to regain its feet, Marie slammed into it, pinning the terrified deer to the ground with her forepaws before darting her dripping maw down. The deer squealed as Marie's jaws closed around its spine, snapping it like dry wood. Then Marie tore out the deer's throat and began to feast.

It took a great deal of willpower to force herself from the freshly slaughtered carcass of the fawn. Marie had consumed the creature's heart, liver, and most of the muscle tissue from one of its flanks, but her wolf was far from satiated. However, she needed to leave enough meat on the bones to be attractive to the other werewolf, and the moon was just clearing the horizon. Wherever the other wolf was, if they hadn't changed since the last attack, they would be transforming now. She hoped that the still-warm carcass would be sufficient to tempt it, or her efforts would have been for nothing. At least she would have the remains of the deer to console herself with if her plan didn't work.

She didn't have long to wait. The glowing disc of the full moon had barely crested the valley shoulders when a long, shrieking howl echoed across the rock-strewn slopes that made Marie's heart race and the wolf part of her tense up, ready to flee or fight as the situation dictated. Alongside the surge of adrenaline, there was unmistakable excitement. At long last, it seemed that she would finally encounter someone else like her. Another werewolf. Another howl rang out, and Marie thought that it was probably around half a mile away, back toward the pub. The wind whistled through the valley from west to east, and she caught a little of the other creature's scent — an acrid, bitter and musky animal odor that made the hackles on her neck rise. Unfortunately, the wind direction meant that the other werewolf was unlikely to catch the scent of the freshly slain deer without assistance. Her original plan had been to lure the other creature out to the carcass of the deer, then keep upwind of it and trail it until morning, when she would introduce herself after they turned back. Marie now realized that would be unlikely, so instead, she began racing up the steep valley walls, bounding over loose rocks and sending screed tumbling to the floor below, until she reached a large standing stone overlooking the valley.

Then Marie let out her own howl, a long lament to the moon that echoed along the valley, reflecting back on itself so that it rang out for almost five seconds after she'd closed her muzzle. The response, however, was not so much a howl as a roar of rage that almost rooted Marie to the spot with terror. She could smell the other werewolf clearly now. Hear its frantic ascent of the valley walls. And when it crested the ridge and stood before her, Marie realized that she'd made a terrible, potentially fatal mistake.

This werewolf was not like her. Not one little bit. It stood on two legs, not four, and was almost seven and a half feet tall. The creature seemed to be caught in a halfway stage between man and wolf and was nothing less than the physical embodiment of pain, rage, and sheer bloodlust. Blood-streaked froth spumed from between its vicious glinting fangs, and its snout curled up into a snarl. Then the creature began stalking toward her.

Oh, Fuck!

***

Marie decided on a course of action in a microsecond. Using her powerful hind legs, she launched herself into the air while her upper body twisted to point her away from the advancing monster. Then, ears flat to her head, Marie raced south, across open scrubland, and tried to get her bearings. She knew that her best bet was to lose her pursuer in the thick woodland to the northwest, but she would need to get past the monster and down the screed slopes to have half a chance of evading it. If she missed her footing and fell, she would heal quickly, but it might give the other werewolf enough time to catch her, and she was under no illusions as to how she would fare against it in a straight-up fight. There was a large artificial lake to the southeast, but there was open moorland for almost a kilometer directly east of her position. She should be able to outdistance the other werewolf there and then cut north into the woods, where the creature's size should work against it. Marie risked a glance over her shoulder and, to her horror, found the werewolf almost upon her. She veered sharply to the right, just as a massive clawed hand slashed through the air. She remembered the female deer she'd hunted earlier, uncomfortable with the reversion of circumstances. The other werewolf was bigger than her, stronger than her and, to her dismay, faster as well. She needed a new plan, or her fate would be the same as the unfortunate fawn that she'd feasted on earlier.

Marie veered to the southwest, rapidly changing direction on instinct alone when she sensed the other creature was about to attack. She didn't have many advantages against it. She was more agile and accelerated faster than the lumbering beast, and she had her intelligence. It remained to be seen whether these could be turned to an advantage against raw power and animal instincts, but she had no choice if she wanted to stay outside the creature's jaws. She changed direction again, almost doubling back toward the ancient menhir where she'd started, when the werewolf's claws connected with her flank, opening deep tears in the muscle and sending her crashing into a hawthorn bush. Her mind reeled with pain and panic — a panic that increased when she realized that her wounds weren't healing. Warm blood oozed from the four tears in her flesh, filling her nostrils with the thick metallic stench of her own mortality. She tried to scramble to her feet and ignore the burning agony in her leg but knew there was nothing she could do. The werewolf would be on her in seconds. She looked up into the flat phosphorescent discs of the monster's eyes and felt peace wash over her. Acceptance, even. This was it. She was going to die. Marie closed her eyes and waited for the werewolf's fangs to find her throat.

When a few seconds had passed without her being torn apart, Marie opened one eye and found the gigantic bipedal werewolf had its back to her. Facing not one, but two other werewolves — a huge black beast and a smaller silver-grey wolf, positioned perhaps fifteen meters away from her assailant. The four-legged newcomers were circling the monster from opposite sides. The black wolf feigned an attack, and when the creature reacted, the grey werewolf darted in and slashed at its flanks before retreating out of range again. Then, once the grey wolf had the beast's attention, the black werewolf would attack. Within minutes, the legs and lower abdomen of the bipedal werewolf were scored with dozens of small wounds, each one staining its brown fur with blood. They were wearing the monster down, slowly bleeding it in the same way that a regular wolf pack would attack a large prey animal, and it seemed to be working. The beast's movements already seemed slower, its counterattacks less coordinated.

Unfortunately, the enormous brown werewolf also seemed to sense this and changed its tactics. Rather than attempting to fend off both of its assailants, it waited until the grey werewolf feigned its attack, and then spun around, sweeping its terrible clawed hands out in an arc that connected with the black werewolf as it leaped in to attack. The counterattack opened four terrible wounds across the black werewolf's side. Loops of intestines glistened in the moonlight, and it let out a cry of terror and pain. The injured wolf tried to turn and flee, but the beast was too fast for it. Its jaws darted down and tore a mouthful of muscle tissue from the black werewolf's leg in a spray of blood and gore. Then it swung its taloned hand back in the opposite direction, raking its claws across the face of the silver-grey werewolf that had launched its own attack.

Marie couldn't believe what she was seeing. This massive bi-pedal monster had taken on two other fully grown werewolves, and it was winning. The black creature lay prone in a spreading pool of its own blood, with clouds of its breath puffing out from it in the cold autumn air. The silver wolf was hurt, but not fatally. However, it wasn't much bigger than she was, and she didn't think it would last long now that it had the brown monster's undivided attention. And once the creature had slaughtered both newcomers, it would turn its attention back to her.

Marie had two choices. Neither of them particularly good. She could have turned and fled, hoping to gain enough ground on the monster while it finished off the two newcomers, or she could join them, make a fight of it, and hope that they were both better disposed to her than the bi-pedal monster once the battle was over. Assuming they survived.

In the end, it was no choice at all. For now, the creature seemed to have forgotten about Marie as it stalked toward the silver-grey werewolf. The grey beast had regained its footing and shook the blood from its eyes while growling a warning at the advancing monster. Marie picked herself up, ignoring the flare of pain from her wounded leg, and launched herself at the creature, leaping high into the air, jaws wide open in a last, desperate attack.

The werewolf didn't even see her coming. Marie's fangs closed around the back of its neck, and it let out a roar of fury, slashing wildly at her with its razor-sharp talons until the silver beast darted in and raked its own claws across the monster's abdomen. As the brown werewolf watched its intestines unravel out onto the frost coated grass, Marie bit down as hard as she could, thrashing her fangs from side to side until the brown monster's head came away from its body in a fountain of warm blood and landed with a wet splash in its own innards.

Marie and the silver-grey werewolf stood then, for a moment, eyeing each other with caution. She couldn't help but notice that the silver wolf kept flicking its eyes toward the fallen black beast. Marie decided that the last thing she needed right now was another fight, so she cautiously she lay down next to the cooling corpse of the dead brown werewolf (which was in the throes of returning to a more human form) in what she hoped was a submissive posture, while remaining ready to fight for her life if she needed to.

Fortunately, the other werewolf didn't seem to be in the mood to fight either. It nodded its head toward her in acknowledgment then bounded over to its injured companion, transforming back to human as it went. By the time it reached the werewolf's side, the silver wolf had vanished, and a grey-haired, muscular man knelt beside the fallen creature.

"Fucks sake, Gregorz," he hissed with a distinct German accent, "you've really gone and done it this time." He turned to Marie, who was still flat in the grass. "You, girl. I need your help, or he's going to bleed to death."

Marie considered the possibilities for a moment and then began her transformation back into a human. She hated the change from wolf to human far more than the reverse. Not only did every inch of her skin burn as the thick fur pushed itself back into her pores, but the muting of her senses seemed almost like a mutilation. She whined more at the loss of self than the pain of her bones reforming and the electric agony of fangs pushing their way back into her gums. Within a matter of moments, she was nothing more than a fifteen-year-old girl again, suddenly conscious of both her naked body and the frigid wind that whipped across the moorland. The man's urgent voice snapped her out of her momentary uncertainty. "Girl, please. If you don't help me now, then he's going to die."

Ignoring her own injuries, she raced across the moorland to where the stricken werewolf lay. Up close, its wounds were far worse than she had realized. Four tears across its abdomen had come close to disemboweling it. She could see the slippery tubes of internal organs through

228

the rips in its flesh, and dark blood pumped from the gaping cavity. Worse by far, however, was the damage to the werewolf's leg. Muscle and sinew had been torn away from all the way down to the bone, and despite the German's best efforts to stem the blood loss, dark jets of coppery ichor squirted from between his fingers.

"Here," he said, taking Marie's hand in his. "Put pressure here. As hard as you can. We need to stop the blood."

Marie did as she was instructed, pushing her hands down into the sticky fur with as much pressure as she could until the blood pulsing from beneath her fingers slowed down.

Another voice came from the shadows, startling her. "Oh, for goodness sake, Daniel. What the hell have you and that idiot Gregorz done now? And who is the girl?"

Marie turned her head to regard a blond-haired man, dressed in a heavy winter coat and carrying a large hunting rifle, step from the shadows.

"Nice to see you get here at last, Oskar," Daniel growled. "You seem to have missed the action again."

Oskar ignored Daniel's tone, stepped forward and regarded the injuries to the black werewolf, then shook his head. "Gregorz, you bloody fool. I'm going to need you to change back before I do anything to your injuries. Because what I'm about to do to you is going to hurt, and I'd rather you weren't in wolf form when I did it."

The black beast, while apparently unconscious, must have heard the man's instructions, because Marie felt the bones begin to shift beneath her hands, and the thick, sticky fur retreated back into flesh until she was left pushing down with all her might on the ruined thigh of a heavy-set, black-haired and bearded man.

Oskar turned to her. "You, girl. Sit on his legs, but keep putting the pressure on the wound. Daniel, hold his arms down."

Marie looked to Oskar, then Daniel. "I don't understand. What are you going to do? Why isn't he healing?"

Oskar gave her a thin smile and produced a hunting knife from the backpack he'd been wearing, then began cutting away the ruined flesh around Gregorz wound. "We don't heal from injuries inflicted by other werewolves. Not until the next full moon," he grunted as the knife sliced through muscle and sinew, "so I'm removing the affected tissue."

Gregorz eye's snapped open as the blade bit into his flesh, and a cry of anguish escaped from his lips. Marie struggled to keep his legs pinned, and she could see that Daniel was having similar difficulties. Then Gregorz's eyes changed from dark brown to bright yellow, and she could feel the bones beginning to shift beneath her fingers.

"Oh god, he's changing again. He's..."

Oskar paused his impromptu surgery and struck Gregorz between the eyes with the hilt of his knife with such force that Marie heard the bones of his skull crunch under the impact. The yellow eyes crossed, and the big man slumped back to the ground, unconscious for the time being. Then Oskar returned to his work, slashing away thick ribbons of muscle and flesh until the wound began to heal of its own accord. Then he started work on the unconscious werewolf's abdominal injury in the same way.

After a few moments, Oskar stepped away from the unconscious man, looking in disgust at the blood-soaked arms of his jacket. Then he turned his attention to Marie. "Your interference ruined a perfect plan to destroy that moonstruck. Who the hell are you, and what the hell are you doing here?"

Marie was taken aback by the venom in the man's words. "I... I'm... My name is Marie Williams. I've been looking for you... or... at least... others like me..."

Daniel got to his feet and tilted his head as he regarded her. "Of course. I didn't see it at first, but now... tell me, Marie. Do you have a brother? Michael?"

Tears sprang unbidden into her eyes. "I did. He died years ago."

Daniel smiled and offered Marie his hand. "*Liebchen*, I think you had best come with us."

31st October 1993. U Sedmi Svabu Medieval Pub. 01:25

Marie sat huddled in the alcove of the old pub and cautiously eyed her surroundings. She didn't like that there was only one exit to the pub that they had adjourned to. After the battle, Gregorz, Daniel, and Oskar had retrieved her clothing and then taken her back to their rented apartment. There, Marie had showered for the first time in what felt like weeks, and Daniel had dressed her wounds as well as he could manage. He had loaned her some of his own clothes that, while far too large, were at least clean and, as Oskar stated with a look of disgust, *didn't stink of her accumulated filth*. Oskar had left to tie up some loose ends, leaving her in the company of the other two werewolves, and she did not feel comfortable at all. Perhaps it was the fact that she was inside an establishment that would have chased her out with a broom twelve hours ago. Or it could be that she was sitting across from two killer werewolves, and they were between her and the exit.

She picked up the mug of spiced hot chocolate that Daniel had bought her and looked from one man to the other. "So," she said, "you three are werewolves that kill other werewolves?"

Gregorz seemed to struggle to find an answer to that question and looked to Daniel for help. The German took a sip of his beer and smiled. "Not exactly. What you saw tonight is what we call a moonstruck. It's a werewolf that tries to suppress their wolf nature and fights against it, either consciously or subconsciously. When the moon is full, the wolf side of them becomes too strong to contain, and they end up caught in a halfway state between man and wolf. They are nothing but pain, rage, and instinct, and, as you saw, are very dangerous. So, when we hear about one of them, we hunt them down and deal with the situation."

Marie drained half of her drink in a single draught, enjoying the warmth that seeped through her body, then thought about what Daniel had said and narrowed her eyes. "I don't get it. Why not just leave them alone? Or track them down when they are just people and try to help them?"

Gregorz downed a shot of Slivovitz, poured himself another from the bottle, then leaned forward. "It's not that simple, little one. We live far away from the world of men. We have a community. A family. But if people knew of our existence, then we would be hunted down and exterminated. There are still enough of those who know the old legends and would know where to look. If a moonstruck were to rampage through a town, for example, then the damage could be catastrophic. People would not be able to deny our existence anymore, especially at the next full moon, when the survivors changed for the first time. So, when we hear of a moonstruck, we hunt it down and kill it. It's the law and has been that way for over a century. We do it for our survival. Do you understand?"

She nodded. "I get it, I suppose. I can't say I like it much, though. Do you all do this? The hunting?"

"No," Daniel said. "Only a few of us are on what we call field teams. The rest of the pack are just families. Husbands and wives. Children. Like any other community, really."

"Listen, child," said Gregorz, "you saved my life tonight. Daniel's too. If you wish it, there is a place for you with us. With the pack. That is what you were searching for, yes?"

"I... I don't know. I thought it was, but now that I've found you, I'm really not sure. It scares me. I've been on my own for so long now that I don't know if I'll fit in. I don't tend to play well with others."

Daniel smiled at her. "There is something else you should know before you make your decision. You mentioned your brother, Michael, earlier. What if I told you that he wasn't dead? That he was with us and had been since he was a boy?"

The German's words were like a slap to the face, and Marie felt anger boil up inside of her. "I'd say you were full of fucking shit! I was there when he died. How do you think I got these?" she snapped, showing the four silver scars that circled her wrist.

Gregorz shook his head. "No, child. I brought him back to the pack myself, after the unfortunate incident in High Moor. He had been poisoned by a hunter, but not fatally. I smuggled him out of the country and back to the pack, so he could be with his own kind."

"You did what?" Marie snarled, throwing her half-empty mug at the big man. "You took my fucking brother from me. You left me alone. Every single thing that happened to me since then is your fucking fault! And you expect me to trust you? Fuck you!"

Daniel stood up and put his hands out in an attempt to placate her, "Marie, if we'd left him with your family, the chances are that he would have become moonstruck. Most do, if not trained. He would have killed you, your parents, and god knows how many others. And then we would have had to kill him. What we did, we did for him."

"And what about John?" she spat. "Did you kidnap him too? Or did you just put him out of his misery?"

The two men exchanged uncomfortable glances. "You mean John Simpson? No. We sent a field team to retrieve him and never heard from them again. We never found a

233

trace of them or the boy. Please, Marie. Try to calm down. I can understand why you are upset, but you have a chance here. You can be with your brother again by this time next week. I know that it's difficult, but I'm asking you to trust us."

Marie's head surged with conflicting emotions. These strange men were offering her everything that she'd ever wanted. Not only a place to belong, with others like her, but the return of her brother, whom she'd believed dead for years. The street kid in her screamed that it was a scam. That it was all too good to be true and was some kind of setup. And even if it wasn't all bullshit, these bastards had taken her brother away from her and left her to deal with her father's attentions alone.

She clenched her fist and looked first at Daniel, who wore a pleading expression of concern and then to Gregorz, who was wiping hot chocolate and melted marshmallows from his beard. *Fuck It,* she thought, *If they are playing me, then I'll rip their throats out and burn their village to the ground.*

"OK," she said, "I'll go with you, but you'd better not be talking bollocks, or there'll be hell to pay."

Daniel seemed to relax a little at this, and Gregorz smiled at her, despite his wet clothes and chocolate flecked beard.

"But before we go anywhere," she said, "There's something I have to do."

31st October 1993. Jižní Město Housing Estate. 03:11

The temperature had dropped significantly as Marie had made her way back toward the center of the city. She hadn't been in a hurry to make the journey. The coat that she'd borrowed from Daniel kept the worst of the cold away, and the icy air helped clear her head. She'd had a lot to think over, and the long walk from Lesser Town to the housing estate had allowed her to mull her decision over. Measured thought was not one of Marie's strongest attributes — she had a tendency to commit to action and go with her gut instinct rather than think things through, but after a few hours weighing things up, she was confident that she was making the right move.

Spider fingers of frost were forming across the windshields of the old Skodas and Ladas parked outside of the grim concrete buildings, and the grass crunched beneath Marie's feet as she walked. It already felt like the coming winter was going to be an especially cold one.

It had only taken her a few minutes to go into the flat that she'd been squatting in and retrieve what meager belongings she had. She'd liked Prague but wasn't the kind to be sentimental about a place. Or people, for that matter. Still, the city had been kind to her in the end. She picked up her backpack from where she'd left it, pocketed the flat key, and stepped out into the cold pre-dawn air.

There was still one thing that she needed to do.

Marie made her way down the icy concrete ramps, taking care not to slip on the patches of black ice that had formed. Her injured leg had throbbed constantly on her walk across the city, and the last thing she wanted was to pop the stitches that Daniel had put in place. Being hurt was an odd sensation that she really wasn't used to, and Marie was in no hurry to add to the existing pain by falling flat on her backside. Once she reached the ground, she made her way across the park where she'd spoken to the street children a few days earlier, lifted the corner of their makeshift shelter, and ducked inside.

The children were huddled together beneath a pile of coats and blankets, deep in sleep. One of the younger girls coughed for a few moments, then settled back down again, lost in her dreams. Marie crouched and watched them until the older boy that had challenged her a few days ago sensed her presence and woke with a start.

"Who... oh, it's you, English. What the fuck are you doing back here? Didn't you find your *vlkodlak*?"

Marie smiled at the boy. "I found him, all right. In fact, I bit it's head off. You don't need to worry about werewolves anymore after tonight."

"You didn't answer my question. What are you doing here? I told you last time, we don't have any room here, no matter how many pastries you try to bribe us with."

"You don't need to worry. I'm leaving the city tonight, and I wanted to give you something first." She nodded toward the young girl who had been coughing. "To help the little ones." She handed the boy the key to her old flat, along with the money that she'd stolen from the American tourist a few days before.

The boy's eyes widened. "What... Why? There's so much money here..."

"Just take care of them. That flat isn't much, but it's still got running water and power for now, and it's a bit warmer and safer than being out here. As for the money — I don't need it anymore. Just consider it thanks for helping me find my *vlkodlak*."

Marie turned to leave the shelter when the boy said, "Wait, English. Where will you go?"

She grinned at him. "I'm going to my family. I think I'm going home."

** This story is set between Parts 2 and 3 of High Moor.**

ABOUT THE AUTHOR

Graeme Reynolds was born in England in 1971. Over the years, he has been an electronic engineer in the Royal Airforce, worked with special needs children and been a teenage mutant ninja turtle (don't ask).

He started writing in 2008 and had over thirty short stories published in various ezines and anthologies before the publication of his first novel, High Moor, in 2011. This was then followed by High Moor 2: Moonstruck in 2013 and High Moor 3: BloodMoon in 2015

When he is not breaking computers for money, he hides in a out in South West England and dreams up new ways to offend people with delicate sensibilities.

You can find Graeme online in the following places.

https://www.facebook.com/graeme.reynolds2

https://www.facebook.com/GraemeReynoldsAuthor/

Twitter: @GraemeReynolds

http://www.graemereynolds.com

Hybrid: Bloodlines

Nick Stead

Screams rang through the night, shrill and piercing. Mangled body parts glistened darkly in the thin beams of moonlight shining through the forest canopy, the scent of blood and death thick on the air as man fell to beast, prey to predator, mortal to immortal. Bloodied jaws struck with unnatural speed, ripping and tearing through pale flesh until it hung in useless strips from ravaged limbs and the living became the dead. And the carnage had only just begun.

Cromus rose from his second victim, inhaling deeply and savoring the tantalizing odor of men reduced to meat, no doubt repulsive to humans but full of allure for one such as he. His ears were tuned to those cries of agony and terror and the rapid beating of his victims' hearts, music to which his own primal heart sang. The intense taste of crimson juices tingled on his tongue, bringing that same savage delight first discovered centuries ago, the night it was awoken by his father's blessing. With all that fresh death dominating his senses, it threatened to cloud his mind, giving rise to his bloodlust, ever-present in the darkest recesses of his being and straining to run rampant even after all these years. But he had long since learned to control that monstrous desire for senseless slaughter.

Another scream rang out, marking his blood brother's latest kill. The forest was crawling with humans, and it took him a moment to wrestle his yearning for more bloodshed into submission. There were times when he still allowed himself to give in to it. When he would lose himself in the feral joy of massacring humanity, but this was not one of them. For this hunt was not all it had first seemed, and the stakes were higher than ever.

Gunshot tore through the night, bullets thudding into

the trees around him. Cromus snarled and turned to face his enemies, wanting nothing more than to fall on them until every last one lay dead or dying in pools of their own blood, but there were too many. All it took was one bullet to find its mark in his heart or his brain, and his unnatural life would finally come to an end, his passing celebrated by those hunting him but mourned by none, except Magnus. That was not the death he wanted. Reluctant as he was to flee, he knew it was his only choice that night, and so he turned away, dropping to all fours even though his body was still mostly humanoid, save for his lupine head, paws, and tail.

More bullets sought to end him, but even in that halfway state between man and wolf, he was too fast for his enemies, and he escaped without even a flesh wound, bounding effortlessly over the dirt and twigs as he wove his way between the trees. Then came another gunshot, followed by a high-pitched yelp of pain. Cromus skidded to a stop, ears swiveling toward the sound, straining for more clues as to how severely injured his last surviving packmate might be. Three more shots thundered in his ears, the third sounding with an awful finality before all went quiet. Cromus' heart pounded with fear of his own now, and a worried howl escaped his jaws, even though deep down he knew it was already too late for Magnus.

The minutes stretched on with no reply from his brother wolf, and a second howl left his bloodied muzzle, this one voicing his grief for his fallen packmate and a sense of all he had just lost. Cromus was old enough to remember a time when the night would have rung with answering howls from his brethren, but now there was only a terrible silence as his voice trailed off.

Shouts from his left and the crashing of feet through the undergrowth spurred him back into action. That bestial rage burning at the core of his lycanthropy blazed through him, the darkness that came from his humanity demanding vengeance. But Cromus was no longer ruled by such base desires as he had once been in the early days of his gift, and he was as much a wolf as he was a man. The lupine side to him knew better than to rush headlong into a group of humans with enough guns to kill him, and so he took to fleeing once again. He would honor his fallen brother by surviving and continuing on their bloodline, living to fight another day when he would face better odds and not certain death. And when that day came, then he would have his revenge.

***

Magnus's death hit Cromus all the harder once he was permitted a brief respite, his thoughts fixed solely on his lost packmate. In the gray light of dawn, the shape of the black-furred werewolf began to recede, lupine might shrinking into the weaker form of the man he had once been, centuries ago. The pain of the transformation always felt more intense whenever his body returned to its human state, as if his flesh never wanted to give up the greater strength of the wolf. But his human form had its uses, and so he endured the pain, made bearable in the knowledge he could shift back to wolf at any time, as long as his body had the energy required to fuel the transformation.

He had lost his pursuers some time ago, and his flight had taken a more purposeful direction, across the untamed wilds of the Scottish highlands and toward the one they'd come to this accursed island to see. Even without the night's tragic events, Cromus was already regretting the decision to journey to this land so far from the country he still thought of as home. The climate was cold and wet, and the sky remaining dreary even after the sun had begun its ascent towards the peak of midday. It only made him gloomier as he stalked across the wilderness, sweat beading on his bare skin, despite the crisp air, running red with the dried blood and gore covering his flesh. He would have presented a fearsome sight to any unfortunate enough to cross his path if it hadn't been for his skills at evading prying eyes.

Cromus thought back to the moments before the attack the previous night.

"I still say it was a mistake to come here," Magnus had said. "We do not even know the boy really exists."

"That is precisely why we are here," he had answered. "If there is even the slightest chance that my dreams are visions of a surviving wolven descendent, then we have to find him. Our great race is all but gone. If the boy has somehow slipped through the grasp of the Slayers and he yet lives, we must awaken the wolf in him, before our enemies condemn us to extinction."

"But what difference can one more truly make? You would have us risk much for little. I do not like this, brother. For all we know, it is a trap, and even if your dreams are genuine, we both know this is a desperate move. We have successfully avoided our enemies for three winters now. Why venture back into the world of men, where they are sure to find us, when we can continue on in the wilderness, undiscovered and unchallenged by any but the occasional vampire in search of similar natural refuge?"

"We both know it is only a matter of time before one of them stumbles upon us once more. Our race stands a far better chance at survival with three instead of two, and perhaps it will allow us to successfully breed with a human female and start a new pack that way. Raising cubs might be possible with a third pack member."

"You know I would follow you to the ends of the earth. If this is truly your will, then I am with you, as always; I just hope your dreams prove true, and we find this boy before the Slayers find us."

The boy: He was there every time Cromus closed his eyes now, as if the Fates themselves had decided to intervene and send him on this path.

And what if Magnus had been right to suspect a trap? It was no secret the Slayers had spellcasters among their ranks. The visions might have been no more than dreams sent to trouble him through witchcraft; no more than a means to lure the only two surviving members of his father's once-great pack to their deaths. They had barely set foot on British soil when their enemies had found them, baiting them into an ambush with a few of their own, confident the human prey would prove too irresistible for the two werewolves to ignore. And he had been foolish enough to play right into their hands, leading his brother to his death.

A feeling of such loneliness settled over him, the thought that his visions could be false almost too much to bear. And if the boy had never been more than a dream, what did that mean for the werewolf race? He could not remember the last time he and Magnus had come across the trail of another, it had been so long, and so many years had passed since they'd had any dealings with other packs. Could it be that he was not just the last of his pack, but the last werewolf alive? Were they doomed to fade into legend, never again to answer the call of the moon or roam the earthly plane as flesh-and-blood beings, but instead reduced to stories, no more than echoes of a bygone era? The thought of that saddened him as much as the death of his pack.

There was only one way he was going to get the answers he sought. He had to consult someone with the power to interpret dreams and visions, someone with the foresight to interpret his destiny and give him some advice as to which direction his future path should take. And there was only one man alive with those abilities whom he trusted. But would he still have chosen this path if he'd known it would cost Magnus' life? That was one question he might never know the answer to. All he could do was continue on the course the Fates had set him upon and pray to the gods it had not all been for naught.

***

A house loomed up ahead, the dwelling of the man he'd

come to see no different in appearance to any of the other human homes he'd passed. Cromus approached with caution, ready to bolt at the first hint of danger. But he detected no signs of life in the immediate vicinity, save for the lone heartbeat his ears picked up from within the building. Even in the form of the black-haired man he'd started out as, his senses were far better than those of a human, and he was emboldened by the apparent lack of unwanted company, his hand reaching for the handle of the front door and twisting to find it was unlocked.

The ancient slab of wood creaked open to reveal a gloomy interior, wreathed in the strong scent of incense and lit only by the glow of a lone candle, despite the electric lighting built into the place. Cromus padded across the stone floor toward the table, where the house's only occupant sat gazing into the small flame flickering on the end of its wick. In times gone by, he might have been known as a cunning man in those parts, while others might have called him druid, shaman, healer, or even priest, but in modern society, he was generally thought of merely as psychic. Regardless of his title, he came from a long line of mystics skilled in dealing with spirits and visions, once revered long before Christianity began to confuse such as the work of the Devil. In present times, he was likely met with more in the way of skepticism than he was fear, but that did not stop him practicing the ancient arts of his family.

"You are here about the boy," the man said without looking up.

"So he is real," Cromus answered.

"Yes, he exists. But be warned: He will be your undoing."

"So the vision is a trap? Is he human, after all, invading our dreams through some trickery of the Slayers?"

"The wolf blood runs strong in his veins — you should have no trouble turning him if that is your wish. But it is not just the Slayers you need fear. Dark powers are at work. I see the shadow of a demon looming over your dying race."

"A demon?" the werewolf growled. "They returned to Hell centuries ago. What mischief can they possibly work from down there?"

"A great deal. This is no minor demon limited to torturing souls in its own realm."

"Still, why should I fear them? Do they not wish to see the Slayers brought to an end and mankind forced to its knees once more, as it was in the time of my father? Oh, how men cowered before us as we slaughtered them by their thousands, the streets turned red and decorated with raw flesh. I am sure the demons want a return to those glory days as much as all those who call themselves undead."

"Demons are not to be trusted, and the reign of your father has long since passed. Even if you could somehow spread lycanthropy to a new generation, the world will never again know an era like that. Not even with the last surviving son of Lycaon to lead them. You would do well to forget the boy and return to your exile in the wilds before it is too late."

"I can't turn back now. Magnus already gave his life to bring this boy into the pack. And if Hell is taking an interest in us, that has to mean something greater is at work here — this demon you speak of must have seen something in our race, some kind of potential as yet undiscovered to give us a chance at victory in the battles still to come. I have to see this through."

"A newly turned werewolf is a volatile thing. The boy will bring about much death and destruction; I need no visions to see that. But will that rampaging force be enough to defeat the Slayers and their guns? I very much doubt it."

"I did not ask for your doubts, Aran. Tell me where I can

find this child, and I will be on my way."

The cunning man finally chose to look up, his face lined with the burden of seeing so much that would come to pass and the knowledge he was powerless to change most of it, his hair grayer than Cromus remembered. "Twenty years since I last saw you, and you look the same as ever. Not even the smallest of scars to mark your hardships, let alone a wrinkle. I would almost be jealous of your lycanthropy if it weren't for the blood covering you from head to foot."

"The name of the place where I can find the boy, Aran. Before our enemies find him, or me."

"That will require another vision to discover, which may take some time. You might as well take a seat while you wait. There's steak in the fridge if you're hungry and towels in the bathroom for you to sit on — I'd rather not have your bare arse on my chair if it's all the same to you."

"Thank you, old friend."

"Friend," Aran grunted. "I curse the day our paths first crossed. And I tell you now, the boy will not thank us for this. You may call it a blessing, but to him, it will be a curse."

"He need never know of your involvement," Cromus answered, stalking over to the fridge to investigate the meat on offer. "No more delays now. It is surely only a matter of time before the Slayers strike again."

Aran did not look happy, but he lit more incense and began the preparations to induce another vision, as promised. There was nothing for it then but to wait.

***

Fully wolf in form, Cromus bounded across the countryside, the grip of his four paws unrivaled by any human technology and his speed and stamina greater than any mortal creature. It had been late afternoon by the time he'd left Aran's home, and night was already falling before he crossed the Yorkshire border. But he wouldn't rest until he reached the area the cunning man had seen.

Roads cut through the landscape like ugly knife wounds carved through the flesh of the natural world, impossible to completely avoid though he kept out of sight as much as possible. But the signs he passed proved useful for navigation, and he found the town he sought without too much difficulty. Only when he began to near his destination did he slow, taking the opportunity to hunt in the fields on the outskirts of the human world.

With the waxing moon overhead and the aching hunger in his belly after the long run and the second transformation earlier that day, his craving for human flesh burned as strongly as ever. Cromus watched from the shadows as his unwitting prey walked the quiet country roads to their local pub, mistaken in their belief this was still their domain and they had nothing to fear from the surrounding darkness. They had lost that animal alertness to the signs of danger lurking in the blackness, their arrogance soon to cost them their lives. It would be so easy to take one of them, drag them away to their deaths before their friends and family could even realize what had happened, and his mouth watered at the thought, threads of drool hanging from those great jaws with the longing to rip into the succulent meat. But not that night.

Cromus drew away from temptation, prowling across the fields until he picked up the fresh scent of deer. Moments later, he had caught up with the animals and made his kill, warm blood splattering his body with a fresh layer of gore and matting his fur as it congealed, limbs scattered and still twitching with the need to run and guts strewn across the grass. He savored the rich taste of the hearts, kidneys, and livers as the slippery organs slid down his throat, and the sensation of raw meat on his tongue felt divine once again, even if it was not quite the meat he hungered for. But once he had eaten his fill, that hunger quietened, and he loped away from the grisly remains, toward the heart of the town.

The stink of the smog hanging over the world of men was thick in his nostrils, particularly unpleasant after the years spent living in fresher air far from the foul fumes their machines spewed out and the pollution they insisted on coating the earth in. Constant background noise battered his eardrums, from the roar of cars on the roads to the incessant pounding of modern music, annoying and distasteful to his ancient ears. But it was the orange glow of streetlamps he was especially wary of, knowing how much humanity relied on their sense of sight. It would not do to be seen roaming the dimly lit streets, for news of his arrival in the town would surely be quick to reach his enemies, and then he risked missing his chance to find the boy and turn him.

Keeping to the shadowy back alleys, Cromus prowled the town, searching for the scent of the last surviving wolven descendant able to be turned. He might not know the boy's scent yet, but he would certainly pick up the smell of wolf blood the moment his nose found a fresh enough trail to detect it. Then it was just a matter of following it to wherever the lad happened to be.

So he worked his way outward from the center, the streets devoid of humans after a while. And he was soon rewarded with a hint of the smell he was searching for, nose pressed to the ground as he located the trail. Ideally, he'd turn his prey that very night and take him to one of the remoter areas he'd already passed through on his journey to the town, where they could manage his first full moon in relative safety and then flee the country and return to safer lands. But the Fates had other ideas.

More of that annoying music filled his ears, blaring out from a house on the street the trail led him down. It was loud enough to mask any sounds of approaching danger, and he became increasingly uneasy for as long as his hearing remained useless. So it was that he rounded the corner to find a woman just suddenly there, the wind blowing in the wrong direction to carry her scent and give him any forewarning through his sense of smell.

Cromus froze at the sight of her, his hackles raising in alarm. She seemed similarly surprised to find herself facing a huge wolf, but when he growled, there was no hint of the fear in her eyes the feral sound should have raised. Instead, he thought he saw recognition, not of who he was but rather for what he was. She knew he was no wolf, just as she was no defenseless human to fall helplessly to his teeth if he chose to attack.

The woman was the first to recover, but she drew neither gun nor blade. Instead, she grabbed her walkie-talkie, calling for backup and confirming she was a member of that hated faction who had taken it upon themselves to hunt down every last creature of the night — the same group who had killed Magnus, and all the other werewolves he had once called pack. Cromus saw his chance to avenge his fallen brother and began to advance, intending to kill the woman as slowly and painfully as time allowed, before more of them showed up.

"I do not fear you, son of Lycaon. Kill me if you wish, but I will not give you that added satisfaction. And ultimately, it will accomplish nothing — my people will be here in minutes, and you will suffer the same fate as the rest of your wretched pack, except there will be none left to remember you."

Cromus paused, feeling uncertain. How did she know who his father was?

"Did you cry for your packmate?" she continued, a mocking tone creeping into her voice. "Did you cry when we gunned him down like the filthy animal he was, or are such emotions beyond monsters like you?"

Cromus snarled and started forward again, his anger quick to rise to the surface. There was much he would have said if his vocal cords had not been fully lupine, but the words were impossible to form without changing back to something more human. He would have to settle for such bestial sounds of rage, and the acts of violence he intended to indulge in.

"And who will cry for you? The vampires? Not likely,
given your history. The ghouls? They only hunger for flesh.
Poor lost wolf, doomed to die alone. Your name will soon be
forgotten, your race finally brought to an end. Maybe you
should run, so you can live for a while longer."

The werewolf was about to lunge and rip the taunts
from her throat, her words turned to gurgles of panic as
the blood pumped from the gaping hole he would make of
her neck. But once more, the sound of gunshots filled his
ears, the backup she'd called for appearing just as she'd
promised. And for the second night running, there were too
many of them for him to fight, forcing him to flee yet again.

Her screams of rage filled his ears as he made his
escape, the reprimands she yelled at the other Slayers
clearly audible over the din of the music still blasting out
from the nearby house. It seemed they'd panicked when
they'd seen him moving towards her, shooting before they'd
had time to aim and giving him the warning he'd needed to
flee before it was too late. No doubt she would order them
to hunt him down, but her shouts were already growing
fainter as he headed back to the sanctuary of the fields
where he would find somewhere to hide and rest awhile
before resuming his own hunt.

***

Cromus spent the rest of the night dreaming of revenge.
It took all his willpower not to give in to the rage and the
bloodlust when he awoke the next day, such dark emotions
stronger than ever with the moon only hours away from
rising as full. But he had not survived for so long by being
reckless, and so he returned to his human form once more.

Continuing to search the streets as a wolf was not an
option in broad daylight, so he went in search of clothes
and a stream to wash in, though he made another quick kill
to replenish his energy first. Once his hunger was sated, he
cleaned the thickest of the blood off, the water running red
with the taint of all the lives he'd taken over the last two
days. There would be plenty more to follow if he had his

way, but he reminded himself the boy was more important than avenging Magnus. No amount of bloodshed would bring his fallen brother back, and the boy would soon become his new brother and ensure the continuation of their race — as long as they both survived long enough for him to turn the lad.

A few people had washing hung on lines in their gardens, and with his abilities, it was simple enough to sneak up and steal what he needed to pass as human. Then he took to the streets again and risked returning to the area where he'd found the trail the night before.

There was an even fresher trail that morning. A surge of excitement filled Cromus as he closed in on his prey, his thoughts still turning to vengeance. If only Magnus had survived as well, but they would soon honor his memory. His heart beat faster with the anticipation of such slaughter, the boy almost within his grasp.

The wolven descendant must have realized he was being followed because he turned then, his eyes wide as he took in the demonic visage the werewolf must have presented. Even clothed and relatively clean, Cromus knew there was still a sense of his predatory nature. He'd seen it in his own reflection in the hunger that prowled behind his eyes, even before they bled back to their lupine amber. But as their eyes met, he was given another surprise. For this was not the boy of his visions. This lad was younger, and suddenly he recognized the scent he was breathing in as not just the one he'd detected with wolf blood but familiar on another level as well. The child was a relative of none other than the female Slayer he'd encountered the night before!

The boy had already begun to back away, perhaps regretting the decision to wander the streets alone. Cromus merely smiled his wolfish smile. What were the odds of finding not one, but two wolven descendants in the same town? And he could think of no better form of revenge than turning the family of one of his enemies.

His prey turned to run, but with the lad's inner wolf still

dormant and awaiting the bite to set him free, he never stood a chance of escape. Cromus was on him in minutes, sinking his fangs into the soft flesh of the boy's neck and passing on his father's blessing.

A scream and footsteps running toward them forced him to abandon his new packmate and flee once again, but no matter. Sometimes one bite was not enough, but in this instance, he sensed it was. The boy's fate was sealed. He would soon die to the bite, only to be brought back by the wolf in him, changed and stronger for the awakening of the lupine side to his nature. It was in his blood. It was his destiny...

***

Cromus resumed his search for the one from his dreams on the other side of the town. It was here he encountered the Slayer woman for the second time, just a few hours after biting her kin. And like the night before, he had no forewarning of her coming, though there was some safety to be had in the number of witnesses on the streets around them. He did not think she would pull a gun on him in the sight of so many people, not if the Slayers still wanted to keep the existence both of themselves and the creatures they hunted a secret from the rest of mankind.

"You again," he growled. "How did you recognize me this time?"

"Did you really think you could bite a child while wearing your human mask and get away with it?" she hissed, her eyes filled with a new level of hatred. "We saw everything."

"Who is he to you? Son? Nephew? Cousin?"

"It no longer matters who he was. If he turns under the full moon tonight, he will be no more than another slavering monster to kill, before he kills us."

Cromus smiled to himself, enjoying the thought of her being forced to murder her own blood to prevent another werewolf running loose and taking more human lives. But the survival of his race was more important than his own personal need for vengeance, and so he said, "There is another option. Let me take the boy, and I swear you need never see us again. We will leave the country and make our home as far from humanity as possible, where we will live off the animals of the land for as long as we are left in peace."

"Leave you alive, and at risk of infecting any more people with wolf DNA we might have missed? I think not. Especially when we are so close to ridding the earth of your unnatural taint at long last. But I will make you a counteroffer. Come with me and submit yourself to experimentation, then perhaps our scientists can find a cure and save the child from the same fate as his brother."

"And why would I do that? If escape is not an option this time, then I would rather you give me a quick, clean death now and be done with it."

The woman reached into her handbag, glancing around to check no one was paying them any attention. She withdrew something wrapped in bloody tissue and offered it to him without any words by way of explanation, letting him take it from her and discover what it was for himself.

Cromus had the sense to shield the thing from the view of any who happened to pass by, though most kept to the opposite side of the street, perhaps subconsciously aware that something was amiss and eager to keep their distance. The package was only small, the tissue sticking to it where the blood had dried as he peeled back the wrapping to reveal a severed toe. A human might have recoiled in horror and dropped the gruesome digit, but the werewolf merely turned it between his fingers, noting how it had been removed with a clean-cut, the flesh dull and lifeless around the ghastly paleness of the blood-streaked bone.

Sight didn't tell him much, so he raised the ghoulish offering to his nose, feeling a jolt in his stomach as he recognized the scent.

"Yes, your packmate is alive," the woman confirmed. "And if you agree to come with me so we might search for a cure, I give you my word we will release him. You shall be taking his place."

Cromus eyed her with distrust. He sniffed the toe again to be sure, though there was no mistaking that scent, and the flesh showed no signs of the decay that should have set in if it had been removed from Magnus's corpse. But suspicion drove him to ask, "Why do you need me if you've already captured him?"

"Our scientists believe we need the werewolf that passed on the curse if we are to hunt for a cure. And you are the last surviving son of Lycaon; he who was believed to be the first of your race. If you were truly bitten by the first of your kind, your flesh could tell us much of how the lycanthropy is passed from host to host."

"And how do I know you will keep your word once you have me in your custody?"

"You don't."

Trusting her was out of the question, but if there was even the slightest chance his packmate had been taken alive rather than killed, he felt honor-bound to try and save him. Maybe they could even find a way to escape together, and then seek out the boy from his visions. The relative of this female Slayer might have to be left behind, but at least if they left the country as a pack of three, then the journey to Britain would have been a successful one.

He was about to agree when his vision became oddly clouded, and when it cleared, he was no longer on the street but inside a darkened room. There was the outline of something humanoid just ahead of him, but the light filtering in from the doorway behind was too dim to make out who it might be, and the smell of death was overpowering, masking any clues in the being's scent.

He took a step closer, light flooding in as he neared the

room's other occupant and bathing them in its artificial glare. But it did not hurt his eyes as it should have done, and he had no trouble focusing on the shape he'd glimpsed in the darkness.

The man had his back to him, suspended by chains hanging down from the ceiling so that his arms were outstretched above him, his hands hanging limply in the shackles around his wrists. His bare skin was almost flawless except for the birthmark on his right shoulder, a mark Cromus knew well.

"Magnus?" he whispered.

There was no answer. The black-haired werewolf sensed something was wrong, remaining cautious as he stepped round to look upon his brother's face. Except there was no face left to look into.

A gory crater was all that remained of the front of his skull, lined with fragments of shattered bone and pieces of brain matter after it had exploded from the impact of a bullet fired at point-blank range. Somehow, the entry wound had not been visible from behind, or perhaps he'd just not wanted to see it until looking upon the undeniable.

Two more bullets had pierced his pack mate's chest, and there was another hole in his thigh, the three shots that must have felled him. And while he'd lain there at their mercy, they'd shot him in the back of the head. There was no coming back from that kind of damage, even with the healing powers of the transformation.

Cromus felt his anger rising once more as the chamber of horrors faded, and he found himself back on the street with his enemy. And though he had never been blessed with the gift of scrying before, other than the occasional dream vision granted to him, he knew with a terrible certainty what he'd just seen was real.

"Lies," he snarled, throwing the toe back at the woman.

She seemed to have been rendered speechless, shocked

that he had seen through her ruse — so much so that she made no move to stop him as he turned and ran, his anger straining to break free once again. But once again, he forced it back down. The time had still not come for more bloodshed, and his revenge would have to wait a little longer.

***

He knew they would be out hunting him after that. He knew he should leave the town far behind before night fell and they came out in force. But something overruled that strong survival instinct which had kept him alive for so long. Something would not let him leave without finishing what he'd set out to do. And so he continued in his search for the boy.

Dusk came with not even a trace of the other wolven descendant. Cromus could feel the power of the full moon overhead, filling him with energy until he felt more alive than he had all month, every fiber of his being yearning to change into the shape of the wolf so he could run free and hunt the prey he longed for. All it would take was one beam of moonlight, and he would be powerless to resist the transformation back to full wolf form. But the cloud cover was thick that night, and the moon remained hidden behind the blackness of the night sky, made deceptively empty by that overcast blanket. And for as long as the choice remained his, he resisted the temptation to give himself over to the lunar madness, trying to keep his focus on finding the one the Fates seemed to have been steering him toward.

The hour grew late, the streets quiet. Still the moon would not show itself, Cromus' thoughts turning to the child relation of the Slayer woman. He did not envy the uneasy transformation that the boy faced, his body in turmoil as the lycanthropy fought to take hold and force his first change. But in the absence of the moonlight needed to trigger it, his humanity would undoubtedly be fighting against the wolf stirring within. It was regrettable he could not be there to help his new pack member, though the torment it must be causing his enemy still brought him a grim pleasure. He wondered if she would put the boy out of his misery as his body writhed with the wolf straining to break free, or whether she would wait until he did change, only firing the killing shot when his small body lost all trace of its humanity to the might of the beast.

Approaching footsteps reached his ears, the scent of gunpowder marking the humans as armed enemies. He could sense them preparing for a coordinated attack, moving in to trap him in a circle of death. And again, he knew he should not risk the greater odds brought against him, knew he should slip away before they could get into position. But he was done running. If they wanted a fight, he would give them the violence they craved, the slaughter his own darkness desired. He would have his revenge for his fallen pack.

Cromus ripped off the stolen clothes and finally allowed the transformation his body had been pressing for all night, embracing it now and welcoming the anger that rose with it. The rush of the life force in his veins seemed to sing with the call of the hidden moon, his blood boiling not just with the strength of his wolfish nature but also with the rage gripping him, voicing itself in a bestial roar as black fur burst from his skin like the physical manifestation of that darkness of his soul. Pain lanced through his gut, forcing him to his knees as organs began to shift, while the familiar deep ache of his bones stabbed through his entire body as some began to shorten while others lengthened into a more lupine shape. Long ago, it had been an almost unbearable agony to be endured three nights every month while the moon reigned above, but no more.

The odd sensation of his ears growing pointed and sliding upward was no longer a discomfort. Teeth elongating into fangs and nails into claws brought indescribable pleasure, and the throb of his face stretching outward into the powerful muzzle of his lupine side only heightened his excitement for the hunt and the kill. But he severed the flow of primal energy before it could take him to full wolf form, choosing to remain a hybrid of wolf and man once again, for as long as the moon kept out of sight.

New strength rippled through the werewolf as he rose to his full height, eyes blazing amber in his skull with the rage coursing through him. The humans were almost upon him now, these mortal fools who dared to take the role of the hunter when they were born to be prey, especially on this night that belonged to his race. He didn't need the touch of moonlight to feel its call, and he would answer in blood and death, as he'd been made to do.

The Slayers did not open fire as one, lacking the discipline to work as a unit. One of the men panicked, attacking before the rest of them were ready in response to the fear Cromus's presence invoked. And who could blame them? He was the real predator, his body made for killing. He needed no guns or blades like these pitiful pretenders, and too late, it seemed they were beginning to realize just how vulnerable their frail mortal bodies were without their crafted weapons.

Cromus charged the man, taking only minor flesh wounds as he bounded toward his target, two bullets grazing his arms and a third nicking his shoulder. The pounding of his enemy's heart came as a summons, a call as strong as the moon beckoning him to the slaughter and driving him to greater acts of brutality than any real wolf would indulge in. Then he was on him, sinking his fangs into his victim's flesh and shaking his great head from side to side so that his teeth shredded muscle and sinew with devastating efficiency. He worried the man's arm until it was reduced to bloody tatters, the bone snapping with a sickening crack from the force of his bite. His prey was too lost in the world of pain and horror he'd dragged him into to remain a threat, and he wanted these people to suffer for what they'd done to his pack. So he left him shaking and screaming and moved on to his next victim, attacking with similar savagery.

One by one, the humans fell to his predatory might, ruined limbs pumping their lives out onto the concrete, a spreading pool of blood appearing much darker under the dim streetlights than the crimson it should have been. Ribs poked through shredded torsos and torn faces, robbed of their human features, cried for help that would not come. Even with medical intervention, they had to know the Reaper was near, their chances of survival slim when their bodies had been transformed into ghoulish sculptures of their own mortality. And still, Cromus savaged his victims until the last dying breath rattled through those broken bodies, the near silence left in its wake like a void their screams had been sucked into.

His bloodlust slaked for the time being, the werewolf turned away and loped toward safer hunting grounds, his only regret that the female Slayer had not been among them. But there was still time to unleash his fury on her yet and to find the boy. Not that night, though. He felt staying in the town would be too risky, so he returned to the fields, where they would be less likely to find him. There, he would await the dawn when the sun would bring more human shields to hide behind as he continued his hunt for the wolven descendant. And he felt confident he would find him eventually. It was only a matter of time.

***

A man once again, Cromus found himself wandering the same streets he'd already searched, with no greater success. The day was almost spent when his path took him back to the town center, the sun low in the sky and surely only a couple of hours from setting, the moon soon to take its place and call him back to the hunt. He'd all but resigned himself to having to wait at least one more day before finding the lad, when finally the scent he sought carried to him on the breeze.

Cromus felt a sense of triumph as he followed that scent down the street he was currently on and around the corner to the shops lining the main road, his quarry just up ahead.

261

He was granted a quick glimpse of the boy's face as the lad turned toward the girl he was walking with, enough to confirm this was the one Cromus had seen in his dreams. But he would not make the same mistake as he'd made with the child he'd already bitten, determined this time to grab the wolven descendant before the Slayers or any other humans could intervene, and to do that he would have to wait until the boy was somewhere quieter than the busy road. So he trailed far enough behind that they would not realize he was stalking them, his sensitive ears picking up every word of their conversation, though most of it seemed to be teenage nonsense. He began to doubt his visions when they reached the side of the road and debated how this wolven descendant, perhaps the last hope for werewolf kind, was going to die. Could this really be the future of lycanthropy?

"Maybe I will end up splattered across somebody's windscreen, I don't care," the boy was saying. "Or maybe I'll be flattened on the road by a bus, squashed roadkill."

"Yeah, well, just don't get yourself killed while I'm around 'cause I'm not ready to die trying to save your sorry arse yet, okay?" his friend answered.

But at least Cromus had learned his name, the female referring to him as "Nick."

After a while, they came to a large building teeming with humans of all ages. Nick and his friend went through the main entrance, leaving the werewolf to wait in whatever shadows he could find outside.

From what he understood of the modern world, it was some kind of a complex filled with various merchants and taverns and places to indulge in other pastimes. The sort of human establishment he would be out of place in since he had no money to spend on whatever leisurely activities it had to offer, let alone food and drink. And if the faintest sliver of moonlight found its way inside and brought on the transformation, he would soon find himself surrounded by enemies once more while the boy slipped away from him.

So he kept his head down and wandered around the area while he waited, though he didn't stray too far for fear of missing his chance to turn the lad that evening.

Night fell, but the moon was hidden once more, and again, he chose to keep his human form while it was behind the clouds. He caught a glimpse of it once or twice, climbing ever higher as the hours passed, though it did not break completely free of that wispy blanket, and he was able to fight the urge to shift a while longer.

Finally, the boy emerged with the same girl he'd entered with, plus four others. The moon chose that moment to find a gap in the blackness to shine through, and Cromus sank to his knees as the familiar pain took hold, unseen by the group of youths. His body was beginning to change to full wolf, and there was nothing he could do to fight it, though he cursed the bad timing, knowing it would be more challenging to kidnap the boy on four legs rather than two. But it seemed the Fates were with him that night, for a moment later, the moon passed back into darkness, and he was able to reverse the changes with his clothes intact.

His luck continued, the teenagers foolish enough to walk to their homes instead of letting their parents pick them up, and he decided to strike the moment they left the main roads behind. Their conversation was filled with more inane teenage subjects while they walked, and he learned little more of consequence as he tailed them from behind, but all that really mattered was the boy's lineage. With both of them descended from wolf rather than ape, Cromus would pass on their gift, and they would soon be hunting together beneath their lunar master. It was in their blood.

They had not gone far when Nick came to a sudden stop. The black-haired werewolf darted behind the hedgerow growing on the side of the road just as the boy turned to peer uneasily into the darkness, seemingly sensing he was being followed. Cromus decided it was time to make his move while there was no one else around, or risk missing his opportunity. And the longer he stayed in the town waiting for his chance, the greater the threat of the Slayers, for they would surely keep sending more and more until one of them managed to land a killing shot.

He crept along the hedgerow, intending to step out in front of the group and send them running back down the street, away from the help they might find in the town center. Despite his love of human flesh, he had no intention of killing the five other humans. He wanted nothing more than to grab Nick and turn him, then get him as far from the town as he possibly could before the next night. Then, when the full moon rose for the third and final time that month, the boy would experience his first transformation. Assuming the night sky was clear, of course.

But his luck was quick to turn, the moon breaking free of the clouds a second time and the throb in his stomach beginning anew. The transformation was coming whether he wanted it or not, and he stumbled back out onto the side of the road, running past the group with his head down, forced to rethink his plan. He heard one of the girls asking if they should help as he sought somewhere safer to change, picking a darkened footpath devoid of any other life more substantial than the rodents cowering in the vegetation around him.

Once it was clear he would have to spend the rest of the night as a full wolf, he embraced the transformation yet again, the changes coming a little quicker than if he'd tried to resist, though it was never as smooth at full moon as a voluntary shift. The pain was more noticeable without the anger ruling him, the bones in his hands and feet elongating to form paws with a throb of such intensity it would have made most beings pass out. Other bones ground together, most noticeably his femurs, which were becoming shorter and more suited to walking on all fours, while his face stretched into a muzzle once more and a tail shot out of his spine.

His internal anatomy altered once again, organs shifting to become fully lupine, until moments later, the pain faded and hunger crashed over him, the desire to rip into human flesh returned. But he fought it as he circled back round to cut off the youths on the next street, focused on the boy.

They could only stare in shock when they laid eyes on him, and for a moment, they each stood frozen, the humans struggling with their fear of coming face to face with a dangerous predator, and he still wrestled the hunger which demanded he slaughter the five who would only ever be prey. But the moment soon passed, and the humans began to back away, breaking into a run when he charged them.

One of the girls turned to look back and crashed into a lamppost, Nick and the girl he'd walked to the complex with running back to help her. But she was never in any danger, Cromus fixated on his target and resisting the temptation to attack any of the others, passing the stricken female without even slowing. Nothing was going to stop him from turning the lad now, least of all the small stone which bounced harmlessly off his side.

Nick raised an arm to try and protect himself, and Cromus latched onto it, but he was wary of causing too much damage and was careful not to bite down too hard, his teeth barely raking the skin beneath the jacket the boy wore. Suddenly the garment was hanging limply in his jaws, but he couldn't be sure the slight scratch his fangs had made was enough to awaken the lad's inner wolf, so he pounced, sending them both crashing to the concrete. There, he fought the outstretched arms trying to keep his jaws away from the vulnerable flesh of the boy's throat, but while still human, the lad was no match for him, and his fangs were soon sliding into his neck.

Something stabbed into his shoulder seconds later. Cromus yelped and twisted his head to see the glass from a broken beer bottle protruding from his flesh, but he couldn't reach it with his jaws, and the pain called his rage back into being. The friend was determined to drive him off, and for that, she would die. Or she would have done, had it not been for the sudden scent of something worse than Slayers. His enemies had returned, and he had no option but to run.

***

The glass in his shoulder was a constant source of discomfort, throbbing as he limped across the town and slowing him down. But his enemies were coming for him, and stopping to lick his wounds was not an option. Cromus would be lucky to escape with his life now.

His flight took him across private land, its borders defined by a fence crowned with vicious-looking metal spikes. There was plenty of vegetation, which might have offered cover if his pursuers had only been human, but there was that scent again, carrying a hint of the grave though this being was not quite dead. He knew all too well what manner of creature hunted him, but they were supposed to be allies in these desperate times, united against their common enemy for as long as the Slayers posed a threat. Yet there could be no doubt about it, this vampire had chosen to side with the humans. And Cromus only had one word for that, his fangs bared at the very thought. *Traitor!*

Too late, the werewolf realized he was cornered. The vampire had all the advantages if it came to a fair fight, but there was nowhere left to run unless he could jump over the fence. But with the glass embedded in his shoulder, he was not sure he would clear it, and landing on those spiked tips would only weaken him further, his body not able to heal until the transformation reversed with the dawn. And then another scent carried to him, and he turned to peer out through the vegetation and the bars of the fence to look at the street on the other side.

Unlikely though it seemed, the Fates had delivered the boy to him a second time. If Cromus could just reach him, he might be able to find a way to grab his new pack member and flee with him as he'd first planned, before his enemies had driven him off. It would mean he'd have to take his chances with the fence, but seeing Nick walking just on the other side of it filled him with fresh confidence. Their eyes locked, the boy's filling with a fear which drove him to his knees to search the ground for another makeshift weapon like the broken bottle his friend had found. And Cromus knew then that this was destiny, and somehow they would escape together as a pack.

So the werewolf bunched the powerful muscles in his three good legs and leaped as high as his injury allowed, but something was wrong. An invisible force seemed to tug at him as he sailed through the air, pulling him back just enough that his momentum was lost much sooner than it should have been, his weight suddenly pressing down on the top of the fence, those wicked spikes impaling his chest. Another yelp of pain tore itself from his throat, blood gushing down the metal, holding him there. His breath turned ragged, rattling through punctured lungs, while his heart struggled to continue pumping around the sharp object stabbing through it, forcing more blood from his body and hastening the shroud of darkness closing over him.

Despite the full moon overhead, the transformation back to human kicked in as Cromus hung there, helpless and feeling his life slip away. But with the damage to his heart, it would not save him.

"He will be your undoing," he heard the cunning man warn him once again, as though Aran were there with him in his final moments. His eyes locked on the boy he was going to die for as that spark of life began to fade, a last smile flickering across lips wet with his own blood. Cromus had done his part. The blackness closed in, and he died knowing that at least his father's legacy would live on.

ABOUT THE AUTHOR

Nick Stead began writing at the age of fifteen. His love of horror and werewolves in particular led to the creation of Hybrid, following a brainstorming session with his cousin to get him started on the first three chapters. Twelve years later at twenty seven and after two major redrafts, his dream of seeing Hybrid published was finally realized.

Now thirty one, he has completed the first three books in the Hybrid series and is hard at work on the fourth. He has also written several short stories and has had work published in anthologies, as well as a short story arc in Bryn Hammond's The Complete History of the Howling.

Nick lives with his two cats in Huddersfield, England, where he spends most days chained to his desk, writing to the scream of heavy metal guitars.

For more information about Nick, Hybrid, and other works visit:

www.nick-stead.co.uk

or find him on Facebook at -
https://www.facebook.com/officialnickstead

and Twitter @nick_stead

Evernight Circle

Matt Serafini

Chris wakes up, startled, hammering heart, clipped breaths. The dream crumbles like sand as he tries to keep it intact. It's gone like that, leaving Chris distracted by the blur of seemingly permanent forest as Charlotte speeds on. She never asks if he's all right.

"Where are we?"

"Passed some signs for Billings a ways back," she says. "An hour ago."

"You're sure?"

Charlotte's hands tighten around the steering wheel. Her knuckles glow white. Just like that, there's tension again.

Chris isn't going to play that game. "If that's true," he says, throat climbing over her sighs, "then, I was going to compliment you on making good time."

A long pull of silence. Even the smallest things have to be hard. "Thanks."

Chris turns toward the window. He grumbles something about "forgetting it" and watches acres of desolation roll past, certain now this is the biggest mistake of his life.

They'd gone west, leaving Philly behind and in it, every single person they'd ever known. Chris doesn't know why. What about *this* is worth saving? When he and Charlotte lay together at night, stiffer than boards in bed, he mulls it over without ever finding an answer.

"We're close," Charlotte says.

The car slows and rolls off what passes for the main road out here. Headlights stare into an eternal forest.

Overhead, dark clouds slash the sky like animal claws. The GPS stopped working miles ago. The flashing icon on the screen is a blue car circling a screen of deep white.

Charlotte cracks the door. Immediately, there's a dog's growl.

"Jesus," Chris says.

"Forget it." Charlotte slams the door back into place and points at the glove box. "Hand me the map."

The folded gas station paper sits on top of the owner's manual, a stockpile of Dunkin' straws, and extra napkins from all the fast food they'd hit on this cross-country sojourn. Charlotte snatches it with a vicious sigh.

Chris turns toward the backseat as she searches for bearings. He stares at their belongings. Fifteen boxes, crammed tight, seat-to-ceiling.

"We need to go back the other way," she says. "Guess I missed a turn."

Six snarling dogs stand in the middle of the road as the car loops around. Their mouths flash hungry grins.

Even with the windows up, Chris hears harsh growls vibrating in their throats. "Drive toward them," he says. "They'll move."

Charlotte edges forward, tires churning on gravel. The dogs stand their ground, and headlights chase every last shadow off their agitated bodies. Mottled fur streaked with blood. Accordion snouts. Saliva dangles off their chins like translucent beards.

Damn things refuse to move.

Chris' balled fist hits the horn. Finally, the dogs scatter for safety just beyond the lights. Their growls commence there, somehow louder.

It buys Charlotte the space she needs to go back the way they came. "There's something you don't see every day."

"It's probably business as usual out here."

Her side-eye is Ginsu sharp. Chris looks away for fear of being slashed. *I can't even joke around without it being read as a warning shot*, he thinks. Because in her mind, it's more than a joke. He's diminishing her accomplishments, she'd say. Laughing at her career because she's taken up "working for the man."

What Chris doesn't have the heart to tell Charlotte is that this insecurity haunts her head. Not his. He made peace with reality long ago. You can't be rebellious twentysomethings when you're mid-thirties. Try and do that, and you just become assholes.

They have to retrace the last eight miles. Charlotte takes it slow, determined to catch the elusive turn. Each time she brings the car to a near stop, the specter of snarling dogs grumble in the distance. Which would be worse? Those same dogs following mile after mile? Or an area so overloaded with them that it's another pack looking to tear their throats clear.

The stacked boxes in the backseat prevent them from checking the rearview, and neither of them feels like sticking their heads out the window to see where the noise is coming from.

"Here it is!" Charlotte says, more triumphant than she's sounded in years. Cuts the wheel. Overhanging trees slouch. Branches scrape their roof as they pass beneath. This road looks brand new—pavement that's smoother than a newborn's ass—but also secretive, as if determined to remain hidden away from the world.

Chris drops the window a couple of inches to confirm the newfound silence. The growling dogs aren't following.

The road climbs over treetops and wraps around a small

mountain, where manmade lights glow in the distance. Moonshine bathes Charlotte's face. She senses Chris' eyes and glances over, managing a movie star smile as she sparkles. In this moment, she suddenly seems renewed.

Chris feels relief. For a second, their chemistry resurfaces.

A wordless moment passes.

The road evens out as it takes them to the summit. The area here is clear of all foliage—just flat earth and those distant lights growing brighter by the mile.

"Evernight Circle," she says. The car slows before an iron gate. "I think we're home."

A broad-chested man steps from the vinyl-sided gatehouse. Charlotte puts the window down, and he leans in, forearm on the door. Grins wide as he looks them over.

The tattoo on his arm is a jewel-hilted dagger with one strand of blood wrapped all the way around it.

"Let me guess," he says. "Charlotte and Christopher Tepper?" His accent is vaguely European.

"That's us." Charlotte rummages through her purse, but the guard waves his hand.

"We got your personnel file," he says. "So no worries. You're who you say. I see that." An overly familiar grin as he points to the road. "Through the gate, straight down. Number five." He drops a key ring into her lap and pushes off the door. Disappears inside the guardhouse, and a second later, the gate slowly begins to groan.

Charlotte waves her thanks as they pass into their new community. There's a strip mall just beyond the gates, exclusive to residents of Evernight Circle. A grocery store and pharmacy, a pizza shop, a couple of smaller storefronts Chris cannot make out at this distance.

The paved road leads to a small rotary and, beyond it, a

strip of suburban homes in various stages of construction. They pass six or seven in-progress lots before reaching a cul-de-sac of five completed homes.

Charlotte pulls into the closest driveway, number five, and kills the engine. She knocks her head back and takes a deep breath like she's been holding it the entire drive.

"We made it," she says, then laughs. "Fifteen hours? Holy shit, I'm so tired."

Chris cracks the door and steps out, glad to get boots on the ground. "What do you think?" he says. "Leave the unpacking for daylight?"

Charlotte climbs out and stretches her fingers toward the sky. Her back cracks and her nose puffs. The air up here is like nothing else. Her eyes close as she savors it, grinning over the hood of the car.

"How about breaking in the shower?"

***

Their home is partially furnished, per the agreement.

A kitchen of brand-new stainless-steel appliances, a dining room set that neither of them much likes and a king-size memory foam mattress that sits in the center of the floor inside the master suite. Bed frame not included.

They can't believe how much energy they've stashed away as they break in their new home. They break in the master shower. They break in the staircase. They break in the kitchen island top, and finally, break in their new bed.

Charlotte sleeps like a brick, using Chris as a pillow. Her sweaty cheek is pressed against his chest hair, and the rhythm of her slow beating heart calms him. Yet even now, he can't sleep. He tries, and maybe he dozes a few times, but the panic is always worse at night because there's nothing to distract you from the truth.

The truth that something bad is going to happen. He's

carried that feeling like a spare tire for years. Each time Charlotte loses her temper, forcing him to lose his in retaliation... dogs more rabid than those wild packs back there. The reality of them has always been uncomfortable. And yet, neither will address it. They only keep moving forward like nothing's wrong, trying new things and hoping for the best while deep down—

A knock at the front door roils them, morning come early.

Charlotte's eyes flutter and then widen. "Is someone knocking?" she asks. "What time is... oh crap!" She springs up, suddenly wide-awake. She reaches around for her clothes and finds only Chris' tee. It drops just below the curve of her bottom, and she's apparently okay with that. Hurries downstairs without giving Chris a shot at getting ready.

He sits in the raw at the top of the steps, listening to Charlotte's employer roll out the red carpet. Central Alchemical, or centrAL as their logo reads, has sent an emissary from the public relations office, a woman named Dayne, whose demeanor is defined as "two cups of caffeine before eight am."Her jittery spiel is a hundred decibels louder than it needs to be, focused mainly on area amenities and company perks.

Charlotte attempts to explain away their clothes strewn all over the house, but Dayne only giggles over it and continues. "You can choose to have our shuttle bring you to work," she says. "It's a luxury afforded only to those in Evernight Circle, and you can set a specific arrival time so that it comes when you're ready." She taps the paperwork placed on the counter. "Instructions for setting up your MycentrAL app can be found in here."

"You're going to spoil me," Charlotte says.

"That's the idea," Dayne says. "We want you to get the most of your new life."

"I intend to."

"Good," Dayne says. "Great! The company wants you to get situated before you get started, though we are asking you to attend an onboarding presentation tomorrow. Nothing crazy. A little paperwork, a tour of the facilities located just up the hill, and a special a meet-and-greet with senior management. Many of whom are on site this week and eager to meet you."

"Would love to," Charlotte says.

"I'll let you get settled, then. The shuttle will see you at nine tomorrow."

And that's that. Chris comes downstairs once Dayne is gone, and Charlotte strips his shirt off and hands it over.

"Come on," she says. "Let's get unpacked."

***

Chris dreams that night of hungry dogs. Of snarled mouths, red paws, and one silhouetted figure, slender and obviously feminine, standing beyond them like the animals are protecting her. Like they'll never let him reach her.

He springs up in bed, sucking air. Lacquered in sweat, not from heat, but panic. He should be glad to be awake, realizing he's safe and sound in the comfort of his new home. But he feels worse now because the animal snarls aren't inside his head.

They're outside.

"Do you hear that?"

Charlotte is on her side, rolled so far over she's about to fall off the bed.

Chris gets up and goes downstairs. Just beyond the front door is where the snarling is loudest. He peers from the kitchen window. The streetlamps are on, but they're muted and seem to be mostly for cosmetic purposes. The snarls are as constant as a lawnmower.

He walks around the house and pulls each window curtain down, desperate to blot the noise. From the living room, the moonlight is so bright that it projects forest branches as a gnarled claw on the naked wall behind him.

Chris is nearly back to the bedroom when a full-throated howl rockets into the sky and stops him cold. The hairs on his neck stand at attention. Not because of the noise, though. But because of the sight in front of him.

For a second, he swears Charlotte has been watching him through squinted eyes. A thin smile baked into the edges of her mouth.

"You up?" he says.

But she's back to sleep or pretending to be. Even as the howling goes on.

He climbs back beneath the thin linen sheet, nestling into the supposed comfort of his pillow. But he can't stop hearing it, even after it ceases and Evernight Circle goes back to silence.

It's a long time getting back to sleep. And as soon as he does, he's back to dreaming about dogs.

***

Charlotte's gone when he wakes up. The note on the refrigerator says, "Orientation—be home later!"

Evernight Circle is ever determined to impress. The concierge service left a carafe of fresh-squeezed orange juice on the counter, along with a foil-wrapped breakfast sandwich and two sleeves of perfectly crisped hash browns.

Chris eats breakfast while fiddling with his phone. Has to connect to centrAL's wi-fi, which he doesn't especially care to do, given that he's a VPN and DuckDuckGo kind of guy, but figures he can make do for now. He texts a few friends to let them know he's arrived safely and waits for replies that never come.

The thought of fiddling with boxes for an entire day is too depressing to consider. He changes into jogging shorts and decides to foot it around "town" to get the lay of the land. There's no better way to feel at home than to know what's around.

There are four additional homes on Evernight Circle. Each one is allegedly occupied, though he's seen no evidence of this. If any of his neighbors owned cars, they're cloistered inside garages. And nobody ever seems to come or go.

Chris jogs the cul-de-sac for a closer look, thinking it might be nice to say hello to another face or two. The house directly beside his is number three, and all of the shades are drawn to the sills. He dares himself off the pavement and crosses the yard.

"Hello," he calls, more for the benefit of any spying eyes and ears. "I think I heard some water running, and I just wanted to do the neighborly thing and let you know."

He sees inside through the bottom of the one curtain that hasn't dropped all the way down. There's almost no interior decoration that he can see, and he wonders if he isn't mistaken about anyone living here.

Number one is next. That house sits at the very center of the curve. It appears similarly vacant at first, but as Chris trots up the stone path to the porch, he sees the front door beyond the screen partition isn't a door at all but rather a solid steel hatch. An ill-placed eyesore, unnerving in this AstroTurfed suburbia.

Each of the windows is barred. The iron is painted to match the house's pale crème vinyl siding to camouflage it more.

Chris remembers the howling from last night and thinks whoever lives here has heard it more than once. Thinks he needs to speak with them. From the way this place is reinforced, there's a pretty good chance that terrible noise is more than just a freak occurrence.

The house with the brass number two on the mailbox is mostly nondescript. Chris grows more brazen, half doubting that anyone lives in any of these pine boxes.

He goes straight to the door, this one typical fiberglass, and knocks twice. A startled bustle sounds just behind it, a perked and waking animal. Chris knocks again, and the commotion grows louder, clacking nails failing to catch on a wood floor.

Chris waits a full minute and figures no one's coming to answer. Then he starts across the lawn toward the fourth house. One of the front windows is slightly raised. He starts for it, calling, "Hello," as he goes. "I'm new to the area was hoping you might be able to—"

Somebody stands just beyond the window there, veiled only by billowing curtains flapping around like startled ghosts.

"Hi," Chris repeats, his mind cycling, eager to fill the air with something, anything else.

The air is already filled with an elongated, scraping groan.

"You okay?"

The silhouette lifts a hand to the glass, and Chris sees the outline of a pulsing forearm. All of it a prelude to three simple words:

"Take the bite."

Before Chris can question it, the silhouette falls away, screaming in surround sound.

The startling noise - screams layered on top of other screams - pushes Chris into the street, where he takes his cell phone from his pocket.

And dials 911.

**

Chris retreats back to his side of the street. Drops to the curb and waits for the police.

He never takes his eyes off that window, tensing for something to come smashing through it.

The police arrive in just under three minutes.

Only it's not the police. The approaching sedan is branded with centrAL's logo. It rolls up casually, no sirens blaring, no lights flashing, and pulls directly into the driveway. Two uniformed men get out. One wipes donut power away from his mouth with the back of his hand before he goes to the door. The other comes across the street sucking iced coffee through a straw like this ain't nothing but an afternoon stroll.

"Concerned neighbor," he says, blotting Chris' view of the number four yard.

Chris recounts what happened. The guard makes bored, thoroughly disinterested faces, barely listening. Does everything but check his phone.

"Won't be the last time it happens," the uniform says. "Gentleman living there rarely comes out. Works graveyard shift at centrAL. Prone to seizures. Sometimes he forgets to take his medication, like today, and... well, it's good that you called."

"He's okay now?" Chris asks.

"We're going to contact his supervisor, see if HR can't make better arrangements to ensure he's getting the treatment he needs. On behalf of the company, we apologize for the disturbance."

The officer spins and walks back to the car. Once he's all the way there, he turns back. "centrAL thanks you for being the kind of neighbor we pride ourselves on having."

The other officer comes out of the house and closes the door behind him. Tries to knob again to ensure it's locked. He trots back to the car at the same time, leaving a silent house in his wake—no more groans.

But now that window is all the way down.

The car makes the circle, and both officers wave as they pass.

Chris watches them coast off down the street.

"The same thing happened to me when we first moved here."

A female voice startles Chris into a clumsy jostle.

A blonde steps down off number three's porch. She wears a loose patterned skirt and a white top. Her heels clop down the sidewalk in a way that pleases Chris' ears.

"I should get used to it?" Chris says.

"Depends." She shrugs. "When I first moved here, I used to hear his growls all night long. Sounded like the guy would stand in front of his opened window, gargling fucking mouthwash or something."

"Security told me he worked nights."

"Yeah," she says. "Now, he does. Pretty sure they rotated his ass because the nine-to-fivers were sick of putting up with it." She gives a lopsided smirk as she approaches. "Ashlee," she says with the offer of her hand.

"Chris."

"Welcome, neighbor. Meant to come over yesterday, but move-in days are tough. Didn't want to be a bother."

"Glad for a friendly face," he says. "Was beginning to feel like nobody really lived here. One big Potemkin Village or something."

"Oh, hey, I'll give you the tour." Ashlee points to number

one. "Gregor May lives there. You'll never see him because he works a hundred hours a week up at centrAL— practically a slave. Oh, wait, I mean, he's upper management. Only moved here to show the peons that everyone in the company's a team player."

"Right," Chris says. "So when cube slave Johnny Smith hears he needs to work eighty hours every other week, they can run a guilt trip down on him. *We're all doing it, don't you know*?"

Ashlee laughs and slides her finger over to yard number two. "The Sundstroms live there. Kind of old-timers. He's facilities, and she's an artiste. What that really means is she stays up all night binging Netflix and making really long Facebook posts."

Apt, Chris thinks. Covers just about every person back home who considered themselves a practitioner of the arts.

"Now, the charming gentleman you tattled on is Harry Freeman."

"Are you on the company dole?"

"I'm a trophy wife." Ashlee makes air quotes. "My husband works up there, though."

"What's he do?"

"He's a buyer. The rest of the company hates him because every external purchase needs to pass his desk."

Chris begins to ask what she does, but Ashlee reaches out and touches his arm. A surprising burst of contact that stops his question dead.

"Have a drink?" she says. "Nothing funny, just... well, save me the trouble of bringing you a bottle of wine later on."

"Yes, please."

"Right this way, then." Her hips do a cute little sway as

she walks, and Chris likes the smooth and clean shape of her thighs—plenty of which is visible beneath her sashing skirt. She seems determined to keep ahead of him, and Chris wonders if her motions aren't for his benefit.

They go inside, and he sits at their kitchen counter. Their homes share almost exactly the same layout, only this one's in reverse.

Ashlee is quick to return with two oversized wine glasses and places the bottle between them. She twists the spiraled blade down inside the cork and pops it free. "Was beginning to feel like this was the most suburban place on earth," she says. "Like I was going to have to have to get addicted to opiates in order to have a proper life struggle."

"Goals," Chris says.

They clank their rims together, and she smiles, tilting the glass to her lips.

"Life that good here?"

"Good as anywhere."

"Happy to meet you, Ashlee," Chris says. He listens as she fills him in on life on Evernight Circle. How the grocery store is well stocked and reasonably priced. Concierge service is effective in getting other items very quickly. But she cautions about ordering anything too personal because they use Amazon Prime and then just slash open the shipping boxes and deliver the items in person.

"Isn't that sort of obtrusive?" Chris says.

"You think?" she scoffs. "You want to buy a dildo, you're going to look into the eyes of some judgmental deliveryman who'll wonder what your o-face looks like."

"Jesus."

"Just saying, you're buying batteries, go for it. You want sex toys, UPS is still your friend, even if it takes a little longer because all those packages sit in the gatehouse until centrAL feels like sorting it."

centrAL provides most things, turns out. Full-service generators, appliances, and they'll even deliver breakfast with a simple phone call and request if you want it. All of it complimentary—centrAL's token of appreciation for its most loyal employees.

They polish off one whole bottle, and Ashlee quickly replenishes their supply. This time with an older vintage that's far pricier. Clearly, she's as grateful for company as he is.

Chris steers the conversation to history, asking how long she's lived here. Three months. Nobody's been here more than six, but the company is rapidly looking to expand. Evernight Circle will sustain thirty homes in all, and the company has plans to grow the shopping strip into a full-fledged retail center, so nobody ever has to leave this wonderful little community of recluses.

It's an ambitious plan. One that makes Chris feel a bit better about his decision to follow Charlotte here. centrAL is serious about longevity. You wouldn't sink a billion into this kind of settlement otherwise.

"Can I ask another question," he says once the conversation lulls.

Ashlee shrugs and chugs.

"What's up with the animals around here? Last night, there was howling so loud I couldn't get back to sleep."

"Not sure if you know this, Chris, but we're in the woods."

"Hardy, har, har."

"Like, deep in the woods."

"Okay, it's nothing, right?"

"The animals are shaken up," Ashlee says. "The people

285

in town are pissed off about it. Mad at centrAL. They claim the company displaced a bunch of wildlife to develop this mountain. Some of the creatures get confused and come wandering through their old stomping grounds because they don't understand what's happened. I feel sorry for them."

"That makes sense."

"My advice? Get a shotgun or a rifle." She disappears into the living room and returns with a shotgun cradled in her arms. Brings it to the table and plants it between them. Her fingers stroke the barrel with baffling suggestion.

Chris hasn't touched one of these things ever and doesn't intend to start now. He's always been terrified of guns, figuring he'd blow his head off the second he touched one.

"The gates around this place are pretty serious," she says. "But one night, I'm having a drink in the yard, and a coyote comes snarling out of the forest. I have no idea how it got over the fence... they're supposed to have sensors that trip the company any time there are intruders."

"So, what'd you do?"

"Shot the fucking thing in the face."

"Is that true?"

Ashlee nods. "Only time I've ever killed... anything. But now, I'll fire a warning shot. Usually, that's enough to make them shut it. Clear them out."

Chris thinks about the way he blared on the horn to get those feral dogs to scatter. "How much would it cost to keep you on retainer?" he says. "To come over and fire off a shot next time I hear that kind of noise?"

"You continue being good neighborly company, and it's on the house whenever you need it."

Another clang of glasses formalizes their agreement.

They drink and indulge in plenty of small talk until Chris brings the conversation back around to the house at the end of the street. Number one.

"What's up with the barred windows? The battleship door?"

Ashlee shrugs. "Saw him once. I don't even think he lives there, just had to be the first one on the block to show the company lemmings that this was for real."

"Makes sense... it's just..."

"Weird, right? And totally, condescending. Like, the rest of us have nothing better to do than sit around thinking about breaking into his house?"

"Yeah, but aren't you curious?" Chris says. "I mean, why have all that physical security if there's nothing to see."

"Forget it," Ashlee says. "I'm not that curious. I feel like that's the best way to put these people in line. Show we don't really give the slightest shit about them."

Chris glances at the clock over Ashlee's shoulder. Charlotte is going to be home at five, and he wants to have dinner ready to celebrate the start of her new career and, more importantly, their new life.

They speak for a while longer, and then Chris excuses himself, but not before they make plans to walk up to the strip mall tomorrow and see what else Evernight Circle has to offer.

***

Charlotte comes through the door at six, dropped off by that centrAL shuttle. Dinner is caprese chicken, slow-roasted asparagus, and a bruschetta starter.

She smiles at the gesture and sits at the sparse dinner table, listening to the particulars of the day in astonished silence. After which, she says, "You called the police on our neighbor?"

"I thought he was in trouble."

"That's one way to meet people."

"Also met the woman who lives right there."

"She cool? We need some new Saturday night friends."

"You tell me," Chris said. "Her husband works with you."

"Haven't met anyone except HR and management." Charlotte's day was traditional corporate onboarding. "I have an office," she says, unable to contain a prideful smile. "Not just a high cube, but like, an actual corner office. My view is all mountain ranges, oh, and a little koi pond that wraps around to the front."

Chris glances at his phone, sitting face down on the table. "Have you spoken to any of your family?"

"Called my mom for about three minutes at lunch," she says. "Why?"

"Texted a few of the guys, and they never wrote back."

"Probably still mad at you for moving to the middle of nowhere."

"Yeah, they think I'm going to start watching NASCAR."

It's a good dinner that inspires better conversation. For the first time in a long time, there's mutual interest in one another, and it's hard to say what's driving it. Perhaps just a simple change in scenery, was all they needed to rekindle their lost feelings.

Charlotte insists on doing dishes. Chris watches her work, motivated by the way her work pants cling to her curves. He approaches on his heels and slides his palms beneath the waistline, cupping her beautiful cheeks together. "I love the way your ass looks in those pants."

She moans and giggles and lets him fondle for another

moment, steadying herself on the palms of her hands, but ultimately discouraging him with a gentle nudge of her back. "I'm still wiped out from the drive... and from our marathon session the other night. But I've got tomorrow off, so how about a really short rain check for now?"

"Promise," he says with breathlessness. "Really short?"

They do a little more unpacking and watch the sunset from their backyard patio. Chris glimpses Ashlee across the way, on her hands and knees with a trellis in her fist as she tends a small rose garden. She offers one cursory wave but refuses any more eye contact.

Upstairs, Charlotte takes a long bath with the door locked. That's unusual, given her usual playful habit of teasing Chris with glimpses of her body.

He goes downstairs and puts the trash in the garage, opening the bay door to better see Evernight Circle beneath the pale moon. If any of his neighbors had actually come home from work at the end of the day, he can't tell.

He goes back in and finds Charlotte standing nude in front of the head-to-toe vanity. She pops a pill and chases it with a glass of vodka. Her eyes droop once she realizes Chris is watching. Tears stream down her cheeks.

"What's the matter?" he asks.

"Nothing." She wipes her eyes with the back of her hand. "Nerves."

"What'd you take?"

"Something for the anxiety."

"Anxiety? You were just telling me at dinner how you've never felt better."

"What can I say, Chris?" She refuses eye contact. Just saunters past and drops onto bed. She rolls onto her side and stares out at the moon.

"I'm committed to making this work," Chris says. "You've got your thing. I'm going to start contracting again."

She might've said something, but it was muffled, and she doesn't bother repeating it.

He climbs into bed and places a hand on her naked hip. Nothing sexual, just comfort.

Charlotte doesn't answer. She's already sleeping.

***

She wakes up with a fever the next morning.

Chris hasn't slept at all. New worries heaped on top of old ones.

Charlotte refuses any help. No aspirin, no juice, nothing. She just pulls the sheets tight around sweaty shoulders and wraps herself like a mummy. Determined to sleep it out.

Chris hears spattering vomit on ceramic more than once. Then she begs him to leave her alone. "Just for a few hours, let me sleep." He doesn't want to, but it's seemingly the only thing he can do that will make her happy. So he showers, dresses and heads for Ashlee's, only nobody's home.

Chris decides to walk up to the strip mall anyway. He's lived in Evernight Circle for just a few days but has already grown sedentary. Living in Philly meant you walked everywhere. Even as his metabolism slowed after crossing north of thirty, he never had a problem maintaining himself there.

Now he worries he's about to pack it on.

There's a lot of commotion as he approaches the rotary. An angry roaring crowd he doesn't yet see. Chris makes his way to the strip mall and decides what's happening at the front gates is more interesting than shopping.

Five centrAL police cars are parked on this side of the fence. Officers wear riot gear, body armor, helmets with visors. They block the entrance, staring down an angry crowd on the other side.

A few handmade signs jut up over the bars.

centrAL MAKES THE WORLD WORSE!!

OUR WILDLIFE DESERVES A PLACE TO LIVE!

IT'S NOT JUST OUR PLANET, YOU ASSHOLES!

Chris agrees with these things in theory but is annoyed by the disruption. Aren't there bigger problems in the world to worry about first? He wonders if this is what it's like to grow old...

One of the officers notices him hanging back and starts moving toward him. "Sir, could I ask you to go back to your home, please?"

Chris nearly laughs in his face. He wants to say there's nothing to worry about but catches himself now that he glimpses the people standing behind the gate.

They're more than just angry protestors. They look like soldiers, even if their uniforms aren't very uniform. They're all dark clothes, sweatshirts, and jackets, supplemented with shoulder pads and surplus helmets... a few have sacks slung around their shoulders, and Chris can guess what's inside.

"Yeah," Chris says, turning back. "Maybe I'll go home."

The officer gives a nod of solidarity and returns to the gate. Some of the protestors have zeroed in on Chris, shouting threats he hopes are idle.

"Walls aren't going to keep you safe forever, you scab!"

This rattles him. His hairline starts to sweat. How could anyone think he's a problem just for living somewhere? The world is happy to go mad, and there's no room for nuance anymore. You're either good or evil, depending on the person casting aspersions.

Chris hurries back and is glad to see his front yard, forgetting for a second what's waiting for him inside.

Charlotte begs for water a couple times that afternoon. Her voice is a ghost: faded and infrequent. She sweats through every inch of bed sheet, soaking through the fabric and making it translucent. Her teeth chatter like a skeleton's.

Chris fills a plastic cup with ice water and places it bedside. Every few hours, he goes upstairs to freshen it up. And each time he goes, her breathing is shallower than before.

He's not concerned. Not at first. Everyone gets sick. At nightfall, he decides to change the bedsheet and leave a plate of toast on the end table. He finds Charlotte sleeping stomach-down, which he's never seen in six years of mutual domestic life.

"You okay, hon?" Chris helps ease her to the side to get the sopping sheet free. Her eyelids fling wide at the electricity of his touch, revealing milky white orbs beneath. He leaps back as she springs up. Her mouth falls past the point her jaw can naturally distend. Drool floods down her chin, and her incisors are somehow the size of small spikes.

She's growling like those wild dogs and seemingly as eager to bite.

Chris takes a large step back, watches her features twist. He retreats until he's in the hall. Pulls the door shut and listens to that guttural stutter.

She sounds a lot like the guy across the street.

Chris doesn't move until he hears the sound of a shuffling body turning over in bed and then, eventually, the shallow breathing that comes with sick sleep.

"Holy shit," he whispers. Goes downstairs and gets a craft beer from the fridge. Sits out on the porch where at least silence is guaranteed.

Quiet takes Evernight Circle like fingers around a throat. There isn't so much as an insect to chirp out of place, and if the protestors are still out front, he can't hear them this far back.

It's unnerving because he looks one way and another, and he sees this street for the façade it is. This is not Anywhere, USA. It's a mockery of it.

Two shadows skitter in the distance. They move like ballet dancers, leaping through the night from one shadow to the next. They appear out from behind Harry Freeman's work shed and vanish once more behind his house.

Chris stands up at the sight. He thinks he'll go inside and lock the doors. But curiosity gets the better of him. He thinks he'll go next door and have Ashlee get her gun. But he's too petrified to move that far. His nervous foot tips the beer bottle over, and it goes rolling down the cement steps in slow motion. Clanks have never echoed so loud, and the foam rushes free in fizzing waves.

He freezes like he's guilty. If the shadows continue to move undeterred, he doesn't see them back there. But the way the street curves allows for larger pockets of darkness to exist between Freemans' place and the Sundstroms' house, and so he wouldn't necessarily see anything.

Not until they brazenly reappear on the Sundstroms' doorstep. One keeps watch while the other hovers over the doorknob. Chris doesn't dare move out of fear of being seen. He thinks he's far enough away from the closest streetlight to remain anonymous, though motion will surely give him away.

Chris reaches for his phone, careful to keep it inside his pocket until the sentry turns back around. He wants to be on the phone to the police as soon as that happens. After today's scene at the entrance, he thinks those maniacs will come rushing, and Chris feels a surge of violence in his blood.

And just as he's thinking about how satisfying it would be to watch these criminals get grounded into dust, an animal's shriek spikes the night.

It comes from the porch. The trespassers have managed to open the front door, gusting audible hell sweeps as soon as it swings wide. They retreat with their backs to Chris, down the steps, and to the pavement as two hunched figures fill the doorway, light fleeing their bodies as they stride into the night.

The trespassers begin to scream. Their retreat takes them beneath the streetlight. Their stretched faces show only madness. The two figures rush them, and it's the first time Chris sees the Sundstroms.

Two people on the cusp of old age, shriveled and naked, come snarling onto the pavement. Their hands are down at their hips, overturned and outstretched, flashing gnarled fingers to verify their intentions. Their faces are battle-ready, mouths scrunched into snarls that reveal gnashed teeth.

Chris nearly laughs at the absurdity of the sight. Two tough-talking protestors being driven back by grandparents whose features twist as if in service of frightening their own grandchildren.

When one of the trespassers trips and goes down on one knee, and the older woman pounces. She takes her victim down with a slash to the face and then falls atop the body, pinning it in place.

The protestor tries to scream, and her female voice is severed with a snap like crunching carrots. Her body convulses as the old woman drops against her face, wet tearing sounds thunder down the street like a bowling ball.

Chris has taken his eyes off the other two. Mr.

Sundstrom is gaining ground on the other trespasser who's now trying to talk him down. The old man isn't having it. He lunges for the young man, capturing his arm and yanking it toward him.

The old man winds his head back, opens his mouth wide and closes it right over the young man's forearm. Breaking bones snap, and the arm falls away, a rush of blood coating the old man like a busted fire hydrant on a summer's day.

The body face-plants, glug-glugging onto the tarmac. The old man crawls up onto him, a gleeful thrum in his throat. Mr. Sundstrom chomps straight through his victim's clothes to reach the bounty of flesh beneath.

Chris holds his breath. Closes his eyes. Can't close his fucking ears, though, and that's where everything's happening. Cold, wet snaps—flesh being picked clean off bones. Wet, satiated chews. Ferocious sneers that become satisfied pants. It seems to never end, and Chris has seen too much.

He opens his eyes in a squint and sees the body a few hundred feet away. In the distance, the other corpse has also been abandoned.

There's the Sundstrom's, walking hand-in-hand back toward their house. To the little slat of glowing light beyond the door.

That's when Chris finally rushes back inside his house and slams the door. Starts upstairs and then remembers that Charlotte is one of these people.

He rushes to the side windows where Ashlee's house is visible. He doesn't know what he expects to see, hoping to find her staring back at him.

The shades are drawn, and the house is dark.

God, he thinks. *I need to talk to someone.*

Chris lies on the living room floor, hyperventilating.

Afraid to run but more terrified to stay.

Never once does he sleep.

***

Sometime before dawn, a large shadow appears on the far side of the living room. It moves stoically across the front yard, slow stomps in front of the circular bay window.

Chris' back is to the glass, but he hears it. And before he can process anything, he's paralyzed by the inhuman shadow gliding across his wall. He holds his breath again as if this thing might otherwise notice him. His lungs tighten; his eyes water. But there's something so primal and threatening about the shape that he knows he's got to keep his breath pinned down.

Once it finally passes from view, he empties his lungs like a wheezing balloon. It's not over yet, because now there are heavy breaths on the doorstep. One thin piece of wood and fiberglass is all that separates them.

Chris turns and sees slivers of fogged glass on the top part of the door, where the small window glazings bring daylight into the foyer.

One yellow eye hovers in the glass, widening as their gazes lock.

An enthusiastic howl follows. The rumble from its throat is like a distant passing train. Pots and pans on kitchen shelves tremble, and the front door stutters in its jamb.

I'm dead, Chris thinks, and can't even muster the preservation required to defend himself. He's too stunned. Too terrified.

A second howl follows, this one muffled by the ceiling overhead.

"Charlotte," Chris whispers and then plants a palm over his mouth, remembering that animals hear everything.

Each time he blinks, her perverted and monstrous glare stains his mind's eye.

He plugs his ears with the rounds of his palms, but the noise seems somehow louder then.

He stays like this until daylight comes and the howling upstairs recedes into sandpaper wheezes.

***

"Guess you forgot about our date yesterday?" Ashlee stands on his doorstep, where the monstrous eye had been just a few hours earlier. She smells like lilacs on the warmest spring day ever. Promises of a future that's otherwise slipping away.

"Did you see what happened last night," Chris says.

Ashlee gives an expected smile then rises on her heels to check the stairwell. "Is your wife—"

"Resting," Chris says. "Weird thing, though?" He turns to look for himself. Sees empty risers. Thinking better of all this, he opens the door wide and steps onto the porch. Closes it behind him and walks all the way to the curb.

The street is so clean, he's already trying to find other explanations in his mind. But that's what they want, isn't it? He knows damn well what he saw.

Ashlee follows, hands outstretched. "What is it?"

He tells her. And she's not surprised. She pretends to be, but not at first. In that split second before her performance has a chance to kick in, before the feigned shock gestures and wide eyes, there's the sad acknowledgment of reality.

"What's happening?" Chris says. "Please."

Ashlee looks around. Careful eyes scrutinize Evernight Circle with well-earned distrust. At long last, she says, "How's your wife doing?"

"centrAL had their doctor come out first thing today. I didn't even call him."

"What'd he say?"

"That she's fine. Particularly bad strain of flu going around."

Ashlee leans in close—this next bit of info is too privileged for anyone else to hear. "I think you should come over and talk to me."

Chris turns and stares up at his bedroom window. Charlotte is up there, hands to the glass, glaring down. He thinks her lips are curled around long and jutting fangs, actual animal's fangs, but his mind fights what his eyes are seeing. There's got to be someplace more rational to land, right?

"She'll be fine," Ashlee says. She looks up at Charlotte, too. Takes Chris' hand between her palms and gives a gentle tug that agitates the woman in the window. Her hands slap the glass louder, throwing muted growls that befit a caged animal.

Chris follows Ashlee back to her place, beyond the kitchen countertop that had been the sight of their last meeting. They're going upstairs, and into the spare bedroom. Last door on the left, where the walls are lined with so much soundproofing foam that the actual space has been reduced a size not much larger than a walk-in closet.

All that's in here is a small work desk with a laptop. A silver butcher's knife sits beside the mouse. The bottom of that blade is stained with little flecks of dark brown.

Ashlee shuts the door and leans against the puffing foam on the back of it. She pushes a finger to pursed lips. "They hear everything."

"centrAL?"

She nods.

"What is all this?"

"We're rats. Evernight Circle is the maze." She chews the inside of her lip to stop it from slumping. "Any chance you'd get in your car right now and drive? Away from here?"

"You mean... take my wife and go?"

"I mean leave your wife. And go."

Chris laughs. Not because this is funny, but because it's the only thing you can do when the world shows you how indifferent to your fate it truly is.

"I'm serious, Chris," she says. "You'll die if you stay."

"I'm not leaving Charlotte."

"She's already dead."

"You don't kn—"

Ashlee strips so fast, Chris can barely process what's happening. She isn't smiling. There's nothing seductive about her nudity. Somehow the gesture has made her more graven.

"I'll show you," she says in a voice that isn't hers. Her register has moved to the basement, growling baritone. "Now look at me. Don't worry. Just look."

Her body fluctuates. Pockets of air moving up and down her skin, making it look like she's got a million pustules rising up out of her flesh at once. Her neck stretches, and her jaw snaps. Bones keep snapping until all of them there are broken and the jawbone swivels around inside the flesh net that's holding it in place.

She lurches forward, and Chris staggers back. She isn't coming for him, though, even when her eyes swivel up into hiding, leaving two empty cotton white orbs. Her hands are sheathed inside tufts of blond fur, and she takes the silver blade in her fist, closing her fingers tight and falling to her knees.

"Watch, Chris," she says. Her words are loose and watery.

The tip of the blade digs into the soft part of her wrist, slicing up toward her elbow. Her whimper is that of a beaten dog. As soon as the knife reaches her shoulder, she brings it back to her wrist and digs in anew.

These slashes chase the fur away. Her broken jaw snaps back into place on tightening skin. She continues to cut, moving the action to her other wrist. Her human eyes drop back into place like casino slots, and she looks at him with a desperate plea for help in her eyes.

She continues to cut until her arms are stained crimson, and the blade slips from her fingers. She falls onto her side, crying into the carpet now that she's temporarily exorcised the wolf.

Chris kneels. His hands hover because this woman is unfamiliar to him, and though she needs comfort, he doesn't have the slightest idea of how to provide it.

"You do this every time?" he says.

Ashlee only nods. Once she recovers enough of her voice to speak, she whispers. "It starts with a drug. A drug they're testing. Prescription transformations."

"Charlotte took a pill the other night," Chris says and then stops himself. Scared to continue. It's the truth, and he knows it, but somehow saying it out loud is far worse. Like maybe there's still a way back if he holds his tongue.

But now that he's kneeling in blood over a body that slowly shrivels back into human shape, he knows it's too late.

"Did your husband do this?"

Ashlee shakes her head. Lifts one frail finger to signal there's more to say, but that it's going to be some time before she can. "I did something bad," she says at last.

"What?"

"...in the basement."

Chris realizes why he's never spent much time trying to accept these events. In his mind, he already believes them. Like much of the world does.

Because of the video.

A video that was posted online a few years back. One that took the Internet by storm. It showed a young woman alone in some cabin or cabana. She answered the door and let another woman, probably her lover, inside. There's a cut in the video, and then we see the naked guest move from the bedroom to the bathroom, where the other girl eventually comes looking. As soon as she gets close, the door explodes in her face, and a hairy creature's arm pulls her against the splinters. Then the door breaks away, and a massive wolf lurches out, shredding the girl to pieces, mauling her until they both struggle out of frame.

The video's authenticity is in constant debate. It's the most viewed thing on YouTube and seems to be directly responsible for the explosion of religious rebirth happening not just in this country but all over the world. It's become the source of a million Internet urban legends, spawned a dozen documentary specials, and even a Netflix limited series that's close to unwatchable.

Many have hunted for the exact location where the video takes place, with one leading theory suggesting it's impossible to find because it was sourced in that Massachusetts town that burned to the ground right around the time the video appeared.

Chris always thought that part had to be fake. Only because he never wished to consider the ramifications of the truth.

Until this moment.

Now there's no choice. He swallows hard and helps Ashlee to her knees, and then to her feet. He hands her clothing, and she uses his shoulder for leverage while she dresses. The wounds on her arms are already closing.

"Show me," he says. "Let's look in your basement."

***

They go downstairs. Ashlee is slow to walk. She places her elbow on the wall every few steps while she wipes tears from her eyes.

A case of the chills keeps her arms perpetually trembling.

"It's either that..." Chris slides a thumb across his wrist with a *ffft* sound.

"Or a big, hairy hangover," Ashlee confirms. "That's right. I've become a cutter 'cause the wolf doesn't like it."

The cellar stairwell is narrow. It's lined with the same sort of soundproofing panels that recede the space. Chris starts down but turns, afraid that Ashlee may decide to trap him here.

His paranoia is muted because Ashlee is already on the way down, too.

"I don't understand this," Chris says. "If everyone on this street is..."

"Your neighbors are werewolves, Chris," Ashlee says without a trace of irony. "At least in theory."

"Right, so, if that's the case, why all the soundproofing? Everyone knows what you are."

"It's not the wolf I'm hiding," Ashlee says as she reaches the floor and taps a six-digit code into the industrial number pad that has been retrofitted to a heavy meat locker door.

It detaches, and Ashlee pushes in, stepping into a finished basement. It's all padding, floors, walls, and ceiling. Every inch is soundproofed. Much of the floor wears dark brown spatters, little drips and drabs leading to a naked man's body slouched in the corner, fashioned in place with silver chains around his ankles and wrists.

The body wears blood like most wear clothes, and the smell in here is worse than a well-used portable toilet.

"Meet my husband," Ashlee says without a trace of irony. "Say hello, Robert."

Robert stirs at the disruption. He lifts his head to the air, tilts shoulder-to-ear. His eyes are missing, two clean and gaping holes as if they'd been scooped out. Thick red tears crust his face.

"Jesus, Ashlee—"

"No," she growls. "Before you even start…"

Chris backs up, spins for the door. Ashlee races to block him, pushes it back into place. Her grin is a tiny bit sinister, the wolf inside unable to resist.

"Let me give you the Cliffs Notes. I'm your Ghost of Christmas Future. Get me? Nobody in this little strip of paradise is here for any other reason. That means the love of your life is committed to jumping species and then gnawing you right down to the bone."

"How can centrAL not know he's missing? If he works there—"

"Nobody who lives on this street works there. Look, I lied to you about number three being rotated off the day shift… if I gave you too much truth right off, you'd freak. But it doesn't take much time here. And yours is running out. Once your wife wakes up, I mean, really wakes up, you're Alpo."

Charlotte's betrayal makes sense, and it kills Chris to

admit this. Her change of heart felt like some distant fantasy, and now he realizes just how much she'd come to despise him over the last few years. All this time, and it was never about putting the marriage back together.

It was about finding the right revenge.

"Robert built this room," Ashlee says. "As soon as he turned, he realized he couldn't control the beast and didn't want centrAL studying his every move. So this space was just for him. And his toys. People from town. Girls, mostly. That was until he couldn't contain himself any longer and came after me. Let me live. Some gift."

"This is *your* revenge."

Ashlee doesn't answer. Instead, she says, "Spent the last month figuring out how I can get my ass inside centrAL. I need to know if there's a cure."

"I think I should go," Chris says.

"Home?"

"Yeah… back to Philly."

Ashlee smiles. "That's good. Because we probably won't meet again."

Chris starts to say that's fine with him when the world overhead goes to hell.

***

It's all booming voices as soon as they reach the top of the stairs.

"Hey, hey! Ho, ho! centrAL has got to go!"

"Whose forest? Our forest!"

"Say it loud, say it clear, get centrAL out of here!"

It's not quite sunset, but the black bloc army marching down Evernight Circle is clad entirely in black pants and sweatshirts, their faces covered with bandannas and cheapo Halloween masks. Many carry bottles stuffed with rags, while others clutch tire irons and flaming torches.

"Holy shit," Chris says.

"They're going to ruin everything."

"Maybe we can—"

"They look like they're here to talk?"

Ashlee bolts the door and rushes around the house. She shuts all the windows, draws every shade, and moves furniture to form makeshift barricades.

"It won't be enough," she says.

Chris watches like a helpless child. Does he stay and help Ashlee defend her roost? Or take his chances with the protestors who surely see him as the enemy? And what of Charlotte? Does he have any allegiance to her?

Ashlee reappears with two rifles and a machete, spilling all of them on the kitchen counter. "If you're going to leave, you'd better go now."

Chris is fixated on what's happening out there. A mass of angry people march over Henry Freeman's lawn. Steel-toed boots break the door and storm inside.

They return almost instantly, dragging an unwilling person by his flailing legs across the concrete.

In the torchlight, Freeman is barely human, but not exactly wolf either. His torso is elongated, covered in patches of gray hair. His hands and fingers are stretched in perpetuity and ditto his haunches. The tips of his fingers aren't quite claws but like swollen nubs. He swipes at the protestors, who kick and punch him into submission while those outside the immediate circle ready more lethal weapons.

The night flashes then swallows the scene in a thick

mass of enveloping smoke. The black bloc scatters as centrAL security floods the street. One armored riot vehicle branded with centrAL logos is flanked on either side by ten men. Erupting machine gun fire transforms this suburban mock-up into a warzone.

"They'll kill to protect their secrets," Ashlee says.

Freeman is close enough to their side of the street that Chris sees him crawl out of the smoke cloud and get to unnatural feet. He moves like a thin man on stilts. Well on his way to becoming a wolf when nature hits the pause button, freezing him forever in between two worlds.

He's barely to the shadows when two black blocs rocket out of the smoke cloud as if fired from a cannon. They brandish silver blades that flash sinister glints as they pass beneath the streetlamp. They hack the tall man's neck, chopping at him like a cherry tree. One thunk, and blood erupts like a geyser, springing high into the moonlight.

"Kill the freak!" someone shouts.

Backup appears alongside the attackers, chopping at Freeman's flailing hands until the tortured man is swallowed beneath a flurry of red-stained silver hatred.

Ashlee picks up her shotgun, loads it. "That's what's waiting for us if they decide to break in here."

"Decide?"

"No," she says. "They're coming. Goddammit, so much of this is Robert's fault. He put this... disease in me." She goes to the far windows and glances up at centrAL HQ. Sighs loud enough for Chris to hear it across the house. "Now or never, I guess."

"You're going up there?"

"Security will only be tighter after tonight."

centrAL's security forces are being swarmed by people with nothing left to lose. Loved ones lost. Their hometown made worse. Area wildlife forever affected.

Both sides are whittling each other down. The bodies strewn across the streets are a mix of parties. But the protestors have sheer numbers on their side. And now they're scooping machine guns off centrAL's dead. They resume their sweep, storming the Sundstroms' yard.

"What do you say, Chris? Come with me, you might still make it."

He doesn't get the chance to answer.

One howl sweeps through the chaos of Evernight Circle. And every noise that follows is screams.

***

One last look. Chris needs one of those.

Face to glass, he watches the steel-reinforced door that belongs to house number one fly off its hinges. It rockets into the night, pancaking at least three protestors off the front steps.

The rest of the black blocs scatter to avoid what comes rushing through, but it's too late.

Gregor May is a wolf the size of a gorilla. His fur is darker than tar, and he moves on his haunches, upright with eyes that swirl green and yellow. He lifts his nose to the air, puffs once, and then descends on the crowd.

Bladed claws slash through darkened makeshift uniforms, watering the front lawn with glugs of spraying blood as bodies spill everywhere.

The thing moves like a tank through the crowd, delivering too much damage for any kind of regrouping.

In the chaos, Chris sees a smaller group of black blocs on the Sundstroms' doorstep, dragging the old, naked couple from their sanctuary—both of them snarling and growling like animals, but still very much human. They

307

slash and snap, but their very human limbs render them mostly harmless.

"Side-effects," Chris says. "Of the drug."

"You catch on quick." Ashlee reappears with a shoulder bag of likely essentials slung over her shoulder.

"Freeman was caught in mid-transformation... the Sundstroms have the instincts and minds of wolves, but their bodies refuse the change. And you can guess what's happened to Gregor..."

"Permanent wolf." The hatch on number one was never about keeping people out.

"Let's go. We can slip out through the backyard if we hurry..."

The carnage has spread to their side of the street. The massive, dark wolf has two corpses pinned on Ashlee's grass, talons smashing through faces and stuck in the wet earth beneath them.

Errant gunfire sounds like firecrackers. Bullets sink through the permanent wolf, but the creature pays them no mind. Adrenaline has him, and the animal wrestles his killing hands free. Goes rushing off into the fringe of smoky silhouettes fanned out across the tarmac.

Chris and Ashlee slip into the darkness, moving all the way to the edge of her yard toward the tree line beyond it.

"We'll find the wall back here."

"Knew some of you shits would try and run." One man in a hoodie and paintball goggles stands between them and the wall. "I told them we had to watch the perimeter." He holds a six-shooter on them.

"We look like those fucking things?" Ashlee says, spreading her arms out.

Black Bloc seems more concerned with Chris, whose

khaki shorts and Target tee screams anything, but "*I'm ready for action.*"

"I'm getting him out," Ashlee says. "He's a friend of mine."

Black Bloc isn't buying. He comes toward Chris for a closer look, and Chris thinks maybe this was one of the guys who insulted him yesterday.

As soon as he's passed Ashlee, she lifts the gun barrel to his head. One pump. It's somehow louder than the entirety of the warzone at their back.

Black Bloc's eyes pop wide beneath the goggles. The realization of this miscalculation is short-lived. She pulls the trigger, and his head becomes a blender of skull and blood.

They scale the wall without another word, leaving the corpse to spill out over its pine grave.

***

centrAL is several miles up the incline. Evernight Circle is a perpetual battleground. Chris doesn't want to turn back, but does anyway and sees several fires where the houses had been.

He thinks about Charlotte, lost and confused, and feels despair for the situation in his stomach.

Ashlee senses his conflict, touches his arm. "You can't do anything for anyone but yourself, Chris."

"I know."

"You made the right choice."

"Did I?"

"You'd rather be dead back there?"

"No, but..."

"Someone you loved betrayed you. Scrape it off and let's go."

"You never told me how you're planning to get inside."

"I... oh shit."

They can now see the entrance to centrAL, and it's clear they're not getting in at all. The company's in lockdown. Front doors barred, parking lot floodlights so bright the place looks like Lincoln Field at halftime. And while centrAL may have a paramilitary unit entrenched below, there's another one up here, just waiting in the wings. Half of the parking lot is a military command center with a perimeter of armed guards.

"I need this," Ashlee says. Her voice is distant, like a decision's been made.

"Then let me," Chris says. He starts into the parking lot as Ashlee grabs him.

"They won't let you leave."

"Let me worry about that. You just stay hidden... and close."

Chris steps into the clear with his hands raised. He doesn't need to work that hard to show his fear. His legs wobble from scaling the mountainside, and the images from that warzone are fresh in his mind. He draws on them to sell his panic.

"Help me," he screams.

Mercenaries rush toward him in silhouette. They look like linebackers, wearing double their weight in armor and padding. Chris anticipates their command and gets on his knees.

"My name is Christopher Tepper from number five Evernight Circle. I escaped once the killing started and never looked back."

"Check him for bites."

They do not afford him the dignity of privacy, stripping him on site. Gloved hands rummage his skin, his folds, while eager gun barrels press against his skull, his neck, his heart.

Once they're satisfied, they drag him across the parking lot to a satellite of mobile command trailers. He's taken to the one at the end, dragged inside and told to dress and then sit.

The room is all monitors, several of which are tuned to the chaos on Evernight Circle. A few others show settlements that look almost exactly like it. Cameras spy down on suburban tracts, monitors cycling through several angles, inside and out.

Chris sits for what feels like forever, drawn to the chaos on his street, watching helplessly as the dark wolf continues his assault. From what Chris sees, the black bloc is decimated, leaving Gregor May to puff his nose and hunt down stragglers.

centrAL's soldiers seem to have pulled back to the entrance gate, no real desire to engage the wolf.

His house is the only one unburnt. He watches the filtering monitors, most of them showing only grey snow patterns, to catch a glimpse inside the place he briefly called home. The place he stupidly thought would define the next phase of his life.

At last, the monitor clicks over and shows black bloc corpses littering his kitchen and stairwell. He finds Charlotte hunched over one of the protestors, gnawing at his neck, the moment timed just right to show his head snap free and go rolling down the stairs like a child's toy.

Charlotte glances up, and the camera catches her face. A delighted smile on razor blade lips. Yellow and inhuman orbs where her eyes had been. Tufts of hair cover her forehead and cheeks. The same pulsing flesh he saw on

Ashlee.

His wife's gone.

The dark wolf stumbles inside and growls as if to greet her. Charlotte stands up, side-stepping the mass of fallen bodies. Her nostrils puff in cautious anticipation.

Chris feels disgust in the pit of his stomach. But the curious part of him refuses to look away. So he sees the large wolf meet the new one, watches them embrace, and fall snarling to the ground, where the triumphant beast mounts his wife, her own features breaking and expanding as it happens.

An animal's snout reaches out of her skull, replacing the area where her nose had been. The moans are pure ecstasy, and soon they share a howling so loud he hears it on the monitors but also thinks that he hears it in real-time, booming up through the forest below.

"It was always going to be this." A figure appears in the doorway. In backlight, all Chris sees is a short-cropped silver head of hair sitting atop the broadest shoulders he's ever seen. This guy's so big it seems like the trailer's shrinking.

He sits opposite Chris with only a small slab of Formica separating them.

"I learned a lot from the last time, you know. The first time."

Chris' attention is on watching his wife assume her new form, a wolf with a light brown mane, growling as the larger, dominant creature mounts her and thrusts away while chewing playfully on her back.

Chris feels tears on his cheeks and cannot understand why, though he accepts this as truth. He's hurt by the sight. Devastated, even. Now understanding what all those restless nights and lousy sleep were trying to tell him. It's a mistake. All of it.

The man with the silver hair cranes his thick neck toward the monitor. Veins bulge against his flesh.

"Afraid it's true," he says. "She's got no love for you. Came here seeking transcendence. And she's got it." The man places a small white pill on the table, no bigger than a Xanax. In his other hand, he's got a gun.

"Two choices, Christopher." He doesn't elaborate any further.

"My wife," Chris says. "Charlotte... sent me here to ask about a cure."

Silver Hair looks back toward the screen. "She look like she wants one?"

Chris doesn't answer. He reaches for the pill because he'll do anything for one more sunrise.

"That drug's come a long way," Silver Hair says. "From a tab to a pill. Takes a little longer to pass through your digestive tract before it's absorbed into your bloodstream but... I'm proud of our work."

"This is a one-way trip?" Chris says.

Silver Hair nods. "Nobody ever comes back."

Chris drops it on his tongue, swallows. Once Silver Hair sees the lump in Chris' throat, he asks him to lift his tongue just to be sure.

The trailer door opens again, and a mercenary with a thick accent sounds off. "Mr. Fane, the outbreak on Evernight Circle has been contained."

"Good," Fane says. "Is PR in touch with local authorities and government?"

"As we speak."

Fane gets up, places a hand on Chris' shoulder and squeezes. "For the inconvenience, and for your willingness to cross over, I am letting you go. Of course, you're only good as long your silence. Break that and..."

"I won't."

"I know."

Fane exits and leaves the door open. Chris follows and crosses the parking lot like a ghost. Nobody pays him any mind.

He enters the forest and moves away from Evernight Circle. The rustling beside him gives way to a familiar body once he's far enough away from the action.

Ashlee looks curious, too afraid to ask.

"There's no cure," he says and keeps walking.

"I figured," she says. "Damn."

"They made me take the pill."

"Why?"

"I..." That's all he says. He doesn't know why death wasn't preferable.

"Okay," Ashlee says with a deep, accepting breath. "Guess this is life now. Let's hoof it to town. If we hurry, we can get there by dawn. I'm going to help you cross."

***

They reach the outskirts of town before daylight, then check in to a dive motel. The first thing they do once they get the keys is shower the stink of smoke and blood from their bodies.

Ashlee sits nude on the bed when Chris comes out, shivering, beginning to feel feverish. She embraces him immediately. He cries as she lays him down. Cries as she takes him in her mouth. Cries as she mounts him.

Then moans.

Her body is soft, even as it begins to change. Her eyes remain kind, even as they turn demonic. "Stay with me, Chris," she says as her voice becomes a snarl.

Chris has never felt anything like her. He pushes up in rhythm to her hips, and Ashlee's moans are electric even as they recede into inhuman baritone.

"I lost everything," he says.

"No," Ashlee growls, slapping his face with an open palm. Her lips peel back to show primed killing teeth.

It only turns him on more. The taboo. The forbidden. He realizes he's wanted her all along, and only more so after discovering her secret. It's more exciting now because he's not yet the same.

That will change. But for now...

"You're beautiful," he says. "Just like that. Perfect."

She drops against his nose, and her pulsing flesh tickles him. Their bodies continue to dance, harder and faster as their groans inspire one another to keep at it, finding the crescendo.

He explodes inside her, and at once, her teeth shred through the soft flesh of his stubbly neck. He feels himself bubbling into her mouth, spilling down her throat. She gnaws away appreciatively. The wet smacks on her tongue please his ear.

"What now?" He can barely speak, and thinking's twice as hard. He's freezing cold. In shock. Maybe dying.

"You sleep." She sits back upright, letting his blood spill down her face and chest. "The dreams will be hard, but you'll make it. I'm here."

And that's what he does. The dreams are bad. But not like before. At last, he's found someone to help him meet them head on. He's no longer alone.

ABOUT THE AUTHOR

Matt Serafini is the author of *Rites of Extinction, Ocean Grave, Under the Blade,* as well as the werewolf novels *Feral* and *Devil's Row.*

He has written extensively on the subjects of film and literature for numerous websites including Dread Central and Shock Till You Drop. His nonfiction has appeared in Fangoria and HorrorHound magazines. He spends a significant portion of his free time tracking down obscure slasher films, and hopes one day to parlay that knowledge into a definitive history book on the subject.

His novels are available in ebook and paperback at all fine retailers.

Matt lives in Massachusetts with his wife and children.

Follow Matt on Twitter @mattfini

Instagram https://www.instagram.com/mattfini/

or visit https://mattserafini.com/ to learn more.

Lifeline

Paul Kane

She was in pretty serious trouble.

Not her, personally, but the woman on the other end of the phone line. The woman she'd been talking to — no, listening to — for some time now. Gauging how best to help her. Trying to persuade her to either go to the authorities or just get the hell out of there before she got herself hurt. Before she got herself dead.

Because the man she lived with, her partner Caleb, was going to kill her before too long. That much Beth could tell, and not just from her story — which had built up over the course of a few months, whenever the lady who called herself Norma could get away from him (usually when he'd passed out drunk, which could be at any time of the day or night). She could tell from the way Norma was talking, because for as long as she could remember, Beth had been able to pick up on such things.

It was easier in person, of course. When that person was in front of her, it was simpler to get a sense of what was going on in their lives. Whether they were hurting, reluctant to admit something, whether they were thinking about ending it all. It was incredibly hard to hide that kind of thing from Beth. It was one of the things that had secured her the gig here at the Women's Crisis Lifeline. She'd been able to pinpoint exactly what was troubling Pamela, the woman who'd interviewed her. Surprise, surprise, it was down to a guy.

But Beth's insight had been so uncannily accurate, right down to the fact that her ex had left after spending all of Pamela's savings and that she was still struggling to keep her head above water all this time later.

"My God!" Pamela had said, hand going to her mouth.

"You're absolutely right. All that from just a few simple questions..." Then she'd frowned, wondered if maybe Beth had been doing some digging, asking around. She hadn't needed to, but Beth could understand Pamela's wariness.

"Just give me a chance. *Please*," Beth had said to her, pushing a strand of her dirty-blond hair — which always seemed to have a life of its own — behind her ear. "See how I do." So she had, and Beth had proved to be one of their most popular and successful employees. That name felt wrong somehow, like it was just another job. Yes there *was* a wage, but it wasn't fortunes — and those who didn't need the cash came in on a voluntary basis to help out. Beth made enough so that she and her son could get by. Luckily, one of her neighbors — Amy — was happy to watch over her eight-year-old while she was here in the evening; otherwise, the childcare would probably cripple her. That would mean she'd have to look for something else, wouldn't be able to devote so much time to women like Norma. Women on the verge of some really serious trouble.

Beth could relate. Because she'd been there herself, had got out from under it eventually, escaped before anything drastic could happen to either her or her child. It had taken a long time to get there, though, and she'd had to do it on her own because she'd had no friends who could help. She'd had no mobile phone, no access to a landline, so calling somewhere like this would've been impossible. Every aspect of her life: controlled.

Hadn't started out like that, but when did it ever? At first, Owen had been *her* lifeline. Lovely, kind, sweet: everything she could have hoped for in a man. Older than her, sure, but then he was bound to be when she was only in her teens and Owen was her teacher. In him, however, she thought she'd found that family she'd so longed for. That safety and security which had eluded her all her life.

Being abandoned at birth, nobody wanting her right from the start, hadn't done her confidence any favors. Then being put down and bullied by the other children at the orphanage had made things worse. Calling her ugly or stupid, or just plain beating her up when the folks who ran the place weren't looking. There was one in particular, a hateful bitch called Kathy, who made her life a misery. Never letting up, always putting Beth down. Sometimes literally, on the ground. Beth knew why they were doing it, of course — felt their pain to some extent — but that didn't make it any easier to take.

Her only escape had been in her dreams, where she was free to run, to jump. To get away. Wasn't the mouse she was the rest of the time, the one they'd forced her to become.

Was there any wonder she'd been more than ready to grasp at the happiness Owen was offering when it came along? "Grooming," they called it now — she recognized it for what it was — but back then, it had simply made her feel special at a time in her life when nothing else really did.

All that staying behind to help with after-school activities, those lunchtimes they'd grab in empty classrooms... Part of her knew it was wrong, and so did Owen — who was, as he often reminded her, putting his job, his whole life, on the line for her — but during the first flush of it all, neither of them had cared. She would have done anything for him, looked up to him. How was she to know what would happen eventually? How it would all turn out? She had nothing to compare it to but the romances in those fairy tales where Prince Charming would ride up and sweep a girl off her feet. Wasn't that what was happening here? It was the one and only time that intuition of hers had failed her.

There were rumors, of course, started by Kathy and others jealous of what they thought was going on. Didn't matter whether it was true; the notion of it was enough for them to go into overdrive. Then, of course, in the run up to her sixteenth birthday, she'd missed her period. Her time of the month. As careful as they'd been, there were never any sure-fire methods — not when you weren't even on the pill

— and Owen definitely hadn't been firing blanks. She often wondered if it had happened that one time after the summer ball, when Owen had fallen foul of some spiked punch. Beth was feeling miserable because she was the only one there without a date, not able to say anything of course when the other girls were teasing her for it. So, when he'd caught her on the way back from the bathroom, slurring his words but telling her how gorgeous she looked, how much he *wanted* her, pulling her into the supply cupboard, she hadn't really been able to say no.

That was the first time it had hurt, that he'd been rough with her, and she thought then maybe it was a really bad idea to do what they were doing. That he was in such a state he'd probably messed up taking precautions, messed up the protection (though in Owen's head, and as he was forever telling her afterward, it had been her own fault; something she must have done).

It had forced their hand, Owen's hand anyway. Forced him to contemplate getting out of town before the scandal was discovered. He could have just gone off on his own, leaving the whole mess behind him — and Beth worried so, so much that he'd simply do that. Abandon her like the parents she'd never known (had her mother found herself in a similar situation, perhaps? If so, then Beth could forgive her for what she'd done; she would understand now...). He didn't do that, but in the end — by the time it was all over — she wished he had. Would have been better than the alternative.

Which meant going off with Owen before everything hit the fan, "starting afresh," as he called it. Stopping dead in her tracks was what Beth would later come to think of it as. Trapped. Reliant on Owen for everything, especially when it came time for the baby to be delivered. He'd taken her to some backstreet place, and she'd almost died giving birth, but Beth had pulled through. Her son had pulled through. Though there were times in the years to come when she thought it might be better if neither of them had.

Owen got by on agency teaching work, mostly private gigs, whatever he could find. But he wasn't happy. He'd changed dramatically in such a short space of time (or maybe just showed her his true self). From Prince to controlling Ogre. Oh, it was *all* about control. And the resentment was there quite early on, laying the blame of what had happened well and truly on Beth's doorstep. At the same time, he was doing more to undermine her confidence than any of the kids at the orphanage had. Sometimes she'd long for the days of Kathy! He made all the decisions, from where they lived — they rented, moving around quite a bit — to what they ate, how she and the little one dressed. When he was out, he'd very often lock them inside the house without a key, locking all the windows as well in case she ever had any "funny ideas" about trying to leave.

And yes, there was violence. If she'd thought he was rough in the supply cupboard, she hadn't seen anything. Not just in the bedroom, but if he thought she was answering him in a tone he deemed disrespectful (she never did, never dared), even looked at him the "wrong way" (whatever the hell that was)... Beth did her best to keep the place tidy, to cook — though God help her if it wasn't right, underdone or overdone (he'd thrown the plate at her on more than one occasion, though fortunately she always ducked, and it hit the wall; good reflexes, hers).

She did her best to be a good mum, too. Gave her son all the love she could, which again was a problem. Owen got very jealous, accusing her of caring about the boy more than him (which actually was true). Yet he refused to send him to school when the time came, probably because he was worried about what might slip out accidentally about their home life. "I can teach him all he needs to know," Owen assured her, which in itself was quite chilling. Beth didn't want her son growing up to be like his father, not in the slightest.

When he wasn't teaching him, Owen was using the child as leverage to get Beth to toe the line. Threatening their kid became a way of getting what he wanted, but again over time this was taken to extremes. Sometimes, usually when he'd had a drink or several, Owen would tell her he was going to hurt the boy, even kill him. Many was the time when Beth had to stand between them, taking the beating instead, while her son would look on, virtually catatonic. Withdrawing into himself, protecting himself from what was going on around him.

She suspected Owen was doing to some of his students what he'd done to her, as well. He'd get in late from work some days, or she'd smell the scent of other girls on his clothing. But he never went off with any of them, never made them his property like he had done with Beth because she was so... special. She felt guilty when she hoped that he would, because Beth wouldn't have wished this life on anyone. Owen was growing increasingly paranoid, to the point where just leaving them locked in the house wasn't enough. Sometimes he'd even bind them with plastic ties until he got back — "For your own good, just to make sure," he'd say. It was a method he was increasingly using in the bedroom as well.

In the end, it all came to a head, and she finally woke up. The threats to do something serious to her, and especially to her son, became too much. Beth couldn't stand up to him. She just didn't have the strength. So she knew they had to run away. Before it was too late.

It was then she hatched the plan to put some of Owen's pills — the ones that made her dopey if he felt like he needed even more control — in his food. She'd broken into the drawer he kept them in, crushed them up and sprinkled them over his roast... one of the few times, ironically, he'd complimented her on the meal. Just before he fell head-first onto the table, unconscious.

Beth stole some money, grabbed the keys to get out and fled with her boy. She had no idea where she was going, just got on the next bus out of town taking them anywhere. They stayed in a hotel the first few nights, but then the money began to run out. Beth found the address of a rescue mission in the phone book, and they went there. The women who ran it were lifesavers, had welcomed them no questions asked and pointed them in the direction of a shelter, a place to stay for a little while. Helped with things like changing their names: hers to this one, her son's to Robbie. They were also the ones who'd set up the interview with Lifeline, who'd got her this work — and she'd never looked back since. Her life was relatively normal now, a second chance, and although she still didn't have much confidence, she was determined to pay it forward, pass on the help to others... like Norma. People who were in pretty serious trouble themselves.

She recognized the signs, which was why she was advising *Norma* to finally wake up, get out of her home. Get away just like Beth had managed. Before it was too late. Before her husband did something to her that couldn't be undone.

"Listen to me, Norma, I know what I'm talking about... Do you have anywhere you can go, a relative perhaps?"

"My... my sister in Illinois, maybe."

Lucky. Some people have nobody, thought Beth. "Then go there, please. I want you to get as far away from Caleb as possible."

"But my things, my job. I—"

"The rest can be sorted out later on, trust me."

It took some persuading, but Beth finally got her to promise to leave while she still could. She gave her some numbers of local organizations that would be able to help her once she hit Illinois. Gave her a shot at a second chance.

"I... I don't know how I can ever thank you."

"Just be safe, Norma. Just be safe."

She gave a sigh of relief when the call ended; she'd done her part for now and hopefully set Norma on the path to freedom. *Hopefully.* It didn't always take, but Beth could hope.

"Beth!" her workmate Fiona was calling out to her from a few booths away, hand over her own mouthpiece. There was only a skeleton staff on tonight, just them and a handful of other operators scattered about the room, occupied with their own problems — or more accurately, other people's.

"Yeah?" Beth shouted back.

"Got a lady here asking for you by name, sweetheart." Just like Norma always did, one of her regulars probably. "Who is it?"

"Someone called Diana?" Fiona said.

Beth frowned. She didn't have any regulars called Diana. Fiona caught her look of puzzlement and shrugged. Could it perhaps be a recommendation from someone? "Patch her through," Beth told her, and the other woman nodded. "Hello? Diana? How can I help you tonight?"

"Beth," said the voice. It didn't sound like any of the other women she dealt with. Sounded... strong, confident. More confident than Beth, even — which wasn't that hard, granted. And it wasn't a voice she'd ever heard before, to her knowledge.

"Y-Yes?"

"Beth, I need you to listen to me," said the voice, Diana's voice. "You're in serious trouble."

"Who is this?" she asked.

"That doesn't matter. You just need to trust me when I tell you you're at risk."

"Trust you? I don't even know you. I don't know anyone called Diana."

"No, but I know who you are," the voice informed her. "Who you really are."

Beth paused for a moment, a shiver running down her spine. "You know... Look, do you need any help tonight, Diana? Because there are women out there who—"

"I'm trying to help *you*," said Diana. "You're in terrible danger."

"I... I'm in..."

"He knows where you are."

"Who?" asked Beth, voice cracking, though there was only one person Diana could possibly be talking about. But that was impossible.

"Who do you think?" Diana told her. "But look, he's not the real problem. Men are coming, they're going to your house. You need to get to your son. Get your son out of there."

"Wait... wait, what?"

"There isn't time to explain," Diana insisted. "These men, they know who you are too. What you can do."

"What I can... I can't do *anything*!"

"We both know that's not true. Those abilities of yours, being able to tell things? You're like me. We can all do it... Comes down to smell when people are in front of you, to hearing when you're talking over the phone. For example, am I lying to you right now?"

Beth didn't reply.

"What's your gut telling you?" Diana prompted.

It was telling her that this woman was speaking the truth.

"I know what I'm talking about. You're special, Beth... I'll call you Beth, right? Even though it's not your real name. I mean, we're all special — my mom used to call it magical — but you can do things the rest of us can't. Things you don't even... You're important. You have control like I've never—"

"Control? What are you talking about? I don't have any..." *Control. It was all about control.*

"Doesn't matter. You just need to believe me, get to your son before it's too late. *He's* even more important."

Then the phone line went dead. Beth rose instinctively, her chair falling over backward.

"Everything okay?" asked Fiona from her station.

"Er... yeah. Yep," said Beth, but she wasn't fooling anyone; even without her powers of perception, Fiona could tell that was bullshit. "I-I just have to check on something."

Then she was yanking off her headset and grabbing her coat, making for the exit behind her.

***

When she arrived back at her place, out of breath, there was a black van outside.

She raced up the path, toward the—

The blame well and truly on her doorstep...

—open door, calling out for Robbie and Amy. It was the babysitter she came upon first, sprawled in the hallway, limbs at weird angles. Beth let out a yelp, though even before she saw the first of the men in her living room, she knew the girl wasn't dead, merely knocked out — tranqed actually.

"She'll be okay," said the guy with the bull-neck in the khaki trousers and cable jumper. "We don't kill our own."

"What have you done with my..." But then she sensed —

saw — Robbie, behind the man, being held fast by another member of the group. This guy was shorter, with spiky hair, and had a huge hunting knife to the shaking boy's throat. There were three more in the room as well, a guy with a pockmarked face who was aiming a pistol in her direction, a second with his mouth wide open — breathing through it — who just looked confused, and another one with a limp who was ordered to cuff Beth... just in case.

"Saved us the trouble of picking you up," he grunted.

"Is this... Did Owen send you?" she asked them as they placed the shiny bracelets on her, ones which matched Robbie's.

"Your ex?" said Bull-neck, then nodded. So what was this, some kind of revenge thing? He'd finally found them and wanted them punished? Wanted his property returned to him? She tried to figure it out but was having no luck for some reason. Her intuition blocked somehow.

One thing she did know, and it didn't take a Sherlock Holmes to work this out: She. Was. In. Serious. Trouble.

Her. Personally.

And her son.

"Now, are you going to come quietly, or do we have to cut the kid?" Just like Owen, the threats. The control. She'd go with them, Beth agreed, as long as they didn't hurt Robbie. They'd laughed at that, as if they couldn't promise anything.

Special. Important...

Beth tried again, but it was... it was all so foggy, terror clouding her mind and her judgment. Or something else, something they were using?

The pair of them were bundled into the back of the van next, which the limping man drove — the pockmarked guy sitting beside him. Bull-neck, Mouth-breather, and Spike rode in the back to keep an eye on their charges.

Trapped again.

Also scattered around inside were bits of chains with shackles attached to them — like you might see in a dungeon — boxes and boot-lockers. One of them was open a crack, like her door had been, and Beth thought she saw the muzzle of a rifle poking out. If she didn't know it before, she did now: These were seriously dangerous men.

Robbie was crying, so frightened he'd wet himself.

"Shh, it'll be okay darlin'." Beth said the words but knew it would be far from all right, especially when the men in the back all laughed again. Robbie was already shutting up, though, withdrawing into himself like he used to do when he was younger. "What do you want with us? Why don't you just let us go?" she asked but was scared to hear the answer.

"We've gone to a lot of time and trouble to find you," Bull-neck replied. "Both of you. Spent money. Now, why ever would we want to let you go after all that, bitch?"

"Because... Because..." Beth shook her head. It didn't matter what she said, there would be no reasoning with guys like this. Yet she still had to try; it was what she did all the time on the phone back at Crisis (and if ever a situation warranted that name it was this one, right here and now), attempting to get through to people. "You don't have to do this."

"Oh, but we do." Spike piping up this time. "We do, or one day, it'll all belong to you lot."

"My lot? I don't understand. What are you talking ab—" A slap then from Bull-neck to quiet her down. Again, just like Owen. All cut from the same cloth.

"You don't have to pretend anymore, bitch. Don't you understand? We've killed more than our fair share of your kind."

She thought about asking him again what he was talking about but would only have received another smack for her trouble. Instead, she just shook her head, confused.

"You... Hey, you don't think that she..." Spike was rubbing his chin. "She must know what she is, right?"

These men, they know who you are too. What you can do.

Bull-neck peered at her. "Sure, she does. How can she *not* know? She'd at least know once a month."

Once a month? Her time of the month? What were they talking about?

"S'why we chose now," said Spike, nodding and laughing. Mouth-breather still looked bewildered, but she was beginning to suspect that was just his default. "Waited till the Cycle was over."

Cycle? thought Beth.

"Course, you can never be too careful," Bull-neck said to Spike. "Which is why we take precautions. Why we slapped those on 'em."

Spike nodded, but Mouth-breather still seemed none the wiser.

Precautions?

"None of 'em can resist it, though," continued Bull-neck, possibly for the benefit of the guy with his mouth hanging open. "That full moon rolls out and *bam!*" He nodded sagely. "She knows what she is, all right."

It was Spike's turn to frown then. "He didn't seem to, though, did he? Thinking about it."

"Who?"

"The ex. That Owen guy..."

Bull-neck shrugged. "Didn't care. Not after we'd—"

There was a sudden thump on the roof of the van, which made it rock. "The fuck was that?" shouted Spike. Then ahead, to his comrades: "Glynn? Tobe? The fuck was—"

Another jolt, and the van shunted sideways — the driver (Glynn or Tobe, Beth didn't know which) tugging on the steering wheel so hard the vehicle nearly tipped over on its side.

Then there was a cracking sound, the glass splintering on the passenger side window. Pockmark had his pistol out again, waving it in that direction, but he didn't even have time to get a shot off before the glass caved in and he was being dragged out of the van through the hole.

The guy with the limp was stamping on the brake, so hard the burning rubber was making squealing noises and smoke was rising from the tires, blocking the view through the windscreen.

Stopping them dead in their tracks.

"It can't be!" shouted Spike. "Can it...? How can it...?"

Bull-neck simply shook his head, began scrabbling around, rooting through the boxes there, and ordering his friends to arm themselves.

Precautions. Protection...

Spike pulled out the hunting rifle, tucking grenades into his belt. Mouth-breather unsheathed a machete, while in his other hand, he held what looked like some sort of harpoon as if he were fixing to take on a whale. Bull-neck himself had plumped for a shotgun. All of them tooling up, expecting trouble themselves.

Pretty serious...

The Limper was opening the driver's door now, practically falling out — and Bull-neck was sliding open the back door, letting the light from inside spill out. "Bring them too," he ordered, nodding at Beth and Robbie. "We might need them to bargain with."

Leverage to toe the line.

Beth still had no idea what was happening. Bargain with who? Whatever had attacked them, taken Pockmark? And even now, his screams could be heard above everything else, tailing off into strangled gurgles.

"Christ! Tobe..." whispered Spike.

They'd ended up on a patch of scrubland, but as Beth cast an eye back down the road they'd been on — heading out of town, away from the population centers — she saw the bridge they must have passed under. The one whoever had been following them used, a length of rope or something still dangling over its edge. Must have been following and then got ahead of them, got to higher ground, and...

The Limper — who was, by process of elimination, surely Glynn — had drawn a revolver, the biggest handgun Beth had ever seen in her life (not that she'd seen many) and was shooting randomly into the night-sky, wherever he heard a noise.

"Save your ammo!" cautioned Bull-neck, but then it didn't matter anyway because something had hold of Glynn, a large shape pulling him over the bonnet of the van. He continued to fire up into the air until his chamber clicked on empty. Beth thought she saw fur as whatever it was dragged him down out of sight.

More screams, more gurgling sounds. And a roar. Mouth-breather made a move to go and help, and Bull-neck told him to stay where he was in the light coming from the van. There was a noise from the top again, so Bull-neck motioned for them all to move back, away from the vehicle: Beth and Robbie — who was still virtually catatonic — being dragged with them by any available hands.

"One of your little friends?" spat Bull-neck, but Beth still didn't have a clue what he was talking about.

Then it was there, on the roof, poking its head over —
snout first.

A wolf. An honest-to-goodness wolf! They weren't that
far away from town, not into wild animal territory anyway,
and Beth had never heard of anything like that in this area.
The odd stray dog maybe, but not this. It snarled, revealing
its gleaming white teeth: so many of them, some still sticky
with redness. Its claws hooked over the edges of the van,
where the door was open, and they too were wet with the
blood of its victims, Tobe and Glynn. Yet it was struggling
somehow, Beth also felt that. In pain, injured by one of
them, maybe?

Something was thrown up toward the creature, Spike
tossing an object onto the roof: a grenade that he'd already
pulled the pin from. It dropped onto the top of the van with
a clanging sound, bouncing a couple of times before going
off. But it wasn't any ordinary blast when it came, more like
a cloud — not of smoke or anything like that, but sparkly.
Fragments of something that shone and twinkled in the
light from the van.

The wolf had already started to leap by then, but it was
a clumsy action, and the reach of the explosion was too
great, spreading outward the longer it went on.

At the same time, Spike had his rifle up and was aiming
— tracking the beast and letting off a couple of rounds.
Beth couldn't tell for sure, because all this was happening
too quickly, but it looked like those missed the wolf entirely.

What didn't miss was Bull-neck's discharge from his
shotgun. But, as with the grenade, this wasn't an ordinary
weapon: Instead of firing shells, it spat out gleaming metal
darts. When one of these ended up in the wolf's leg, it
looked like some sort of tent peg sticking out.

Definitely hadn't been firing blanks.

The wolf howled in pain, landing awkwardly but
scrabbling to try and get to its feet before it could be

targeted again.

"Put it down!" shouted Bull-neck.

Never letting up, always putting—

Mouth-breather's turn was next, and he fired his harpoon gun, which caught the animal in the side. A length of twine attached to the spear bolt embedded there, connecting the wolf to his weapon. He tugged on it, pulling the creature closer and readying his machete. But even with the damage it had taken, the wolf was stronger and, in turn, tugged back. It yanked on the twine and dragged Mouth-breather nearer, almost pulling him off his feet. When he was close enough, the wolf swiped with one of its claws and cleaved off both his hands: the one holding the harpoon, and the other gripping the machete. Mouth-breather sank to his knees, holding up the stumps, which were pumping out viscous liquid. The wolf cocked its head as he looked up at it, his mouth still gaping open. Then it swung again, leaving that bottom part of his face hanging off: jaw, chin, the works.

Robbie was being pulled sideways by Spike, using him almost like a human shield. "*No!*" called out Beth.

While the wolf was distracted, Bull-neck pumped a couple more of those tent pegs into it, one catching it in the shoulder and sending it spinning like a ballerina. It tumbled to the ground, rolling and rolling. As it did so, it changed — and when it came to a stop, Beth could see it was the figure of a woman. A naked woman, maybe in her 50s, with reddish hair.

"I don't know how the hell you did that. You shouldn't be able to... But, well, it won't help you any." Bull-neck was skirting around and heading for the van again, reaching inside and grabbing lengths of chain. The woman was breathing hard, pushing herself upright and glancing across at Beth, at Robbie — who was being held by Spike, arm around him.

"B-Beth..." she managed, and it was then Beth recognized the voice. The same voice that had spoken to her on the phone, that had warned her.

"Diana?" Beth whispered, and the woman nodded, almost imperceptibly. How she'd heard was anyone's guess. Or was it? A second or so ago, she'd been a wolf, and now—

You're like me...

We're all special — my mom used to call it magical...

There was a whipping sound, and Bull-neck had suddenly unfurled the chain, the silver chain, and was striking Diana with it, causing her to howl in agony. Beth took a step toward her, to help in some way, but Spike whistled to get her attention. "I wouldn't if I was you." He'd dropped his rifle and once again had the knife at her boy's throat.

She stopped. What could she do, anyway?

The chain flew out once more, this time wrapping itself around Diana's throat. Bull-neck tugged on it, just like Mouth-breather had done with his harpoon, except this time it was tightening, cutting off her air supply.

"You... you can do things... the rest of us can't..." Diana wheezed, barely audible, and yet Beth could still hear it. "The control... you... you have to let it out, B-Beth. Y-You're stronger... much stronger than me. Stronger than you realize..."

What the hell was she talking about, let what out?

What can I...? I can't do anything.

We both know that wasn't true.

She looked down at her wrists, at the cuffs — the silver cuffs. The ones they thought would put *them* in control.

Which is why we take precautions. Why we slapped those on 'em.

The threats, the—

You can do some things the rest of us can't. Things you don't even... You're important.

Beth looked at Robbie, saw how out of it he was, just like he used to look when his father...

The knifepoint had drawn a bead of blood.

You just need to believe me, get to your son before it's too late. He's *even more important.*

In. Serious. Trouble.

Her. Personally.

And her son.

Beth knew now what fate these men had in mind for them once they were finished with their tests and examinations. Had known it all along, regardless of their attempts to block her senses. To mask their scents.

Tell her he was going to hurt the boy — even kill him.

You don't have to do this.

Oh, but we do, or one day it'll all belong to you lot.

We've killed more than our fair share of your kind.

Beth glanced across at Diana, who looked her squarely in the eye. "You... you can do this..."

Y-You're stronger... much stronger than you realize...

The chain was pulled tighter, the knife-blade brought closer.

Beth closed her eyes. And when she opened them again, everything was different: She saw things differently. Targets instead of threats. Hunters becoming the hunted. Cuffs that should have been burning her by now, that should have kept her subdued, but she was them pulling apart — snapping them like they were made of paper. Breaking free. No full moon in the sky, and yet she could suddenly feel its influence out there after all these years of denying it, of repressing what she was. Feeling like she was nothing, less than nothing. Now it was filling her up, empowering her.

Giving her the strength to save her son. To save Diana as well.

And as soon as she was thinking it, she was doing it. Almost like something else was taking over, something that had bided its time, waited until she was ready. Until she woke up.

Showing her true self. No mouse this time, but an altogether different beast.

Dirty-blond hair — *fur* — with a life of its own, prickling as it pushed its way to the surface, clothes ripping. Most didn't have a choice — when the moon was out, they *had* to change — but she had more control than that. Could choose not to, even when it was at its fullest. Could decide to change now, too, even when it wasn't.

All this time thinking that she had no power at all, when, in fact, she had the most; she was just using it to suppress the urges. To such an extent that she didn't even realize she had them at all.

Diana had been struggling even before they attacked her, barely holding on to the change — and it was impressive that she could even do that. Because Diana was weaker when there was no full moon. Beth wasn't. Nowhere near. As these two idiots were about to find out.

Free to run, to jump...

Spike first, because he had her kid — her cub. Twice he'd put a blade to her child's throat, and he would pay so dearly for that. Before he could even react, she was leaping at him, grabbing his shoulders and pushing him back, forcing him to release his grip on his hostage. The knife was swatted away like it was a piece of cutlery, and Beth stared down at Spike's terrified face. Ignored his pleas to spare him, and simply bit into it, ripping a huge chunk of that face away with the massive, sharpened teeth she now had. He twitched, spasmed, then lay still.

Looking up and over, she saw that Robbie was okay — still in shock, but physically fine. Snarling, her gaze swept across to Bull-neck, who was only now realizing that something else had happened. He dropped the chain, snatching up his shotgun again and rounding on this new enemy.

"You... you can't... it's impossible!" He fired one round, two, three. All of them hit Beth, those darts, those tent-pegs, but she barely felt it. They barely scratched her. "Fuck me!" shouted Bull-neck, searching around for something else to use against her, but it was too late. They didn't have anything that could harm her anyway. Not really.

Beth was on him seconds later, clawing and biting, savaging him until there was hardly anything left of the man that had abducted her and her son. Hardly anything left of him that could be identified as a human being.

Then she rose, stepped back. Changed back... now that the wolf wasn't needed. It served her, not the other way around — which was certainly different. Beth went over and helped Diana remove the chain that had been choking her, helped her pull out the darts still in her, the harpoon spear. The bullets would need removing with a scalpel and tweezers, but somehow Beth knew she had those back in her truck along with spare clothes. The truck she'd parked on the bridge and had let the tow-rope down from. The line she'd used to swing onto the van.

"He... he okay?" Diana nodded over to her boy.

"He will be," Beth said. "He's alive."

Diana nodded.

"How did you... I mean, what did..."

"I'll explain everything, that's if I even need to. But first I think we... we need to get out of here."

Free to run...The rest could be sorted out later on. "Right."

Beth helped her up, helped her across to where Robbie was. Robbie, who looked at her with gaping eyes — shocked, but coming out of his fugue state. Who now ran to her side, let her free him from the cuffs then hugged her. They all made their way back up to the road, back toward the bridge.

"Thanks," said Diana finally when they got to the car.

"I think I should be the one... I don't know however I can... I mean, is there any way of repaying you?"

Diana shook her head, then stopped. "There *is* something you can do."

"Name it," said Beth.

"Not something for me. For yourself. There's something you need to face, to stop running away from... Mary."

Beth paused then, but she shouldn't be surprised the woman knew her real name. After all, she seemed to know everything else.

"Then we can talk," said Diana.

***

She looked across at her passengers.

The woman who'd called herself Beth, who'd hidden for so long behind that name, hidden what she really was for much longer. And her son, Robbie... No, Jason. Jay. Asleep, head resting on his mother's shoulder as they traveled up the long and empty backwater road. Poor mite still didn't really understand everything about all this, but they had time to teach him. The important thing was they'd pulled through; it had been a week now since their brush with death.

Mary hadn't gone into details about what she'd done, what she'd needed to face when Diana had dropped her off at that bar a few nights ago. Even if Diana hadn't been able to "read" her scent, it was only what she'd been planning to do to Owen herself. That was how this whole thing had gotten started. Diana, choosing another one of her victims — someone who deserved her attentions, another guy who'd wronged women. Who'd abused young girls, in fact! She was more careful these days, of course. Didn't just rely on the scent to tell her what she needed to know about a person, because that could be fooled — she'd been fooled before. Scents could be masked; they could be faked, as she'd discovered to her cost.

But this guy had checked out, and he'd had a run-in with some old friends of hers recently. People she'd escaped from herself, who were becoming more and more organized. Whose network was spreading, not just across America but abroad as well. She'd kept tabs on them since her first encounter, just as they kept tabs on her kind. Tracked them, slaughtered them for the monsters they figured they were.

"I was just paying it forward," Diana had told Mary. "Someone saved me once too." Offered her a lifeline. "A male wolf. Didn't even get his name — but he gave me a second chance."

Mary was on her third, which could officially start now that the woman had done to Owen what Diana had done to her own abusive ex so long ago, ripping him to shreds. So much in common, more than either of them imagined, finally standing up for themselves and cutting the ties...

Cut from the same cloth, as Mary might say. As young as she was, there was more wisdom in there than someone three times her age.

Diana had seen that when she encountered Owen. Had sniffed out memories of their life together, of how Mary had escaped with her son. Had seen how Owen had been looking for her ever since, how he'd eventually found her. And how — after a few threats and a payoff — he'd sold her out to those hunters. No questions asked.

It was then Diana began putting two and two together, recalled the stories she'd heard on her travels. Rumors, myths really about a woman and her child who would prove vitally important to their kind and their future. Mary had filled in the rest, which she'd gleaned from tasting the hunters' flesh: another thing she could do that the others couldn't. Digesting information along with the meat, stuff that went back generations, anyone they'd ever had contact with.

From them, she'd learned it had been hunters who'd killed her parents, but the couple had made sure she was safe first (had loved her more than anything, as it turned out). The hunters had lost track of Mary at that point, until Owen's blundering investigations had tipped them off.

And *they* knew the rumors as well, the legends. Needed both mother and child dead... just in case it all turned out to be true. A woman abandoned, brought up alone, who would give birth at an early age. Someone who would go into hiding because she could change the course of history. Someone they'd woefully underestimated, who had powers they couldn't even imagine. Immunity to silver, could change at will... and Diana had never seen a wolf move so fast!

But it was clear Beth — Mary — didn't even know what she was, or at least she wasn't admitting it to herself. Owen certainly never even suspected. That left both her and her son at risk, vulnerable. So Diana felt compelled to try and help.

She'd rung the Crisis Lifeline to warn her, because she knew she wouldn't get there in time. Indeed, she'd only just arrived as the van was pulling away — and it was too public anyway for a fight. Was able to follow, skirt around and wait on the bridge to mount a rescue away from prying eyes.

The hunters hadn't known what hit them, thought because it wasn't a full moon, they were safe. But Diana had picked up a trick or two herself over the years, meeting other wolves — around the time she'd heard those tales, as it happened. Learned how to "store" some of that lunar energy, like a battery. How to summon it, tap into it — and especially just after the Cycle. It was hard, painful, and she couldn't maintain it for long, but she hoped it would be enough to get the job done. Either that, or Mary might snap out of her reverie in time, Diana's coaxing and the threat against her son finally doing the trick.

It had been a gamble, but a gamble that paid off — thankfully. Now they were heading away from everything in her truck, from any unwanted attention. From the investigation the authorities would mount.

"It's not running away this time. It's not hiding," Diana told her. "We just need to keep you safe. Keep you *both* safe." That and hone her skills, teach Jay.

At the very least, now this mother and son had a family; they knew that there were others like them out there. Diana, for starters, who'd always wanted a family of her own. But if the myths, the legends were true, then in the battles to come, this pair would prove vital. Might even lead to the defeat of the hunters altogether... If not, then they were in trouble. Not just the three of them or the others Diana knew about — had connected with — but the whole of their clan. All of them, in the worst kind...

Of pretty serious trouble.

Paul Kane

ABOUT THE AUTHOR

Paul Kane is the award-winning, bestselling author and editor of over ninety books — including the *Arrowhead* trilogy (gathered together in the sellout *Hooded Man* omnibus, revolving around a post-apocalyptic version of Robin Hood), *The Butterfly Man and Other Stories*, *Hellbound Hearts*, *The Mammoth Book of Body Horror* and *Pain Cages* (an Amazon #1 bestseller). His non-fiction books include *The Hellraiser Films and Their Legacy* and *Voices in the Dark*, and his genre journalism has appeared in the likes of *SFX*, *Rue Morgue* and *DeathRay*.

A former British Fantasy Society Special Publications Editor, he is currently serving as co-chair for the UK chapter of The Horror Writers Association. His work has been optioned and adapted for the big and small screen, including for US network primetime television, and his audio work includes the full cast drama adaptation of *The Hellbound Heart* for Bafflegab, and the *Robin of Sherwood* adventure *The Red Lord* for Spiteful Puppet/ITV.

Paul's latest novels are *Lunar* (set to be turned into a feature film), the Y.A. story *The Rainbow Man* (as P.B. Kane), the sequels to *RED — Blood RED & Deep RED* — the award-winning hit *Sherlock Holmes & the Servants of Hell*, *Before* (an Amazon Top 5 dark fantasy bestseller) and *Arcana*.

He also writes thrillers for HQ Digital/HarperCollins as PL Kane, the first of which — *Her Last Secret* — came out in January. Paul lives in Derbyshire, UK, with his wife Marie O'Regan and his family.

Find out more at his site **www.shadow-writer.co.uk** which has featured Guest Writers such as Stephen King, Neil Gaiman, Charlaine Harris, Robert Kirkman, Dean Koontz and Guillermo del Toro.

Ivan's Night Out

A Wolf Hunt Prequel

Jeff Strand

Ivan sat in his car, watching the house across the street. Inside were a father, mother, teenaged son, and teenaged daughter, all probably asleep. He wasn't sure that they were sleeping, and he didn't know if there were others in the house—the uncertainty and risk were part of the fun.

He took his knife out of its leather sheath. It was a hunting knife with a six-inch serrated blade. He'd polished and sharpened it before leaving his apartment, and there was no trace of blood. Ivan figured that if he was going to stab somebody to death, they at least deserved the respect of a clean blade. Yes, there'd be blood from four different victims—at least—on the blade before he left that house tonight, but hey, they were all in the same family, so they wouldn't mind mixing crimson. Anyway, the idea of respecting his victims was something he used to amuse himself, not an actual code of ethics.

He could do this very easily if he wanted. Walk in there, transform into a scary-ass wolfman, rip them apart, slurp up some blood, and be on his merry way. But he didn't want to do this the easy way. If he was on the prowl for a thrill kill, he was going to do a thrill kill. Murder everybody in the house with his knife. No guns, no transformation. Up close, human against human. Warm blood felt better splashing against skin than fur.

Of course, Ivan also wasn't suicidal. If things went bad, he'd change. He could do it pretty much instantly—no long, drawn-out, painful *An American Werewolf in London*-style transformation for him. Tonight was a personal challenge, but he knew he'd walk out of that house alive.

Time to go. He picked up his lock-picking kit, got out of

the car, and walked across the street. He quickly moved to the back of the house. A light turned on automatically because of a sensor, but Ivan wasn't going to be frightened away by a bit of illumination. He stood patiently by the back door until the light went off.

He gently tested the doorknob, just in case they'd left it unlocked. They hadn't. No big deal—Ivan could pick an expensive lock with little difficulty, and this door had a shitty one. A few moments of poking around in there, and the lock popped open. He slowly opened the door, stepping into their garage.

He walked over to the door that led to inside the house. Also locked. He appreciated their half-hearted attempt to provide him with a challenge. Ivan popped that lock as well, then opened the door. It creaked a little. He didn't know if anybody in the family was paranoid enough to come downstairs to investigate a soft creak, so he continued to open the door until he could slip inside.

Now he was in a dark kitchen. He opened the refrigerator and took out a bottle of beer. Ivan didn't like beer very much, but he liked the idea of drinking somebody's beer before he murdered them.

He could transform his head—just his head—and quickly bite off the top of the beer bottle. Was that breaking the rules? His goal was to avoid using his sharp fangs on tender flesh, not on glass and a bottle cap. But if he did this, he couldn't tell himself that he committed the entire murder spree without ever using his gift. Though it would make a little more noise, he'd find a good old-fashioned bottle opener.

Ivan opened the correct drawer on the third try. He popped off the bottle cap, took a long swig of beer, and poured the rest out into the sink. Then he went upstairs.

He went into the first room on the left. The teenaged girl lay in bed, eyes closed. He would've expected to find her texting her boyfriend or exploring her sexuality, so this was kind of a surprise. What kind of teenager was asleep before midnight on a Saturday? She deserved to die just for that.

Ivan crouched down beside her bed. She was definitely asleep, not just faking it thinking he might be one of her parents. He listened to her breath as her chest gently rose and fell. Only a few more breaths left for her, the poor thing. He wondered if she'd die a virgin.

She'd never graduate high school, get married, have kids, or achieve any of her life goals. On the other hand, she'd also never suck off some guy for meth. Ivan liked to think that she would've been her class Valedictorian and gone on to cure diseases or some shit like that.

He plunged the blade deep into her throat.

Her eyes flew open.

Blood spurted out onto her white pillow. Ivan pulled the knife out of her neck, though not the way it had gone in. After the blade tore free, she gurgled for a few more seconds before going still.

Nice.

He ran his index finger across the gash in her throat and touched it to his tongue. He swished it around in his mouth. *Type A-negative,* thought Ivan. All blood types tasted the same (to him, anyway), but it was a fun, private joke.

In a perfect world, he'd slice off her head and leave it on the foot of the bed to increase the shock value when her body was found. But there wasn't time for that. He could transform and tear it off, but again, that wasn't in the spirit of this evening. He supposed the onlookers would be horrified enough by the sight of a beautiful young girl with her throat slashed open.

He went into the bedroom across the hall.

The teenage boy was also asleep. There was no evidence that Ivan had interrupted him masturbating. What an awful family.

Ivan crouched down next to his bed. He tapped the boy on the nose with the tip of the knife.

The boy groaned and rubbed his nose but didn't open his eyes.

Ivan switched from a tap to a jab. Not enough to break the skin.

The boy opened his eyes. Then he opened them even wider as he saw Ivan. Ivan slammed his hand over the boy's mouth.

"Shhhhh," he said. He held the blade up to the boy's eye. "Don't make a sound," he whispered. "You may think I'll run away if you call out to your parents, or you may even be dumb enough to think that they'll get here before I stab you, but I promise you, you're wrong. Do you want to die tonight?"

The boy shook his head.

"Then do you swear not to be a complete fucking idiot?"

The boy nodded.

"Good." Ivan removed his hand from the boy's mouth. A drop of blood fell off the knife onto the blanket. "Does that blood look familiar?"

The boy looked confused by the question. Ivan chuckled.

"I'm just messing with you. Of course, you wouldn't recognize your sister's blood. That would be crazy. Now, to answer the question that I'm sure you're thinking, yes, she's dead, yes, it was gross, and no, she didn't suffer very long. I mean, she was conscious for part of it, and I'm sure the pain was excruciating, and there was sheer panic in her eyes, but it was over pretty quickly, all things considered. A few seconds, maybe. Ten. You can handle pretty much anything for ten seconds, right?"

The boy began to cry.

"That's fine, that's fine," said Ivan. "You're allowed to cry. Just keep it quiet, or your death will take way longer than ten seconds. Oh, shit, did I give away that you're going to die? Damn. I should've had a spoiler warning. That was very inconsiderate of me. Do you accept my apology?"

The boy continued to cry. He was getting a little too loud.

"There, there, young one," Ivan said, gently running his hand through the boy's hair in a gesture that both of them knew wasn't really meant to be soothing. "I understand the desire to weep for your lost sister, but keep the noise down, or I'll bite your fucking face off."

Ivan *really* wanted to transform right now. Change this kid's perspective about the existence of monsters right before sinking his jaws into the kid's face.

Maybe he should. Did it really matter if he was able to slaughter a family in human form? He was a goddamn werewolf—he should take advantage of it!

No. He'd stick to the plan. He'd grown too complacent. The killing was too easy. For a truly satisfying evening, one he could look back upon fondly, he needed to do this without cheating.

Anyway, the boy looked plenty scared without gazing at a werewolf.

"What's your name?" Ivan asked.

The boy didn't answer.

"If you don't answer my question, I'm going to stick this knife in you. And when I stick this knife in you, you won't be able to stay quiet. Which means you'll break my rule about making too much noise, and so I'll have to stick the knife in you a bunch of times in a bunch of places. That's a

351

Jeff Strand

lot of suffering just to get out of telling me your name. What's your name?"

"John."

"John? That's a pretty generic name, John. Did your parents just assume you were going to be boring as hell? John. Fuck that. Your new name is Tiberius. We're obviously not going to go through the whole process of having your name legally changed—just know that in God's eyes, you are now Tiberius."

Tiberius' body quivered as he wept.

"Oooh, this is awkward, but you've got some snot right there. Some people wouldn't tell you that. They'd let you go on with your day with snot on your face and never say a word. Not me. I care enough about you to let you know. Oh, by the way, your crying volume is starting to get a bit excessive. I get that this whole situation is traumatic, but you've got to work with me here. You're only number two on my list. I've got four people to get to tonight. I'd hate for your bawling to interfere with my meticulously planned schedule."

Tiberius didn't stop crying, not that Ivan expected or wanted him to.

"Okay, enough chit-chat. As I accidentally revealed earlier, I'm going to kill you. But don't worry, I'm not going to cut out your eyeballs or anything like that. That would be awful, wouldn't it? Having your eyeballs cut out? Ugh. I'd never put you through that experience. No, your death is going to involve this knife slamming into your throat. Like your sister, you'll have maybe ten seconds of agony. It's worse for you because of all the anticipation, of course, but it's still way better than having to lie there while I carve out your eyeballs, right?"

"Mom! Dad! Get out of the house!" Tiberius shouted.

"Wow," said Ivan. "I honestly thought you'd be too paralyzed with terror to try anything like that. I actually admire your bravery. I'd consider letting you go, but I broke into your house planning to kill you and the rest of your family, and that's what I'm going to do. G'night."

He slammed the knife into the boy's throat. There might not be time to watch him completely bleed out, but Ivan could spare a few seconds to watch the geyser. He got a nice up-close look, stopping short of actually trying to get any in his mouth. Then he hurried over and stood next to the doorway.

The mother screamed before she came inside the room.

She wailed her son's name. The sound gave Ivan almost as much pleasure as the actual murder.

She *should* have noticed that the blood was still flowing, which meant that whoever had committed this atrocity was nearby, which meant that she should not be entering the room of her late son. Instead, she rushed over to the bed. To be fair, she may have believed that she could stop the bleeding and save his life. He couldn't blame her for not thinking clearly at this particular moment.

He also couldn't blame her for being so distracted that she didn't notice when he walked up behind her. She did notice when he yanked her away from the bed and held the knife to her throat.

"Don't move," Ivan said, both to her and to her husband, who stood in the doorway.

"Take whatever you want," the man said.

"Including your lives? Thanks."

The man didn't seem to have noticed the gory scene on his son's bed yet. Ivan stepped out of the way, taking the woman with him, to give him a real good look. The man looked horrified, but to his credit, he didn't scream or puke.

"Jane!" the man called out.

"John and Jane?" asked Ivan. "Jesus Christ, you guys

have no imagination. I'll save you the trouble of going into Jane's room. Just take what you see on this bed and swap the mental image out for your daughter. Probably redder because she's had more time to bleed."

The woman tensed up as if she were preparing to do something very stupid. Ivan pressed the knife more tightly against her neck to dissuade her of that idea.

"What do you want?" the man asked. He was doing a remarkably good job of remaining calm.

Ivan shrugged. "The respect of my peers. Somebody to grow old with. A grilled cheese sandwich. If you were asking what I want right now, in this specific moment, I want to murder your wife like I murdered your children. And then, of course, to murder you. Did that answer your question? Do you need more details?"

Now the man was looking a bit wobbly. Ivan hoped he wasn't passing out.

"Please don't hurt her," he said.

"I just said I wanted to kill both of you. I know you asked nicely and all, but why would you think that would change my mind? You've got to do way more than that to make my heart grow three sizes tonight."

"What can I do?"

"Nothin'."

"Take me instead."

"You're not making logical sense, sir. I've already said that both of you would be dying tonight. Your offer doesn't come from a place of negotiating power. Now, if you'd offered to deliver a busload of orphans here in exchange for your wife, I might consider it, but your offer is quite honestly a little insulting."

Then the woman did something stupid.

She bashed her head against Ivan's. She was shorter than him, so it was her skull smashing into his jaw, but she did it really hard, and he bit his tongue. She did this without moving her neck much, though the blade still cut into her flesh.

Ivan hadn't expected this, despite the earlier warning, and biting his tongue hurt like hell even when it was with his human teeth. The mix of pain and surprise caused him to lower the knife. He didn't *drop* the knife, just lowered it, but that was apparently enough for the woman to see an opportunity to bash her head against him again, even harder this time. *Now* Ivan dropped the knife.

She lunged at him. Her fingernails may not have been as long and sharp as werewolf claws, but they were pretty goddamn savage as they tore across his face.

He started to lose his balance. Then he lost it completely when the man tackled him.

Shit!

He'd accept failure if it was because Granny lived with them and called the cops. He'd even be okay with it if the man had fled and got to the phone before Ivan could mutilate his wife. But he'd had a knife to the woman's neck. She'd gotten the best of him when he had a fucking knife pressed against her fucking throat. That was unacceptable.

The man slammed Ivan's head against the floor.

Ivan transformed.

He got no enjoyment out of the man's expression upon suddenly discovering that he was on top of a werewolf. Felt no pleasure when he slashed his claw across the man's face, removing his nose and both eyes.

Ivan gave the woman a head start, but still, there was no glee in the pursuit. When he pounced upon her and her body broke as she fell down the stairs, it did nothing for him. He tore her apart and scattered her around the living room with absolutely no sense of accomplishment.

He changed back into a human and went upstairs in his shredded clothes. Grabbed his knife off the floor. Stomped his way down the stairs, into the kitchen, and out the back door. Returned to his car. Screamed with rage.

He screamed and pounded his fists against the dashboard and kept screaming and screaming until he noticed that he'd changed his hands into wolfman hands and really fucked up his car.

Ivan drove home, filled with a fury that he'd have to release soon.

ABOUT THE AUTHOR

Jeff Strand is the author of the WOLF HUNT trilogy, cleverly titled WOLF HUNT, WOLF HUNT 2, and WOLF HUNT 3. His other lycanthrophic fiction includes "My Werewolf Neighbor" and "Werewolf Porno," the latter of which continues to get the most hits on his website.

He has also written lots of books without werewolves.

You can visit his website at www.JeffStrand.com.

He's on Twitter (@JeffStrand)

Instagram (JeffStrandAuthor)

Facebook (JeffStrandAuthorFanPage).

THANK YOU FOR READING

Thank you for taking the time to read this book. We sincerely hope that you enjoyed the story and appreciate your letting us try to entertain you. We realize that your time is valuable, and without the continuing support of people such as yourself, we would not be able to do what we do.

As a thank you, we would like to offer you a free ebook from our range, in return for you signing up to our mailing list. We will never share your details with anyone and will only contact you to let you know about new releases.

You can sign up on our website

http://www.horrifictales.co.uk

If you enjoyed this book, then please consider leaving a short review on Amazon, Goodreads or anywhere else that you, as a reader, visit to learn about new books. One of the most important parts about how well a book sells is how many positive reviews it has, so if you can spare a little more of your valuable time to share the experience with others, even if its just a line or two, we would really appreciate it.

Thanks, and see you next time!

THE HORRIFIC TALES PUBLISHING TEAM

ALSO FROM HORRIFIC TALES PUBLISHING